I0819671

THE FRANCHISE

THE FRANCHISE

THOMAS ELROD

Tor Publishing Group
New York

This is a work of fiction. All of the names, characters, organizations, places, and events portrayed in this work are either products of the author's imagination or used fictitiously.

THE FRANCHISE

A Tor Book
Published by Tom Doherty Associates / Tor Publishing Group
120 Broadway
New York, NY 10271

www.torpublishinggroup.com

EU Representative: Macmillan Publishers Ireland Ltd, 1st Floor, The Liffey Trust Centre, 117–126 Sheriff Street Upper, Dublin 1, D01 YC43

The Library of Congress Cataloging-in-Publication Data is available upon request.

ISBN 978-1-250-40658-3 (hardcover)
ISBN 978-1-250-40659-0 (ebook)

First Edition: 2026

Printed in the United States of America

10 9 8 7 6 5 4 3 2 1

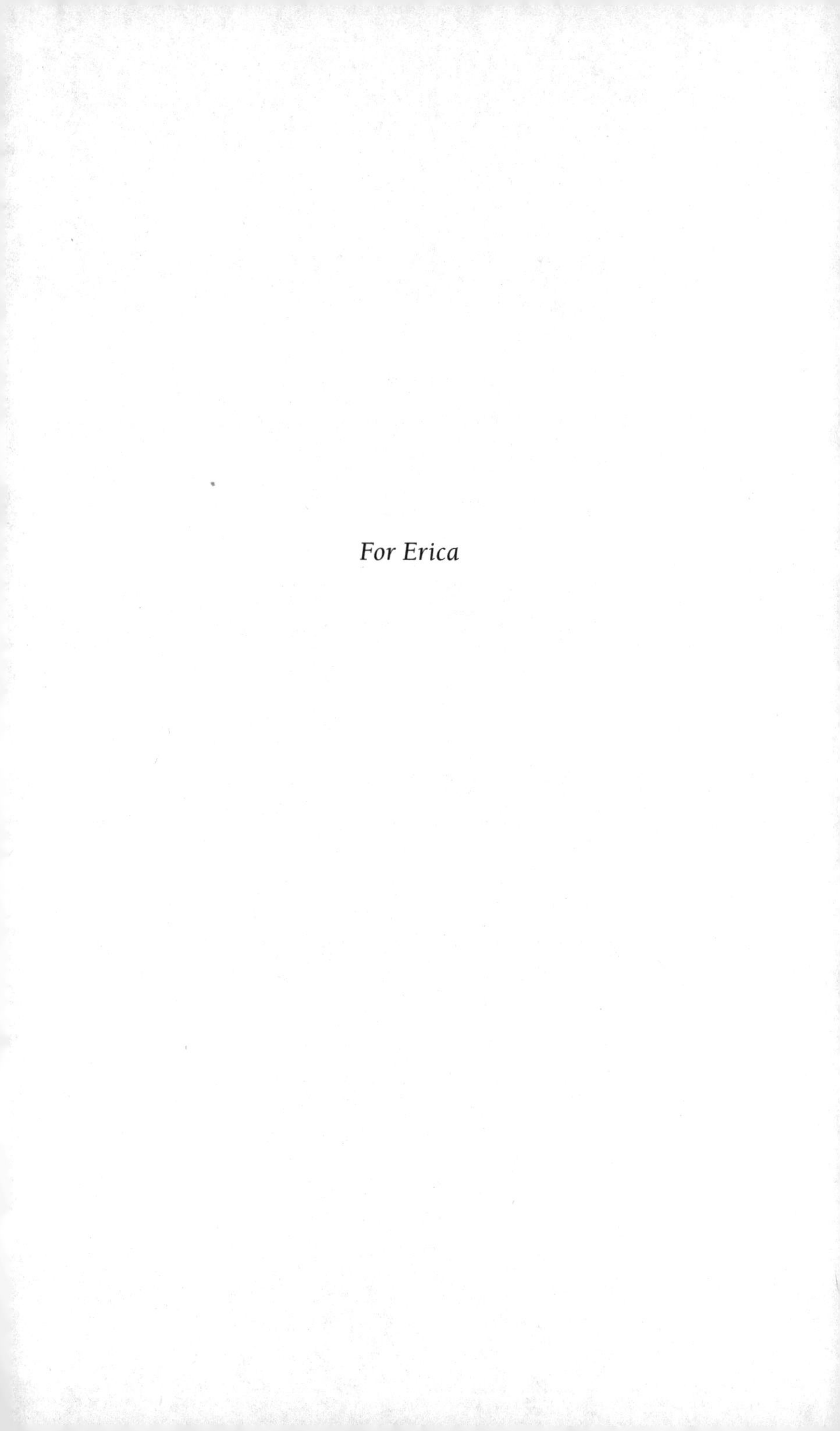

For Erica

Besides, do any of us understand what we are doing? If we did, would we ever do it?

—George Bernard Shaw, *Pygmalion*

THE FRANCHISE

NEW YORK CITY

October 23, 1962

Nobody remembers this, but the weather had been so nice the day before. A cool fall breeze, a few clouds in the sky, golden leaves still on the trees, and a darkening evening anticipating, not yet permitting, the coming of winter. It was an autumn day that suggested the possibilities of a world still becoming. So as men and women in Manhattan crossed on their daily errands—and one marveled at the looming canyons of steel, their promise of American ingenuity and greatness, the rest of the century still to come and what would it be?—the fact that the whole time men in dark suits smoked cigarettes and placed telephone calls and made plans for the end of the world, any small pleasures afforded by the weather were rendered not just insignificant but possibly dangerous. Better to forget it entirely. The world was not anticipating winter. It was anticipating death.

The publishing offices of *World Science Fiction and Fantasy Magazine* sat above the park, so when Wendell Highsman looked out his window and saw children playing that Tuesday morning, despite the now-overcast skies, he wondered why they were so damned foolish. Had they not watched the president's speech the night before? Their parents had, at least. Here was a thought that made Wendell even more upset: that the children's parents knew the truth—Khrushchev had planted nuclear warheads in Cuba, Kennedy was setting up a blockade, and the final, inevitable clash was now imminent—and the children themselves hadn't been told. That the parents didn't want to worry their little ones too much on the final day of their lives. That it was the only way to keep them safe.

Wendell was not safe, either, he knew that. But at least his office building was stone, built by some titan of industry the previous century. If the blast was from downtown—and it would be, if the Soviets were smart and accurate—then in these walls Wendell might actually live, at least until the radiation took hold. But in the park you were exposed, and vulnerable, and Wendell did not want to think about children dying. He turned away from the window.

Mrs. Olson sat in the next room, behind her typewriter filling out rejection notices for the afternoon mail. Wendell didn't tell her to stop. She hadn't said anything all morning, hadn't mentioned her son, even though he was in the navy and Wendell knew she had seen the speech because she watched Brinkley every night before *Bridge*. Preparing the mail was probably the best thing for her. It kept her focused, distracted, not thinking about her son sitting on a carrier in the Gulf watching the end begin. Let her stay busy. Wendell knew the mail would never arrive at its destination, of course, but maybe that was a good thing. It meant that H. W. Ferry or Jonathan R. Kellerman or Susanne Popovorich (she needed a pen name for sure) would never find out that their stories about sex-crazed astronauts and delusional dragonslayers and genius scientist-politicians had been rejected. They would die believing that publishing glory was just around the corner. That their ticket had come up and the October skies were harbingers of a big, bright American tomorrow.

The typesetters hadn't even shown up for work today.

"That man is here," Mrs. Olson said, not bothering to stop typing, when Wendell wandered out of his office. He thought he might head down to Kelvin's for lunch. Kelvin's was safe enough from the bombs. Safer, probably, if they had to hide in that basement. But Wendell had forgotten that there was an appointment, one Mrs. Olson had scheduled some days ago, before the end of the world. Well, before they knew about it.

"He still came?" Wendell asked.

"Why wouldn't he have come?" Mrs. Olson typed a letter

informing Mary Jackson of Tupelo, Mississippi, that her work showed "much promise" and that Wendell Highsman wished her the best of luck on her future endeavors.

"Well, send him in, I suppose." Wendell walked back into his office and sat down, facing away from the window.

The man who walked in, dressed in a shaggy brown coat and sporting a thick, black mustache, carried a cardboard box with him. Wendell was annoyed already. Mrs. Olson's job included not letting prospective authors in to see him. If you let one man in, they'll all want to come, pleading their case for why your rejection was so cruel, so unjust, so callous and unappreciative of their work. In the past, Wendell considered allowing only solicited submissions. Maybe he would again, if they all lived.

The man was very forward. "Excuse me, sir. I am from Boston, and I must speak with you."

"You're not from Boston." Wendell meant it as a question, but it came out as an accusation.

"Oh, yes, I am. I live there with my wife and infant son. I just rode down on the train this morning."

"No, your accent. French?"

"Yes, that is where I grew up. My name is Jean-Danton Souard."

"Never been to France, sadly. During the war I was stateside. *Stars and Stripes*. You know it?"

"No."

"Fine outfit. When did you come to the United States?"

"1946."

"Hmm. Not Vichy, were you? Oh, never mind. How can I help you, Mr. Souard?"

Jean-Danton fumbled with the box in his arms. He placed it on Wendell's desk, then sat in a wingback chair in the corner. Wendell looked at the box and sighed.

"I can't just read manuscripts off the street," Wendell said. "We have a system, a way of doing things here. You understand, it's only fair."

Jean-Danton nodded. "Yes, I have read the magazine. I

understand your policies, but this is my only copy. I spent all our savings to get it typed."

"We have policies about returning manuscripts, too, you know. It's all in our submission guidelines."

"It is just too important to send through the mail. I cannot just leave it with anybody." Every manuscript was always the most important thing in the world.

"So you expect me to read this now, while you sit there?"

"I must take this manuscript home if you reject me, yes."

Wendell sighed and looked out the window. "Mr. Souard, I really do not have time for this today. We are very busy. I am waiting on proofs for the new issue, we have plenty of other manuscripts to review, plus I need to provide some editorial feedback on—"

Someone laughed outside his window. They were all going to die and people were laughing.

"I'm very sorry, Mr. Souard. It is a bad day. You should go back to your family in Boston. If something should happen, you should be with them."

"If something should happen? Do you mean the bomb?"

"Yes. Is there even anything else right now?"

"No, I suppose not. But, it seems to me, if it is all so hopeless, why not read my novel?"

Wendell thought he should call his sister in San Francisco. When something happened, she would be far enough away. Maybe he would call his lawyer, his accountant. Make sure his affairs were in order. His sister would close the magazine, most likely. She had always hated it. When they were children she complained how it took up their father's time. Just as well. What would be left of it anyway, once Wendell was dead? Old issues in an A&P somewhere in Minnesota. There's a fun discovery for future archaeologists: Look at these primitive stories full of horny astronauts! What a bizarre culture!

"You know," Jean-Danton interrupted, breaking Wendell's reverie (he was looking out the window again), "during the war I was a prisoner in a German camp. Me and many other French soldiers. We knew we were going to die. *Knew it*, even if we hoped otherwise. But until you are dead you still need to live."

Read my book because we're going to die anyway. It was a novel approach, Wendell gave him that. He considered that Jean-Danton was a man comfortable with the current state of the world, who wasn't distracted by the certainty of death. Or at least, he could spin a little yarn and convince you of that. For the first time, the manuscript intrigued Wendell.

"You can't sell stories in an American magazine with a foreign name. We can only sell issues if people have good strong American names."

"Will you read my work?"

"Perhaps. What is it about?"

"The end of the world."

"Well, now, that *is* very topical."

"It takes place in a medieval, magical kingdom."

"I don't do that sort of thing right now. Sputnik, you know. Kids want to go to the moon."

"But this land is unique. There used to be magic, but it's been outlawed. And some of the inhabitants want to see it return. So there is an internal rebellion, and the story becomes an exploration of politics and society and—"

"Wait, wait," Wendell said. "This is all too much. You said it was about the end of the world?"

"Well, metaphorically, perhaps."

Wendell laughed. "The French."

"It's the end of their world, the world they know. You see, at the end of this whole rebellion, magic *does* come back, but it isn't what anybody expected. It changes the entire realm, everyone's relationship to one another, to themselves. They end up in a world they didn't expect, and couldn't foresee."

"How long is it?" Wendell pried open the top of the box. It was entirely filled with paper.

"It's, well, typed it is over two thousand pages. Two thousand, one hundred and sixty-three to be precise."

"Christ, I got Proust over here."

"I know it is quite long, but every word is perfectly chosen, I assure you."

"You speak English very well."

"I had an English tutor. Before the war. She lived with us."

"You were wealthy then?"

"She was a communist. We all were."

An ambulance drove past, sirens roaring. Somebody in the city was going to die and they wouldn't even get to see the bomb. "Well, Mr. Souard, I am not going to lie to you. We don't serialize novels very often, certainly not ones as long as this. But I'll take a look at it. Politics and the end of the world are on my mind, too, after all."

"I appreciate that, Mr. Highsman. I really do. Is there any chance for a decision right now, and an advance? I spent my last dollar on my train ticket."

"I didn't say I would buy it, Mr. Souard, just that I would read it. And anyway, what good is money going to be soon? I'll tell you what, though. I can pay you fifty dollars today. If I don't buy your novel, take it as a commission for a new story. I'm feeling generous." He was, too. The sounds of people chatting on city streets on the last day of their lives had inspired in him a charitable spirit.

"Thank you, Mr. Highsman. Very much. Is it all right if I smoke?"

"Yes, yes, go ahead." Jean-Danton lit a cigarette and Wendell found himself, like a magnet, pulled to look out the window again, back down to the children in the park.

He should give Souard more, what did it matter? He would give him a hundred dollars, maybe a thousand. He would bet the whole future of the magazine on this sprawling, ridiculous novel. He would need it to be a major hit, an unexpected sensation, for such a decision to make sense. Perhaps it would be, there was no way of knowing. Nothing about the future can be known at the end of time, only imagined. Wendell could certainly imagine the novel a success. Imagine a future where they serialize the whole thing and sell out issue after issue, readers demanding to find out what happens next, what twists and turns of fate await their favorite characters. Wendell could imagine the eventual publication of the book, in a handsome hardcover, then a cheaper but bestselling mass-market paperback. Then the sequels, each one another hit. Poor Mr. Souard's children become wealthy inheritors of this massive, popular series. Hollywood makes movies, they make television shows, people read the books to their kids and tell them, "My parents used to read this to me." Everyone knows the names of the characters and the author and, of course, the place where it all began. On the pages of *World Science Fiction and Fantasy Magazine*, Wendell J. Highsman III, Publisher and Editor in Chief.

It was a nice thing to imagine, on the day you were going to die.

"Hell, how about two thousand dollars? And I buy it right now. If it stinks, you'll just have to rewrite it, right? Ha."

"Two thousand? My good sir, I say, I mean I do say . . ."

"Never mind that. Oh, Mrs. Olson? Can you come in here? Now, Mr. Souard, there will just be some paperwork for you to sign. Say, what is the name of this mythical realm of yours? We need a good name. For you, too. Maybe just abbreviate your Christian name. J. D. Souard, doesn't sound too bad? Even a little American. But your world, what do you call it?"

"It is the same as the title of the novel. It is called *The Malicarn.*"

THE MALICARN

THE SIXTEENTH WINTER IN THE REIGN OF QUEEN HANNAH I

1.

There are two types of historians. The first looks at an old uniform and asks, "Who wore that?" The second looks at that same uniform and asks, "What does it feel like to wear that?" Buck Douglas was the second type.

Buck's father kept his old army uniform under the bed. When he was out, drinking at the inn until late, Buck would sneak into the crate, take out the uniform, and slide it over his clothes. The sleeves were too long, and hung awkwardly off his sides, but Buck liked the smell of it. It was musty, dirt still on it. There were medals on it, too: one for meritorious service, another "Emblem of the Malicarn," and a dark-bronze circular medallion with the phrase "Order of the Magi" emblazoned on it, awarded because his father served with a wizard in battle.

About which wizard, and which battles, Buck never did learn much. Frank Douglas did not speak of the past. When Buck's father wasn't drinking, he worked their small farm in the valley. And when he wasn't cursing his mules and pushing his plow, he was hitting Buck and shouting about how worthless he was.

The farm yielded potatoes and carrots mostly. The orchard washed out in a flood, and the pigs all died of fever. When Buck turned two the queen's inspectors came and fined Buck's father for keeping too many chickens. The inspectors confiscated three, and that winter—with the crop failures and the lack of meat—Buck's baby sister and mother died. His father drank more after that.

Sometimes his father would stumble in late, breath reeking of ale, and other nights friends of his dragged him home. They'd pour a bucket of water over his head and toss him into bed.

"He was never like this during the war." They wouldn't say more about it than that.

When Buck was seven, his father lost their lease on the farm and moved to a small room in one of the boardinghouses in Kingstown. Buck started working, first for city granaries during the harvest and then as a hauler for stonemasons. He lugged stone from quarry to worksite. He was young but he grew strong. One of the masons suggested he take an apprenticeship, and when he was twelve he moved out of his father's room into a small shack on the master mason's land, attached to a barn, where he rose early every day and learned how to cut and shape stone, how to mix mortar, how to place the stone and bind it into place.

At night the master would invite the journeymen and apprentices to supper with his family, and that is where Buck first heard real tales of the old wars. How there used to be hundreds of wizards, how the late King Prion, himself once just a lowly sheepherder, became the one to unite them against the Dark Mages, how the many men of the Malicarn were called to fight. The master himself was a captain in the cavalry and told long stories about the glorious days of the war.

The only time Buck heard these stories from his own father was his final winter when he fell ill. Old army friends rode up to the mason's house in a hurry to find Buck. When Buck came to his father's bedside, the old man sweating while frost formed on the window outside, he talked for the first time about the past. About Buck's mother, the farm, and most of all the war.

"We used to sleep in a circle, shifts of three at a time on watch, sitting on the edge of the camp. A whole company sleeping that way. We could never set up secure defenses, not unless the wizard was able to perform a hex of some kind. But usually the wizard kept to himself, sleeping and eating in his tent. Ours was named Ferguson. He would come out for marches, riding a horse, and of course he led us into battle. But even the generals rarely saw or spoke to him at other times."

Buck wanted to know all the details: what they ate, what weapons they carried, how they lined up in formation for a battle. There were things his father couldn't remember, details he seemed to confuse, mix up, or repeat. But still he talked. He could no longer drink, so nostalgia was the next best thing to distract his mind.

"One day we were searching a village for a company of mages. The houses appeared deserted, but my commander and I searched each room anyway. In one small hut, we found a shelf leaning against a wall. When we moved it back, there was a small child hiding in a tiny closet. With him were hundreds of spellbooks, wizard staffs, magical amulets. The mages were hiding all their artifacts there. The child was young, no more than six, but when he saw us he shot an arrow at my commander, who fell dead. Through the neck. I struck the child down with my sword. Later that night, the mages returned, but we were ready. We surprised them, and slaughtered them all."

Buck's father died after a day of sweating agony, screaming things Buck could not understand. "Free me!" were his final words. Buck paid to have his father's body carried back to their old farm to be buried beside his mother and sister. It cost all the money he had in the world, and he had to dig the hole himself.

When he finished his apprenticeship, Buck heard about the young queen's masonry renovations on the old castle. He had never seen the queen, only knew her from his father's curses, but the money was good and so Buck returned to Kingstown. The town that had grown up in the few years since Buck and his father first moved there was remarkable, a maze of streets and a mix of styles that screamed chaos and meant life. Kingstown was vibrant and alive and full of possibility. The streets were also filled with the wretched, the poor, and the damned.

Buck worked hard there, helping lay the foundation and constructing the south wall of a new nave. Some of the other masons he knew from the master's house, former apprentices or journeymen, also came looking for work. They heaved and sweated during the day and drank and caroused at night. Their favorite spot was a brothel called the Broodmare, where Buck lost his virginity.

It was at the Broodmare where Buck met his first guildmember, a carpenter named Wallace, who overheard Buck telling a story about his father's time in the war.

"You should come to one of our meetings, if you appreciate history," Wallace said. "I think you would enjoy it. We have a special speaker at our next meeting."

The Wizarding Reenactors Guild had dozens of chapters throughout the Malicarn, but Buck visited one that met in the antechamber of a church on the opposite side of the river, a respectable neighborhood of merchants and tradesmen who did business in Kingstown but preferred not to live in the middle of the mess. The chapter was an all-volunteer group of about thirty men, a mix of the trades and wealthy benefactors, including one named Kreek, the smartest and most knowledgeable man there.

Kreek was famous, so Buck was told, for training the Council of Heroes in the final years of King Prion's reign. A knight himself, he continued to train young highborn children the art of swordplay by day, but in the evenings he preferred the company of the common man, those who were interested in the old tales but had never experienced magic themselves. When Buck arrived at the church for the weekly meeting, Kreek was already there, standing in front of a row of chairs. He was shorter than Buck expected, but strong and broad, built like an ox. Buck himself sat toward the back, in the corner. He nodded politely at Wallace and a few of the other men. Shortly after, Kreek turned around and addressed the crowd.

"Thank you for coming out tonight," Kreek began, as the last members filed in. "A few announcements: If you have not yet decided to attend the Battle of Pine Run Reenactment, make sure you tell us before next week so that you have a spot in the carriage. We cannot afford more horses, so if you do not let us know you will have to walk. It is a full-dress event. If you do not have a uniform, please let myself or Wallace know and we can find a spare for you."

Wallace, in the front row, gestured at Kreek. "Oh," Kreek continued, "and Wallace reminds me that afterward we will congregate at a pub to be determined. So be sure to bring some extra deniers for that. All right, well, with no further delay, let me introduce our speaker. I know a lot of you have been asking who it is, but we have kept it a secret so that we were not overrun with non–historically minded folk. Gentlemen, please welcome, to speak on the inner experience of wizarding and combat, the Last Wizard himself, Gregorian the Great."

The place erupted in thunderous applause, but Buck was too shocked to clap. He had seen glimpses of Gregorian, wandering to and from the castle, but the wizard was mercurial. He would appear suddenly in a city square and then vanish again. He often holed up in his tower, a black obelisk in the Old Village, sometimes missing for weeks on journeys far from the Malicarn itself. His business was mysterious and unknowable. There were always whispers that he was secretly in thrall to the Necromancer. But the young queen trusted him, and so he remained a figure of respect throughout the realm.

Only once had Buck seen him up close. As a young child he went hunting with his father and they ran into Gregorian, who was on some errand. The wizard, always renowned as charitable to the common folk, gave them his cart and horse and continued his own journey on foot. This was shortly after his mother and sister had died, and Buck could not remember the words his father passed with the wizard as this kindness took place. He was so young that the memory itself was mostly his father's retelling of it. But Buck always held a fondness for Gregorian in his heart.

Now Gregorian stood before them. He was not a particularly old man, but he had the face of someone who took too many walks in the sun, wrinkled and sallow, with beady eyes and a hunched and crooked back. He wore a bright blue cloak—not as thick as the one Buck's father had owned, but just as long—and held a wooden staff in his right hand. His beard was short and patchy, and he spoke slowly, a croak in his voice, as if he was always on the verge of forgetting what he was saying.

"Now, what I have here is a typical sorcerer staff. Probably a level three or four would have used this. You see one end here with a small obsidian orb, the other side this purple gem, shaped a bit like a spike. This gem, it is called a 'collector,' that is because you would stick it into a body"—here he mimed stabbing a corpse on the ground—"and draw out the energy needed for your spells. This orb is the 'enhancer,' and the actual spell is focused here. It does not always come out as a blast of lightning necessarily, but it is directional. Now, a real strong sorcerer, a level seven or eight, say, could do most of his spell-making without a staff, if he needed to, but the staff would still give him extra control, better focus, more efficient uses of energy."

This was more information about wizarding than Buck had ever heard before. His father and others had always spoken in such generalities—that the wizards were mysterious, or treacherous. Buck realized he had heard very little about *how* the wizards worked, what they did exactly, and in what manner they did it. Buck glanced at the other men in the little room, all nodding their heads and staring raptly ahead. Only Kreek looked skeptical, stroking his beard and leaning back in his chair.

Gregorian held up his cloak. "Now this is a handmade cloak. You can still order it directly from many tailors. Most master tailors can do the hand-stitching. Though of course it is cheaper if you want to order one from one of the mass-produced shops. But the more authentic ones are nice because they are a little heavier, gives you a bit of the feel of what it was like to wear. Most people think the cloaks are only decorative, only nostalgic since they harken back to the prewar cloaks, in the days of the Old Kings. But there was more to it than that. On the battlefield, they do the same sort of work as a battle flag. The secular troops could see their wizard through the smoke and debris. They could follow him when he moved, see him give orders. And since the Dark Mages, the few of them there were, did not wear cloaks at all, you knew exactly where the Alliance Wizards were at. Of course, it made them targets for the longbow marksmen."

Gregorian demonstrated some classic wizard stances with his staff, what a reanimate spell would look like (staff at forty-five degrees, slowly thrusting forward), or a defensive spell (usually a Necromancer specialty, it involved squaring your legs and holding the staff perpendicular to the ground). Buck watched with interest but kept hoping to see one of the spells actually work. They never did.

"Now," Gregorian continued, "while I would of course like to show you a real spell, all magical energy in the Malicarn is banished. That is how we keep the peace with the Necromancer, which is why we don't train wizards anymore, and why this is a lost art. But I assure you, it was real once, and quite beautiful. However"—he paused and smiled—"a little taste never hurt?"

He raised his staff and waved it above his head. It sparkled, white streaks like lightning crackling from its tip. The crowd applauded. Buck wiped a tear from his cheek.

When the meeting ended, the attendees mingled with one another, a few badgering Gregorian about some obscure point of staff lore. Buck was standing awkwardly toward the rear of the room, unsure whether or how to engage, when Kreek approached him, hand out and smile wide.

"Good evening," he said. "I am Sir Kreek, Master of Sword. You must be Buck? Wallace told me you might be coming." Kreek had a strong grip.

"Nice to meet you," Buck said. "Quite a show. Educationally, uh, interesting."

"Mostly bollocks, if I am being honest. Gregorian has done this same speech at a few of the monasteries. Part of his campaign on behalf of the queen, hoping that some magic would be enough for people to stop clamoring to end the bans. But it is mostly smoke and mirrors."

"What do you mean?"

Kreek smiled. "It is all propaganda. Magic is not gone, it is just suppressed. See how he does his little tricks? Gregorian is harmless enough, but he is an old man who protects himself before he protects the people of the Malicarn. Never forget that."

That is how Buck Douglas ended up a member of the Wizarding Reenactors Guild. He sat in pubs twice a week listening to Kreek lecture about magical heritage, how every man was entitled to it, how it had been stolen from them. How this heritage was suppressed by the Necromancer, the real ruler of the Malicarn, a hidden menace who kept men poor and magic outlawed. It all made sense to Buck.

"Yes, the old king kept us safe," Kreek would say at meetings. "Prion handled the threats of demons and attacking dragons well. But his rule only dealt with external threats. What about internal ones? Are your pockets safe? Your sweethearts in their beds while you are away? And hasn't it gotten worse under the rule of the young crippled queen? Buck, were your mother and sister killed by magic? Was your father? Or was it not rather due to the ravages of the land, of poverty? Magic could solve all our problems, could save our farms and our families."

He would complain about the goblins from faraway lands who were flooding into the Malicarn, taking over dead farms, farms which had once belonged to Malicarn men. Goblins kept to themselves, secretive and devious. Buck saw them only rarely, sometimes passing them on the road. But there were more of them every year, and fewer farms for men of the Malicarn. "These goblins," and Kreek would sneer when he said those words, "are brought here by the Necromancer and his men. Another way of keeping down the common folk of the Malicarn." He did not say it himself, but others would whisper about how much the queen resembled a goblin—dark-skinned, crippled, full of secret plans.

Everything connected. Buck's family farm, its failures, his

father a broken veteran with no support, no prospects. Buck's own life, hacking away at stone, his young joints already aching as the queen and her advisors sat in the castle and enjoyed comfort. He listened to Wallace talk about his theory that the Necromancer planned to replace the citizens of the Malicarn with demons from the netherworld. "Maybe these goblins are demons too," he would say. And Buck listened to Kreek go on about his own ideas: how the only way to get magic back would be for the people, the common folk, to take it back themselves.

Once a month the Guild held reenactments at various sites across the realm. Sometimes only on open fields, random spots where they could host a gathering. But sometimes they held events on the sites of the actual old battles, where wizard had faced off against wizard: the Siege of Crooked Creek, the Engagement at Sutter's Point, or the Battle of the Morlon Kastaun, where the Great Wizarding War reached its climax in the years before Buck was born. The Morlon Kastaun was Buck's favorite historical battle, so when he learned they were planning a winter reenactment he was especially excited.

Reenactments were full-day affairs, with chapters of the Guild all coming together to camp, drink, and battle together. The Morlon Kastaun was perhaps the largest event they had ever put on, nearly three thousand men all told. Each man was assigned to a company, and within that company to a platoon. Historical accuracy was paramount, so each platoon was given specific instructions on where to march and how to behave during the battle. Most guildmembers could not read, so the scripts provided to the platoons were of little use. They just had to memorize their movements. One man in each chapter was designated to be the wizard. In Buck's, that was Kreek.

On the morning of the battle, everyone lined up in their respective formations. Buck and the other grunts wore outfits they either bought or made themselves. Buck wore his father's old uniform, an authentic relic that impressed the other men. Each reenactor carried a wooden sword as well, something that could be wielded in a historical fashion but not actually hurt anyone.

Then the fun began. At the sound of a trumpet, the guildsmen marched forward. The Morlon Kastaun took place on a large, hilly field beside an old, dark forest. The original Temple of the High Wizards had once stood here, though now it was merely a ruin. These fields were sheep pastures now, lightly sprinkled with a recent and rare snow flurry. The only other nearby inhabitants were the monks of the Dollories Monastery on the far end of the battlefield.

Buck held his sword out in front as he walked over the grass, keeping pace with the men lined up beside him. No one was overly focused on speed or accuracy, each man falling a bit behind or ahead as his attention drifted to other parts of the field. Buck could see Kreek, in full wizard regalia, at the center of their line, holding aloft his staff. Buck's platoon followed up a hill, toward an old temple ruin where they were supposed to clash with a platoon from one of the other Guild chapters. But when they arrived, they found no one else there. Buck's platoon wandered around the ruins for a few minutes, stepping over old stone walls and the remnants of statuary before finally deciding to continue down the hill in the direction of Kreek and the other platoons. As they approached a line of trees, another chapter president, not dressed for today's event, ran up to them, shouting and waving his hands.

"What are you doing?" he yelled. "You are supposed to be dead!"

"But there was no one back at the ruins for us to fight," said Buck's platoon commander.

"It doesn't matter, this whole flank is destroyed. Just die now, and it will be fine." And so, without encountering any enemies or swinging any swords, Buck's entire platoon was wiped out. They lay down on the field and played dead for two hours.

Later that afternoon, after the potluck lunch and a series of historical speeches, Buck and Wallace agreed to walk the perimeter of the battlefield and retrieve any garbage or personal artifacts strewn across the grass. They trekked toward the northern edge of the field. Many Guild chapters were heading home, and Buck could hear their carts rattling back to their villages, the calls of their men echoing beyond the hills as they rode away. The sun was setting and an orange dusk settled over the land.

Buck and Wallace split up, each canvassing a different side of a line of trees. Buck pulled behind him a small wagon, half filled with dropped scarves and broken wood swords heaped in a messy pile. As he bent over to pick up someone's discarded mug of ale, a screech broke across the sky. Right above him was a ball of fire, arcing over his head, plunging toward the earth. Great wings, the color of emeralds, stretched out from the flames. Buck found himself under the shadow of a dragon.

No such beast had been seen within the Malicarn for a generation. Dragons fed off magic, and so in a land devoid of magic such creatures were scarce. Yet here one was, falling to the ground. Buck leapt behind a small rock and covered his head. The ground shook when the dragon hit it, a deep groan bursting forth like a guttural scream.

Buck remained behind the rock for a long time, even as the noise calmed and all he could feel was the heat of the dragon's breath. Slowly he peeked over the rock and looked at the beast's remains. Buck did not know how dragons died, but it made sense that they would die in fire. Where before was a grassy field was now a crater, smoking and filled with the fiery, ruinous corpse of the great creature. Only a few visible remains of its armored hide could be seen amid the smoke. Buck had never seen its head, could not tell from the terror in its face what had caused it pain and distress.

As he watched the smoking remains, he noticed something else. A small figure, stumbling out of the crater. It was a man, a mask flung down at his side, tearing open the shirt he wore and falling half naked onto the ground, a few feet from Buck.

A dragon rider. A true harnesser of magical forces. In legends and histories nearly as powerful as the wizards themselves, and some of the wizards' greatest enemies. How incredible that one would come now, and fall among the Guild!

Buck rushed over to the rider, grabbed him by his arms, and dragged him behind the rock. The man was shouting, babbling in a tongue Buck could not comprehend.

"You are safe," Buck said. "Do not worry, you are safe here."

From the line of trees Buck saw Wallace running toward him, waving his hands and shouting.

"I am here!" Buck yelled, then looked again at the dragon rider. The man had no beard but his face was calm.

"I am safe?" the rider asked, haltingly, in a strange yet beautiful accent.

"Yes, you are safe," said Buck. "This is the Malicarn. Don't need worry about wizards. The Guild will protect you."

2.

Before her lessons, Queen Hannah liked to sneak away to the royal menagerie below the stables. The castle warden filled it with plants, animals, and birds gifted by visitors. Hannah's favorites were the bright colorful ones, with feathers that popped out of their heads or scales that sparkled in the sun. There were the singing birds, who chirped sweet little melodies. And there were the water creatures as well, frogs who hopped and swam and dove in the large pool at the center. The whole building was made of glass, and when Hannah walked inside the air was always warm and wet. Hannah assisted the warden with cleaning and feeding, and she liked to sit on a stone and hold out her hand full of seed as dozens of birds flocked to sit on her arm and nibble at her palm.

She lingered too long, and the stern figure of her tutor appeared outside, above on the hill, shouting her name.

"Best be off, Your Majesty," the warden said to her, and Hannah brushed off her hands and trudged back toward the castle. It was a winter morning, with a bit of fresh overnight snow on the ground. Hannah's weak leg stung in the cold, and she limped as she walked up the hill. Her leg bothered her always, but the pain was sharper when it was cold outside.

Hannah's tutor, an old frail man named Fennick, was responsible not just for instructing the young queen but for chaperoning her around the castle grounds, ensuring she was on time to appointments and properly dressed for royal visitors. Fennick did not talk much about himself, though he seemed to know at least a little bit about everything related to castle life.

Hannah's lessons took place in her private chambers, in the upper level of the castle's old tower. Hannah and Fennick sat on opposite ends of a small desk, reading passages together from the Book of Knowledge and discussing theology. Hannah massaged her leg as Fennick read through a series of verses.

"This one here: 'Ye shall not partake in the whims of the enchanter, nor learn by his side.' And this—" He flipped to another page. "Here: 'He that useth divination shall be cursed, as shall the witch, and the wizard, and the driver of enchanted beasts.'"

Hannah had heard the verses before. Fennick liked to read them, and today he did so with a special urgency. He would go on long explanations about how the Malicarn was better now without magic, how her advisors had brought order and stability to the realm, unlike the reign of her father, which was full of terrors. It was all academic to Hannah, who didn't remember the old days of magic anyway.

"You should be happy we are rid of those times," Fennick said. "There were terrible deeds. Wizards of all kinds; stones called dreamtalkers, which warped the minds of common men. There were horrid beasts, demons of the underworld, dragons, who—"

Fennick stopped, as if he was going to say something else, but instead he put away the book. For whatever reason, Fennick seemed reluctant to mention dragons in front of her today.

"Well, we do not worry about such things now. The Citadel is dangerous and fearsome, but it is no threat to us." The Citadel, a black-walled castle in the west, was the home of the Necromancer. No man ever approached it, but it loomed menacingly over the valley below. So Hannah had heard.

After studying theology, Hannah and Fennick worked on arithmetic and geometry, conducted some discussion of scientific principles, and then ended with a lecture on history. Fennick pontificated long and loud about the Great Wizarding War, the renowned acts of the Council of Heroes, and much more lore besides. Fennick had lived through much of this historical era and could recall it in vivid detail.

"At the Battle of the Morlon Kastaun, two factions fought against one another, the Red Mages and the Blue Sorcerers. They met at a spot, in the north of the valley, where the black walls emerged from the foot of the mountain, the old wizarding temple—" Even for Fennick this was proving to be a long and digressive anecdote, since they were supposed to be discussing the history of monastic orders. "—and one side faced against the other in the greatest display of wizarding magic the world has ever seen. The ruins of the Morlon Kastaun stand still as a monument to that slaughter." Fennick liked to talk about wizards, no matter what the Book of Knowledge said.

Mornings were for study, but afternoons were for royal business. Not that Hannah's advisors needed her present. She had just turned sixteen and so for another year, until her regency was over, she had little direct authority and her advisors managed the realm. When she left Fennick—and was relieved that he did not insist on escorting her directly to the Privy Council—Hannah took a detour and headed for the yard to watch weapons training instead.

Hannah was not permitted to train but enjoyed watching her knights do so. Kreek, the old swordmaster, stood in his usual place in the castle courtyard atop a small wooden stool, arms crossed as he surveyed the yard. He had been away for over a week, and there had been no fight training in his absence. But as

Hannah hobbled toward him, Kreek glared at her. He never said good morning, and if anything seemed more angry than usual today.

Kreek was renowned as the greatest fighter who ever lived, and had trained her father and the rest of the Council of Heroes before Hannah was born. Hannah knew these stories well. All the great victories of the Council in the years since were due, in part, to Kreek's guidance. And now he had to train young knights to protect a crippled queen. Hannah could sense his constant rage.

"Today you will practice with a two-handed sword," Kreek bellowed to one of the pages, handing him a wooden sparring sword nearly four feet long. "Sir Kellington will spar with you."

Kellington was the youngest member of the Queen's Guard, only eighteen years old but already a knight, and a full head taller than Hannah. He approached from the stables, wielding an even longer sword, and smiled at his queen.

"Ready for some fun?" he asked Hannah.

"Give me a good show," she said.

With her bad leg, Hannah could never move fast enough to effectively wield a sword, and her advisors would have balked at her requests to do so anyway.

"Young girls do not train to battle," they insisted. "Certainly not young queens."

"But kings ride into battle all the time."

"That is different."

"Why?"

"It just is."

Hannah watched the page parry blows from Kellington, circling around as he needed to, attempting to keep up a strong defense. But he never attacked. Holding the large sword with two hands was extra tiring, and each of Kellington's swings hit with more force, the wood vibrating in the page's hands.

"Strike!" Kreek yelled at him.

The page dropped his sword and yielded. Kellington stood

back, and Kreek stepped off his stool, grabbing the young page by the collar.

"Too slow, too stupid! You'll be sliced in half the first time you ride out with the Council of Heroes. To think this is the quality of man I have to train." He raised his palm and slapped the boy across the cheek.

"That's enough, Sir Kreek," Hannah shouted. "Let the boy have a rest."

Kreek said nothing but glared at the queen. He let go of the page and walked away.

"Good effort," Kellington said to the boy. "You impressed your queen."

Hannah walked toward the center of the courtyard. "I will have to speak to my advisors about Sir Kreek," Hannah said to Kellington. "That was not appropriate."

"It was how I was trained, Your Majesty. The old man is tough, but he knows how to make warriors."

"He *is* old. I should find my guard a younger swordmaster."

"I doubt your advisors will approve."

"Another year," Hannah said, "and this queen will make her own decisions."

"Well, I suppose Kreek may have been a bit rough today, but I don't blame him, with the dragon and all."

"What dragon?"

"Oh, your advisors did not tell you?"

"They forget to tell me a lot. But I have not seen them yet today."

"Oh, well then I should let them tell you. It is not my place."

"It is your place, if your queen orders it so."

"Please, Hannah, come on. I do not want to get in trouble."

"You will not. Tell me about this dragon."

"Well, Kreek's been away, on some hunting trip or something, up near the Morlon Kastaun ruins. The day before last, there's this dragon flies overhead, dies or is killed, and its body falls onto a field. Fire spewing everywhere, quite dramatic. Scared the monks up there something bad. Kreek saw the whole thing, so I heard."

This explained Fennick's digressions that morning. "A dragon? In the Malicarn? Why wasn't I told immediately?"

"Don't look at me, Hannah. I only heard about it from one of the squires this morning."

Above them sat the tower keep; a small window on the north end was the Privy Council chamber. Hannah knew her advisors were in there, discussing these important things, without her.

"Well, Kellington, I think it is about time for my royal duties."

There were two places in the castle where business was conducted. One was the main hall, a large and light-filled room also used for meals and entertainment. That was for the public, the hearing of queries from local landowners and the bestowing of titles on noble men and women. The other place for royal business was the Privy Council chamber, a smaller space filled with bookcases, a large round conference table, and a plethora of chairs. Not all the chairs would fit around the table, and many of them were stuck in various corners and nooks between piles of manuscripts. The Privy Council was where the real work happened. Charters were consulted, levies debated, and secret handshakes made between disputing factions about how to best proceed with running the realm.

Sanderson and Quentin, the royal advisors, were arguing with one another in the Privy Council chamber when Hannah walked in.

"Good morning, Your Majesty," Sanderson said, standing and bowing toward her. Sanderson had a long, poorly trimmed beard. His eyes were always bleary and he got out of breath easily.

Quentin merely nodded. He was sterner, clean-shaven, more focused, and despised Sanderson despite spending almost every waking minute with him, hashing out the minutiae of running the kingdom. The two old men had been the queen's regents since her birth and would remain so until her seventeenth birthday. Whether or not they would stay in the queen's service after that, Hannah had not decided.

Hannah sat down on a cushioned chair in front of the small table where the men were arguing. The stone walls were icy cold, the air in the chamber so chilled they could see their breath when talking. There was no fire lit because of all the documents surrounding the hearth and Sanderson's fears of records accidentally lost in the flames. The table in the center of the room was piled with scrolls, maps, and papers of various sizes. Quentin held a quill and scratched some notes on a parchment, while Sanderson paced with his hands clasped behind him. Hannah had walked in and interrupted them in the middle of an argument, and they quickly went silent. They did not like to yell in front of the young queen.

"Are you discussing the dragon?" Hannah asked.

"Ah, yes, Your Highness," Sanderson said. "So you have heard about that."

"Not from you, unfortunately."

"Well, we were going to discuss it with you, whenever you chose to arrive at council. But there is no need for concern. The creature is dead."

"There is much need for concern!" bellowed Quentin. "Do not try to present your queen with a false picture, Sanderson. Your Majesty, the creature is dead, that is true, but there is much more we do not yet know. Are there others? If there was a dragon rider, what became of him? Why was there a dragon in the Malicarn in the first place? The monks at the Dollories Monastery are hard at work searching for solutions to these questions, but this is a grave threat to the Malicarn. There hasn't been a dragon seen in the Malicarn since your father's, um—"

"Since his death," Hannah said. "Yes, thank you."

Quentin looked back at Sanderson. "You see? You think she is still a child and will not think such things! She knows how dangerous this situation is!"

"It is not dangerous!" Sanderson replied. "The dragon is dead.

There is nothing we need to fear and nothing we need to do, save wait for the monks to finish their research."

"What about Gregorian?" Hannah asked. Both men stopped and looked at her. Sanderson sighed, and Quentin dropped his head into his hands.

"What?" she asked. "Why not speak with him? He's a wizard, he'll know more about the dragon than any of us."

"Your Majesty," Sanderson said, "whatever power Gregorian once held, it is long in the past."

"But Gregorian has knowledge no one else has. Maybe he understands—"

"He knows nothing," Quentin snapped. "It is best to not engage with him and his old ways."

"The Councilors trust him."

"The Council of Heroes are warriors and do a fine job protecting us from dangers. But they work in the borderlands and do not interact with Gregorian regularly. They do not see that Gregorian is . . . old."

Sanderson and Quentin had always disliked Gregorian, but Hannah could never figure why. Gregorian was not an official regent and did not sit on the Council of Heroes—in fact, he did not have an official position at all—but he was always free with advice. Especially with Hannah. Gregorian would visit court and sneak Hannah books when Sanderson and Quentin were not looking. Gregorian's books were illustrated and colorful, full of daring heroes in distant worlds of magic, about fantastical people who had the powers of animals, and tales of great wizards who could fly.

"You have to keep these hidden," Gregorian would tell her, sliding the small books inside the pages of a long historical chronicle. "Only read them alone at night. You never know who may be watching and wish to take them from you."

"Are they banned, like magic?" Hannah asked.

"Yes, but they are not dangerous. They are fun. I enjoyed them when I was young and I want you to enjoy them too."

Sanderson and Quentin thought Gregorian sinister, and if they knew of his secret gifts to the queen their suspicions would be confirmed. But Hannah believed there was much more to the wizard, and the world, than what concerned her two advisors.

"Well, I still think Gregorian should be consulted," Hannah said. "I order you to do so."

Sanderson smiled and sat in a chair across from Hannah. "My queen, while I am charged to serve you in all ways, I must remind you that until you are seventeen the regency has bestowed upon myself and Sir Quentin the powers of the Crown, for your protection as much as anything. Since the day you were born we have endeavored to rule fairly and wisely in your stead, and though we will always take your preferences into advisement, we simply must follow the binds of our own conscience."

Sanderson liked to give this speech, and it had become more elaborate over time.

"So you will not consult with Gregorian then?"

"No, Your Majesty. We will not."

"Very well, I will speak to him myself." She raised her voice and shouted to the ceiling. "Gregorian, the queen formally requests your presence for royal council!"

Sanderson and Quentin groaned. This was some bit of magic Gregorian had long ago given Hannah the power to conjure. She did now know how it worked, exactly, but if she simply shouted the words loud enough, Gregorian would soon appear. It was technically against the law, but the magic was subtle enough that no one could ever prove its existence, much as Sanderson and Quentin wished to, if only to force Gregorian into exile.

Sanderson stood back up. "This is a waste of time, Your Majesty."

Hannah could have said the same about the rest of the afternoon, which was spent reviewing tax rolls, boring and tedious work that Hannah hated but for which Sanderson insisted she be present. Afterward she had a break before supper, so she walked back down to the castle courtyard to find Kellington.

But Kellington wasn't there. Instead, sitting on the wooden platform Kreek had used earlier, was Gregorian, dressed in a plain brown robe and scratching his short beard. Gregorian had never had a very long beard, which made him different from other wizards. Of course, Hannah had never met any other wizards, so she supposed it was possible that Gregorian was just like all of the rest of them.

"You came quick," Hannah said.

"You asked me to." Gregorian stood up, yawned, and stretched. "Let me guess. This is about the dragon?"

"Yes, Sanderson and Quentin did not know much about it. Took their time even telling me."

"Well, there's not much to tell. What is left of it is well charred."

"You have seen it?"

"Oh yes. This morning. I planned to come and give you and the regents a full report. But like I said, there is not much to report on." He walked over to a pen where a few horses were standing and leaned against the post. "There will be some Councilors, perhaps some knights, who are going to want to ride out hunting for more dragons. I would discourage this, when they come to you."

"You know this already?"

"Yes."

"Quentin thought there might have been a dragon rider. Do you know about that?"

"Hmm." Gregorian paused, petting the mane of a nearby horse. "Not all dragons have riders, you know. And if there was one, he must be dead, too. Incinerated, like so much of the dragon itself."

"I think I should see the remains. Reassure the people—"

"No, it is really not necessary. Trust me, the faster the people forget about the dragon the better."

"I disagree. They are only now recovering from famine, and the flooding last summer was a hard blow. Any other signs of doom will surely be taken as bad omens. But if I reassure them, as their queen—"

"What will happen, do you think? Have you ever addressed the people before, as their queen?"

"You know I have not. But I should begin to practice."

"The people won't like it. They don't like highborns speaking down to them. You can stamp your feet about it, but I am simply telling you the truth. I have been speaking to them on this goodwill tour for you and people are very angry."

"I have not done anything."

"Yes, that is their main point of contention."

"But I cannot do anything until the regency ends. They must get to know me. I will be compassionate, you know that, Gregorian."

The wizard tapped a few rhythmic beats with his fingers on the post and then turned back toward the yard. "I do. I am only trying to be honest, in order to protect you. Tensions are high, let's not exacerbate them. That is all I am saying."

"You believe I do not know what I am doing."

"I think you *want* to know what to do, but you don't want to admit that you do not."

"And you? You know how I should rule?"

"Yes. If you listen to me, you will see that."

"Well, I expect this politicking from Sanderson and Quentin, but not from you, Gregorian." She turned and walked back into the keep.

"Hannah, now, listen, that's not fair—" But she didn't hear the rest of what he had to say as she passed into the stone tower.

Hannah took supper in her private chambers. Eating alone helped her think. She pulled out some maps from Fennick's stash of texts and scrolls, charting a path from Kingstown and the castle to the Morlon Kastaun battlefield. It was only a day's ride, assuming you had a fast enough horse. Someone could make it out there, leaving at dawn, and make it back by dusk. You wouldn't get to rest, of course, and you would need to know where best to change horses, but a skilled rider could do it.

"Please ask Sir Kellington to visit me after he eats," Hannah told one of her servants.

Kellington walked in an hour later, slightly drunk, but still dressed in full mail with his sword at his side. "Your Majesty! I come to serve you!"

Hannah realized this late-night assignation was about to be misinterpreted, so she got to the point. "Sir Kellington, I need you to take me to the Morlon Kastaun to see the dragon corpse. I trust you have a fine steed on which to ride, and can do so with some stealth?"

"Uh, yes, Youe Highness. It is a long ride, though—"

"I do not wish to stay long. Simply to see the corpse. We travel light and fast so as to avoid a royal retinue that would slow us down. If we leave at dawn we can make it back within a day. My advisors will be upset but by the time they figure out what to do we'll have returned."

"With respect, Highness, that kind of hard riding is certainly possible for a knight in times of war or on an urgent quest, but it is likely to prove wearying to one, like yourself, who is not used to such trials. I say this with all respect, of course."

"Nevertheless, you will do it."

"I must get permission from the regents, or else—"

"You will not. In a little less than a year the regents will have no more power, and I expect to spread my favors far and wide, but only to those whom I know I can trust."

Kellington nodded. "Of course, Your Majesty. I suggest you sleep as much as possible. I will have the horses prepared in the morning."

Hannah was pleased with her authority, though she had trouble falling asleep. At first she just thought it was excitement, but after some hours in the dark she noticed there was a slight hiss, as from a teakettle, emanating from within the walls.

"If that is some magic of yours, Gregorian, I demand you to stop it." She said this aloud in jest, but the hissing did indeed stop. She had trouble sleeping, rolling on her bed and trying to tamp down her excitement. She finally dozed a bit toward morning, and had dreams of a dragon flying above her at the Morlon Kastaun as a battle raged below.

Just before dawn, Hannah put on a riding dress—the most modest she could find, but encrusted with jewels in the fringes even so. She snuck down to the courtyard. The guards at this hour were posted mostly around the perimeter, making it easier to move about the castle grounds undetected. Kellington was waiting there for her with a horse, a large chestnut.

"There is a garrison along the way," he said, "where we can change for another. It will not slow us down too much."

"Thank you," Hannah said. "What did you tell the horsemaster?"

"Just that I needed to run an errand for the queen."

They both climbed onto the horse, Hannah behind Kellington, clasping her hands around his waist. She hid her face as they passed through the castle gates. There was a path that wound down the hill through Kingstown. Kellington took it slowly, since the streets were clogged with the destitute sleeping against buildings and doorways. The walls were covered with graffiti, mostly obscene and disparaging remarks about the queen and the Council of Heroes, along with some unrelated pornography. Outside the walls they crossed through a large, semipermanent tent city of migrants and then finally into an open field. Kellington kicked the horse into a gallop, and they were off.

Hannah did not ride much. Her leg prevented it, and when she did travel abroad it was typically in a carriage, slowly, surrounded by knights. The sun rose over the hills and Hannah's eyes watered as the sharp, cold air hit her face. The fresh morning breeze made all things feel new.

But the ride was short. Only a few miles in, Hannah noticed a company of horsemen descending from a northern ridge. The horsemen rode straight toward them, fast and fleet. They were knights as well, and they surrounded Kellington, forcing him to a stop. The lead knight rode up beside him. It was Kreek.

"Sir Kellington, who is it you are riding away with?"

Hannah took off her hood. "Sir Kreek, it is I. Do not blame Sir Kellington. I ordered him to take me to see the dragon."

"Yes, I know. Kellington, this should be a killing offense, kidnapping the queen—"

"I was not kidnapped."

"—but I think it may merely be a demotion back to squire. You are clearly not ready for the responsibilities of knighthood."

"Sir Kreek!" Hannah shouted. "You have no such authority! As queen, I decide who is fit for knighthood."

Kreek leaned in toward her. "My authority here is invested by the regency! You are under the care of the same!"

Kellington's hands held the reins, but were shaking. "I am sorry, Sir Kreek, I, I—"

"Save your apologies. Turn around. We will escort you home."

Hannah would not keep Kreek in his position as royal swordmaster, not once she was old enough to change it. She knew that now. She would just have to wait another year, and Kreek would not be able to talk to her like that ever again. Next time he found out—and suddenly Hannah felt a drop in her stomach. How had Kreek found out where they were going? How did he know they were headed to see the dragon corpse?

The sun rose higher and the frost baked off the grass on the open fields. The snow that still clung to branches and trunks under shade glistened in the morning light. It was not long before Kingstown and the castle came into view again.

Kreek had ridden down from the north, not from the castle. But still he knew they were gone, knew where they were going. Somebody must have told him. Somebody who might have been able to see Hannah, watch her, make sure she wasn't doing anything she wasn't supposed to be doing.

Somebody like a wizard.

LOS ANGELES

April 20, 1981

"Don't swim in the pool," Ted said. "There's something weird growing in there."

Someone handed Rex Donaldson a cocktail and he craned his head over a cabana chair to take a look. The pool water was a little cloudy, but it looked fine. Ted stared at it glumly.

"I know, it looks okay, but there's something wrong with the filter. It was all green yesterday."

"Well," Rex said, "I didn't bring my swim trunks anyway."

Ted went off to meet some freshly arrived guests, and Rex approached the edge of the pool, sipping his drink alone. This house was far too large. Four bedrooms, an extra-large garage for all the classic cars Ted didn't own. In an especially expensive neighborhood off Laurel Canyon. Ted would never be able to keep up with it. Rex had seen this happen a bunch of times before. Somebody gets a little bit of success, their first minor hit, and they overdo it on real estate or women or drugs.

There didn't seem to be any drugs at this party, though. That was a shame. Rex could use a pick-me-up.

A day of development meetings, always draining, followed by an executive-only screening of the new Lenny Pinkus picture. The film was all right. Pretty funny, too long. Rex was going to have to tell the director to cut it down about twenty minutes. But it should be okay. Rex had kept the budget under control. Oh, everyone had bitched at him constantly during production. Even the cinematographer had threatened to quit, but that was an empty threat. No one more replaceable. Pinkus didn't complain, though. He at least was getting paid well. The studio head laughed often during the screening, so that was positive. The picture wasn't going to sell like gangbusters, but Rex could keep it in the black. Give him enough time and Rex Donaldson could make anything a hit.

After lunch he went to Peppy's apartment in North Hollywood for some cocaine, but Peppy was out. Rex hadn't hit any lines all afternoon. He was starting to get itchy.

Back at the office, Ted had left a message with Rex's secretary, reminding him he was having a little party. Ted always hosted little parties with fifty or so people. Rex figured it was a good way to score coke. Ted bought this new place two months earlier, and his parties were probably costing him more money than whatever pool repairs he needed. But Ted was a screenwriter, and therefore one of the neediest figures in all of Hollywood. He got points on last year's Lenny Pinkus hit, and he was going to ride that financial wave as long and high as he could. Ted did not, as far as Rex knew, have any additional work lined up.

The last call Rex made before driving to the party was to his brother Dave. Dave lived in Rochester and had never done cocaine. He was an accountant, or an actuary, or something. Rex admitted that he did not like to talk to his little brother, because Dave talked a lot about Rochester and Rex always hated Rochester. It was cold and snowy and gray. When he moved to LA he never expected to spend any more time thinking about Rochester. But now their mother was sick and Rex figured it was his weekly duty at least to keep up with Dave for news on how she was doing.

"Second round of chemo went well," Dave told him over the phone, as Rex sat in his office flipping through script notes. "Still pretty sick for about two days, but today she's feeling much better. Doctor seems optimistic."

Rex was happy to hear that. If his mother died he would have to fly back to Rochester for the funeral.

"Oh, did you hear about the Red Wings?" Dave asked.

"What?"

"The Rochester Red Wings were playing the Red Sox this

weekend. The Pawtucket Red Sox, of course. The game went thirty-two innings. Thirty-two! They didn't even finish playing. It's still tied two to two. They finally let everyone go to sleep at like four AM. They're going to have to finish it the next time the Red Sox are in town. It's the longest baseball game ever, they're saying."

"Wow." Rex desperately wanted to get off the phone.

Now as he looked at Ted's dirty pool and surveyed the crowd growing around him, wondering who among them had cocaine, Rex couldn't stop thinking about that game. A game that never ended. Maybe when the teams kept playing someone would finally get a hit, but maybe they wouldn't. The game could just keep on going, forever. Why not? There was no rule it couldn't. The players would have to keep coming up to bat, keep pitching, keep fielding. There was no way for it to ever end. Rex tried to imagine a film that never finished being produced, that kept going. Studio screening after studio screening, note after note, cut after cut. How long could something like that last? Did the universe even last forever? Rex found the whole idea terrifying.

A man Rex hadn't noticed before was standing next to him at the pool's edge, smoking a cigarette. He had a sallow face, a thick mustache, a round pair of glasses, and an old, shabby suit.

"Not much of a party, eh?" Rex asked him.

The man blew a puff of smoke and looked at Rex. "It seems like a party to me." He spoke with a hint of a French accent but Rex had a feeling he didn't have any cocaine.

"Rex Donaldson," he said, sticking out his hand. "I'm a producer at WBC Studios."

"Ah." The man shook his hand. "Jean-Danton Souard. Nice to meet you."

"Souard? The writer?"

Jean-Danton sighed and took another drag of his cigarette. "Yes. You have read my work?"

Rex had not, though he had read the notes from his assistant. Souard was a hot item. A mega-selling book, two sequels. For years everyone in town had tried to bid on options to adapt it, ever since the first book was a surprise serialized hit in a small magazine. Rex personally knew a producer at an animation studio who wanted the rights really bad. Rex was interested, of course. Any property that sold a million copies and was translated all over the world interested him. But he didn't have the slightest idea what the books were really about. Some kind of fantasy story, something about magic and dragons. Would be expensive. Did kids like dragons? But Rex knew if he optioned the rights then none of his rivals would be able to adapt the books, either, and that would still be a win.

"I have read them. Loved them."

"Who was your favorite character?"

"Hard to say. So many good ones. What are you doing in Los Angeles? Taking meetings?"

"No. My wife and I are vacationing in Santa Barbara."

"Lovely town."

"The wine is good. And our son is going to the university there, so we can visit him."

"So you know Ted?"

"No, who is Ted?"

"This is Ted's house. This is Ted's party. He's a writer."

"What has he written?"

"Oh, a few movies. Do you know Lenny Pinkus? He's a comedian."

"I have heard of him. He does funny voices?"

"Yes, he's very popular in France."

"I have not lived in France for a long time."

"Well, you should watch one of his films. They're very popular."

"No, I do not think I will." Jean-Danton threw his cigarette into the pool and lit another. "I am only here because my literary agent had some meetings in town. I told him I would drive down and see him, and now he wants me to keep him company. So I follow him around for the night. As a favor, I suppose. He likes to show me off." Jean-Danton gestured to a well-dressed gentleman talking to Ted inside the house. Rex would have to make his way over there to say hello.

"Well, Mr. Souard, I hope I'm not being too forward, but I would love to take a meeting and talk about your books. You know, of course, how interested everyone is in them."

"No one has optioned my books."

"Ha! Well, an error I can assure you won't be too long in being remedied. I know some real smart young directors who would love to speak with you about—"

"No, you misunderstand. No one is going to option my books. You can keep bidding on them, but the answer will always be no."

"Oh, if you're worried about some Hollywood big shot butchering it—and why not, right? certainly this town has ruined many properties in the past—I want you to know that's not my intention. Hell, it might be unadaptable! That's always a possibility. I would never force something into production that's not suited for the big screen. But you have to at least come take the meeting, while you're in town."

"No, Mr. Donaldson. This isn't a negotiation." This was a strange man, Rex suddenly noticed, to come to a Hollywood party and smoke cigarettes at the pool, ignoring everyone and claiming no interest in taking meetings. Hollywood was nothing *but* meetings.

"I'm sure your literary agent wants—"

"What he wants doesn't matter, either. He's made quite a bit of money off of me, so I'll come out and dance sometimes to appease him." Souard's French accent came out stronger when he was upset. "But my books are my life. I will never let you adapt them and turn them into some piece of *property* for you to profit off."

Rex smiled. "Of course, Mr. Souard, no pressure." It wasn't worth alienating the guy. There would always be more time. Baseball games can last forever; so can movie development.

Jean-Danton flicked another cigarette into the pool. "Such a filthy pool," he said, and walked back into the house.

"Enjoy your time in Los Angeles!" Rex shouted after him.

Rex stayed beside the pool, nodding to no one in particular. His charm was all off today. He really did need some cocaine.

THE MALICARN

THE SIXTEENTH SPRING
IN THE REIGN OF QUEEN HANNAH I

1.

The wall collapsed during the night. Maybe the mortar wasn't setting, maybe Buck had placed the stones wrong. Maybe it was sabotage, though Buck couldn't figure why anyone would want to knock down a retaining wall on the far side of a horse pasture.

Buck told Otto right away, but Otto had to finish milking the cows before he could walk over and inspect the situation. By then another row of stone had fallen off the wall and the entire structure looked like little more than a pile of rocks.

"You gotta deal with this, Buck," Otto said. "I don't have time for it right now."

"I'm supposed to be getting on watch duty."

"Someone else can do that. Kreek promised me help, this wall is the help I need."

Otto was curt, but Buck knew it wasn't directed at him. He was curt with everyone. The presence of extra hands on his farm hadn't compelled him even a little bit to moderate his temper. If anything, it made it worse. He was always complaining, shouting about the extra mouths to feed, the damage they were doing to his vegetables by overeating, his cows by overmilking, and his horses by overriding. It was true that the Guild was taking up a lot of space and resources on Otto's farm, but Kreek was insistent that it was the safest spot in the Malicarn.

"Otto is an isolated loner," he had explained. "Nobody much likes him, which means nobody is going to be checking on him. I'll make sure he's compensated for whatever losses he accrues due to our presence. In the meantime, if he has work for you to do, do it."

That would now include rebuilding a wall. It took most of the morning for Buck to clear the fallen stone, clean off the day-old drying mortar, and sort everything to figure what else he might be missing. Buck wanted to return to the granary, but he still needed to mix the mortar and set the first few layers. There wasn't enough quicklime for even one full row of stone, which Buck unfortunately didn't realize until he had already relaid half of it. The mortar would have to set as it was, and if tomorrow he came back with more lime and things didn't line up correctly that was just the way it was going to be. He wasn't a bad mason—he just wasn't very good.

After he ate supper with the other guildsmen, Buck took his break and walked down the hill to the granary, an old building Otto had also been meaning to repair but never got around to. Wallace was standing guard outside today, and nodded as Buck approached.

"Thought you were coming earlier?" Wallace asked.

"I was working on that wall for Otto."

"He's a lazy old bastard, that's for sure. Kreek ought to find another place, one with fewer chores."

"I am sure he has his reasons," Buck said. "Kreek here?"

"Nah. Haven't seen him in two days. You relieving me?"

"I don't know. I think I was supposed to be inside."

Wallace shifted his feet and leaned against the stone wall. "I can't stand for much longer, I'm getting sore. Find out if someone's coming out, all right?"

Buck walked inside, and up a set of wooden stairs to a landing at the top of the tower. Two more guildmembers were in here, sporting short swords. Sitting against the far wall, blanket over his lap, head slumped on his shoulder as he napped, was the dragon rider.

When Buck first found him, bleeding and screaming on the field of the Morlon Kastaun, he knew that the man was in danger, but only when he and Wallace carried the dragon rider to Kreek, kicking and yelling the whole way, did the full extent of the danger become known.

"I always feared this day would come," Kreek said, "when the peace forged with the Necromancer would be forfeit. I suspect Gregorian has betrayed the realm, perhaps planning on seizing power for himself, and now our enemies will soon invade. This dragon is but a harbinger of their power."

These were dark prophecies, but they did not scare Buck. They thrilled him. War was coming! Perhaps he would live to see wizards in battle after all.

Kreek soon spirited the dragon rider to Otto's farm, hiding him in the granary and placing the guildmembers as his wardens and protectors. Most men would sit on watch for a day or two then cycle back to their homes, but Buck and the younger guildmembers remained on the farm. It was exciting, being so close to magic.

"What is it we will do to him?" they asked Kreek.

"We must keep him hidden for now. I will work my influence in the realm, find what information I can, and see how we can use this to our advantage."

Otto himself was not part of the Guild, but he found Kreek's appeal very satisfying. "Never did like that old wizard, always hanging over us common folk, making us feel low. Who is he? Not a lord, no, not even a real warrior. He's the one bringing in goblins to take over our farms." Buck noticed Otto was prone to long diatribes against the queen, the court, the Council of Heroes, basically anybody with any sort of authority. He hated them even more than the guildmembers stomping around his farm.

But whatever Kreek's plan was, it was taking time. The prisoner had been nearly three months in the granary, growing thinner and weaker despite how well they tried to feed him. Kreek wouldn't permit the man to be taken outside, not even after dark, and grew angered and paranoid whenever anyone suggested it.

He had to stay in the granary, and the Guild alternated watching him between chores on the farm.

"I think it's your turn in the cow pasture," Buck said to the man seated at the top of the stairs. "I was supposed to be on guard duty this morning."

"Yeah, well, you're late. I ain't going to work for that jerk now. He'll just yell at me more."

"You gotta go."

"Nah, I'm headed over to the barn. I'm taking a nap."

The other guard was ready to leave too. "It's too hot up here. I can't breathe."

"Could you relieve Wallace, then?" Buck asked. "He's been standing out there all morning."

"Yeah, fine, I could use the fresh air."

They left. Buck remained alone with the dragon rider, who was still asleep. Buck sat in one of the half-rotted chairs beside the granary window and picked up the little sword the Guild kept there for the guards.

"Buck?" The dragon rider had woken, and was pointing at Buck.

"Yes, Buck, that's right. It's me again." At first the dragon rider could not speak much, save for "Hello" or "Yes" or the occasional "Help, please!" But he did seem to know that he was in the Malicarn. "Malicarn! This is Malicarn!" he shouted, not without excitement, when they first carried him to the granary.

Slowly, he was getting better at longer conversations. Last time Buck was on watch, the rider had mentioned the late King Prion, and Buck told him the story of Prion's reign—or what he could remember, anyway. The rider had listened attentively, but without, as far as Buck could discern, much reason.

"Prion!" he shouted again, smiling and nodding at Buck. "He was king. But not now."

"Yes, your speech has improved tremendously. Prion was king. But he is dead. Now Queen Hannah, his daughter, is ruler.

Do you remember? We spoke about it. Dead. That means, uh, not living. No more."

"Prion, dead. Yes, yes." He sat up and pointed at Buck. "Do you have water?" he asked. "Thirsty?"

The rider was chained by his legs to the wall, but the chains were not very tight and he had plenty of slack. The Guild needed to keep him here but they had no desire to hurt him. Here was a potential ally, after all. Buck took his skin of water from the rope around his neck and handed it to the rider, who drank from it. He spilled as much as he swallowed. He handed Buck back his skin, then stood up and looked out the small granary window. The view was blocked by a nearby tree, but if there was wind you could sometimes see a hill beyond.

"All Malicarn?" the man asked, pointing.

"Yes, Malicarn. This is the realm of the old Carnas, ancient forest folk. You know, Malicarn actually means 'Land of the Carnas,' though the Carnas themselves are long since—"

"Malicarn, I saw it. A long time ago, at home."

"Oh, with a seeing stone? You have that magic?"

"Ha, yes. Seeing *box*. You do not have a word for it." He pointed out the window. "See? I see nothing."

They had chained him near the first window precisely because there was no view, and thus no way for any spies to see into the granary and discover the Guild's prisoner. The window by Buck had a wider view of Otto's farm, especially the wheat field. Kreek was very firm on the fact that the rider must never look out that window, or exit the granary, but Buck glanced outside and couldn't see a single person—not even a guildmember—on the entire hillside.

The rider was their ally, or was going to be. Wasn't it cruel for him to remain tied up for three months with only the view of a tree to sustain him?

"All right, hold up," Buck said. The key to the manacles hung at the top of the stairs. Buck pulled them down, unlocked the restraints from the man's ankles, and then slid them off.

The rider hobbled over to the window and looked at the field. "Malicarn!"

"Yes, that is the Malicarn!" Buck replied. "A once-great country, that will be great again if—"

Buck had not come up with the rest of his sentence yet. Like most things he said, he was making it up as he went along, finding each appropriate word based on what came before. So it wasn't so much that he was interrupted when the rider shoved him down the stairs, rather that he was denied the opportunity to continue.

Buck hit his head hard against the stone wall as he fell. He remained conscious, but was disoriented enough that he was unable to stop the rider as he leapt over him, down the staircase, and out the front of the granary. There was yelling, the sound of a struggle, and when Buck managed to stand back up he saw, out the window, the dragon rider disappearing into the wheat field.

2.

Even with the window closed, Hannah could hear the shouts from the street. She flipped through a book of maps, slumped in a chair in the corner of the Privy Council chamber, ignoring Sanderson and Quentin's bickering. It was Sanderson who had closed the window, despite the warm spring day, tired of listening to the mob outside the castle gates.

"The key to mobs is to ignore them," Sanderson told the queen. "They only grow stronger if you pay them any mind."

Why was everyone telling her to ignore the people? There had been angry beggars nearly every day since the dragon fell, the crowds slowly growing. Instead of people forgetting about the dragon, rumors were spreading that war was imminent, or that the dragon heralded more crop failures, or that the queen was planning on murdering children to appease the dragon gods. At first this was out of fear, but lately, Hannah suspected, it was more out of anger. The spring rains had not come, and the heat was baking newly sown fields. It would, in fact, not be a fruitful harvest, and children would die.

"We have to send a contingent to the armories in the lower valley," Quentin shouted as Sanderson riffled through papers. "We cannot risk another—"

"No, no! We start moving knights and armed men through the valley and the people will take it for what it is: an occupation."

These conversations, which had been happening with increasing frequency, took place with Hannah present but silent. The silence was a mutual and unspoken agreement between the queen and her advisors after her attempt to sneak away. Listening but saying nothing meant that Hannah was going to be obedient, that she wasn't planning on doing anything rash. Allowing her to listen meant that the advisors weren't going to exclude her from any discussions or sensitive matters of the realm. They would make the decisions, but Hannah would know what all of the decisions were. For the time being, that seemed to placate everybody.

Someone knocked and the door opened. A page walked in. "That man is here. The old blacksmith."

"Oh, now he decides to arrive?" asked Quentin. "Fine, fine. Bring him in."

Hannah turned the page in her book, looking over a map of the Malicarn. There was very little detail, and the map faded off soon after crossing into the eastern frontier. The seas which surrounded the Malicarn on every other side did not indicate what lands might be beyond them.

A moment later a short man, older than Sanderson, entered the room. He was dressed casually, as if he had worked a forge that morning. He bowed to Sanderson at first, but then realized his error and turned to bow at Hannah.

"My queen."

"Sit, please," she said, putting away the book. The man

remained standing. "These are my advisors, Sanderson and Quentin."

"Ah, yes, we have met, when you visited the River Lands last spring. I was in the crowd when you addressed us in the square."

"I don't recall," said Quentin. "Did Alfred send you? He is the reeve in those parts?"

"No, no. I come of my own accord. My name is Jasper, and I have an urgent matter."

"We do not usually hear petitions in the Privy Council," Quentin said. "Certainly not from men of your, um, station. Why did you not present this to your queen at the hall this morning with the other petitioners?"

"Well, to be frank, sir, I found myself delayed. The crowds outside the city have grown thick. People traveling from their farms, unable to feed their families. And the mobs outside the castle gate itself. It was quite difficult to find a way past them without suffering a blow. They are quite heated."

The public petitions were being curtailed anyway. Hannah spoke to only half a dozen people a day or so now, usually men known to the court, nobles or others of high renown. The common folk were being kept outside, for her safety.

"Well, you've made it this far," Sanderson said. "What is it that's so important?"

"My queen," Jasper said, turning toward Hannah, "it concerns the dragon."

"Speak directly to us," said Quentin. "Your queen will still hear you, but we'll be the ones with the answers."

"Uh, yes, of course. My lords—"

"We're not lords."

"My good sirs, then. Since the dragon's appearance rumor and fear has swept through the realm. Stories about goblins stealing children in the night, the dead walking, great beasts rising from the depths. Nonsense, of course, most of it. But there is one rumor that I believe is true: that the man who rode the dragon to the Malicarn is alive. He's alive, and he is still in the realm. An omen of war, they say."

"War?" Hannah asked. "Who ever said anything about a war?"

"Now, now, Your Majesty," Sanderson said, "there's no war. Some people are worried about this dragon, that's all. Maybe anxious about the next harvest, but that's still some months off. Plenty of time for the rains to come. No, I think what Jasper means to say is, some people heard a rumor of war, but like all the other rumors there is nothing to it. Isn't that right, sir?"

"No! That is not right! There are whisper networks all over the realm. An underground, if I may call it that. I mean no disrespect, Your Majesty, but it is the truth."

"How do you know of this underground?" Quentin asked. "Are you a part of it?"

"Not so much, no. But I do know of it. All men do."

"This is an outrage! How dare you threaten your queen!"

"I come not to threaten. I seek help. I talk to people from all places, and they are afraid. Afraid of outsiders coming into their homes, goblins stealing their farms—"

"Those are citizens of the Malicarn," Hannah said. "I do not like this tone."

"Residents of the Malicarn, perhaps," Quentin interjected. "But not citizens. A goblin is not a man, and—"

"I do not wish to hear such vile slanders!" Hannah shouted. She tried to sound firm. "I do not even like the term. The outsiders are people, not goblins. Call them what they are. *Men.* This is known throughout the realm, though many choose not to believe it." Gregorian had been pretty firm with Hannah about this very point, and he rarely got animated, so she followed suit whenever the topic came up.

"My apologies," Jasper said. "I am simply repeating what I hear. People do not always trust the Crown, because of, well, because—"

"Because I am a young cripple who looks like a goblin?"

"Not my words, Your Highness. Simply what I hear. Believe

me when I tell you that there is a dragon rider out there, somewhere, and enemies of the Crown hold him captive. It is not just a rumor."

"What good could it possibly do," Quentin asked, "even if it were true? The dragon is dead, they can't get much use out of a rider now."

"My theory is they plan to parade him about and incite the mobs to revolt. Whatever it is, if you haven't anticipated it, you can be sure that your wizard hasn't anticipated it."

"What the hell does Gregorian have to do with anything?" Quentin shouted.

"But it's just a rumor," Sanderson said. "You may have heard it from someone you trust, but you haven't seen this rider yourself, have you?"

"No," Jasper said. "But there are, uh—" He paused, looking at Queen Hannah. "There are lots of people upset with the way the Crown has been run. No offense to you, sirs."

"People are always upset with the Crown," said Quentin. "That's why we have a Crown."

"I've heard just about enough of this," Sanderson said. "You've gotten dangerously close to treason. I should have you hanged. Leave us."

Hannah watched Sanderson push the man back out of the room, and Jasper looked at her, pleading with her to interfere. But she said nothing and a moment later he was gone and the door was again shut.

"Should we take him seriously?" Hannah asked.

"No," said Quentin. "This is all a waste of time. Better to forget it. No more commoners in the castle, that's what I say. The sooner everyone forgets about this dragon the sooner these crowds will calm down and go home, and—" He looked out the window and let out a heavy sigh. "Now what is that?"

A building was on fire, just beyond the castle's outer walls.

"Looks like the Inns of Court," said Sanderson. "Do you think it was set intentionally?"

"I'd rather not find out. We better deploy the barracks. Stop this from becoming a riot, or at least more of a riot than it already is."

Both men left, ending Hannah's official business for the afternoon. She reopened her book of maps, trying to remember what Gregorian had told her about the lands across the sea. It was very vague, just that great nations lived there, and it was safer to ignore them than try to establish diplomatic relationships. She should have pressed him on this. He knew more than he was letting on.

She stood up and looked out the window at the fire, a large conflagration which was already spreading down a street. Bells tolled as the city fire brigade leapt into action. They would probably have to raze several blocks to stop the fire's spread. How many homes would that be? How many more people forced to live outside the castle gate, yelling at those inside? Hannah imagined their rage, imagined someone bringing forth a dragon rider, demanding to treat with the queen. She couldn't imagine what they would do after that. Her imagination didn't stretch that far. But for the first time, Hannah was afraid.

3.

Buck and Wallace rode off on two of the older horses. They didn't have time to choose differently, what with Otto yelling after them and the sun quickly lowering toward dusk.

"You lousy, goodfornothing sonsuvbitches!" Otto was screaming, covered in mud and shaking a pickax. "You ruin my farm then take my horses! I see how it is! I see!"

"We'll bring the horses back, straightaway," Buck shouted back at him. "Just need to take care of some Guild business, all right?"

Buck and Wallace didn't send anyone to tell Kreek about the rider getting away. Frankly, everyone tacitly agreed it would be best not to raise Kreek's ire. If the rider was still missing by daybreak, then sure. They would tell him. But Buck and Wallace were going to ride after him first. It wouldn't take long to find him. Where was he planning to go anyway?

They followed a recently blazed path through the wheat field of down and damaged stalks, which ended at the tree line. The lack of rain had made the ground hard and stiff, and this was where their tracking plan immediately ran into problems.

"Well, you've really done it this time, Buck." Wallace got off his horse and walked in a circle around a large oak, hoping to see something on the ground. "Yes, you have really gone and done it. Kreek's certainly going to have some words with you. Oh yes, he's going to kick you out of the Guild for sure."

"He can't have gone far. We'll find him." Buck liked to say things that he knew weren't true.

They rode a little way into the woods, hoping to find some sign of something or someone. After about an hour Wallace saw a column of smoke over the treetops. They approached and found a small cottage with a chimney, and two young children playing in the garden outside. Behind the home sat a blacksmith's forge. The mother emerged from the door as the men approached.

"I'm not paying no more soldier tolls. I got two little ones out of that already, I can't afford to do it again. I can't—"

"Ah, no," Wallace said. "That's not what we're here for. We're looking for a runaway. A man on foot. Dressed sorta funny. Speaks a foreign tongue. Perhaps you've seen him?"

"You king's men?"

"No."

"How do I know that?"

"I mean, look at us."

"You're on horseback. You have a sword."

"What? This?" Buck held up the small sword he had taken from the granary.

"That's hardly a sword at all," Wallace said. "Look at it, it's so small."

"Yes," said Buck. "Sir Kreek's is much bigger, much better made."

"Sir Kreek?" the woman asked. "The royal swordmaster? So you are king's men?"

Wallace sighed, but Buck began babbling, words falling out of his mouth at random. If he babbled enough he might say something smart.

"No, no! We've never even been inside the castle at Kingstown. I mean, I helped build part of it, being I'm a mason, you know. So if I've been inside that was only the parts I helped build, as I was building them. Wallace, though, he's a carpenter. Didn't work on the castle at all, did you? We know Kreek a bit, but not from court or nothing. Not the friendliest chap I admit. We're guildmembers, see, members of the Wizarding Reenactors Guild. So is Kreek. We like history and magic and learning about magical history, but we don't ever really do much with the queen or anybody like that. No one at court, no Council of Heroes. Just regular folk, you know, like you. These horses are from old Otto's farm, you know Otto I expect? Lives just beyond the woods? Bit of a hermit, most of the time. Probably not very friendly. I'm sure you told your kids not to go near him or nothing. Maybe made up stories about how frightful he is to scare them to stay away? But he's quite nice actually. Been helping us. See, truth of the matter is, there's this dragon rider. Real dragon rider. You heard about the dragon, that fell up at the Morlon Kastaun? Well, he had a rider, that's true. And we captured, or rather we rescued him, and now he's escaped and all alone in the great wide world and if we do not find him soon I fear something terrible will happen to him and—"

"Shut up." The woman stepped forward and looked at the clearing around her home, searching for any other men. "My father is out, on an errand to Kingstown. I expect him back tonight. If you can wait, you might find what you seek."

Buck and Wallace got off their horses and sat on a stump.

The woman brought them some tea but then went back into her house.

"Think she's seen him?" Buck asked Wallace.

"I think you're a damned fool, blabbing to anyone who will listen about the dragon rider. Get us all thrown into the stocks, you will."

They waited a long time. Buck nodded off at some point after dusk, woken finally by a man shouting from the front of the house. It was very dark out.

"You kept him here? Gina, this was unwise. I just spoke to the queen myself, trying to get her to take these rumors seriously. Now it'll look like I was plotting against her all along, which is what she was figuring, anyway."

An old man, fresh from travel on the road and holding a lantern, was talking to the woman, pointing at Buck and Wallace and trying not to shout too loud.

"Father, I was only trying to help. He was in such a state, I—"

"Gina, please, keep your voice down."

Buck and Wallace stood and approached them. "Hello, sir," Buck said. "We're guildsmen, looking for—"

"What guild?" The man stood in front of the doorway, blocking his daughter and the inside of the house itself. He did not want them to come in.

"The Wizarding Reenactors Guild. We—"

"That's no guild. That's not a trade. Did the queen send you after me? Tell her old Jasper never meant to harm her, never meant anyone harm. Just trying to help the people. You know what people have been saying about this dragon?"

"It's a sign of the end."

"You know why they say that?"

"No."

"Because a dragon's a god," said Jasper, "and when gods fall, kings and queens are sure to follow."

There was a long silence. "Ah," said Buck.

"I've seen this day coming," Jasper said. "I've dreamed of dragons. Dreamed of a lot of things I can't figure. Ever had dreams of vast stone canyons, void and empty like the end of time? Plague and disease, ending the world, and the soldiers of the dead descending upon you? No, I figure not. You're young. Young ones don't dream like that."

"Sure, I dream," Buck said, though he didn't rightly remember if he did.

Suddenly Jasper took out a knife. "Stop!" he shouted, and Buck was ready to protest but then noticed Jasper pointing to something in the trees. Buck turned and saw two men emerge from the darkness, dressed in dark clothes, each holding a short black wand. Wizards.

"All right now, you did a good job hiding him, but it's all over."

"Who are you?" Wallace asked.

"Move aside, please."

"They're wizards," Buck said. "They wield dark magic, I'm sure."

One of the men, the taller one, snorted. "Yeah sure, that's right. We're wizards. Now get out of the way."

"No!" Wallace shouted. The wizard held up his black stick. A bolt of lightning emerged from the end, hitting Wallace in the chest. He fell to the ground, convulsing.

"You killed him!" Buck shouted.

"Calm down, he's fine," the other wizard said, then held up his wand toward Buck. "You want some, too?"

"You're in league with Gregorian, aren't you?"

"Yeah, sure kid. He's our best friend. Now if you can just move out of the way, give us the pilot."

Jasper continued to block the door. "The Malicarn will never again be ruled by the evil magic of wizards! I tried to reason with the queen, but a storm is coming, one which will wash your kind away, and cleanse this realm of—"

The wizard shot a bolt at Jasper, who yelped and fell out of the doorway. He dropped the lantern, which smashed and began burning a small bush by the doorway. Gina shouted and ran inside. The men followed her. Buck heard a scuffle, and a minute later they reemerged, dragging the dragon rider out by his collar. The man was screaming and shouting, thrashing about. Gina ran out with a pail of water and doused the fire.

"Calm down, you're going home," the wizard said to the rider. "It's uh, how do you say it, Gene?"

The taller wizard pulled out a small book, emanating a blue light, and read something slowly. "Uh, nǐ yào huí jiāle." It was some sort of spell, for the rider suddenly stopped screaming and stood up.

"Stop right there," a voice bellowed from the darkness.

The wizards turned. "Is that you, Brian?"

But Buck recognized the voice, and the figure who emerged through the smoke of the smoldering bush was, at that moment, a sorely needed sight. Kreek sat upon his horse, dressed in full mail. His sword was still sheathed, but he held in his hand a staff. Not a walking staff, but some staff of great magic.

"Your little band of rebels really kept this one quiet," the tall wizard said. "Would have been real trouble if we couldn't find him soon."

"You cannot leave with him," Kreek said.

Wallace and Jasper were both rising to their feet, out of breath but watching Kreek with the same awe and terror as Buck. Buck was wondering how Kreek had found them, of course, but also where he had gotten that staff. There was only one conclusion. Kreek, it seemed, had become a wizard too.

"Come on," the short wizard said. "It's getting late. We gotta—"

With the sound of a great thunderclap, fire burst forth from Kreek's staff. It hit the short wizard, who fell backward on the ground, instantly dead. The dragon rider leapt back.

"Jesus!" shouted the other wizard. "Why the hell did—"

But before he could finish, another thunderclap flew from Kreek's wand, and the second wizard was dead as well.

Jasper ran to the rider, grabbed him, and looked him over for injuries.

"I am so sorry, Sir Kreek," Buck said. "I did not mean for him to get away."

"Silence," Kreek said. "What's done is done. The time of revelation draws near. Jasper, spread word throughout the underground: The dragon lords live. Soon they will descend upon us. You must be ready. Tell the leaders to gather their banners and meet us on the Morlon Kastaun. I will raise the people."

"I can't believe it," Jasper said. "I told the queen. I told her but she wouldn't listen."

"Of course not. The queen is one of the damned, a goblin come to destroy us. We cannot trust her. Or any of her supporters."

Wallace and Buck rode back to Otto's farm in silence. The dragon rider, arms and legs tied, rode with Kreek. When they arrived it was dawn, and they took the rider to the granary to put him back into chains. Kreek forced Buck to unload a new batch of supplies from a cart. They were boxes filled with magic staffs like the one Kreek now wielded. Once he had carried them all into the barn, he approached Kreek, who was speaking to Otto from his horse.

"I know I failed," Buck said. "I know I made a huge mistake. But please, please do not kick me out of the Guild. This is all I have in the world, these men and this Guild. What would I do without them? These new magic staffs, I think—"

"Silence," said Kreek. "There will be no staff for you."

"But I can help, I—"

"Enough! You have failed me. In fact, we were so much closer to utter destruction than you can possibly know. This dragon rider is the key to what happens next. Without him, I dare not even imagine what would occur."

"If there's a plan, you can tell me. I can—"

"You *cannot* be trusted. I know that now. It is not your fault.

It is simply your nature. You are not malicious, merely stupid. When the revolution comes, Buck Douglas, you may still be a part of it. Every man, woman, and child in the Malicarn may be a part of it, in their own way. But when it comes, and I assure you it comes quickly, you will not be a member of the Guild. Now finish your work for Otto. I have promised him your labor for the rest of the day. And then tomorrow you will be off."

"But where should I go?"

"Elsewhere. Anywhere. I do not care. I assume you can find work as a mason, which is what you are. And Buck, if you speak of the Guild or our activities to anyone, be warned. I will know. I will find you. And you will meet the same fate as those Dark Mages in the forest."

Kreek left, and Buck returned to work on the wall, which once again had completely collapsed.

BOSTON

July 21, 1993

Embarrassingly late. He would have to come up with some kind of story. Train delay, perhaps, except half the room was full of New Yorkers who hoofed it up for the night and none of them had any problems. Something with a client, you understand, couldn't be avoided, I hope the service was lovely. Had to be something big, family emergency? Well, that was partially true, if getting your girlfriend off to the Hamptons without the wife finding out is a sort of emergency. Maybe he could just go with an old standby, I forgot what time the funeral was. I'm getting old, I really need to keep my own calendar, not rely on the old noggin anymore. Oh, where is my secretary? She's in the Hamptons.

Peter Sanford, it turned out, didn't have to deploy any of these excuses, because Jean-Danton's widow could barely speak, she was crying so much. Wendy Souard sat in the middle of the large den right past the foyer, a group of old friends and extended cousins circled around her, rubbing her shoulders and handing her tissues. Peter laid a consoling hand on her arm and told her how sorry he was, how much he was going to miss Jean-Danton. She smiled, the pained sad smile people manage to express when they aren't actually happy, and told her friends, "This is Paul Sanderson, John's attorney."

In any other situation, Peter would have assumed malicious intent on the misremembering of his name, and maybe the bereaved woman really was digging into him for missing the funeral, but Peter let it go. He was more taken aback by her calling Jean-Danton "John," but then again she was from Wisconsin. She didn't even speak French.

Peter walked into the adjoining dining room, where the mourners with less of a personal stake in the deceased's passing were gathered. It was a wide room lit by a chandelier constructed out of blown glass, hanging over a table of golden mahogany. Peter was wondering how much of his firm's labor went into offering services which directly or indirectly paid for that table and chandelier when he recognized Chet Bauman and Benjamin Long, Jean-Danton's agent and accountant, standing in the corner over a plate of shrimp.

"I was wondering if you were coming," Chet said to Peter as he walked over. "You missed a nice ceremony."

"Well, a ceremony anyway," Benjamin said. "They held a full mass and had four eulogies. It went on forever."

"I didn't know Jean-Danton to ever set foot in a church," Peter said.

"Well, you know, at the end sometimes you hedge your bets a little."

"Did you speak, Chet?"

"Oh God no. Nobody wants to hear from me. What am I going to do? Brag about foreign translation rights?"

"Say something about Hollywood, people like that."

"You think his wife's going to let you chase those deals now?" Benjamin asked. "I mean, once she has time to consider it?"

"His son's the literary executor," Chet said. "I haven't gotten a good read on him. But maybe, I hope so. Dying has certainly increased interest and demand. I've been getting calls from this producer Rex Donaldson, have you heard from him? He was behind a big push to option the series a few years ago, now he's trying to tell me to watch *Jurassic Park*, says the technology is right to adapt."

"The price is right, that's what it is."

They began chatting about Benjamin's boat and the Knicks, the inherent business of attending a client's funeral well understood among all three of them. Peter had known them both for almost two decades, when the firm Jean-Danton hired to manage his legal affairs plucked Peter, then a young associate, out to handle "that writer's shit." Peter never made partner but then he didn't need to, since he ran his own firm now handling the affairs of dozens of writers, and even a few actors too. He was excited to see what dividends Chet's Hollywood connections would yield.

Peter eventually needed to piss, but didn't pay enough attention to the twist and turns toward the bathroom so on his way back he ended up in a dark shelf-lined room of books. There was a single desk next to a fireplace, and one chair under a window. The desk was bare save a few blank pages and a pencil. He was in Jean-Danton's office. Jean-Danton never did like writing with a typewriter. In the chair sat Daniel Souard, nursing a scotch.

Peter had never met Jean-Danton's son, though he had certainly heard the writer complain about him enough. Complaints about him dropping out of one college then another, complaints about his inability to find a job or move out. Complaints about his general lack of goals or ambitions or even interests. Daniel Souard was thirty-one years old and still lived, last Peter heard, in a spare bedroom on the top floor of the house.

"Oh, sorry, got turned around," Peter said when Daniel noticed him. "Didn't mean to disturb you."

"Oh, don't worry about it. You're not one of my mother's friends?" It was less a question than a hopeful inquiry.

"No. You must be Daniel? I was your father's business associate. His lawyer. He talked about you a lot."

"Ah, you're Peter. Yeah, I have all that paperwork about the estate somewhere. I haven't really looked over any of it yet."

"There'll be time enough for that. I wouldn't worry about it. I'm very sorry for your loss."

"Thank you. You know, the thing is, I'm not very sad. Not like my mom. She's distraught. She really didn't think the cancer was going to kill him. But he smoked two, three packs a day, long as I can remember. I mean, you can smell it in the walls down here.

Everything here is probably encrusted with smoke." He ran a hand over the spines of the books and records on the nearest shelf.

Peter leaned against the writing desk. "I knew your father a long time but I've never been to his home before. Never seen where he worked."

"Well, he didn't have a lot of friends. Those are all my mother's friends out there."

"I see."

"He always seemed like an old man to me. Always had a decade or more on all of my friends' dads. And I think the war had made him older still. There really wasn't anybody else around here like him. You liked my father, though, right? You liked his books."

Peter didn't want to lie to him, but he had never found Jean-Danton particularly pleasant. He was an anxious, morose person, paranoid about the status of his literary estate and cold to anyone he thought did not share a similar care or concern. But he had made Peter a great deal of money over the years.

"Yes, your father may have been a client but he was also a dear friend. And he was very talented."

"Which book was your favorite?"

That was another problem: Peter had never read any of Jean-Danton's novels. Peter did not read much for pleasure. After spending a full working day looking over wills and trusts and briefs, he preferred to spend his evenings watching basketball, often at his secretary's apartment. If he did read, he preferred nonfiction, usually a book of history about Churchill or Gettysburg or something he could start and not feel bad about when he didn't finish. He didn't much care for novels.

"The first one, definitely," said Peter. "You can't beat the original."

"You know," Daniel said, "I wanted to be a writer once. My dad was never very encouraging, I don't know why. It was hard to live in his shadow. Not a lot of writers have kids who are writers too."

Peter had no idea if that was true. "Well, you're going to get to carry his legacy forward now. That's quite an honor."

Daniel laughed. "Chet's already talked to me about selling rights for movies. Dad hated that. He didn't want to disturb the 'integrity' of the series. But he never finished it, you know? Supposed to be seven books, but he only wrote five. He outlined the next one, but he was already on oxygen and could barely get out of bed. Now they'll never be finished."

Peter did not have Chet's salesman-like ingenuity, or Benjamin's analytical gift for financials, but he did have the lawyer's sense of opportunity. He could smell where there was a gap in the documentation for an attorney to plow right through.

"You know, Daniel, your father was always very proud of you. Maybe he couldn't always show you that, or you couldn't see it, but he was. I'm not a literary person myself, I'm just here to advise. And I'm not your father, either, so take this for what it is, a suggestion. But it seems to me your father left you a gift. Who better to finish his series than his own son?"

Daniel had lifted the scotch glass to his mouth, but stopped when Peter said this. Despite how much time he must have spent sitting in this room, in the dark, in the days since his father's death, this idea had never occurred to him. The literary estate was going to be his burden, his cross to bear for the rest of his life. Now, and Daniel had never even remotely seen it this way before, it was also going to be his salvation.

"You know, Peter, I think that would actually be a really special way to honor him. Right? His fans would appreciate it. I wouldn't act like this is my thing, really. It's his outline, his ideas. I'm just finishing what he started. A son seeing to the end his father's legacy." Daniel set down the glass of scotch, sat up straight in his chair, and smiled.

"Wow," Peter said, "that's beautiful."

It really was. Peter was going to make so much money.

THE MALICARN

THE SIXTEENTH SPRING
IN THE REIGN OF QUEEN HANNAH I

1.

The royal stablemaster waited for Hannah in the courtyard, a horse hitched to a large green carriage. Three knights sat on their steeds behind it. Hannah buttoned a cloak over her dress as she climbed in. The sun had not yet risen, and there was a chill in the air. Hannah had not felt actual cold for weeks.

"I'll be taking you, my queen," the stablemaster said, smiling through several missing teeth.

"You expect rain at all?" Hannah asked.

"Most likely. But not today."

Kellington—whom Kreek mercifully had not reduced to squire—led the retinue. He insisted the stablemaster come because it would be conspicuous for one of the queen's guards to be driving a carriage. The whole point was to exit the city without drawing attention to the fact that she was leaving. The trip, naturally, was Sanderson and Quentin's idea. The rioting following the fire had subsided somewhat, though the crowds in the city remained and more strayed in daily. There was certain to be more violence, especially as the rain stubbornly continued to not fall. So Hannah would be shuttled off to the Mountain Keep, isolated but protected in another royal castle way up in the hills. Hannah didn't want to go, partly because she found the keep sad and boring, partly because it felt cowardly for the queen to leave the city. But of course she had no say in the matter. Sanderson and Quentin stayed behind, promising to send documents and briefs up to the Mountain Keep as needed until the mobs subsided. Fennick, to her relief, stayed behind as well. Hannah traveled with no other officials, just Kellington and a few guards dressed down to resemble common travelers. They rode out of the castle courtyard after dawn. A few commoners, waking in the streets of the city, watched the carriage roll past, but said nothing.

The train moved slowly. Kellington led, riding in front as two other knights rode behind. They did not raise the royal standard, even once they were clear of the city and its outer encampments. Near midmorning, Hannah peeked out the side of the carriage. The morning dew was baked off the grass, and they were passing down a road near the river. They would soon reach a fork that would take them up to the hills toward the Dollories Monastery, an old leaky church where Hannah had, unfortunately, stayed overnight many times when traveling. Other than looking at the stained glass there was little to do there. The monks were expecting them for the night, and the next day they could continue up the relative isolation of the mountain roads toward the keep itself. But there were two roads up the mountains, and if they stayed on the main road they would come instead to the Old Village, and Gregorian's tower. A different path stretched toward the Mountain Keep from there, a wider if somewhat longer one. Quentin had given orders to take the road to the Dollories, in hopes of them making it to the Mountain Keep faster. But Hannah suspected Gregorian might be at home tonight.

"Ah, Sir Kellington?" Hannah shouted. Kellington slowed his horse and rode beside the carriage window.

"Yes, my queen?"

"Have you been on the road to the Dollories recently? Have they repaired it from the flood last summer?"

"There have been workers on that road all winter. I believe it is quite repaired."

"Even if we finally get some rain tonight, as it appears we may?"

Kellington looked at the sky. "I am not sure of that. It is cloudy but not with storm."

"Should we not take precaution, though? Head toward the Old Village and spend the evening? It is nearer. Gregorian would offer lodging, if there is none to be found at the inn."

Kellington grimaced, and Hannah knew she had overplayed her hand. "Maybe, Your Majesty, but that north road is less friendly. Runs closer to the Citadel."

"Masons are working at the mill," the stablemaster said. He was listening in. "They will know the road."

"Thank you," Hannah said.

Kellington sighed. "We should stop when we reach the mill anyway. To water the horses. But we should not linger, and you should remain out of sight, Hannah." He only used her name when he was being very serious.

The mill was a few miles ahead, down a small embankment. The miller's wife served food to passing travelers as well, and the mill was widely renowned as a brewery. Several tables were arranged outside an awning on the west side. The mill itself sat not far off, in a wooded grove next to the river. The wheel was turning, but several men worked on the west wall, patching cracks and placing stone over a large hole.

Hannah wrapped a shawl around herself as she and her company disembarked and approached the pub. The miller's wife appeared from within, at first with an exasperated, chiding tone that instantly went soft when she recognized the queen. Their subterfuge had already ended.

"Oh, Your Majesty! Take a seat, please. Inside, we have much finer—"

"Our men can sit outside," Hannah said. "We just need to water our horses and we'll be on our way." As she spoke, Kellington and the other knights began walking the perimeter of the house and the mill, quickly inspecting the patrons and masons for weapons or anything dangerous. Everyone's sympathies were suspect these days. The miller's wife watched them warily, but Hannah continued to smile. "I am sure our men could all do with an ale, if you could spare a few pints."

"Yes, of course! To serve the queen and her knights would be an honor!"

Hannah sat and Kellington returned. "A few of the masons have an ill look, my queen. I advise we not stay here once we have our drinks."

"What kind of look?"

"Angry? I don't know. Unkind."

"You cannot tell a person's politics based on their face, Kellington. Did you speak to them about the road?"

"Pardon? No, I did not. I do not believe—"

"No matter," Hannah said, standing back up. "I can ask."

"Hannah! You must remain concealed!"

Hannah ignored him and walked down to the mill, where three men were working by the wall and a fourth was mixing mortar in a large stone pot. Hannah approached the mortar mixer. If people knew their queen better, they would not stand so angrily outside her castle. So she reasoned.

"Good afternoon."

The man looked up at her and stopped suddenly, his eyes wide and amazed. He was covered in the fast-drying mortar paste, stained all over his clothes, arms, and legs, and was stirring the pot with a large wooden spoon. He was young, only a few years older than Hannah, but large, with broad shoulders and arms like tree trunks. A pint of ale sat on a wooden stump next to him.

"Huh, good afternoon . . . my highness. Your Majesty." The man bowed, still holding on to the wooden spoon.

"Have you and your fellow masons been faring well?"

The man nodded. "Quite well, yes. I believe so, at any rate. Your Majestyness."

"What is your name?"

"Douglas, sir, ma'am, Your Majesty Queen. Buck Douglas."

"Well, Buck Douglas, have the masons worked on the northern road, the one just up here that heads to the Dollories?"

"You mean the one that got washed out? Yes, I heard that they repaired it. Finished few weeks back, in fact."

"Ah, wonderful. And no injuries?"

"Well, old Gregory, him's of the Derbyville Gregorys, went down with some sort of bad headache, so they say. And Master Felish and his whole family got the pestilience. Not that I saw them, either, but it's what I heard. Missus Felish died, though on account of a bad egg."

"I mean no injuries to anyone working on the road?"

"Ah, no, Your Queenness."

"That is good to hear," Hannah said. "I assume the madame here is looking after all of the masons? You are well provisioned?"

"Yes, ma'am highness." He lifted up his pint of ale toward her. "Keeps us well stocked indeed. Would you like me own ale? For the queen, I would happily part with it."

"No, thank you," Hannah said. "Though I appreciate it."

"For your men, then?"

"They have already been served. If they find themselves thirsty later the Inn at the Old Village will surely provide more drink for them. Best of luck on repairing the mill."

"Please, we have several spare barrels. Take them with you. It is the master mason's special brew. We would be honored."

"Very well. I will have my men fetch and load them. I wish you well. And best of health to all."

"Aye, sir, Queen, Your Majestyness!" Buck bowed again, still holding the stirring spoon with both hands.

Back at the pub, several mugs of ale had been laid out for Hannah's guards, one in front of an empty pillowed chair for Hannah. She sat down at it and took a sip of the drink.

"Well, Kellington," she said. "Sounds like the road is still washed out. They haven't even begun working on it. To the Old Village we must go."

Kellington sighed, but did not dare accuse the queen of lying.

"I did acquire several barrels of fine ale, though, from the masons. They insisted. Perhaps your men would care to put them onto the carriage? I would not like you to be without drink at the Mountain Keep."

This perked Kellington up considerably, and they left the mill with three full casks. By the time the carriage rolled away, a dozen families from nearby cottages and farms had heard that the queen was riding through and walked down to the road to wave her on.

"See," Hannah said to Kellington, "no one is angry to see us."

The rest of the day's travel was uneventful. Dusk was settling over the Old Village when they finally arrived. Kellington, who had been sneaking cups out of the new barrels throughout the afternoon ride, began sharing his dislike of the Old Village well before their arrival. When they finally neared its walls he wound himself up into a sputtering hailstorm of invective.

"Just the worst kind of backward people. No ambition. No foresight. Ever since Kingstown was erected you'd think they'd want to try to improve themselves. But no, just a bunch of wastrels sad that they are no longer the center of attention. Well, you want something, you have to work for it. No one here knows that. Just drunks and layabouts now. The marketplace is barely worth the name as such. No respectable farmer comes here anymore. And you know whose fault it all is? That wizard, I tell you. Now I know, Hannah, he's mentored you, but you're nearly a woman now and you need to see: Nothing good's come of him since before your father died. He's never brought anything but sadness into this kingdom, and the root of it is right here in this rot: the Old Village. The place does not even have a proper name!"

"Sir Kellington," Hannah said, "I do not believe the Old Village is as changed from the days of my father as you suppose, but of course you do have much more experience than me, being nearly nineteen years old."

Kellington blushed and continued muttering under his breath as the retinue passed through the main gate and down a street toward the village square. Hannah admitted that Kellington at least had a point. Unlike Kingstown, where buildings were big and tall and new, and everyone worked at a frantic pace, walking hastily at all times, in the Old Village the buildings were low, sad, disheveled, poorly painted. Villagers ambled slowly through the streets and around the square. And there were many fewer of them than in Kingstown. The roads also felt very straight, a fact Hannah was struck anew by on each visit. Every building was placed exactly where it apparently needed to be, as if the whole village had risen up at once with no mistakes or changes along the way and then been left there until it became shabby. It made the place feel oddly small, even as it stretched over half a mile from end to end. It looked like a town built as practice, a child's play set.

They crossed through the main square and approached the door of the large black tower of Gregorian himself. Kellington slammed down hard on the metal door knocker, and a small woman opened the door.

"Please tell the wizard that the queen is here and we would like room and board for the evening."

The woman said nothing and closed the door. Hannah watched from out of the window of the carriage as Kellington paced back and forth. When the door reopened a few minutes later, the woman looked past Kellington.

"The queen may enter for the night. There is no room for others. You must stay at the inn."

"Oh, for the love of—"

"It is all right, Kellington," said Hannah, climbing out of the carriage. "You and the guard will relax easier at the inn anyway." She approached the old woman. "Can these men arrange to have my trunk and items carried in at least?"

She consented, and a few minutes later Hannah's belongings were inside and the guards rode off with the stablemaster and carriage toward the stables. Inside the tower, Hannah was led up a narrow stair to a small, dark room. A fire burned in the hearth, before which sat a pair of large, worn chairs. The old woman gestured to them. Hannah sat in the closer one, but when she turned to speak to the woman she was gone.

The room felt damp, like a cave, and cold. On the few occasions when she would travel to the Old Village and see Gregorian, Hannah was usually sent to the library on the lower level. Her guard would stay in the tower on those trips, too, but now she was alone, watching the fire and the blank walls and wondering if coming had been a mistake.

"Rather far from the castle tonight, eh, Hannah?" The familiar mellow voice rang from the doorway, and Hannah turned to see Gregorian leaning against a wall, suddenly materialized from the air. His white beard and thinning hair were unkempt, as if he had already been sleeping. The wrinkles around his eyes were pronounced, and as Hannah went to rise, Gregorian yawned, waving at her to sit back down. Gregorian collapsed into the chair next to her. He had visited the castle several times since she spoke to him about the dragon rider, and he looked more tired every time.

"Usually Sanderson tells me well ahead of time when you're coming," Gregorian said. "Did he misplace his page again?"

Hannah laughed. "No, they wanted me to go to the Mountain Keep to get away from the mobs. It has been bad in Kingstown recently."

"Hm." Gregorian nodded slowly. "We should have a drink." He rang a bell, and the old woman quickly appeared back in the doorway. "Two ales, for the queen and myself," Gregorian said, and she vanished again.

"We were meant to take the road to the Dollories Monastery. But I diverted our route, hoping to see you."

"The monastery is indeed quite a bore."

"I am hopeful for counsel," Hannah said.

"Sanderson and Quentin are quite good with that too."

"I am not always so sure."

Gregorian laughed. "Is this about the mobs? I promise, you are safe."

"Actually, I was hoping to speak about the dragon."

"Again? Hannah, I told you, there is nothing to worry about.

The dragon is dead and the common folk will forget about it soon enough."

"What about the dragon rider?"

"What?"

"There is a rumor that the dragon rider lives. The commoners believe it. Surely you've heard."

Gregorian sat quietly for a long moment. The servant woman returned with two pints of ale, and Gregorian picked up his and took a very long drink.

"I do know something about that," he said after the servant left. "But it is not what you think. And it's one of those things I cannot really provide any clarity on."

"Why? Is it the same reason you told Kreek I was sneaking out of the castle to see the dragon corpse? I know it was you."

"Oddly enough, Hannah, that wasn't me. Believe me or not, that's the truth."

Hannah sighed. There was simply no hope of anybody ever treating her like a queen. Sanderson and Quentin were fools, maybe, but where they controlled Hannah out of self-interest and ignorance, Gregorian was doing something else. He wasn't manipulating her, not exactly. But he was up to something, thinking about something, that Hannah just couldn't get a clear sense of. She lifted her poor leg and propped it up on the table, rubbing it as she took a sip of the ale.

"It is very bubbly," Hannah said.

Gregorian watched her leg. "Is it hurting?"

"Oh? Well, after a long day of riding, yes. Especially in a carriage. It is not a smooth journey."

Gregorian reached into his vest and took out two small white items, slightly larger than crumbs. "Swallow these. They will help you feel better. Just drink them back with your ale. Swallow as if they aren't even there."

Hannah put the white nuggets in her mouth and took a large gulp of her drink. She felt them go down her throat and coughed.

"Sorry," Gregorian said. "It is not always pleasant."

"I thought healing was not your expertise."

"Well, maybe I know a little bit."

Hannah took another sip. "Gregorian, why is magic banned? I want to know the real answer. You have hinted at it before."

"You have heard the story. After the Necromancer killed your father, I met with him and we came to an agreement. No magic if he left the Malicarn alone."

"Yes, I have heard that story. But it does not make sense. Why would he care about the Malicarn having magic? Did he not want to capture the Malicarn?"

Gregorian chuckled. "Yes, it is not a very good story."

"So it is not the truth?"

"It is a kind of truth."

"I will be of age soon, Gregorian, and I know there is much that I do not yet understand, but I think for the good of the realm I should learn more. Maybe the dragon means nothing, but people sure think it does. I can't lead them if I don't understand."

He leaned toward the fire, picking up a poker leaning against the hearth, and pushed a few of the logs around. One fire-licked log cracked open, the inside glowing orange, and the flames danced around the newly exposed wood.

"What did old Fennick teach you about fire?" Gregorian asked.

"He said it was 'the devil trying to escape, and so we must be vigilant over it always.' He did not elaborate further."

"Did you tell him what I told you about fire?"

"That it was a reaction of the materials within, transforming solid matter to energy, which gives off heat?"

"Precisely."

"I told him and he just said that was some wizard nonsense."

Gregorian stood up and walked to the corner. He looked up at one dark spot on the wall and stared at it for a long time. Then he turned toward Hannah.

"Quentin, Sanderson, even Fennick—they are not bad men. I need you to understand that. They truly do have your best interests at heart. But I do not speak nonsense, Hannah. I promise you. There is much for you to know, but it is beyond my powers to teach you everything. I cannot explain why—" He looked at the dark spot on the wall again. "—only you must believe that I am intent on protecting you and your rule. Soon, maybe, I can tell you more."

"The unrest, at least?" asked Hannah. "Surely you can help with that?"

"The anger of the common folk is not something you should worry about."

"Of course I should. I am their queen."

"Yes, well, they will all be fine. I am sorry, but that is all I can say." He smiled, and Hannah had the eerie feeling that, somehow, they were being watched.

"Come now," said Gregorian. "How is your leg?"

"It is feeling better."

"Terrific. Now you should get some rest. It is late, and we both have travels tomorrow."

"You are going somewhere?"

"On an errand, yes. One of many I am obligated to, unfortunately. And I must leave quite early. Come, let's to bed."

A feather mattress was prepared in the library. Hannah slept soundly but not long, as the noise of a nest of birds feeding their hatchlings outside a window awoke her just before dawn.

Gregorian was seated at a table in the room upstairs, eating a bowl of oats by the fire, when Hannah entered.

"Good morning, Hannah." Gregorian was the only person who did not ever address her with some royal styling. "I trust you slept well?"

"Well enough," Hannah said. She sat across from the wizard, and the old woman emerged from a side door with another bowl. The oats were runny and creamy—not a particularly fancy breakfast.

"I know you are well fed at the castle," Gregorian said, "but honestly this dish will fill you up and give you more energy than the grease slabs you usually start your day with."

Hannah ate slowly, as the bowl was hot. But she did indeed find it hearty.

"How long will you be at the Mountain Keep?" Gregorian asked.

"I do not know," said Hannah. "Until Kingstown is safe again, I should think."

Gregorian nodded. "Good. When I return I shall check in upon you there."

"Where are you headed?"

"I cannot say. It is not a dangerous matter, but it does need attending to. It will be but a few days. Keep yourself safe while I am gone. No misadventures?"

The servant woman shuffled back into the room. She leaned over and whispered something into Gregorian's ear. Hannah had not heard her speak once.

Gregorian stood up. "Thank you. Hannah, eat quickly. It seems your guardsmen are quite upset."

Hannah slurped down another large mouthful of oats and followed Gregorian out of the room and down the stairs. Kellington was standing inside the tower's front door, pacing furiously.

"Good morning, Sir Kellington," Gregorian said. "Were you well looked after at the inn?"

"I did not want to come this way," Kellington said, speaking directly to Hannah and ignoring the wizard, "and my fears are confirmed."

"What happened?" Hannah asked.

"Someone was seen trying to climb the tower last night," Kellington said. He looked at Gregorian. "You have no guard here, no protection of any kind. How safe was the queen?"

"I promise you she was safe."

"Nonsense. Only because one of the villagers saw this intruder and cried out did he run off. I sent the other guards in search of him, but no one has reported back yet. I think we ought to be on the road quickly, Your Majesty, in case there is more danger afoot."

"You must not overreact," Gregorian said. "The queen is in no danger here. She is less safe on the road with your men, I daresay."

Kellington bit his lip and stared angrily at Gregorian. "Do you mean to say—"

"I mean to say nothing, good sir knight. I must be off early, as well. Your men can attend to the queen's items in the tower. Hannah, be well. Remember what we spoke of. And I will come to the Mountain Keep on my return."

Gregorian bowed slightly, and Hannah exited the tower after Kellington, who muttered under his breath as he stumbled toward the carriage and ranted to the stablemaster waiting atop it.

"Old, fat idiot. Does not know one thing, just sits in his tower and twiddles his thumbs. No sense, no understanding of what is going on . . ." He continued to babble as the other guards filed back in from their search around the village. "And this road is too dangerous, too close to the Citadel. More problems before we reach the keep, I assure you . . ."

Nothing else unusual had been spotted, so Kellington mounted his horse.

"Let us move on then," he said. "If we have no more delays we should make it to the keep before supper."

They loaded Hannah's luggage, then drove quickly out of the village up a steep hill and onto the road that led to the mountain. As the Old Village fell behind, Hannah looked out the carriage's back window. She spied a man walking north, holding a staff and wearing a billowing red cloak. It was Gregorian, and before he disappeared over a ridge he stopped, turned, and lifted his staff in Hannah's direction. A few bolts of lightning shot out from the top, barely anything at all, and then Gregorian lowered it and waved toward her. Hannah thought that was odd. How did Gregorian know Hannah was even looking toward him?

Some old magic, Hannah thought, that Gregorian must still

use in secret. She would have to ask him about that, the next time they spoke.

2.

This was what failure felt like. Loading stone from the quarry into a wagon, pulling the wagon up a hill, down the road. No horses. Just Buck, pulling a wagon of stone five miles up a slow incline, then dumping the rocks in a pile next to the mill where the more experienced masons would cut them into shaped stones and set them. Buck was told not to touch them again, just mix mortar. The master working the mill was not a guildmember, but Buck had once seen him speaking with Kreek on a job in Kingstown, so Buck assumed this humiliation was intentional.

Buck was a journeyman, technically, not even an apprentice anymore, but work had suddenly become scarce. Kingstown was full of the starving and homeless, shutting down all work. The Crown had canceled or delayed a number of planned projects in other towns and castles throughout the realm, leaving the few available jobs open to only the most experienced masons. Buck got this job only because he begged the miller, crying and sobbing, a pathetic spectacle. The miller had known Buck's father—the old family farm was not so far away, though goblins lived there now—and had pity on him. At night, Buck chose to forgo the drinking and revelry the other masons took part in and retired quietly to a tent, where he drank a bottle of whiskey alone and rubbed his sore shoulders and thought about his future.

There wasn't much of one, and so he fell asleep quickly.

Buck had liked to imagine his life as an upward trajectory, rising from the humble beginnings on a farm, surviving the death of his mother and sister, the failures of his own father, to become a masons' apprentice, then a journeyman, maybe one day a master himself, crafting great halls for kings and queens and bestowing onto his own children a great inheritance born of sweat and perseverance. In his time he imagined the whole realm returning to glory, with magic revived under the banner of a just ruler, the Malicarn preserved for the true people of the Malicarn, and the majestic days of his father's youth revived. He would die rich and happy, surrounded by loved ones, in a secure land he helped to build.

But Buck had always known that it was much more likely he'd die young and poor, drunk outside a brothel, after repairing some old stone barn to house a lord's horses. His father wasn't a failure so much as a visionary. His only mistake was bringing Buck into the world. Or maybe that was part of his grand design. How else to share his hard-won knowledge that the world was shit unless you had someone to pass that wisdom along to?

On the job's second day, Buck was allowed to mix mortar. A strange retinue stopped at the pub that the miller's wife operated. They had a large carriage but dressed as poor travelers. The miller's wife could be heard shouting orders to her scullery maids at a pitch usually reserved for knights and highborn men. Buck was working with the other masons behind the pub, and could not countenance what the shouting was about, until the woman riding in the carriage left her seat and approached him directly.

Buck recognized the queen immediately. He had seen her, once or twice, when he worked on the castle's nave expansion in Kingstown. She was tall, of dark complexion, and walked awkwardly, one leg always dragging a bit. She did not seem to be the cruel goblin Kreek had described. He could not believe that the queen would be out of the castle with all of the unrest about, or that she would walk right up and speak to him.

"Have you and your fellow masons been faring well?"

"Quite well, yes," Buck said. "I believe so, at any rate. Your Majestyness."

"What is your name?"

"Douglas, sir, ma'am, Your Majesty Queen. Buck Douglas." He

couldn't make the words in his mind quick enough, they were falling out so fast.

"Well, Buck Douglas, have the masons worked on the northern road, the one just up here that heads to the Dollories?"

"You mean the one that got washed out?"

She asked him some more questions, but he couldn't hear her, couldn't hear himself as he spit the answers out.

"You are well provisioned?" she asked.

"Yes, ma'am highness." What was he saying? He was offering her ale, she was refusing, why was he still offering, being so persistent?

"For your men, then?"

And then she let slip an interesting fact. "They have already been served. If they find themselves thirsty later the Inn at the Old Village will surely provide more drink for them."

He insisted on her taking barrels of ale. But he wasn't thinking about that at all now.

The Inn? In the Old Village? Of course! The wizard lived there. Yes, Buck, you really are a smart one. No, this was not a failure at all. It was, what would they call it in battle? A strategic retreat. And now was the time for a counterattack.

Kreek was going to unveil the dragon rider to the people. When, Buck did not know. Exactly what he hoped would happen Buck was also unsure. Would the rider join their cause? Would other dragons arrive to support him? Would Gregorian raise the Queen's Arms, march out to oppose them? Kreek was a mighty warrior, a wizard even, he knew much about magic and the old ways. But Buck knew some things, too. He knew that no one would be truly free as long as the old wizard roamed, as long as he held sway over court and queen. Magic could never be returned to the people until they took down the wizard. And the best way to draw out the wizard would be to take the queen.

Buck's redemption was here. He abandoned his work at the mill. Yes, that would not endear him to future patrons, but it did not matter. Not if he was the man who took down Gregorian. Once the queen's retinue left the mill he followed behind, far enough not to be seen, hiding on the side of the road, in brush and behind trees.

That night, as the guards slept in the inn, he tried to scale the tower in the predawn hours, but it was too slick, too hard to get a foothold, and some busybody passerby looked up at him and shouted, "You up there? What are you getting at?" Buck had to run and hide before the guards came.

It was for the best. How would he ever capture the queen with the wizard himself present? Better to take her alone. He followed again, as the queen and her guards traveled up the road to the mountain. Buck kept himself hidden in the woods, off the road, but made too many sounds, spooking the knight's horses more than once.

But you are a persistent one, Buck! Yes, you are!

Her guard were few. They were trying to move her in secret. A good plan, a safe plan. But they did not count on Buck Douglas, son of Frank Douglas the hero of the Wizarding War. Hero's blood flowed through Buck. He would not be deterred.

The queen arrived at the Mountain Keep, a small castle in the hills. Buck had never been there before, but he was not scared. That night, it rained. He decided to use the storm as cover, to find if the keep had weaknesses, easy places to sneak in. He stalked around the grounds, climbing trees and low walls. Finally, he made it to the east side of the main tower and noticed a faint light in the window. He climbed, the rain and wind drowning out his groans. He reached the window and peered in, saw the young queen reading a book by candlelight. He could grab her now!

But the queen looked up, straight at the window. Did she see Buck? He fell backward, a long way into the bushes, then scrambled away.

Better to wait, see if the gate opened, find his way in. He set up a permanent sentry post, just south of the keep, over a little ridge where he could see the entire complex. He could wait here. He didn't need food, he didn't need shelter. He had all he needed. The righteousness of a cause. The opportunity to prove himself. He was not the failure of a failure.

He was the man who would save the Malicarn.

3.

A large old structure carved into the side of a rocky hill, the Mountain Keep was colder and drier than Gregorian's tower and much quieter than the castle in Kingstown. A small staff handled the domestic chores, and Kellington's men supplemented a garrison of only a dozen knights. Hannah realized she did not mind the slower pace of life on the mountain, which didn't include daily inquests from the populace or endless meetings with her advisors about taxes and grain levies. She did still have a tutor—a monk named Abbott who lived in and maintained the library on the keep's upper floor.

Abbott had a better sense of humor than Fennick, frequently joking about his inevitable promotion one day to become Abbot Abbott. When Hannah walked into the library, he was reading a large tome and seemed surprised to see her, having forgotten her company's arrival earlier that afternoon.

"Ah, my young queen! Any volumes you wish to peruse today?"

"Yes, I would like to see what texts about dragons you have."

"Dragons, hmm. Not so many. We do have a bestiary. Let me see what else there might be. How long will you be at the keep?" Abbott stood up and began inspecting the shelves of books behind him.

"It is hard to say. Until Kingstown is less . . . distressed."

"Ah, well, do not be afraid! Old Abbott and his books are here to keep you company!"

Abbott did not find any books about dragons, so instead offered her several medical tomes. One was on humors, which

Hannah distrusted, remembering Gregorian scoffing about the subject once. An anatomy book was interesting, so she kept it, as well as one about herbal and liquid remedies. Hannah found a volume on astronomy and the stars, which she decided to borrow as well. She thanked Abbott and returned to her chambers with the books.

That night it finally rained. The storm became fierce and windy. This, alas, did not dim the nighttime sounds of the Queen's Guard carousing in the courtyard. The new ale from the masons kept their spirits lively, and the guards held impromptu boxing matches. Kellington received a black eye, and another guard broke his wrist.

Hannah left them to their amusements as she read in her chambers, comfortable but modest quarters in the keep's east tower. She switched between the illustrated stories from Gregorian and the books from Abbott's library. The medical volumes were mostly nonsense, as Hannah expected. Cures for gangrene by boiling flowers and cutting out flesh. If such remedies had ever worked, Hannah assumed it was because of luck. But if she was going to be stuck in the keep for the foreseeable future, she might as well learn what she could. The Malicarn needed more knowledgeable minds. One time she had inquired to Sanderson about setting up a scientific academy at one of the monasteries, but Sanderson shook his head and muttered about the cost. Hannah would have to be more forthright once the regency ended. She knew that was the only way she could make real changes.

Once their revelry subsided, Kellington and his men would stay in the outer guardhouse, partly to keep an eye on the road during the storm and also to nurse morning hangovers out of sight of the queen. The serving staff slept as they usually did in the lofts above the kitchens, a separate series of buildings adjacent to the keep beyond the courtyard. Only Abbott, deaf enough even without the wind, and Hannah herself remained in the keep.

Hannah read until late, sitting at the small wooden desk in the corner of her room with the book of anatomy by candlelight.

Her back was to her chamber's door, the only sound the wind rattling outside. Hannah paused at one point, looking out the window at the dark shadows of tree branches swaying, when she noticed what appeared to be two dim lights, side by side, floating just outside. In the swirling rain they were surrounded by a deep, round shadow. Only when Hannah lifted her candle did she see them in full. Not lights but eyes. A face. Dark, sharp locks and an angular chin. Hannah thought she recognized the mason from the mill, but then the shadow slipped back, falling away from view. Hannah jumped out of her bed and ran over to the window, but there was no sign of anyone.

She slept the rest of the night with a knife under her pillow.

In the morning Hannah walked out to the guard's quarters. Kellington was slumped in a chair inside by a fire, chewing on a piece of meat and holding his head.

"I think I saw someone last night," Hannah said.

"Eh, yeah, me too. Visions of Mary Alice. Most beautiful girl in the valley."

"No, I'm serious, Sir Kellington. I think someone was climbing up to my chambers. They were at my window."

Kellington sat up and groaned. "Had you too much ale?"

"No. You know I did not."

"Right, right. Yes, well, it is concerning. Maybe it was the same bloke we saw climbing the wizard's tower in the Old Village. Wants an audience with his queen, or something. I'll send guards to look for footprints."

"Can you post some men around the keep tonight? Perhaps take a night off from the ale?"

Kellington rubbed the side of his head. "Believe me, Your Majesty, I never wish to drink again."

The skies cleared and by afternoon the sun was bright above them. Shortly before supper, the watchman's horn blared and Hannah saw Kellington and the other guards rush toward the battlements above the gate. They pointed to something in the distance, down the mountain.

"Someone has lit a beacon," Kellington told Hannah later, when he came to report. "Which means trouble in Kingstown."

"What kind of trouble?"

"Hard to say, Your Majesty. We haven't gotten any messages sent our way."

"They use the beacons for war, I thought."

"Usually, yes."

"Should we leave?"

Kellington thought the guard and staff should stay in the keep, but the stablemaster drove the carriage back to the city to find out what was happening. The rest of the day passed without any more information. No riders approached, and the road before the keep remained empty. Hannah felt ill at ease. Something was wrong. They ate all together in the keep's hall, though without the drinking and singing from the previous night.

After dusk, Hannah sat in her bed, a single candle beside her, and read her book on astronomy. There were many drawings, charts of stars, and explanations for their movements. She hovered over an illustration of the universe: a black hollow orb. In the middle sat the earth, around which circled the sun and the planets. The orb was pricked with thousands of small holes all around, letting in the light of Creation beyond: the stars. The universe was ordered, labeled, contained, and utterly without blemish.

The candle was burning low, the light starting to dim, when she heard footsteps outside her door. The guard spoke, but Hannah could not tell what he said. There was a brief murmur, the scuffle of feet, and then a thump. The door opened slowly.

Hannah leapt out of bed, grabbed the knife under her pillow, and fell against the wall. She was hidden for only a moment. As the door opened the hallway's candelabra illuminated the room, and a torchlight threw away the shadows where Hannah hid. The torch was held by a man, wearing a black shirt emblazoned with the crest of an angry bird.

"Hannah!" Gregorian called out in a whisper. "Hannah, come

here!" Behind him Gregorian dragged in the guard, who was unconscious but still breathing.

Hannah stood up, dropping the knife to her side. "What is going on? What did you do to him?"

"He will be okay. I merely drugged him. He'll only be asleep for a few moments, and other men walk the halls. We must be quick."

"Quick? Quick for what?"

"Lower your voice." His clothes were caked with mud from the road. Gregorian pulled the guard to a corner and set him down gently.

"Is something wrong?" Hannah whispered.

Gregorian did not answer at first, his eyes darting around the room. Then he turned to Hannah, leaned over, and grabbed her arm.

"We must go. Now. It is no longer safe for you here."

"Why? What has happened? Should we return to Kingstown?"

"No, that is not safe anymore, either," Gregorian said. "We must leave immediately."

"Leave the keep?

"No, leave the Malicarn."

Gregorian had never before appeared so spooked. Hannah changed out of her dress and into a riding outfit of shirt and trousers she had borrowed from the stables but never put on. Then Hannah and Gregorian climbed down out of the keep through an eastern window, circled around toward the front, snuck out past the gate, and crossed over a creek into the woods. The wind covered the sounds of boots, and their exit was quick. She wrapped an extra cloak around her to stay warm.

They kept off the road entirely, heading farther up the mountain. It did not take long for Hannah to notice why. From their height she could see the mountain road winding down toward the valley. But where it should be cloaked in midnight darkness it was illuminated by light, hundreds of torches marching toward the keep.

"What is that?" Hannah asked.

Gregorian didn't even look. "Men and women of the Malicarn. They are coming for you."

Hannah suddenly felt tremendous guilt for not sending Kellington and the others away.

They walked through the night; Hannah moved slowly, her leg growing more painful the farther they continued around the mountain. Gregorian did not speak. At one point he turned sharply to look behind them and stopped. When Hannah asked what it was, he shook his head and kept moving.

"I think someone followed me from the Old Village," Hannah said.

Gregorian merely nodded.

"Did you know?"

"No," Gregorian said. "Not precisely. But it does not surprise me."

"Why not? What is going on?"

"We have to keep moving, we will be late."

Soon, the trees began to spread and the ground leveled out, and then suddenly they entered a clearing of high grass. In the middle of the field was a slab of smooth rock, overgrown with weeds, as if it were once a floor of a vanished structure. Hannah examined the ground with interest, but Gregorian looked out toward the horizon, over the hills. The eastern sky shone with a faint blue glow.

"We will wait here," Gregorian said. "They should be here soon."

"What is this place?" Hannah asked.

"An old building from before the Malicarn," Gregorian said.

Hannah sat herself down on the stone and massaged her leg. She leaned back and looked at the early-morning stars above her.

"Is this all about the dragon? There have been so many rumors of a dragon rider, and the common folk are restless—"

Gregorian sat beside her. "The dragon is not real."

"What do you mean? You saw it yourself. So did many others."

"What we saw was not a dragon."

"Gregorian, you sound mad. This is why my advisors don't trust you."

"Hannah, I know there's no way for me to explain any of this to you in a way that makes sense. Not yet. Let me put it to you this way: The Necromancer controls the Malicarn. He controls all of it. And he controls you, too, whether you realize it or not."

"The Necromancer? Does he control you?"

"Even me."

Hannah frowned. "Do the advisors know?"

"No. Nobody does."

"Except for you."

"Yes. And a few others. Kreek among them. Kreek is not his actual name, and he's not actually from the Malicarn. His real name is Brian Doyle."

Hannah stood up, arms crossed, fingers rattling on her elbows. "And is your name really Gregorian?"

"No. It is Glenn."

"You have always been honest with me, in your own peculiar way. That is why I trusted you, even if others did not. But you have never said anything about this before. I thought you maintained a truce with our enemies, not that you did their bidding. Are you my enemy?"

"No."

"I do not believe you. Or, maybe I do. I don't know what to believe. You were not born in the Malicarn, either, were you?" Hannah asked.

"No."

"Where are you from?"

"A place called New Jersey."

"Is it a nice place?"

"Not really."

"What are the foreign lands like?"

Gregorian stood up. "Well, there is a lot of strife. More so than in the Malicarn, in fact."

"The Council of Heroes does a good job of protecting us."

"Yes," Gregorian said. "I suppose that's true. But the Council is not free, either. I don't know, Hannah, how to begin to explain it all. What's real and what's not. Even I don't know anymore."

"Well, tell me about the stars," Hannah said, looking back up at the sky. The sun was getting brighter and only a few morning stars remained visible. "I was reading a book last night about how they are holes in the blanket of the sky, and the light of the heavens shines through them. Abbott gave me that book, and he is well-read."

"Well-read in the types of books he owns, yes. But that's not true, either. Each star is its own sun, like our sun. Far away, with its own worlds."

"Do you travel to those worlds?"

"No, they are so far away even I cannot get to them."

"They must be lonely worlds."

"'Tis new to thee."

Hannah looked at him. "What?"

Gregorian smiled. "Oh, it's just a line, from a play I acted in once."

"You used to be an actor?"

"Used to be? I suppose. But yes, I acted."

"What is the play?" Hannah asked.

"You will find this amusing, but it is about a wizard, and his daughter, who live on an island removed from the rest of the world. But then the world comes to them. The daughter has never before seen people apart from those who live on the island. And she says: 'O wonder! How many goodly creatures are there here! How beauteous mankind is! O, brave new world that has such people in it!'"

"'How beauteous mankind is,'" Hannah repeated. "I like that."

There was a sudden crack from behind them, and Hannah

turned to see a woman emerge through the tall grass. She was wearing an outfit that appeared to be made out of leaves.

"Where is Roger?" Gregorian asked her.

"Circling. There are a lot of armed mobs wandering about. He didn't want to stay still." The woman looked at Hannah. "Why is she here?"

"I had to bring her. She isn't safe."

"Good morning," Hannah said. She bowed her head at the woman. "Are you an outsider?"

"This is Lilly," Gregorian said. "She is an old friend."

Lilly did not bow back. "Where's the scanner?"

"At the Citadel."

"Still?"

"The people are rising. There wasn't time. I had to get Hannah."

"And the pilot?"

"I'm not exactly sure where he is."

"Christ, Glenn. Can you do nothing right? What were you thinking we'd do? You didn't even try to call or—"

"We can go back. I know where the scanner is."

Lilly rubbed her forehead. "Still with *him*, right? Unbelievable. Well, let's go. We'll have to be quick to stay on schedule."

"How much time do you think we have?" Gregorian asked.

"Not much. I will tell Roger to keep circling for now."

Lilly took out a small device, a black box, and spoke to a voice that sounded far away.

"Yes, yes," she shouted at the voice. "Just stay tight. It won't take long." Then she looked at Gregorian. "The access road is still the same?"

"Yes."

Lilly cocked her head to say *Let's go*, and Gregorian and Hannah followed.

"Where are we going now?" Hannah asked as they cut through the woods and onto a large, smooth road.

"The Citadel," said Gregorian.

"What? But the Necromancer lives there, it's dangerous!"

"No, Hannah. It is not. It is—"

He didn't have time to finish. A rock flew out of the forest, barely missing Gregorian's head.

"What the hell?" said Lilly.

There was a brief moment of absolute quiet, then Hannah saw a shadow pass over them and land beside Gregorian. He yelled as the figure wrapped itself around his neck and knocked him to the ground.

"The Necromancer!" Hannah yelled.

But it wasn't the Necromancer. It was just a man. Buck, the mason from the mill, shirt still covered in mortar, his face in dirt. He held a knife in one hand and fell hard against the ground, holding Gregorian around his neck.

Buck and Gregorian rolled down the road, and as Lilly began to run after them another noise flew down from above them. Immediately behind them appeared a dozen, no, two dozen, people with torches, knives, swords. They were marching so fast they were nearly running, frantically looking for someone, something. For Hannah.

Buck had pulled Gregorian behind a tree. The two of them stood between Lilly and the mob. "Go!" Gregorian shouted, his voice choked by the mason. "Go now!" Buck fell backward, off the road, and he and Gregorian disappeared down a steep hill.

"Run!" Lilly shouted, and she and Hannah flew down the road. Hannah's leg shot pain up her side but she kept moving, glancing over her shoulder at the encroaching mob. The road twisted down the mountain, but Lilly took shortcuts, jumping from one switchback to another. Hannah followed.

"We have to go back for Gregorian," Hannah yelled after her.

"No." That was all Lilly said.

The Citadel, whose black frame and smooth obsidian walls could be glimpsed from the top of the Mountain Keep, appeared suddenly before them. They were approaching it from the rear. Legends and tales about the Citadel long haunted children of the Malicarn, and the mere distant sight of it kept most people from ever traveling too far east. The cries of the mob became suddenly stilled by its sight. Even Hannah slowed her run, but Lilly did not.

The fortress was shaped like a cube, and the walls shimmered in the morning sun, but Lilly ran right up to it as if there was nothing to fear.

"Lilly?" Hannah asked. "I don't think this is safe."

"It's nearly empty," Lilly said, approaching a doorway. "I hope we're not too late."

Lilly went inside, so Hannah followed. She didn't know what else to do. The whole building seemed imbued with a deep magic. The doors, made of smooth glass, opened on their own as they passed through, and Hannah was hit by a breeze of cool air. The inside was not threatening at all, but oddly quiet and calm. Seats and tables were arrayed across a brightly illuminated hall. A banner with the letters *WBC* in a grand design hung on the wall.

"Stay close to me," Lilly said.

The building appeared mostly empty, though as they passed down side hallways the occasional person would appear out of a room, gasp, then run away. They traveled up moving staircases and at one point entered a closet that, when they reemerged, left them in a completely new space.

Finally, in a white hall that echoed as they walked through it, they approached a brown door. A sign hung from it that read WRITERS' ROOM, and scrawled in sloppy script underneath was "Pardon the smell."

Lilly opened the door. A large round table and several chairs sat in the middle of the room. Stacks of paper and boxes of various shapes sat on the floor, on the table, and in every conceivable corner, just as in the Privy Council chamber. On the wall hung a dozen or so paintings, lifelike as any Hannah had ever seen. And they were all moving, acting out some scene.

There was only one person in the room, a man hunched over

the central table. He had long hair that fell at his shoulders, and he wore pants but no shirt. He did not seem much like a wizard. But when he turned and saw them he was not surprised.

"It's nice to see you again, Lilly," he said. "After all this time."

Hannah noticed the paintings on the wall changing to different scenes, different people and places. As she watched them she saw that they weren't paintings at all, but mirrors. Mirrors to the Malicarn. She recognized the central square in the Old Village, the castle courtyard in Kingstown, views of the valley, people walking. A man milked a cow, a woman fed a baby, people were running through the Mountain Keep with swords. It was the Malicarn, all of it, right before her.

"Where is it?" Lilly asked the man at the table.

"Where is what?"

"Don't be foolish, Jules. I am not here to play."

The man laughed. He laughed a long time. He laughed and laughed and leaned back in his chair and laughed some more. One of the images above him changed to a new scene. Gregorian, hands tied, dragged by Buck. Hannah watched him drop Gregorian in a dark room, under a colorful window.

"Of course you are here to play," the Necromancer said. "Whatever else is there to do?"

SAN DIEGO

July 20, 2040

"Run it again. It should work. No? Shit. Hold on."

Terry opened his banking app and kept his hand steady, waiting for the face ID to recognize him—didn't matter how sweaty he was, it always worked—and then waited a few more seconds for the account balances to load. There was enough money, he knew there would be, but—

"The room is ready, right? I know I'm early."

"Normally, check-in isn't until three. But you can check in early if—"

"Okay, okay," Terry said. "It's two hundred ten, right? Even with the taxes?"

"Plus fifty dollars a night for incidentals," said the clerk.

Well, that would do it. Incidentals. The two hundred thirty-three dollars in his checking account didn't include incidentals.

"But those come off after you check out," the clerk said, "if you don't use them."

"Well, I'm not going to use them, so that's fine. You don't have to include it."

"Oh, I have to include it."

"But I'm not going to get room service or use the minibar or anything. I won't even ask for more towels. You can just not charge it."

The clerk sighed, and Terry was pretty sure there was at least one person waiting in the line behind him who sighed as well. He had already blown extra money on an Uber from the airport, trying to get downtown faster. The hall was opening soon, and he was still here. It was going to be too late.

"Can I use more than one card?" Terry asked.

"I can't do that, it's policy, I—"

"Well, can I leave my bags here?"

"Only guests can—"

"I'm a guest! I have a reservation! I'll be back to check in at the normal checking-in time."

The clerk didn't really want to argue with Terry anymore, and let him leave his suitcase to get him out of his hair. Terry had one hundred and two dollars on his American Express and forty-three dollars still on the Capital One card. So he could Venmo Geoff, text Geoff to Venmo him back, and once the money hit Terry would put the cash straight into his checking account. Even with the credit card fee and the instant-transfer fee, that would cover the hotel. He could scrounge for meals some other way. Maybe use those incidentals.

By the time he got to the convention center, the line for Hall H was already out the front door. Terry hurried to registration, got his badge with the Special Access sticker, then rushed to the early entrance line, which itself was quite long. But the hall hadn't opened yet. He wasn't late. He would be able to get in.

There were, it turned out, several Even More Early Access and More Important People lines which were served first, some from interior hallways and caverns Terry was unable to see, so his line still waited for over an hour to enter. He high-fived a cool-looking cosplayer and gossiped with a few of his fellow line waiters about what they hoped to see. They weren't there primarily for the *Malicarn* session, but they were interested at least in what was coming.

By the time he was seated, Terry was about halfway back in the large hall. But with the giant screens on either side of the stage, he didn't worry too much about being able to see. The woman who sat next to him commented on his shirt—"I have the same one!"—but she was with a boyfriend or someone, so Terry didn't talk to her much.

He got two texts, one from Geoff (**Money sent. Send me pics, dude**) and one from his mom (**Bobby might have an interview for you. Restaurant Supply store in Rosemont**). He ignored them both but transferred the money out of his Venmo. Then the lights dimmed and the crowd cheered.

The trick with Comic-Con's Hall H was to get there early no matter what. The whole day would be full of sessions for various movies, series, franchises, and properties, but even if you didn't care about one or two or all of them, if there was even one panel you wanted to see—needed to see—then you had to wait. Once the day started, the hall would be full and there was simply no way to guarantee you would ever get in. So Terry spent the morning hearing about superheroes and spaceships and animated comedies and theme parks and horror spectacles and listened with interest and even in some cases delight—Terry did consider his taste quite broad, of course—but the whole morning and afternoon were mere preludes for Terry's main event.

At about three, right when Terry realized he hadn't eaten anything all day except for the pretzels on his early-morning flight, the screens flashed up a logo in that familiar scribal font: "The Malicarn." A low drone over the speakers, the first notes of the indelible "Heroes Theme" from the early films, and on the main screen above the stage began a montage of famous moments from the *Malicarn* film series. Cheers erupted. Terry hooted.

When it ended a second montage began to play, this one acting as a bit of background on the entire *Malicarn* film series. There were a succession of black-and-white photos of a young man in Paris, smoking a cigarette, and some prerecorded narration about Jean-Danton Souard. Terry recognized him, of course, and could even speak fairly knowledgeably about his life and accomplishments, but (and he never liked to admit this, especially around other fans) Terry had never actually read the *Malicarn* books. He tried, of course, but he was always comparing them to the films and, inevitably, got a bit bored with all the landscape descriptions. He didn't really read much in general. His mother blamed his ADHD.

The video then walked through each of the *Malicarn* films, cutting between some behind-the-scenes footage and interviews with the filmmakers. It was mostly recycled stuff. For example, Terry had seen the old clip of producer Rex Donaldson before, where Donaldson clapped his hands together and said "Boom! It was like the big bang!" when he described the impact of the first film.

The clips from all of the films—and the panel's organizers had selected choice, fan-favorite scenes—did provide Terry a nice reminiscence. He recalled the first *Malicarn* film he ever saw, at age eleven in his cousins' basement, which was *The Malicarn Ends*, the climax to the first tetralogy, but which of course was far from the last film. Terry remembered going home and begging his parents to watch all of the other films. He remembered sitting next to his dad as they binged them over one weekend, and he remembered sitting next to him in the theater as each new film came out, and sitting next to him in the hospital as they rewatched some old favorites on Terry's laptop, how he did nothing but watch them over and over again the summer his father died, how watching them freshman year of college led him to make friends, how arguing about trailers and leaks and casting rumors online got him through sophomore year when he wasn't attending classes and the next year when he sat at home and lied to his mom about looking for work.

The audience cheered for each previous film in the franchise as its title flashed across the screen, though the enthusiasm did dim a little bit as they moved on from the original books, through the adaptations of the books written by Jean-Danton Souard's son, and on to the more recent "originals" that the studio had been putting out, including the new prequel series.

"So what's next?" a voice-over intoned over a dark screen.

A talking head faded in. It was Daniel Souard, keeper of his father's legacy, author of over a dozen *Malicarn* books himself, and executive producer on the films. He was an old man now, speaking slowly, as if always about to lose his train of thought.

"I'm so proud to be able to keep this story alive," Daniel said. "In the end, it's not my story or my father's story. It's your story. And we want to give it to you."

The next talking head was Jules Walker, a young, nerdy, but confident man. Previously a screenwriter for the films, Jules was now leading the next generation of *Malicarn* showrunners and producers. Some fans were skeptical of his creative decisions, but Terry had never doubted him. His interview intercut with shots of a new film set. On location in the mountains, castles and villages being constructed.

"We're not just making films anymore," Jules said. "The next step is to create entire worlds. We've had a long and productive partnership with the Portuguese government, shooting on the island of Madeira for over twenty years. People travel to the island just to see locations from the films." A brief montage of tourists snapping pictures in front of familiar mountains, waterfalls, leftover sets in grass fields. "Last year was another devastating year of wildfires in Madeira"—a montage of fires, decimated forests, people crying outside their burnt homes—"and we feel it's our responsibility to give back to this community which has given us so much. That's why, in partnership with the local government and citizens, we are turning the island into the actual Malicarn."

"It's a living set," said a construction foreman, standing in front of a medieval mill being built by his crew. "Everything here is going to work just like it would in the Malicarn. No electricity, no modern technology."

"And the best part"—the speaker was Daniel Souard again—"is that it's going to provide us with new stories. Genuine stories. Stories for years to come."

Terry's phone buzzed. A text from his mom. **Did your plane land? Are you alright?**

"The whole way we tell stories is changing," said Jules. "People don't want to just watch a story, they want to live it. And with our newest technological innovations we can populate this world not just with actors but with people who really *are* from the Malicarn, who live here and work here. If they can exist in an actual living world they understand, then we can create stories for them, too. Challenges to face, evils to fight. And the audience will come along, more than ever. Because the story will be real."

Images of people, dressed as if they live in the Malicarn, riding horses, swinging swords, drinking ale in pubs. They laugh, they hug.

"This is not a theme park. At Disneyland, Mickey Mouse takes off the mask when the day is over. But here, everyone is in character all of the time. We can place cameras and microphones all over, like a reality show. But the characters won't ever see them. They'll never know. And then we direct the story. Things happen, characters react, it's all real. And finally we edit the footage we capture, shape them into films and shows.

"But it's not reality TV. It's *storytelling*, at the grandest and most immersive scale. Imagine going to see a *Malicarn* movie and knowing that *this* really happened. What's more exciting: a real train, or a CGI spectacle of a train?" A short clip of Buster Keaton in *The General*, followed by a badly rendered digital train, flashed up on the screen.

In the next talking head, Jules Walker looked right at the camera. Terry felt like he was looking straight at him.

"You may be wondering, where do all these characters come from? Well, that's simple. They come from you, the fans. Do you want to stop watching *The Malicarn* and start living it? This is your chance."

Terry's phone buzzed again. **Terry?**

"In our new pilot program, you can join up and become a character on our set. It's a minimum six-month commitment, but you'll get free room and board as part of your storyline. And when it's over you'll be able to watch a movie where you are a real part of the action. People always say that their fandom is their life. Well, now it can be."

A scientist stood in a lab, showing off a big piece of equipment sitting on a table. It looked like an old computer hard drive. "It's proprietary technology we've bought from the US Department of Defense and negotiated with Portugal for its use exclusively on the island of Madeira as part of the living set. You will be given the memories and personality of a Malicarn character. I can't say too much about how it works, that's part of the magic, but don't worry. You're still you. When the story ends, you'll always remember what it was like to live in the Malicarn."

A shot of a man, sitting with his wife and kids on the couch at home, watching a movie where he himself was the star, dressed as a Malicarn knight fighting a troll. The man ate popcorn, his kids laughed.

Terry wept.

"I think about my father," Daniel said, looking wistfully into the distance, "and how much of himself he put into this world. Imagine the ability to actually enter it for real, to be a part of something that was only in your imagination. It's miraculous, in its way. I can't wait to see what stories it lets us tell."

"If you'd like to learn more," Jules said, "we're ready to hear from you. Representatives from the studio are taking applications right now, and spaces are limited. If you want to become part of the Malicarn, don't delay. Make the fantasy a reality. Apply now."

The lights went up, Jules Walker himself walked onto the stage holding a microphone. "How about it, huh?" he shouted, pumping his fist. Hall H exploded, cheers and applause shaking the seats.

Another text. **Terry! Are you OK!?**

He would be.

PHILADELPHIA

March 2041

Glenn Mackey had a stock response whenever somebody asked him his opinion: "Interesting," followed by a long, thoughtful pause. If Glenn timed it right, the other person would interrupt with their own thoughts, which they were all too happy to share anyway. Once you got someone going, talking about things they wanted to talk about, it was easy to parrot and cajole them into an extended conversation which made the other person believe you were, in fact, a deep thinker and serious person.

It worked for conversations about television.

"Have you seen *Pierogi Empire*? It got nominated for a bunch of Emmys."

"It was very interesting."

"Yeah, I mean, it's not groundbreaking but I thought it had a unique structure, how it wraps the narrative around a bunch of different characters' point of views. I always enjoy shows that try to push me a little."

It worked for conversations about sports.

"Watch the game last night?"

"Wasn't that interesting?"

"Not sure why you'd kick a field goal at the end instead of trying to throw at least one more time. Run it out of bounds or spike it if you have to. I know they were out of time-outs, but you gotta go for it, you know? Today's athletes. It's like they don't even want to win. They just want to get paid."

It definitely worked for conversations about politics.

"This new caucus is calling themselves the 'Restorers,' and I'm worried there'll be more of them elected after the midterms."

"It's interesting, for sure."

"Scary, but yeah. They effectively created their own political party. And the president is totally in line with their agenda. Every time I think we've hit a new bottom as a country—"

Glenn learned a lot about his interlocutors this way, which made future conversations easier. He knew what people cared about and what they thought was important. He knew who read the news and who only read headlines. He knew who wanted to be flattered and who was genuinely curious about what Glenn thought. This latter group was the most difficult to deal with, since it became clearer to Glenn with each passing year of his life that he had almost nothing of interest to say or contribute in any situation on any topic.

Glenn knew things, of course. He liked to watch plays and movies. He kept abreast of current events and trends in show business and was generally thoughtful in remembering acquaintances' birthdays and children's names. But when he was alone and had the time and the space to search his own mind for a unique or original thought, some new piece of fascinating information or witty observation, he had nothing. His mind was blank, empty, open, waiting to be filled by the rest of the world but incapable of producing anything on its own.

"So did you get a chance to watch the movie?" Jules asked. "What did you think of it?"

"It was interesting," Glenn said. He was still vibrating from the show. Why did Jules want to talk about himself now?

The director and half the cast were singing karaoke up at the bar, a Bowie song none of them knew the words to. This was the extent of the cast party—bad singing and cheap drinks at a dirty bar that didn't card college kids. One of the actors carried a round of shots to Glenn's table, but Glenn was still nursing his beer and Jules wasn't in the mood.

"I can't drink them all!" the actor protested.

"Give one to Becky," Glenn said. Becky was already drunk. She shot back two vodkas and then gave Glenn a hug.

"You were spectacular, just spectacular!" she told him. "You should have been Prospero for our whole run!"

"Don't tell Connor!" Glenn laughed, but she was right. He was great tonight, and he knew it.

"You played Miranda?" Jules asked her. "You were good, too."

Becky poked Jules in the chest. "Are you Glenn's famous Hollywood friend?"

"Famous? Oh, I don't think so." Jules tried not to smile but did anyway. Glenn hated that. "I'm a writer. I'm the showrunner for the *Malicarn* Expanded Universe."

"Ooo, *show*runner," Becky said. "I'm a runner at a Greek restaurant. Bad tips."

The Bowie song ended and suddenly word got around about Glenn's friend. Everyone surrounded Jules, giving impromptu auditions, claiming they could swordfight or ride a horse.

"I don't mind wearing heavy costumes all day long!" "I have directorial experience in film, too. Well, commercials." "My background is improv, you need that right?" "I can do accents."

Someone brought Jules another beer. Glenn wondered how often Jules paid for his own drinks these days.

"What's it like to work on a franchise that big?" someone asked.

"The work's hard, no doubt about it," Jules said. "Long days, especially on set. But this new phase is going to be really good. Lots of innovative storytelling, blurring the line between fiction and reality, some new directions, smart head-scratchers for cliff-hangers on the TV shows."

"Cliff-hangers? Doesn't the streamer release seasons all at once?"

"Yeah, they do. But you still got to keep people watching. There's actually a story guy who comes in and works on episode endings. That's his whole job. The last sixty seconds of an episode. He's got it down to a science, how to make sure you end it right so that the audience keeps watching. He's terrific. Went to the Iowa Writers' Workshop."

"Hasn't the whole steam gone out of that franchise?" Becky asked. "Feels like after you exhausted the source material it's been on fumes. Everything is a prequel now."

"Oh, no!" Jules said, animated but not offended. "I think we're just hitting a new stride. Our new mission goes beyond story. It's all about story *worlds* now. Building them, growing them. Stories end, but story worlds never do. Yeah, we're focused on the prequel space but we have so much we can fill in."

Glenn remembered in college that Jules had considered working in tech, until he failed his first computer science class.

"When you go back to the original movies or books," Jules went on, "they are richer experiences now. Have you watched the latest film? *The Rage of the Red Mage?*"

"I heard it wasn't very good," Becky said. "I don't like titles that rhyme."

"You should see it!" Jules said. "The scanned characters are great! I think they're better than the original actors."

"You're not endearing yourself to us," said Becky. "We don't want to be replaced by brainwashed automatons."

"Speak for yourself, Becky!" Multiple cast members, a few quite drunk, shouted this and similar interjections at Jules's general direction. "I'd kill for a job like that!"

"A lot of people like our new approach," Jules said. "The films are more popular than ever."

"Box office and popularity aren't really the same thing."

"Memory scanning is the future. It's not about the story, it's about the world."

"But it's not art," said Becky.

"No, it's life!"

As if on cue, on the bar TV a commercial played for the new *Malicarn* film. There was a medieval-looking landscape, a lush orchestral score, and a scene of the hero, a knight named Prion, leaping above a stone wall and crashing into a swarm of villainous trolls. Prion looked just as he always had in the previous movies—sturdy and wry, fighting evil while throwing out quips and one-liners. But the Prion in the trailer was not Marvin Powell, the actor who played him for decades. Not exactly. The news had been all over the trades and film blogs and social media feeds for months. Prion and Powell still shared the same body, but Powell's memories and personality had been temporarily altered by a neurological simulation of the actual Prion character, scanned into Powell's brain like a file onto a computer. Powell, despite not looking it, was turning fifty and didn't really enjoy the work of filming medieval fantasy epics anymore. But he still wanted to get paid, and the audiences still wanted to watch Prion. Now they could.

"It's fun to write for these characters," Jules said. "They take every line and note totally seriously. The perfect actor."

"That's because they don't even know that they *are* actors," Becky said. She ordered another beer.

"They're actors all right. They have a role to learn. But the role is the *only* thing they learn. They aren't pretending to be a character. Imagine if Daniel Day-Lewis could inhabit a character by taking on their actual memories, and totally forgetting his own. If he inhabited someone for that long, fully inhabited with absolutely no knowledge of any other life, how extraordinary would that performance be? Total. Method."

Glenn was about to object that Jules didn't have any idea what the Method was, but Jules continued talking.

"The Method's all about bringing your inner emotions into the character," Jules said. "But if you *are* the character, you don't have to work to bring those out. And look, it's this or AI actors, existing only in a computer, we all know it. But AI can't be original. By its nature it just repackages what came before. These are real people, making real, original choices. The truest kind of storytelling imaginable."

"Didn't the military use brain scanning to train supersoldiers or something?" asked Becky.

"Yes, the Pentagon developed the tech first," Jules said. "But it didn't save the Defense Department money. Doesn't really change one's physical abilities, or skill in shooting at a target. A problem for soldiers, but not for us. Plus the military ended up with all sorts of legal problems and lawsuits. So we bought the tech. Short-term it's expensive, but we realized this is valuable IP. Why shouldn't we use cutting-edge tech for art?"

"Oh, so the *Malicarn* Expanded Universe is art now?" asked Becky. But the other actors resumed their own selfish questions and Jules never answered her.

Sometime after four in the morning, Glenn and Jules staggered out of the bar. "I bet they'll be asking after me all day. *Where did Jules go? Did Jules like us?*" Jules laughed very loud. Jules always laughed loud at his own jokes, louder when he was drunk. Glenn helped hold him up, and Jules slumped against his shoulder. Glenn inhaled the conditioner in his hair. Peppermint. Glenn always forgot how strange Jules smelled. They didn't want to wait for a cab, so they stumbled to a bus stop. The driver almost didn't let them on, but Jules bribed him with a hundred-dollar bill.

By the time they walked off the bus in Manayunk the sun was rising. Jules was hungry, so they stopped in a coffee shop. Glenn ordered a double espresso. Jules ate a plain bagel.

"Don't you have a flight today?" Glenn asked.

Jules laughed, mid-bite. "Yes, yes, I do. This afternoon."

"Back to Los Angeles?"

"Nope! Someplace magical!"

"Disneyland?"

"Better!"

Glenn knew Jules was probably going to "the set," as Jules referred to the franchise's new Madeira location, but he was really tired and thought he could delay Jules talking too much more about his own job, at least for a while. He ordered another espresso. "You can shower at my place if you need to."

"Thanks, thanks. Yeah, I might do that." Jules chewed slowly. "You were really great, man. I know I haven't been able to see your work much recently. Things are just so busy, you know. But the show was great. You were great."

Jules never came to Glenn's shows. He hadn't since college. They were always small productions in some tiny theater, so far removed from the studio backlots and location shoots of Jules's life that it seemed ridiculous for him to waste time on them. But Jules was in Philadelphia during Glenn's last performance of the season, and so Glenn texted him, inviting him to a small, half-sold theater in Old City to watch a bunch of hacks and failures.

Larry Pine, Jules's boss and an executive producer of the *Malicarn* franchise, was also in Philadelphia somewhere, taking finance meetings and doing other important business things. His assistant accompanied Jules to the performance, though afterward he disappeared into the back of a black car before Glenn could say hello or invite him to the cast party. Glenn didn't mention it to the other actors. They would have had heart attacks.

"*The Tempest* usually never works for me," Jules said. "Too comic and too serious at the same time. But tonight you really nailed it."

"Thanks." Glenn smiled. "Thanks a lot."

The show ran for six weeks and they didn't sell out once. Poor reviews hadn't helped ("an uninspired and limpid take on Shakespeare," said the *Inquirer*), though Glenn and the rest of the cast placed most of the blame for that on Connor, the lead, who played Prospero with the presence of a children's birthday party magician, loud and confidently annoying. But two hours before last night's show, Connor ended up with a stomach bug and spent the evening puking into a toilet. Glenn stepped into the role at the last moment, and somehow energized the cast into a rousing final performance.

"I loved the whole 'cranky old man' vibe," Jules said. "And Larry's assistant was impressed. I could tell. At intermission he was really excited." Jules continued to talk and chew his bagel at the same time.

"Listen," Jules said, "this brain-scanning tech is the future, it is. I know it's not 'traditional,' or whatever. But you should take it seriously. Did you even watch the movie?"

"I watched it, don't worry. I watch all your stuff."

"While sharpening knives, right?" Jules laughed, and spit up his bagel all over the counter.

Glenn had indeed watched *The Rage of the Red Mage*. He went to a matinee two days earlier after scrounging up enough dollar bills from pants pockets in his laundry bin. Protestors stood outside the ticketing window, yelling at management and holding signs that said CHRIST, NOT COPIES! Glenn sat in the front row and tried to remember the plot of the previous films by reading synopses online until someone yelled at him to turn off his phone.

The film was entertaining enough. The script moved nimbly from set piece to set piece. Glenn recognized Jules's voice in many of the self-aware jokes characters swapped between action beats, but the larger plot was confusing. There had recently been a great war of the wizards (Glenn vaguely remembered this from an older film, *The Battle of the Morlon Kastaun*) and now new and younger characters were being introduced, many with connections to people who had either died or left the series. The small matinee audience applauded when the character of Prion arrived onscreen. Marvin Powell was just as regal in his bearing and as fierce in the fight scenes. The plot revolved around Prion discovering and eventually accepting the fact that he was the true heir to the kingdom, the King of the Malicarn. The film ended with him defeating the last Evil Red Mage from the old Wizarding War, and the final scene showed Prion hiding in a small village, trying to decide when and where to come forward to announce himself as king.

The film ended, but Glenn knew not to leave yet. Another scene played after the credits rolled. A soldier stood guard in front of an old castle. A dark cloaked figure approached. The soldier looked up, eyes wide. "It is you!" the soldier shouted. "The wizard Gregorian!"

But the screen cut to black before the audience saw the figure's face. Glenn forgot most of the movie's details on his way back to his apartment.

"It was interesting," Glenn said.

"You said that already."

"Well, it really was! I'm curious how you make sure the characters actually do what you want them to do."

"Do you want to see how? Come out to the new set?"

"On Madeira? You're not going to abduct me and wipe my memory, are you?"

"Ha! No. I have to clear it with Larry, but you should come. I'll tell him about your performance. I'll get his assistant to vouch, too."

"I have to work, I—"

"Glenn, come on. Don't be daffy. I'll have Larry's assistant call you with the flight details. They can pay you."

Glenn thought to ask how much but didn't want Jules to think he was gauche. "Pay me to do what?" Glenn asked.

Larry's assistant didn't call until a week later, in the middle of Glenn's shift. Today he was Thomas Jefferson, who did not know about phones or radios or global warming or baseball or invasive insects from Asia. He knew only what Glenn had taken the time to learn, a few basic facts about life in colonial America and some choice quotations from the Declaration of Independence, spouted off to tourists wandering in front of the Constitution Center from nine to three, four days a week.

Glenn's phone buzzed loudly in his breast pocket. A sarcastic teenager decided that this was his moment.

"Do your slaves take your phone calls too?" the teen asked, looking not at Glenn but at a girl next to him. "I bet you didn't give Sally Hemings her own phone?"

The boy laughed. The girl was wildly and explicitly unimpressed. Glenn tried to hit the silence button without being too conspicuous.

"And so," Glenn continued, "when it came time to compose a written declaration, Benjamin Franklin asked—"

“Did your slaves drive you to work this morning?” The sarcastic teen half laughed, half snorted. His friends were staring at Thomas Jefferson but not really paying attention.

“I was asked to compose it by Mr. Franklin himself. ‘I do not know if I could execute such a task,’ I said to him, ‘for I am but a humble citizen of fair Virginia, no great orator.’”

“Easy to be humble when you have people do all your work for you!”

Glenn leaned forward and looked the boy in the eye. “Honesty is the first chapter of the book of wisdom,” he said.

“What’s that supposed to mean?” asked the teen. “Is that just some quote you memorized to sound cool?”

Glenn blushed because it was, in fact, a quote he memorized to sound cool. He had a couple of dozen lines by Benjamin Rush memorized, too. But he rarely used them, because he hated playing Benjamin Rush. Nobody knew who that guy was.

When his shift ended, Glenn walked back to the employees’ changing room and took off the Jefferson costume: the breeches, the waistcoat, the cravat. He said goodbye to Betsy Ross on his way out and finally checked his phone, which had several missed calls from Larry’s assistant. He tried calling back but it went to voicemail.

A delivery drone flew low overhead. A few seconds later a police drone followed. Glenn didn’t feel like heading back to his apartment—it was trash day tomorrow so the dumpster outside his bedroom window would be extra foul. Instead he walked into a dimly lit and mostly empty bar. The television was on, and as he thought about ordering he listened to news about water shortages in Phoenix and an update about the knee injuries plaguing half the Sixers’ starters. The weather was going to be hot the rest of the week, and there was an accident on 95 near the airport.

He considered texting some of his castmates from *The Tempest* but decided not to. One had already gone to Chicago for another production; he knew the director would complain about having to wake up early for his day job as an insurance adjuster; and many of the others had gigs or families or excuses. That was always the way of things after a show ended. Glenn never kept in touch.

His phone buzzed again with a text. **Sorry we couldn't connect, Mr. Mackey. Here are your flight details.** It was a private charter.

He texted Jules. **Got the flight info. My own charter?**

The TV played the trailer for *The Rage of the Red Mage*. Glenn pointed to it and gestured at the barkeeper.

"Hey, you want to know something?" Glenn said, not really asking. "My friend wrote that movie!"

"That's nice," said the barkeeper. "You going to order anything?"

Jules texted back. **Well, you're sharing it with staff and some lawyers. First rate, though!**

Glenn ordered a beer and a nacho platter. The cheese on the nachos wasn't melted but Glenn ate it anyway. He waited until the bartender wasn't looking and then ran out without paying the bill.

Forty-eight hours later, jet-lagged and a little drunk from the onboard martinis, Glenn found himself talking about *The Tempest* once again with Hollywood superproducer Larry Pine.

"How did you approach Prospero?" Larry asked.

This was exactly the conversation Glenn hoped to avoid. He wanted to ask about the brain-scanned characters, about how they trained them to act, but he held his tongue too long and now to fill the silence Larry pestered him with questions about process. Larry was an extremely successful person who dressed like a divorced dad at his kid's soccer game—cargo pants, Radiohead T-shirt, and a White Sox hat. Glenn realized he probably was a divorced dad. Larry terrified Glenn, who had never interacted with an actual rich person before, other than Jules. He didn't want to answer Larry's questions. They edged their way across a narrow dirt path, one side dipping down a perilously long and steep hill, and Glenn knew he needed to say something halfway intelligent. Larry chewed gum, looking up at the trees. Jules walked a few feet ahead, a canvas bag slung over his shoulder. Glenn focused on his feet.

"The thing to remember," Glenn said, "is that Prospero is exhausted. He's an old man just ready to be done with all the bullshit. So I leaned into that. I tried not to appear *sad*, exactly, but I played Prospero with a kind of resigned anger. A wizard who hates his own magic."

It did sound intelligent. It was how the show's director described Glenn's own performance to him at the cast party, after his fourth drink.

Glenn wondered if he should get more specific with Larry, if he should talk about pulling his back into a crook and breathing heavily after any slightly strenuous motion. Explain the technical preparation, learning the meter, when to breathe during a line. Talk about making sure his hands had something to do besides always gripping a staff. How important it was to maintain eye contact with your costars, especially as *they* spoke. But Glenn knew Larry didn't really want any technical insights. He just wanted to kill time as they walked through the woods.

Larry nodded and adjusted his baseball cap. "That's just fascinating," he said. "I heard you really brought fresh energy to the part. How long have you been acting?"

"Professionally, since college," said Glenn. "Ten years."

The dirt path turned around a large bend, and after a few more minutes they began to descend. Jules guided them into a thick forest. A silent security guard brought up the rear of their little company, a dozen feet or so behind Glenn. He didn't speak.

"Not far now," said Jules. "If we see anybody at this point, just assume they're in the cast." He pointed to Larry's hat.

"Ah," Larry said, pulling it off and sticking it in his coat.

"Can't have anyone knowing you're a White Sox fan?" Glenn asked.

"Yeah, they'd be too disappointed." He laughed.

The walk was easier now, over flat terrain. It had been nearly thirty minutes since they left the cars, and a half-hour drive from the airport in Funchal before that. Glenn had been expecting a hot tropical climate but Madeira was cool. It rained off and on all morning and now the clouds were clearing. Glenn wondered how much farther they had to go. Jules and Larry didn't want to explain any details about the studio's new set, even after Glenn spent most of the flight signing NDAs.

They approached a low stone wall that stretched in a large arc through the woods.

"Okay, here we go," said Larry. "We'll circle around and you and Jules can continue onward. I'll meet you on the other side." He and the security guard cut around a line of trees to the right and vanished.

"What is this place, Jules?"

Jules set down the bag he had been carrying and pulled out two long cloaks. He tossed one to Glenn.

"You'll see. Put this on. We'll look like monks."

Glenn flung the cloak over himself. It was made of wool and dyed brown, heavy and hot. Jules folded the empty bag and placed it in a large pocket inside his cloak.

"Ready to go through the wardrobe?" Jules asked.

They passed through a small stone gate. The cloak was difficult to walk in, Glenn's strides short and awkward, but Jules moved quick. Through the gate there were several wood-and-grass huts lined up in a row, each with a garden beside or behind it. Past them was a grazing pasture, encircled by a wooden fence, where a dozen goats wandered.

They entered a small medieval village. Or at least what appeared to be one. At the center of this collection of homes was a stone square, with a little inn and a larger wooden building with a wide porch. A fountain sat in the square center.

"That's the town hall," Jules whispered, pointing to the wooden building.

Dozens of men and women wandered in and out of the huts,

tending to their gardens, carrying baskets full of food, or otherwise engaged in talk with each other. There were no children.

"Recognize anyone?" Jules asked.

Glenn looked around. The people in the square did appear familiar. One man, pushing a crate of apples, Glenn knew to have been on the cast of a network hospital drama. And sitting on the porch of the inn, hunched over with a mug of ale in his hand, was Marvin Powell himself, dressed as his character Prion.

Glenn pointed at him. "Isn't that . . ."

"Yes!" Jules whispered. "Refer to him only as Prion. He'll be confused otherwise. Follow me and watch."

Jules walked up to the man and bowed low. "Good day, sir."

"I have had better," Prion said, as he took a sip of his beer.

"A *fair* day, then," Jules said, and pulled out a ring from his pocket, leaning toward Prion so he could see an emblem etched into it.

"*Hrmph*," said Prion, who rolled his eyes and stood up. "Everyone seems to have one of those these days. This way then." He walked through a door into the building behind them. Jules and Glenn followed. Prion led them down a narrow hallway and into a storage closet.

"Are there other accommodations that might be suitable?" Jules asked.

"This will do. What is your business?"

Prion arched his back and leaned against a pole. His mannerisms, his accent, his attitude—all just like Marvin's in the films. Glenn wondered how much of it was genuine.

Jules pulled out a parchment scroll from his cloak, a red seal binding it shut, and handed it to Prion.

"New edict from the monastery."

Prion took the scroll. "You are one of the old messengers. I remember you. Who is this?" He pointed to Glenn.

"He is a servant of mine."

"Hmm." Prion broke open the scroll and read. "The monks

want me to continue to wait in exile? I am tired of this hiding. It is tedious."

"It will not be for much longer. Rumor is there is a new evil massing beyond the Dark Rivers."

"Bad news for the Malicarn if true."

"Indeed."

Prion rolled the scroll back up and motioned to the door. "Care for a drink?"

They walked into a larger hall with a fire burning in the center. A few hungover men lay passed out in chairs before it. Prion tossed the scroll into the flames, then pulled three mugs down from a shelf. A large cask sat in the corner and he filled up the mugs.

"Will you be staying here?" Prion asked.

"No," Jules said, "we must head onward. The rest of the Council must be informed, as well."

"If you see Heloise," Prion said, "tell her that I am safe?" Prion looked almost wistful as he asked.

"Certainly."

They drank the ale quickly—Glenn thought it was very watered down and did not taste good—and said their goodbyes.

"Be safe on your journeys," Prion said to Glenn.

"And . . . I, too, to you," Glenn responded, nodding and quickly turning out of the door before Prion could see the confusion on his face.

Once outside, Jules led Glenn toward the rear of the village. When they were clear of any more people, Jules reached into his robe and pulled out his phone. "Yeah, can you meet us back at the high ridge road? Yes, the one past the hill." Jules hung up and looked over at Glenn. "So, eh? Pretty impressive, right?"

"Powell's memory is still changed? Like in the movie? You didn't restore him after it was over. And he's just waiting in that Renaissance fair until you need him again?"

"'Renaissance fair.' Funny. But yes, he waits there. He's under a two-year contract, and it's easier just to keep him in character, along with everyone else. It creates story challenges but it's easier on the characters. You know, we got some flak for writing the end of the movie as we did, with Prion deserting the army and going into hiding. I agree it wasn't totally natural, but we couldn't have him resume his search for the Necromancer yet. Imagine Prion traveling around the island? Wandering into a grocery store? Hilarious, but potentially catastrophic for his personality."

They started up another hill. The sounds of the village fell away behind him.

"And was everyone else back there was, uh—"

"Neuroscanned? Yes, all of them. We've perfected the workflow. Nearly the whole cast will be scanned now, extras too. We contract with lots of out-of-work actors, but also fans and regular people."

"It's uncanny," Glenn said. "Powell really seems like the character from the movies."

"Well, he *is* the character from the movies. We'll show you the tech. You do it right, have the right balance, they turn out okay. Act like you expect them to."

"How many new characters are you planning?"

"The whole world, buddy."

"Where's Heloise? Prion mentioned her."

Jules shrugged. "Nowhere yet. We're still negotiating with Jen Blakley if she wants to be scanned as part of future projects. Legally we can't force her, even though she's under a five-film deal. So if she doesn't agree, we'll have to write her out somehow."

"You're going to build more, though? More towns and villages, and populate it with other characters, too?"

Jules smiled. "Here, follow me. Larry is going to meet us this way."

Glenn was out of breath when they arrived at the top of the hill. A little dirt road ran in front of them. Jules crossed over the road and into a thick line of trees and bushes. Emerging out on the other side was a steep, bare cliff. And beyond, a wide valley.

The Madeira peaks rose up in front of them, and a river weaved its way between.

"Much of this was government land. And there used to be some towns and villages down there, too. But you know, the trials of our times. Wildfires killed the tourist business. Budget crises. It became too difficult for the villagers to keep going or the government to maintain the parks. So the studio bought them."

"The villagers?"

"No, the villages. For pennies on the dollar. All of the towns and all the state land, across about two-thirds of the island. We're working on more. It's actually a great deal for Madeirans. Lots of jobs coming in. Funchal is still the capital, we're going to base a lot of administrative infrastructure there. The Portuguese are being very helpful. Only a little local resistance so far. Most of the work will happen out here. It was the right spot for it. You know we shot a bunch of the previous films right here? That village was an old movie set we repurposed. There's even the battlefield set from *The Battle of the Morlon Kastaun* still standing, north of here. See down there?" Jules pointed below, to a small group of homes, surrounded now by bulldozers, earthmovers, cranes, and other construction equipment. "The valley is empty of civilians now. We're building a new valley, one just for the characters. It's going to be real, Glenn. It's going to be the Malicarn. *This* is our new set."

Glenn looked out over the land. If he ignored the construction or the few asphalt roads that squiggled along below, he could begin to see that, indeed, the Malicarn was before him. The hills looked like what he remembered from the movies. And the green pastures, too, were not so different from the many fields and plains where battles between wizards and dragons had been fought on screens for decades.

"So when there's not a movie in production, they just keep living?"

"There's always a movie in production, if you think about it.

As long as they can continue to believe their world is real, we can continue to tell stories with them."

"But what if they don't do anything interesting? Or do something boring, something bad for a story?"

"We direct! We can do that through real actors, not scanned ones, helping guide the characters along. We write situations, they act them out, we ensure certain outcomes. There's some improvisation, of course. But it's still *storytelling*, at the grandest and most immersive scale."

Larry and the security guard walked toward them from the path behind.

"A whole universe," Glenn said.

"Exactly. And Glenn?" Jules clapped him on the shoulder as he turned back to the road. "We want you to be a part of it."

"What do you want me to do?"

"Like I said, we need real people living on set to help guide the stories along. We want you to act. We want you to be a wizard."

THE MALICARN

THE FINAL YEAR OF THE INTERREGNUM
(MADEIRA—MAY 2041)

1.

Lilly Kaminsky hated mess. It piled up and overwhelmed, it distracted, it forced her to think about things she didn't want and didn't need to think about. When everything was clean, there was less to worry about. Less to fuss over. There was nothing except what was right in front of her.

In the implementations lab Lilly kept everything in order, lined up, neat, straight. The lab was quiet, two floors underground in the large, black, cube-shaped administration building that the writers liked to call "the Citadel," on the western end of Madeira in what used to be Ponta do Pargo. Unlike the production offices upstairs—messy and busy, full of half-filled whiteboards and pens and constantly streaming monitors—the lab was a model of order and precision. It wasn't fancy: a fairly nondescript space of gray walls and white worktables, a few viewing rooms, and a lot of servers, terminals, and hard drives. But it was tidy, it was clean. There was too much critical work going on—too much to prepare and monitor and deploy—to leave it any other way. Lilly was an implementations specialist, which meant she did much of the grunt work while her boss, a semi-renowned MD/PhD from Stanford named Sue Whitman, took credit. Lilly, after all, merely had a PhD, and it was from Northwestern.

They were responsible for the many characters placed onto the live Malicarn set. The lab processed twenty to thirty characters a day, with the goal of ten thousand characters living and acting on set by the end of the next year. The implementers were well on their way to hitting that target, and had been working on mass implementation for over six months already. With some more staff, the lab could even hit fifteen thousand with a little bit of effort.

The process of implementing a character, streamlined as it had become, was still complicated. First the writers' room sent down requirements. Characters fell into three tiers: A-levels, B-levels, and extras. A-levels were characters with major story arcs, whose bodies were sourced from established actors in Hollywood or London, some who had appeared in previous *Malicarn* films and some whom the writers planned to establish as new characters going forward. A-levels had the most involved instructions. B-levels might have lines or a need to fulfill some story function, and depending on how their arcs went could always be promoted to A-levels. Typically they were sourced from actors with some theater training and saw *Malicarn* character implementation as a big break, though in truth one's thespian background was entirely immaterial to the procedure. Their characters had slightly more simplified personality requirements.

Extras were just that: background actors who were not expected to partake in much, if any, story. Some might never appear in a *Malicarn* film at all but were needed to fulfill the basic duties of running a rural, medieval-like society. They were implemented as farmers, craftsmen, horsemasters, millers, mothers, and wives. There were a standard set of about thirty different personalities used over and over again for the extras. As for their memories, the implementers would mix and match from a prearranged collection: childhoods on a farm, apprenticeships, time served during one of the old films' wars. But compared to the A-levels, who were given elaborate, sometimes novel-length, backstories, the extras ended up with fairly simple, interchangeable little lives. Extras were selected from a pool of volunteers, almost all people who loved the Malicarn and just wanted to live in it for real. They signed long-term contracts and, to Lilly's surprise, were always the most enthusiastic for the procedure.

Lilly herself didn't care much about the personalities. That job belonged to a subdepartment of the lab whose staff were affectionately known as the Brain Coders. They fed each character's stories into an AI language model, which then drew on a vast database of sounds, images, and video—culled from the Web and a number of proprietary archives, along with memories devised by Malicarn writers, producers, staff, and several thousand hours of B-roll from past Malicarn productions—to create a file known as the PersMat: a Personality Matrix. A QA debugger would run the PersMat through another AI, meant to replicate human behavior, to make sure they weren't accidentally building sociopaths or otherwise unstable personalities. Once the PersMat was approved, it moved to Lilly's team.

The biggest hurdle for the implementations team—and what Lilly spent a good chunk of her time dealing with—was that the technology was not only fickle but nearly impossible to fix. If one ran a processing machine too many hours a day it might start to overheat and melt the internal circuits. Everything had to be managed carefully to ensure characters could be implemented on time and the scanners kept running. (The staff had taken to referring to the processing machines as "neuroscanners," even though Lilly found the term unscientific and imprecise.)

There were twelve machines, and only one technician on staff who had any facility with repairing them. But even he could only do minor fixes. If a machine really broke, that was it. There were no more to order, since the patents were sealed under several overlapping cases of litigation in the United States. In fact, the actual specs and documentation for the neuroscanners were held in only one place: a vault in Whitman's office. This was almost certainly illegal, as the US Department of Justice had subpoenaed the studio to get these documents back, arguing that they rightly belonged to the United States government. But that didn't matter if the studio kept all the tech off US soil. The studio had been involved in this legal game of chicken for several years now, and the Portuguese, by authorizing the Special Madeiran-

Malicarn Jurisdictional District, had inadvertently created a sort of legal no-man's-land for themselves, too. With all of the neuroscanner technology in Madeira, the studio didn't have to worry about either government. It was a sort of scientific and technological détente: The United States had the capacity to build more neuroscanners but didn't know how, the studio knew how but didn't have any manufacturing capabilities, and the Portuguese tried their best to appease both parties.

Lilly herself was responsible for tracking the machines' usage and not letting any of them get overworked. There was a complicated spreadsheet and series of workflows she had developed for this purpose, and it took up a lot of her time. But she was also responsible for about one implementation an hour, and since these implementations were the studio's priority they became her priority. It took a lot of organizing to keep her daily tasks ordered and neat, but that's how Lilly liked it. She usually worked twelve or more hours a day, and if anything that wasn't enough. Lilly would have preferred more. It's not like there was much else for her to do, anyway.

The vast majority of implementations were extras—only a few A-levels came through a year, and B-levels maybe once a week. The extras blended together, though a few stood out in her mind: the mother who was very concerned about where her children were, the old man who wanted a drink, the priest who lost his faith moments after implementation.

A few months into the project, Whitman got a directive from the writers' room that the extras needed a bit more spice. They were milling about too much, too passive in crowd shots. Some didn't even try to run away when a few A-levels, as part of an ongoing TV show subplot, fought an animatronic troll at a spring market festival. Each member of the implementations team was asked to contribute a few memories of their own to enliven the extras' personalities.

Lilly, who had grown up in Los Angeles, did not personally have a plethora of rural or agricultural stories she could draw from. There was no need to give a carpenter's wife a memory of a nightclub in Santa Monica or a summer study abroad in Madrid. Instead, she wrote down one of her father's stories about Iraq, one he used to talk about after drinking a little too much.

We were going house to house, looking for a group of insurgents we knew were hiding in the village. Our CO gave us orders to apprehend but also not to put ourselves at unnecessary risk. So we knew we could shoot to kill, no questions asked. Well, we came upon this one little house. Dark, smelled like shit. Someone had been using it as a toilet, just living in there for days. It was empty when we got to it, though. At least it seemed so. We still had to clear it, so I went in first. Nobody in any of the bedrooms, but I noticed a shelf, not flush against the wall, in the back kitchen. I showed it to our captain, who ordered us to move it. Well, we pull it back and there's a hole cut into the wall, and a small little space inside there, like a closet. Piled with guns and explosives, lots of material for IEDs. But the only person in there was this little kid. He must have been about eight. I looked at my captain, wondering what we should do with him, when the kid lifted a gun and shot him in the face. I shot back. They were both dead, my captain and the kid. But we had found where the insurgents were hiding, and when they came back later that night we captured them all.

"Christ, Lilly," Whitman said when she read over it. "This is dark."

"Well, aren't some of these guys veterans of the Wizarding War? I saw those movies, they were violent."

"Yeah, I guess. Just change the details from Iraq to something more medieval. Don't tell the writers, though, unless you've gotten your father's permission for this."

"Oh, I certainly haven't."

The Brain Coders fed Lilly's story into a PersMat for a character they named "Frank Douglas." It was not a name, Lilly thought, that sounded especially Malicarnesque, but there were so many extras now that the teams were just generating basic names for everyone, not worrying since these characters would never appear onscreen anyway.

"Frank Douglas" was meant to be about thirty years old, but the man who was selected was only twenty-four. Lilly didn't worry about it too much. Frank was going to be a farmer, and after a couple of years working in the sun he'd look at least ten years older than his biological age. The volunteer was brought in, already dressed in a hospital gown, hair cut to fit the character, and placed in an examination room, where he sat across from Lilly.

"Hello, I am Dr. Kaminsky. Can you please verify your name?"

"Yes, Terry Prokoff."

"Full name, please."

"Uh, Terrence. Terrence Howard Prokoff."

"Thank you. And can you please confirm the procedure you have been selected for today?"

"I'm going to be, um, implemented."

"Yes, thank you." On the table next to her sat a gray box, like a computer hard drive, with an LED display, various knobs and buttons, and a green cord winding out the top. "This is a Cerebral Cortex Implementations Processor, or 'neuroscanner,' as we call it. It creates new synaptic connections which, once finished, will seem to you as memories and personality traits. Likes, dislikes, social conditioning, that sort of thing. Your present personality and memories will remain intact, but as part of the implementation these will be sequestered to parts of the brain which will not have any active role in your cognitive abilities. Does that make sense?"

"I think so. They explained it like, I'll be watching myself do stuff but can't do it myself?"

"Precisely. We sequester you within yourself. Once your contract expires, we'll undo this sequestration, restore your full self, but you'll always have the memories of your character's actions."

"Incredible."

"Yes. So legally I have to register any objections you may have to this."

"None whatsoever."

"You've already signed consent documentation, but I need to affirmatively receive your consent one more time."

"Oh, I consent!" Terry smiled widely, like an idiot.

Lab assistants administered an intravenous sleeping drug and laid Terry onto a gurney. Lilly left, filled out some paperwork, and returned with the PersMat disk. One of the assistants placed a neural node onto Terry's forehead. Lilly loaded the PersMat onto the neuroscanner.

Lilly took a glass of water from the assistant, who left Lilly alone in the room and closed the door. She set the glass of water down on a table in the middle next to Terry's gurney, then hooked the green wire from the gray neuroscanner box onto the node on the body's forehead. She gave a thumbs-up through the one-way mirror and then flipped the box on. She waited for the electrical signals to slowly charge up, and the readout from the body's brain to appear on the small LED screen on the box. All of Terry's vital functions worked fine. Breathing, heartbeat, sensory perception. He was simply asleep. The sleeping aids would last about another thirty minutes, so Lilly got started. She flipped a switch on the front of the machine, and the soft hum of the box grew into a loud buzzing. The body began to quiver slightly.

In theory, a PersMat implementation could occur when a subject was awake, but the fast flow of images and thoughts would be disorienting, so the procedure was always done when asleep. An A-level subject could take nearly an hour to properly upload, and those implementations were always supervised along with an anesthesiologist and usually one of the writers themselves. Extras only took about ten minutes to implement, and nobody was present except Lilly.

The buzzing eventually slowed down back to its original soft hum, and a small light on the console flicked off. The PersMat upload was complete. Lilly turned off the machine and removed the wire and nodes from Frank's head. An assistant came in and took the machine away. The neuroscanner's hard drive would be wiped, to ensure no future implementations were cross-contaminated with another person's memories.

Lilly then sat quietly in the room for the rest of the hour as the effects of the sleep drugs slowly waned. The next step was the most crucial: QA. Quality assurance. Once this step was complete, the subject would be drugged again, sent to props and wardrobe, outfitted with proper clothes and personal items, and then placed at their location on set. The next time the character woke they would be in their normal life, with nothing but a bad headache and memories of a strange dream.

Terry, now Frank, finally stirred and sat up, blinking and looking around the room. To avoid disorientation, the interior of the observation room was painted to resemble the inside of a wooden hut. His gaze finally fell upon Lilly, the first person he had seen in his new life.

"Hello," Lilly said. "This is a dream. I am going to ask you a series of questions about your life. When I finish, the dream will end. You will wake up in your bed, and your sleep will be over. Do you understand?"

Frank nodded. "Yes."

"What is your name?"

"Frank Douglas."

"What is your occupation?"

"Farmer."

"Are you married?"

"Yes." This was true. His wife was implemented earlier that day.

"Where did you grow up?"

"In the southern reaches." Everybody grew up in the southern reaches, because they did not exist.

"Why did you leave?"

"I fought in the war."

"Which war?"

"The Great Wizarding War."

Lilly worked down through a dozen or so more questions about Frank's life, then moved on to the basic knowledge questions.

"How do you use a plow? When do you plant grains? Beans? Potatoes? How do you deliver a calf? How much would you charge at the market for a bushel of wheat? In what direction from your farm is the Old Village? The castle? How do you make love to your wife?"

Frank answered each question easily, a simple pass. Lilly extended the glass of water to him.

"You must be thirsty. Please drink this."

Frank took a swill of the water. Almost right away, his head began to droop.

"You are tired. Lie down."

Frank lay back down on the gurney and was asleep again.

Lilly left the room, passed off her paperwork, and pressed a buzzer for someone from the props department to come down. A minute later, two runners emerged from the elevator, rolled Frank out, and took him upstairs to begin his new life. Lilly finished entering her paperwork into the system, then reported to Whitman.

"Next one's an eighteen-year-old orphan who lives in the hills," Whitman said. "PersMat's in your inbox. The volunteer's already on his way down."

They were clean, these implementations. Orderly. There was no mess to it. It meant Lilly didn't have to think about what she was doing and what was going to happen tomorrow. This, of course, was all before she met Glenn Mackey.

2.

Glenn's wool cowl itched. He pulled at it but it stuck to his neck, the brim soaked with sweat. His chin itched as well, with stubble from the beard he was growing. He glanced down at the sheet in front of him, the bullet points written out in Jules's messy scrawl. "Knowing surprise. Tell him your name. 'Necromancer has returned.' Get him to commit to helping."

Glenn folded the paper and placed it inside his cloak. The room felt like a crypt—airless, windowless, on the lower level of a recently constructed building the writers were calling "the Old Castle." There was nowhere to sit, so Glenn leaned against the cold stone wall under the lone hanging lamp. It didn't actually make sense for his character to be here, but Jules assured him the lighting would be dramatic.

Glenn looked again at the camera placements, one in each corner, at about shoulder height. Two more in the ceiling, and one low one by the door. They were well hidden, camouflaged and blended in along the stone wall. If he didn't know they were there, or if he didn't know what a camera was, Glenn would never notice them. Jules told him to expect at least one of Prion's bodyguards to carry a camera, as well, hidden in their hat.

Glenn ran through his character's backstory again in his head, trying to recall a few details he could share if pressed. He was Gregorian, the Last Wizard, trained by the Last Necromancer. He defected from the Dark Path and was now trying to make amends. It wasn't much to work with. The writers handed him several binders full of backstory for the world of the Malicarn, but Glenn hadn't read them yet.

He would improvise if he needed to, not that he was very good at that. In college Glenn took acting classes with a Sanford Meisner acolyte where repetition was a frequent exercise. Glenn liked repetition, liked doing something over and over again until he had control over it. But those were theater classes, and this wasn't theater. It wasn't even really film. Glenn had to act completely free, without any concrete preparation for how the scene was going to go.

The scene would be short, anyway. Jules didn't want Glenn's first moments on set to be overly complicated. They had other plans that day. After the scene, Glenn was going to get to see his new apartment. The money Jules had promised turned out to be very good, but even better was the all-inclusive nature of the new set. Glenn would receive his own living space, complimentary meals, and access to basic services courtesy of the studio. The production headquarters had doctors, dentists, yoga instructors, a brew pub. Hours would be long, especially at first, but Glenn wouldn't have to worry about overdrawing his bank account or condescending to teenage tourists. Glenn didn't even care that his contract mandated exclusivity, or that it lasted for ten years. He didn't have to spend another hot summer in Philadelphia, and that was enough.

He fingered the wooden staff the props department had fashioned for him. About four feet tall, it had a small metal tip. When Glenn pushed a small button beneath it, an electrostatic charge burst from the top. It didn't do anything other than shoot off a few harmless sparks, but it looked cool. Glenn had already accidentally set it off twice. He needed to watch his fingers and not scare Prion. Save the pyrotechnics for a better scene.

Glenn heard a clank and the stomping of boots. He stood up straight, flattened out his cloak, and turned so his back faced the doorway. Look solemn and dignified, he thought. The door rattled and opened. Glenn turned around slowly, as if he had been standing in that position for hours and only moved at the sound of his visitors arriving.

Prion walked into the room first, dressed in mail and carrying a long sword in his scabbard. Two imposing knights walked in with him. One of them wore an overly large hat that kept threatening to slip off. Glenn assumed he was the one with the hidden camera.

"I know you," Prion said. "You were in the village, with the messenger."

"I have been many places, my good sir," Glenn said, affecting a faux British accent that needed work. "Or, should I say, my good *king*?"

"If you knew who I was," Prion said, "why did you not speak as such?"

"I had to see you first," Glenn said. "To make sure you were ready. My name is Gregorian. Perhaps you have heard of me?"

Prion nodded. "Yes. I know your past. You were once with the Necromancer." He drew his sword. "Swear to me you are no longer!"

Glenn wasn't sure what would happen if Prion actually tried to kill him. "I swear it!" he shouted. "I have turned from the Dark Path."

"How can I believe you?"

"Because you have been under the Necromancer's control, as well." Glenn waited a moment, giving a pause for Prion to take in this information. Jules insisted that this would come as a surprise to the audience, too, though Glenn thought it felt rather obvious.

"How is that possible? I have never faced the Necromancer."

"His magic has controlled these lands for years, since the Council of Heroes disbanded."

"What do you want from me? What can I possibly do against such evil?"

"I need a fighter, Prion. And the Malicarn needs a king." Glenn looked dramatically at the two guards and then walked closer to Prion, nearly whispering into his ear. "The Council of Heroes must be reborn."

Prion shook his head. "No, that time is over."

"It is not. It must rise again."

"It has been years. They are scattered across the land. Some may not even wish to fight."

"They will fight for you."

"No, I cannot lead them."

"You must. And quickly, too. The Necromancer is gathering his strength. He moves against us soon. If the Council is not assembled he will triumph, and darkness will cover the land once again." Glenn would have to remember to ask Jules how the

Necromancer could be threatening to take over a land he already controlled.

A stereo outside the castle made the sound of a cock crowing for effect, even though it was early afternoon. Prion did not seem to notice.

"Time is of the essence," Glenn said. "I must be on my way." Glenn still wasn't sure how predictable the scanned actors were, but Jules wrote the scene assuming Prion would follow, so Glenn marched out of the room. They passed up the stairs and out into the castle courtyard. A horse was tied up waiting for Glenn, the same horse he trained with the previous week. Wherever the handlers were, they had made themselves scarce. The courtyard was empty, and the sun high above them.

"If I do find them," Prion asked, "if I do assemble the Council, where do we go?"

Glenn strapped his staff to the saddle, then climbed atop the horse, trying to do it in one smooth motion that looked natural. He slid a little too far on the saddle.

"I will be at the Old Village," Glenn said, "in the valley. Meet me there, and together we can turn the tide."

Glenn didn't wait for another response. He tapped his foot against the horse and rode off through a gate. He tried to trot as straight as possible until he was over the hill and out of sight of the castle. Then he bent down and slowed the horse to a walk, riding behind a row of trees where Jules was waiting in a van. Two horse wranglers stood outside and walked up, taking the reins and helping Glenn down. A production assistant walked over with a bottle of water.

From outside the van, Glenn could see an array of TV screens and computers. A number of crew members monitored sound and video from the castle. Jules ran over, clapping Glenn on the back.

"Great first day! Easy, huh? Excellent riding, for a beginner!"

"Can I just ride in a carriage from now on?" Glenn asked. "My balls hurt."

A man jumped out of the van, yelling into a radio. "Which one isn't working? That was our best angle!" It was Clinton Maxwell, the scene's nominal director. Clint had very little actual creative control. Jules provided story notes and the producers worked on casting and organizing the set's logistics. Clint, apparently, got a decent amount of say over the edit. He had directed two small-budget thrillers for a streaming service before the *Malicarn* machine picked him up. He continued yelling into the radio about broken cameras and missing coverage, but did not give Glenn any notes or even acknowledge he was there.

"Isn't it faster than a regular shoot?" Jules said to Glenn. "'Cause you only have one take."

"I don't know," said Glenn. "I've never acted in a movie before."

"Prion's already preparing to leave the castle, too, so your persuasion obviously worked. Once the control room is fully running, we won't need to have these mobile units anymore. There will be nothing anachronistic in the whole Malicarn! You could walk around anywhere and it would seem real."

One of the assistant directors poked his head out of the van. "They're gone, Jules. Heading east."

"Okay! Great! Radio the sector two crew, tell them to prepare. They are probably heading to see Tristan."

"Derek Lambert's character?" Glenn asked. "Lambert's here?"

"No, he's in Maui," Jules said. "We recast him. Wasn't interested in being scanned, or our money. Listen, you want some notes? You hit all the lines we wanted, but it might have been a tad stiff."

"Hard to rehearse when your scene partner doesn't know he's acting."

"Precisely! It's important to keep momentum."

Several other cars drove up. The wranglers led the horse into the back of a trailer, and the production assistants packed the van. Clint waved everyone off. "Second unit has eyes on Prion. That's a wrap for us."

"See, we made our day!" Jules said. "Let's go visit the new site. I want you to see how it's progressing."

Jules and Glenn climbed into a small jeep and pulled away from behind the trees. There was no road to follow here. Any old street had been demolished and cleared, replaced with dirt paths or covered in grass and trees. Every modern building had been destroyed, all power lines pulled down. The landscape looked rural and primitive. They drove for about thirty minutes, the jeep flying fast over rocky terrain. Jules filled Glenn in on the latest developments at the site they were calling the Old Village.

"The inn is constructed, and the stables. Not enough livestock yet. When we started building the set we imported pigs from Britain. They have different pigs over there, did you know? And we'd always used British animals in the films. But you only need, what? Five pigs for a movie? They might be in a shot or two, maybe in the background. You gotta have a lot more if it's a working farm. So now we need to import all these pigs."

"Can't you just use a different pig?"

"No, the fanboys will notice. We may write a scene with a gift from a foreign king who gives us some new breed of pig, just to make the problem go away. There's actually a subreddit about agricultural practices in *The Malicarn*. I mean, Souard does spend a lot of time on it in the books."

"I never read the books."

"Oh, you should. They're quite good. Of course, those storylines are way in the future now. Nice thing about prequels is how much story world there is to explore."

"I read one of his son's books, I think, one of the sequels. On an airplane. Or maybe I just started it."

"Yeah, those aren't as good. But we can do whatever we want now. Have you read the worldbuilding notes my writers gave you? You need to study that, Glenn. Really get to know the Malicarn and its history inside and out."

They climbed out of the car and walked down toward a small

river, where a medieval town was emerging out of the ground with the help of a hundred or so men and women in very modern-looking hard hats. Cranes and scaffolding and dump trucks were spread across the half mile or so where the brand-new Old Village would soon be. The production company had been busy erecting set after set, trying to get them built before Prion or another character showed up. Most of Jules's writing was spent devising scenarios to keep characters on the move, giving the crews more time to prepare.

"Local labor!" Jules said, pointing to the construction workers. "Oh, mostly anyway. We flew in some guys from Morocco, but most of these workers are right here, from Madeira."

"Wasn't Ronaldo from Madeira?"

"What? I don't know, who cares?" They walked toward the village.

"Way I see it," Jules said, "we have about a month to finish up here. Then we bring in all the background characters. When Prion shows up with the rest of the Council, you'll be ready to train them. We're only about ten miles from the castle, which we plan to renovate into the king's palace eventually, so on foot it might be a half-day walk. Far but not terrible."

As they got closer, Glenn realized that the center of town was already finished, and the work that remained was only on the outer buildings. The village was not very large. A smithy, an inn, a few homes. Only a few hundred people could live here comfortably. The central square was set up with a number of market carts and stalls, all currently empty of any produce or goods. Jules led Glenn to a stone tower at the north end.

"Welcome home!" Jules said.

The tower was built out of large black stone, like a looming overseer watching the rest of the village. Glenn had spent the last month sleeping in a company RV while staff residences were prepared, so even a gloomy castle was an improvement. The tower was about fifty feet wide, with a single, large metal door at its base. Jules opened it and they walked inside. The first floor was a library with a couple of uncomfortable chairs and tables piled with books.

"This is where scenes in your house will take place," Jules said. "There's a small kitchen in the back. You'll have a scanned actor as a caretaker, so don't worry about actually making a fire or cleaning up."

There was a winding staircase at the rear of the room. They climbed up to a small loft, filled with more books, two chairs next to another fireplace, and a hay-filled mattress on the floor.

"I have to sleep here?" Glenn asked.

"Oh, no!" said Jules. "This is just for show." On the side wall, he pressed a pattern against a series of stones, and the wall swung open on a hinge. A hidden room lay behind it. This second room was larger, with modern furniture and lighting, painted drywall, a drop ceiling, and a kitchenette with refrigerator and coffee machine. On the far side was a couch, a television, a desk, and a bed. It was nicer than Glenn's Philly apartment. A pile of boxes rested in the corner.

"Is this my stuff?" Glenn asked. He looked at the boxes—hastily assembled and already starting to sag. Glenn had asked his landlord to mail his things to him, as he wasn't sure when he would be getting back to Philadelphia. He opened the top box, and his clothes were clumsily thrown in with random appliances from his kitchen.

"There're more boxes in my office," Jules said. "I'll have them shipped down."

"I don't have to share this?" asked Glenn.

"It's your own private residence," Jules said. "Free room and board! Perks of the job. You gotta keep it hidden from the characters, of course, but other staff can come up here. You get internet service, too. A little spotty but it works."

Jules showed him the amenities, how to work the television and order food. "The cafeteria at headquarters is real good," he said, "unless you'd rather cook yourself." Glenn didn't. His computer was networked to a database of production information:

character locations, ongoing plot arcs, camera feeds. He also had access to most major streaming services and the rest of the Web.

"Scripts and notes will be emailed to you each morning before our daily story meetings. We'll run most of those virtually. I usually won't be able to meet with you directly, unless you come to the offices at headquarters. We can always engineer excuses for your character to leave on some mysterious errand, so you can make it to HQ or you can travel for press and such. The headquarters offices are nice. From the outside, they look like a spooky, magical lair. We're calling it 'the Citadel.' So we may build that into the story."

When they reemerged into the market, Glenn was surprised to see at least a dozen people dressed in medieval garb wandering the square and looking at the empty carts, all seemingly oblivious to the sounds of clanking machinery on the edge of the village.

"Are these all scanned characters?" Glenn asked.

Jules smiled and raised a finger to his mouth to tell Glenn to keep quiet. "Yes, yes. New characters. Mostly bit players here, and extras. We're testing their motor facilities."

"They don't care about the construction?"

"Not currently."

Jules gestured to the side of the square, where one of the villagers was sitting behind an empty cart. She was wearing a plain skirt, and had her brown hair held up in a bun. Her focus was on something in her lap, a gray box with knobs that she turned and pressed.

"How're they performing today?" Jules asked her.

The woman looked up at him. "The basic task functions are working well. If we reimplement and it fails again, they'll have to be retired." She looked at Glenn. "Who's this?"

"Ah, one of our Reals. Glenn, this is Lilly, Lilly Kaminsky from R & D. Implementations. Lilly, this is Glenn Mackey. An old friend of mine."

"Nice to meet you," Glenn said.

"You could screw up the sample by bringing him here," Lilly said to Jules. "Are they going to meet him in narrative or will he be backstory?"

"For this group?" Jules looked around at the scanned actors wandering around the square. "He's backstory for them. This town is going to be where he lives."

"Oh, so you're the wizard?"

Glenn peered down at the box Lilly was holding. It was metal, shaped like an old computer hard drive. Not a medieval prop. "What's that?" he asked.

"It's a Cerebral Cortex Implementation Processor," Lilly said.

"The producers just call them 'neuroscanners,'" said Jules.

"They are not technically scanners," Lilly said. "They don't copy, they implement. We implemented everyone here last week but they had various problems. Forgetfulness, old personalities peeking through sequestration. So we de-implemented, put them into stasis, made sure there's not some underlying neurological issue. We'll reimplement soon, and if there are still problems, restore their base personalities and send them home. Happens to about one percent of all implementations, unfortunately."

"How does it work?" asked Glenn.

"Show him, Lilly," said Jules.

"It's not a goddamn toy, Jules. I only brought it to the field—"

"The *set*," Jules interrupted.

"I only brought it to the *set* in case we have any severe misappropriations on this sample and I have to do an emergency de-implementation."

"So a character's whole memory is in there?" Glenn asked.

"Yes, well, a model of one. You can map their synapses with it but it's never perfect."

"Come on," Jules said. "Show Glenn how it works."

"I'm not doing a field implementation for kicks. You want Larry calling you tomorrow when you have to rewrite half the village because they're comatose? No, you don't."

Jules shrugged and turned to Glenn. "We'll show you later. It's amazing."

"Where do the memories come from?" Glenn asked.

"Visual databases," Lilly said, "narrative code, whatever ideas the writers come up with."

Jules laughed. "I wrote a good one for one of the new monk characters. When he was a child, he fell into a snake pit and was stuck for a week and now has an unhealthy fear of nature. That actually happened to one of our line producers. Kind of."

"Is it safe?" Glenn asked.

"Everyone we've ever restored has been fine," Jules said.

"Well, I wouldn't go that far," Lilly said.

"No, that's true."

"As a scientist, I wouldn't say it's a strong conclusion. We've only restored a few dozen people so far, they've only been restored for a few weeks at most, they were only de-implemented due to other problems, and they were only implemented for a couple of days each. So I wouldn't draw conclusions yet."

"Sounds dangerous," Glenn said.

"It's safe!" Jules shouted. "Lilly is just very . . . precise, with her language."

"I'm scientific," she said.

"Well, it's safe," Jules said. "We're getting droves of fans signing up to join us. It's a real long waiting list at this point. And everyone goes through medical and mental health tests. So it's safe. It's safe, safe, safe."

Lilly lifted the box into a brown satchel next to her, disguised to look like a potato sack, and stood up. "I think these are about done. We've been testing them for three hours."

Lilly pulled out a walkie-talkie and radioed in. A minute later a couple of staff members surrounded the extras and began herding them toward a van that backed up into the square. One of them took the neuroscanner from Lilly and carried it into the van.

"Dinner?" Jules suggested.

South of the town, following the river, was a meadow. With the construction crews behind them, the air was fresh and the scene exceptionally pastoral. The three of them walked for over an hour, Jules continually saying they were almost there even though they weren't. Finally they arrived at a mill next to a small house. The front of the house had a large open patio with chairs and tables sitting out front, and a woman dressed in a brown, muddied dress leaned against the patio's frame, apparently waiting for them.

"We got us a freshly slaughtered ham, today," she said. "If you are hungry."

Jules smiled. "Yes, thank you. We are but weary travelers. We would like your victuals. And three ales, please."

The woman disappeared inside the house and they sat down. Glenn's seat rocked under his weight.

"What's this place?" he asked.

"Oh, it's going to be a mill, once we've written the miller. But we set it up as a little pub, too, with actual food. Trust me, it's good."

"Who's she?" Glenn asked.

"That," Lilly said, "is the miller's wife. I implemented her myself."

"But where's the miller?"

"She thinks he's traveling," Jules said. He looked at Lilly. "When do you think we'll have him ready?"

"Not sure," Lilly said. "The backlog is growing longer. Ten days, maybe?"

"She's going to be worried that he's missing."

"She'll be fine," Lilly said. "Is there anything here except ham?"

"You don't eat ham?" Jules asked.

"Not usually, no."

"Why not? Ham's delicious."

"My parents never ate pork so neither did I."

"Why? They kosher?"

"My mother was, growing up. We just didn't eat pork."

"That doesn't make sense," Jules said. "Either you are kosher or you aren't, right?"

"Not really."

"I didn't even know you were Jewish."

"We were very Reform. We reformed all religion out of our family."

"But you still don't eat pork?"

"No."

"Well, pretend you're not Jewish here. We're still in character."

The miller's wife came back with the food, ham and potatoes, and three pints of ale. She apologized for the wait. "While my husband is out my assistant is minding the mill."

After she walked back inside, Glenn pointed the potatoes out to Jules. "Why are there potatoes here?"

"'Cause they're delicious?"

"There weren't any potatoes in medieval Europe. They're from South America."

"It's the Malicarn, Glenn. It's not medieval Europe."

"It's based on medieval Europe."

"No, because then there would be Jews and we already determined that Lilly isn't Jewish right now." He laughed, but no one else did. "The food is good! Come on!"

The food *was* good, Glenn had to admit. At least in-character he wouldn't be forced to eat only gruel. The ale still tasted watered-down, however.

After they finished, and Jules paid the miller's wife with one of the prop coins he carried with him, they walked down to the river through one of the fields. Jules led the way past the tall grass, Glenn and Lilly straggling behind.

"Sorry about him," Glenn said to her. "He's not really a jerk. Secretly unconfident, maybe, but not a jerk."

"Oh, I know," Lilly said. "Believe me, we've worked together for half a year already. He can't hurt my feelings. He even tried asking me out, twice."

"You can't hurt his feelings, either. He doesn't worry about much. He doesn't seem to care that we're walking through this meadow with, what? Venomous snakes, maybe? Jules, are we going to get bitten out here?"

"Not by snakes. Look out for the wolf spider. They've somehow migrated to Madeira and are everywhere now."

"I don't like the sound of that," Glenn said.

"Well, it's almost extinct," Lilly said. "We'll probably kill it off entirely with all this development and you won't have to worry about it anymore."

"That's the most positive way to say a negative thing I've ever heard."

Jules found a clearing, where they sat by the edge of the water and shared a vape pen.

"This is all going to be farms soon," Jules said. "Real farms, worked by our extras!"

The sun lowered behind the mountains, and Glenn asked Lilly where she came from. A doctorate from Northwestern, a few years in private industry, and after an acquisition or two ended up in R & D for a pharmaceutical firm that was now part owner of the film studio's parent company, some German megacorp.

"Do you like it here?"

"I grew up in Los Angeles, so I actually do. Climate reminds me a bit of home. Wetter, though. Taller mountains."

"Do you like working in the lab?"

"It's a job. It pays well."

"So you don't like it?"

"It doesn't matter."

"I love what I do," Jules interrupted. "You gotta love your work to be good at it."

"I don't think that's true," said Lilly. "At least I never found it to be."

"Well, look at it this way," Glenn said, "at least you get to work in show business now! Did you ever think you would do that?"

"I was in the theater club in high school. But not because I liked acting. A boy I had a crush on ran the lights."

"How did that work out?"

"I think he became an actuary. I quit after my junior year. I hated it."

"She's not a bad actor, Glenn!" said Jules. "Sometimes she's an extra when the lab needs her on set to monitor a character."

"Only small-time stuff," Lilly said. "They never ask me to recite Shakespeare."

"Do you like Shakespeare?" Glenn asked. "I recently did a production of *The Tempest* in Philadelphia."

Lilly laughed. Glenn hadn't seen her laugh yet all evening. She sort of hid her face when she did. "I was Caliban junior year. That's how shallow our casting bench was. 'You taught me language, and my profit on it is, I know how to curse!'"

"That's not bad! I was Stephano. We share most of our scenes."

"You were Prospero!" Jules protested.

"Just that one night you came. I played Stephano normally, you know that!"

"Jules, have you ever done any Shakespeare?" Lilly asked.

"In college I took a Shakespeare course about, like, women in the comedies."

"Don't be modest," Glenn said. "You were the dramaturg for the production of *Much Ado About Nothing* our theater department put on."

"Ah," Lilly said. "So he's not a complete moron."

"Ha ha," Jules said, feigning insult. "I know *The Tempest*, too! Just as well as you remember it, I imagine."

"Great," Glenn said. "Then you can be Trinculo!" Glenn stood and jumped up on a rock.

"Oh, geez," Lilly said. "I'm not sure I remember it that well." She sighed and agreed to run through their scenes. "But I really don't remember." Glenn recited Stephano's lines with verve if not precision. Jules pulled out his phone to read Trinculo's.

"You really know the play that well, huh?" said Lilly. Jules ignored her.

Glenn paced on the rock, pulling up the nervous tics he had used as Stephano. "What is this same?" Glenn shouted.

"This is the tune of our catch played by the picture of Nobody," replied Jules, scrolling on his phone. Glenn pantomimed searching and knocking things.

"If thou be'st a man," Glenn said, "show thyself in thy likeness: if thou be'st a devil, take 't as thou list."

"O, forgive me my sins!" Jules stumbled over "forgive," and said simply "give."

"He that dies pays all debts.—I defy thee!—Mercy upon us!" The two embraced in mock fear. Glenn laughed.

Lilly stood up in front of them. She laughed, too, but then looked into Glenn's eyes. Her cold and frosty demeanor, which Glenn had chalked up to her scientific inclinations, suddenly struck him, with Shakespeare's words coming out of her mouth, as deeply magnetic and charismatic. "Art thou afeard?"

Glenn shook his head. "No, monster, not I."

"Be not afeard," Lilly said. She turned toward the river, as if a rapt audience sat and watched. The field behind them was quiet. "The isle is full of noises, sounds and sweet airs that give delight and hurt not. Sometimes a thousand twangling instruments will hum about mine ears, and sometimes voices that, if I then had waked after long sleep, will make me sleep again; and then, in dreaming, the clouds methought would open, and show riches ready to drop upon me, that when I waked I cried to dream again."

The sun was gone behind the mountains, stars began to sparkle in the young night sky, and Glenn thought he might be in love.

3.

Lilly did not like spending the night at Glenn's apartment, in his tower with empty yogurt cups on the counter and script pages littered in stacks all over the floor. Glenn was always cleaning, so he said, but Lilly never saw any progress.

It was better at her place. She had a one-room studio on the twentieth floor of the Citadel. There was very little furniture—a bed, a small couch, a couple of chairs around a kitchen table. Even here, though, Glenn came in and just *spread out*, taking over with his long limbs, his coat or jacket or shirt flung onto any available surface. He was a walking mess.

Lilly never told Glenn this. She didn't want to hurt his feelings. They moved into some sort of semi-romantic relationship so quickly that, in spite of herself, she had already grown fond of his presence. Glenn made any room he was in more full, even if what he filled it with wasn't productive. He seemed to know about a lot of things—movies and music and trivia about semi-famous people from half a century ago. But none of this minutiae added up to knowledge or insight or even wisdom. Their conversations were about mundane topics—work, pop culture ephemera, memes Glenn found funny—and if Lilly ever tried to talk about politics or the news Glenn grew quiet and a little bored. So she usually just let him talk, filling the air with his chatter. Glenn's mess, annoying as it was, made the rest of Lilly's life a little less sterile.

Lilly of course recognized they were mismatched from the start, even if Glenn did not. When they started sleeping together Glenn was much more invested in the mutual success of their sex life than she was. He talked constantly while they had sex, asking her what she liked, was she okay, should they move or try something new? He was very sincere, which annoyed Lilly.

"Just keep going," she said. "Just don't stop."

But he kept asking questions and wondering what else he could be doing to perform better, and she eventually had to snap at him.

"I want you to not stop! That's what I want you to do!"

She could tell this hurt Glenn's feelings, but Lilly did not find the biological urge for sex something that needed so much discussion. Even afterward, as they lay in bed and Lilly desperately wanted to go to sleep, Glenn liked to talk. Not about their relationship, but about plays he liked or actors he admired or scenes Jules and the writers planned for him to enact on set.

"Do you still talk to your family?" she asked one night. She knew this question would make him quieter, which is why she asked it.

"No."

"No, because you don't like them or because they're, like, dead?"

"Because they're dead."

"Ah, sorry. I don't talk to mine because they're assholes."

"That's interesting."

Glenn truly did want to spend time with her, though. Lilly fell backward into their relationship but Glenn jumped in feet-first. Some days he was the only person in the whole bizarre *Malicarn* project that actually wanted to see her. Even if Lilly was sure Glenn had never had a serious relationship before, and was acting the way he thought a serious boyfriend was supposed to act, Lilly appreciated the effort enough to keep seeing him. The thing about living a life where you make every decision on purely utilitarian grounds is that not very many people make their own utilitarian choice to remain your friend.

The producers constructed a tunnel that ran underground through the set. They connected the Citadel, with all the labs and offices and apartments and administration, to the Old Village underneath Glenn's tower. As the geographic center of the set, the Old Village was a good place for staff to release newly implemented characters or do surveillance. On nights when Lilly finished early or had to run quality assurance on set, she would hitch a ride on one of the electric golf carts ferrying people and supplies from the Citadel to the Old Village. Once in the Old Village, Lilly would visit Glenn in his tower. She had a cheap costume she'd wear for these occasions, so she could walk around the Old Village square and blend in. When lab implementations increased, Glenn spent more time visiting her at the Citadel instead, using the same tunnel but rarely changing out of costume. The Citadel held dozens of dorm-sized living spaces for staff. Lilly was lucky enough to have a window. Some apartments had been constructed underground. One of the implementation assistants lived down there and hadn't seen natural light in weeks.

At the Citadel, Glenn was often called into late-night writing and production meetings. Glenn's accounts of these meetings sounded like a lot of time wasted by writers bullshitting one another, but somehow they still organized three or four different story arcs across different parts of the Malicarn at any one time. Some of these arcs would be spun off into streaming specials or limited series, but everyone knew that they were building toward a major feature film. The writers hadn't quite figured out the shape of it yet.

"All anyone can agree on," Glenn said, "is that it's about the Council reuniting and Prion coming forward as king."

Lilly nodded and only half listened. All the story arcs sounded the same to her.

"The A-level characters are doing what we expect," Glenn told her one night, as they ate Chinese food and watched the small TV hanging above Lilly's bed. "Prion is recruiting the Council characters, who are all agreeing to join up. Slowly, but it's happening. The extras keep interfering in odd ways, though. Like the other day, Prion was trying to ride down to the castle and he got robbed. Actually robbed! The extra knew who he was but didn't care."

"What happened?"

"Well, Prion fought back. Beat him up pretty good."

"Jesus. He fought another character?"

"I mean, it was self-defense. He'll be fine, though. Only a few broken ribs. They might retire him early. Turns out his character had just had a baby, and he needed money to feed her."

Lilly and the other implementers were aware that a baby

boom had begun among the scanned population of the Malicarn. They had expected it, even anticipated it. The characters, after all, had the same desires and hopes as anyone else. There was nothing preventing them from having children if they chose to. But the number of newborns was larger than the producers had anticipated, and the unintended consequences, including a food shortage, were mounting.

Despite how busy Lilly was, Glenn made efforts to see her as often as possible. When she was in the field, they could rendezvous for a few hours in Glenn's apartment. They liked board games, and they had several in progress at various locations: Monopoly at Lilly's apartment, a game of Risk at Glenn's, and several chessboards in the writers' room that, to their eternal dismay, were never left alone between visits. Glenn would also cook for the two of them, usually seafood with a lot of spice, and he'd rattle through conversations at a fast clip, knowing how each time they only had a few hours before one or the other had to rush off to another assignment.

On the nights Glenn stayed over they watched old movies together. Lilly used to think she liked old movies—musicals and screwball comedies and gag-filled silents—but Glenn liked exactly two types of old movies, those directed by horny men and those directed by racist ones. So that was what they watched. There was a lot of Hitchcock, whose grasp of the human psyche Lilly could appreciate as it was considerably fucked up, though Lilly eventually had to tell Glenn to shut up when he babbled on too long about the lighting in *Vertigo*. There were also a lot of westerns, endless westerns with sad men looking off at distant desert horizons. "Well, they're saved from the blessings of civilization," Thomas Mitchell said at the end of *Stagecoach*, as John Wayne and Claire Trevor rode away, and Lilly was relieved the heroes wouldn't have to stick around with the rest of the characters and act depressed about manifest destiny. Glenn liked the ending of *The Searchers* better because John Wayne wanders off alone, but Lilly thought being cast out of society was pretty hopeless even if you had Claire Trevor with you. In any case, at the end of both movies the Indians were dead.

Jules stopped by the apartment some nights. Lilly suspected his visits were partially to see his friend Glenn and partially to gauge the status of Glenn and Lilly's relationship. Jules talked even more than Glenn, chatting incessantly and only ever about work, laying out his theories of things like "benign interventionism."

"The only things we should worry about are the stories," Jules said. "The rest of Malicarn society can do what it wants, apart from them leaving set and discovering the real world. The island helps naturally with that, and the new perimeter guard system should keep them away from the civilian sector of Madeira. But if these people have babies, great. If those babies starve, well, that happens. People live and die all the time, but that's not our concern. Our concern is storytelling."

"But we created these people," Lilly said. "Don't we owe them some support?"

"No," said Jules. "The characters are not machines. They are not AI. We changed their memories but they are autonomous moral actors. We set them up in a working society protected by legal treaties that continues to function well with minimal intervention on our part. Their individual decisions, poor or otherwise, are not our concern. We shouldn't interfere, unless the story dictates it."

"And if the story says to kill them?"

"I'm not a monster, Lilly. The writers have guidelines. Extras don't get involved, ever. They're extras. They are very boring people, as you know. You've seen their personality profiles. They were boring in real life, too. It wouldn't be good drama. I want audiences to feel great escaping into this world, and I want to build the stories they disappear into. When someone watches *The Malicarn*, they need to feel like they are inside of it, just like the heroes are. So no sadism, and no exploitation of boring extras. Plus, all these people signed reams of legal mumbo jumbo excusing us from liability before they were scanned. They knew the risks."

Glenn might have had more complex ideas about the morality of manipulating the people they lived and worked among, but if he did, he never spoke up about it. Lilly noticed during these chats that Glenn was always more concerned about his own role, how much time he would be promised onscreen, how significant his actions would be, if maybe he could get a few more monologues here and there.

Jules and Glenn went on quite long tangents about these things, which Lilly couldn't care about, generally not desiring to talk about work during her few hours off. Instead, as the two men debated with each other Lilly flipped through news channels, watching hurricanes in Florida and wildfires in Oregon, viewing which celebrities got divorced or which teenagers went viral on social media. Glenn and Jules, as far as she knew, never thought about these things. That was fine with Lilly. The outside world was a mess anyway.

Some nights Lilly called her parents, knowing they only picked up when they recognized the voice on the answering machine (they still had a landline), but when her mother's prerecorded "Please leave a message" ended and the line beeped, she never said anything, just sat and breathed silently a few times, hoping maybe one of her parents would angrily pick up the phone anyway and then maybe she would say something. But they never did, so she hung up and sent them an email instead, blaming the time difference for why she hadn't called.

Lilly finally earned a full weekend off, so she and Glenn decided to go camping on the northern edge of the island. Glenn borrowed a tent from the props department and spent over an hour assembling it. Lilly started a fire and cooked their dinner—hot dogs and corn—before Glenn was half finished. After they ate, Glenn insisted that they should have sex in the tent.

"Maybe that seems fun in your imagination," Lilly said. "But it will be super uncomfortable."

It was autumn and the air carried a wet chill. The winter rains had not yet begun but you could smell them. Glenn shivered, regretting coming out to the woods instead of just staying in their apartments. They sat close to the fire, wrapped together in a blanket, and looked up at the stars. Once in a while a blinking light floated past, and Glenn pulled out his phone to check a radar app that told him which plane it was, where it was going, how fast it traveled.

"Funchal to Lisbon. Tenerife to Belfast. Oh, here's one coming in from Caracas, headed to Istanbul!"

"Think they can see us?" Lilly asked.

"There's probably a satellite that can see right here."

"Check Google Earth."

He looked up their location, but it only showed old roads and towns from before they built the Malicarn.

"I bet you can't name any of the stars," Lilly said.

"Well, I know stories about the constellations."

"But do you know how to find them?"

"Um, there's the North Star."

"That's not the North Star."

"What is it then?"

Lilly strained her neck. "Well, there's the constellation Virgo, so that star there? That's Spica. It's a binary star, actually."

"Like in *Star Wars*?"

"If that helps you. I minored in astronomy. I wanted to work for NASA. My dream job was to be an exogeologist and study other planets."

"That's a real job?"

"Is pretending you're a medieval wizard a real job?"

Glenn laughed. "Why didn't you do that?" he asked.

"I felt like doing something with a little more job security, better pay. Federal jobs aren't what they used to be. Plus, being idealistic is exhausting. But I still like astronomy."

Glenn downloaded an astronomy app and tried to identify some stars.

"Can we see other galaxies?"

"Most galaxies you need a telescope for."

"Because they're all moving away from us?"

"Well, everything is moving away from everything else. It appears like we're in the middle, but any other point in the universe would also appear to be the middle, if you were there."

"Whoa, that's a head-scratcher. But it'll reverse eventually? I thought the universe was going to collapse on itself?"

"No."

"That's what the movie *K-PAX* said."

"Is that a real movie? You really have no references for anything outside of pop culture, do you? No, it's not going to do that. The universe is just going to keep expanding until all energy is used up and there's nothing left."

"I feel like I need a cigarette."

"Burn that cigarette and you're just pushing us a little bit closer to the heat death of the universe."

"Well, congratulations. You've convinced me not to take up smoking."

They took the blanket into the tent and fell asleep warm. In the morning Glenn made Lilly coffee and eggs over the fire.

THE MALICARN

THE FIRST YEAR IN THE REIGN OF KING PRION V (MADEIRA—SUMMER 2042)

1.

It was an especially hot day when the king finally returned to the Old Village. Prion sat on his horse, dressed in bright nickel-plated armor, a crown on his head and a flowing white cape off his shoulders. A new scabbard holding his long broadsword hung tightly on his hip. Behind him were the stone walls of Gregorian's tower, and in front of him, ready to train, stood a number of famous faces whom the world had been watching onscreen, in one form or another, for decades:

Ravela, the Dark Witch of the North
Maximus, the Lost Dwarf
Kip and Jip, two drunkards
Bariol, a disgraced knight
Heloise, daughter of the Old Steward
Tristan, a defector from the Necromancer's army

This was the Council of Heroes, the centerpiece of the entire Malicarn universe. Nine Council-centric films had been produced over the years, and the cast had featured in dozens of other properties in different pairings and configurations. Sometimes only one or two would be in a movie or show, sometimes as many as half. But they had not been all together in the same film in a decade. In fact, the character of Bariol died when the original actor wanted out of his contract. He was only recently revived in the story after the actor received a healthy pay increase.

Glenn stood off to the side, watching them from behind a stone pillar. The script today was clear that he needed to *observe* this moment, not be a part of it. As characters, the Council heroes were impeccable. Each of them looked and held themselves to perfectly match prior performances. Glenn watched them closely as they filed into the square. It was uncanny. Maximus cocked his head and squinted, Heloise stood straight with her neck slightly back, Kip waddled a bit when he walked. One thing the Council couldn't do very well, however, was fight. They all remembered how to swing a sword, but the physical act of actually doing it for real, not just in short choreographed bursts for the camera, required a lot of training and conditioning that none of the scanned characters possessed. Even Prion, though he had been scanned for longer and had already starred in one movie as a scanned character himself, was not as nimble as he would need to be to fight the animatronic demon hordes the writers planned for the new film's final act.

"These demons are going to be really scary," Jules had told Glenn, "but they're programmed to react so realistically that the scanned characters will have to fight them for real. They can defeat them, but they'll have to actually fight. It'll look better on film."

The swordmaster and his slew of assistants brought in to train the Council were Reals, not scanned. They were experienced stunt people, cast as characters so the training sessions could be edited together for an inspiring montage. Glenn found the presence of these new actors reassuring. At least he was not the only Real in the Old Village every day. For the most part the stuntmen kept their distance from Glenn. They stayed in character at all times, even when Glenn was alone with them. The swordmaster, a former marine named Brian Doyle who only ever answered to his character name of Kreek, even improvised a moment where he spit at Glenn's feet. Apparently in Kreek's backstory his wife had been killed by a wizard, though Jules later admitted he couldn't remember writing that detail.

Most of the other Reals on set had non-show-business interests, and Glenn gladly allowed them to monologue their passions. Jacob the cobbler was obsessed with the Mets, a condition Glenn learned to pity but not emulate. Jacob was a chronic guest star in TV sitcoms and dramas, a face you recognize but never quite remember. His *Malicarn* role, where he was posted at the castle and acted as the Reals' eyes and ears, was the first stable long-term job he ever had. He even negotiated to bring with him his boyfriend, Darryl, and they lived together on the castle grounds. Darryl was an engineer who specialized in agricultural irrigation techniques and acted as an in-story expert for the local farmers, someone who could talk to them "in character" about how to increase their yield, an important task considering the number of Malicarn farms that were struggling. Darryl loved mushroom foraging and birdwatching, two activities Glenn wasn't quite sure constituted actual hobbies until he and Lilly spent an entire day wandering the forests with Darryl and Jacob tasting yellowing fungus blooms and pointing at a series of identical-looking chirping birds.

These new Reals were all specialists in skills and tasks essential to the running of the Malicarn for which the characters themselves were ill-equipped. Jules, in particular, dreamed of the day when the entire set was completely self-sufficient, able to run as an autonomous medieval society with no assistance or involvement from the outside world, except for whatever story beats Jules deigned to provide. Until then, however, Reals were needed to keep things moving along without massive complications in Malicarn society.

But none of the Reals took their roles as seriously as Brian Doyle, who stood beside Prion on the platform as the king spoke to the Council, his arms gripped together behind his stocky frame.

"Sir Kreek will train you," Prion said, pointing to Doyle, "and remind you what it is like to hold a weapon. Do not underestimate him." Doyle was very stern. He scared Glenn a little.

It was planned that this scene would kick off an extended training montage, which Glenn was not needed for. So he backed away from the pillar at the perfect angle for a long-lensed camera on the other side of the square to capture him falling into a shadowy corner. Then he turned and walked toward the marketplace in search of Lilly.

She was spending the day in the Old Village doing quality-assurance inspections of new characters. The writers planned to grow the population of the valley nearly 20 percent by the end of the current story arc, a more ambitious goal than before. Glenn hadn't seen Lilly in a week, as she had been too busy shuffling between implementations at the Citadel and leading field inspections at a dozen other villages, castles, and farming estates up and down the valley. The harvests were beginning to come in and it would be a test of how well the scanned characters could farm on their own.

Glenn walked through the marketplace but didn't see her. With little else to do, he walked back to his tower. He sent Lilly a text, telling her that he was in the apartment if she wanted to stop by. Then he plopped down on the couch, opened his laptop, and started watching the previous day's dailies.

Dailies and partially edited scenes were sent to Glenn's computer each morning. He spent a lot of time watching them, sifting through footage, scrolling through many moments that wouldn't even end up in a final film. The dailies allowed him to observe various characters in natural moments he wasn't privy to, to see how they acted when they were alone, or how they talked to other characters when Glenn wasn't around.

He learned a few things from this. The wizard Gregorian was not well-liked. Almost everyone, including Prion, thought he was smug and conceited. When Glenn complained, Jules just waved him off.

"Gregorian's a bit of a prig, yes. You're playing him that way because he's supposed to be! But everyone will come to like you eventually, even audiences."

Glenn also learned from dailies that the scanned characters were remarkably resilient. They bought in to their reality wholeheartedly, and even a few slipups—a jeep that took a wrong turn and ended up driving past the Council, or a Doritos wrapper floating in a creek—did not cause much confusion. The explanation for these anachronisms was always something to do with "the Necromancer's Dark Power" or "Old Forest Magic." Characters rarely breached the Malicarn borders out of fear of these legends, though the only places on the island still dense with civilians were in the southeast around the city of Funchal. Airplanes were a constant concern, because there was simply no way to remove all the flight paths of various aircraft that crisscrossed the sky. It did not occur to Glenn that unrelenting air traffic would be a problem for the preindustrial characters of the Malicarn until young children and old men both started screaming and pointing at the clouds. But even that issue had an easy solution.

"Tell them they are the spies of the Necromancer," Jules said to Glenn. "Some kind of evil bird. And if they look too long at them they will be struck dumb by his spells, or something." In final edited scenes, extras staring in horror when a plane flew overhead were simply removed.

An alert popped up on Glenn's screen. Another story meeting. Most of these calls were in the morning, but today Jules wanted to follow up with all the writers after the Council's public reception in the Old Village. Glenn had an hour before the meeting started, so he figured he'd spend some more time on what he called his "historical research."

Glenn was becoming an expert in the fake history of a real place. He read through websites, wikis, and online guides of the *Malicarn* universe, cramming in as much backstory and trivia as he could. He knew the general timeline, how after the movies ran out of source material the producers began making prequels, engineering an arc around the Council and the Great Wizarding War which set up a whole new era of characters and plots. Glenn also knew all of the continuity gaps and character inconsistencies that resulted from this soft reboot, and all of the various fan theories that grew to account for them.

There was the "Anarchist Malicarn" theory, which posited that no one ever really ruled the Malicarn and that it was instead a self-reliant, autonomous entity. The Malicarn kings over the years had no policies, no management issues, and no actual acts of lordship other than fighting wars against various external enemies. For a long time this theory was a joke about how poorly fleshed out much of the Malicarn world was, but after the Great Wizarding War it took on a life of its own, since the king was in exile and no one seemed to be in charge. Even the current storyline, with Prion coming forth as king, seemed to support this, as there was no one to object to Prion's ascension.

Glenn thought this theory was clever and brought it up during a morning story meeting once.

"Stop reading fan blogs," Jules said. "They are just making stuff up."

"Yeah, but isn't it a good point? No one's actually in charge of the Malicarn right now—"

"I'm in charge," Jules said.

When the lore became too complicated, Glenn went back and reviewed older material. The synopsis of the original books, technically in the future of the current story's timeline, felt quite different from the types of stories Jules was interested in. There were fewer heroes, more morally compromised characters, and much more emphasis on ecology and politics. Glenn bought himself a deluxe illustrated edition of the original novel—titled, simply, *The Malicarn*—because he liked the cover art. It featured a painting of a rocky landscape and a black shadow hovering over a mountain.

The book's jacket copy read:

> In the river valley, a prophecy has emerged: The Citadel will fall. In the capital of Kingstown, a mysterious wizard known

as the Necromancer plots to return magic to the realm and install himself in the halls of power. Away across the Mountains, a Council of Heroes fights against the coming darkness. In a story with dozens of memorable characters and locations, empires will crumble, magic will be unleashed, lovers will be betrayed, and wars will be fought.

Since it was first published nearly eighty years ago, *The Malicarn* has sold over a million copies, been translated into more than thirty languages, and given birth to an iconic series of books and films. This new edition includes over a hundred illustrations from artists around the globe, bringing the world of the Malicarn to life in a new and immersive way.

About the Author: J. D. Souard was born in Paris in 1922. He served with the French Army at the outbreak of World War II, but spent most of the war as a German prisoner. Following the war, he moved to the United States and worked as a copyeditor at *The Boston Globe*, where he met his wife Wendy. They married in 1960, and their son Daniel was born in 1962. The first novel in the *Malicarn* series was serialized in *World Science Fiction and Fantasy Magazine* from 1963 to 1964, then published by Oar Books in 1965. Souard wrote four more books in the series before his death in 1993. Daniel Souard continued the series before selling the rights to WBC Studios, which continues to publish *Malicarn* novels in conjunction with the cinematic *Malicarn* Expanded Universe.

Glenn never got around to starting the book.

He had also worked his way back through every film. The quality varied in contrast to the budget. The later, bigger, and more spectacular films—all prequels—felt hollower than the earlier, smaller ones. *The Battle of the Morlon Kastaun*, Jules's first solo screenwriting credit and the climax of the Wizarding War plotline, felt particularly stilted as Glenn watched it one night on his phone. That film serviced a dozen main characters and ran over three hours, ending in a very long battle scene at the old

Temple of the High Wizards, a castle called the Morlon Kastaun. The filming location of this battle was still extant, in the northern end of the valley. Glenn visited it once. The black walls of the castle stuck out of a forest like ancient ruins. The scanned characters, who thought it was a real battle site, had begun erecting monuments to the dead.

When the afternoon production call started, Glenn turned his microphone off and blurred his background, so no one could tell he was sitting on his couch. Larry's box kept freezing up. It looked like he was on a plane. Jules was in the Citadel, sitting at a conference table with four or five other writers, already in an argument with Larry the moment he logged on.

"It's a lot of resources," Larry said, "for it to be taking this long."

"You knew that would be the case," said Jules. "Glenn, where's Brian? Is he still down at training?"

Glenn had nearly forgotten already that Brian was Kreek's real name.

"I don't know," Glenn said. "I left awhile ago, like I was supposed to."

"Fine, fine. We'll check the feed. Better if he stayed there anyway."

These writers' meetings were dry and always too long. They were also relentless and constant. Each day, or multiple times a day, script assignments came with a checklist of things that the Reals had to make happen, a list of things it would be nice to have happen, and a list of what absolutely could not happen.

A writing assistant ran down the wish list for the afternoon. "After training, Prion should visit the armorer. Gregorian insults Tristan over supper. Make sure no one leaves the village. Kip and Jip need to get drunk, but don't let them sleep with anyone. We need to stay PG-13 if we can. Also can't risk any of them getting the clap right before they leave for battle." Someone laughed, but it wasn't a joke. There was a very bad gonorrhea outbreak going on.

Larry grilled Jules about introducing "visitor characters," fans who would only be scanned for a week or less, depending on how much they paid, but Jules always insisted that the Malicarn wasn't ready for tourists yet, that they needed to perfect the story world first, and then under his breath complained about "this Disneyland shit." The visitor-characters program never did get off the ground.

Sometimes specific lines of dialogue were required to be said on set, mostly catchphrases or dramatic beats that would play well in a trailer. Story meetings also included overviews of the current arc and where the writers expected the action would go next. The writers were excited because the training sequence would offer plenty of opportunities for quips and small character beats.

"How about this," Jules said, riffing with the writers. "Maximus tells Tristan not to touch his axe. We'll make it a repeated bit, and then in the final battle Tristan is forced to pick it up to defend himself and says—"

"How do you choreograph that?" another writer asked.

"What, no, listen to the joke. They're at the fight set, then Maximus says—"

"I think we call it the *palimpset*," a writer butted in.

"What does that mean?" said another.

"The demon fight set! Instead of calling it a set, we call it a *palimpset*. 'Cause we built it on top of that first small village set."

"It's pronounced 'palimpsest.'"

"It's a pun!"

"Nobody knows what a palimpsest is."

"I do."

"You're a writer. You're not a real person."

"Let me finish my joke!"

This went on for a long time. Glenn played Wordle. After the meeting finally ended, he got a text from Lilly.

Almost done. Meet me at the inn in 10 min?

He put his costume back on and walked out of his tower,

nearly bumping into Kip, who was pacing furiously, hands twitching at his side. He looked up at Glenn, his eyes blinking as he tried to speak in a whisper.

"Gregorian, I am glad to find you. I need . . . uh, I need to speak with you."

"Of course, Kip. Is your training over for today?"

Kip, one of the more comic Council members, had never so much as spoken to Glenn before. He certainly never looked so concerned.

"Yes, Prion released us. The others went to the inn for drinks, but . . ."

"Oh, you should join them!"

"Yes. It is just, you see, once our training is complete, I suppose we shall be heading out."

"Yes, Prion will need to depart and face the demons as soon as he can."

"Right, this is my concern. I do not think . . . that is, I know I am not ready."

"Perhaps not yet. But I have seen your sword arm, Sir Kip. It is mighty. Kreek will make sure you are ready when the time comes." Glenn was stalling. He didn't know what Kip was so concerned about.

"No, no. You do not understand. I cannot do this."

"You must have faith in your abilities—"

"No. I *cannot*. I have always been told that I am a warrior, a descendant of mighty knights. But it is simply . . . that is not . . . I do not *want* to go."

Glenn bit his lip. "My good man, I assure you, you are more than capable. Put your doubts away—"

"No, Gregorian. Please. You must listen to me. When I think back over my life, all the battles I have fought, quests I have gone on . . . I remember it and I do not remember it. As if they happened to someone else. I cannot explain it, unless there is some sort of secret magic that you know of. I cannot tell Prion this, he would not understand. I fear something nefarious is afoot, and if I go on this quest I will only be an obstacle."

Glenn looked at the short little man before him, his breathing heavy, and felt sorry for him. "I will think on this. But Sir Kip, do not plan to turn your back on your fellow knights. They will need you, even if you cannot see it."

"I will only hinder them. Please, Gregorian. Find a way." Glenn watched Kip sulk away from the square, wandering to nowhere in particular.

Glenn walked toward the inn. Lilly was leaning on a post outside.

"What's wrong?" she asked as he approached.

"Nothing," he said. "Are they in there?"

"The Council? Yeah. And they're getting sloppy already."

Glenn peered into the pub, where Bariol was standing on a table, glass of ale in hand, leading the rest of the Council in a raucous song. Kreek was among them, smiling broadly and singing along.

"Let grasses grow and waters flow in a free and easy way, but give me enough of the rare old stuff that's made near Galway Bay!"

Glenn looked at Lilly. "Did you implement memories of Irish folk songs in them?"

Lilly shrugged. "They know a bunch of old songs. Whitman likes it."

"Well, Kreek missed the writers' meeting this afternoon."

"Oh, is he a Real? I didn't realize. I mean, I didn't remember implementing him, but I can't keep them all straight now. He's very convincing."

She leaned against him, slipping her arm under his, beneath his cloak so no one would notice.

"Nice to see you, Mister Wizard," she said.

"You can't call me 'Mister,'" Glenn said. "*Malicarn* characters don't use that word."

"I'm not a character."

"When you're on set, you're a character."

"You sound like Jules," Lilly said. "Anyway, I did miss you."

"It's been so busy."

Lilly rolled her eyes. "Glad you missed me too." She pointed over to the corner. "See Prion? I think he has a friend."

Prion sat with his hands clasped together with a young extra Glenn did not recognize. She wore a long plain dress, a peasant's dress, her hair braided into a bun on her head. She was Black, one of the first diversity extras the producers had pushed to include, but if she worked at the inn or somewhere else in the Old Village, Glenn did not know.

"Who is she?" Glenn asked.

"Her name is Evangeline," Lilly said. "I implemented her last week. Prion's been quite taken with her."

"With an extra?" Glenn asked. "Why would he be interested in her?"

"Why not?"

"He's supposed to be in love with Heloise, who has a much more interesting personality. I'm just not sure what he sees in an extra."

Lilly removed her arm. "Evangeline's not an idiot."

"No, no, I mean, I'm sure you did a good job. But why her?"

"What does anybody see in anybody, Glenn?" she asked. But by the time Glenn noticed the pique in her voice and became dimly aware that Lilly was not talking about Prion anymore, she walked away. He turned to call out to her but decided not to attract attention, so he let her go.

2.

Whitman put "ANP Briefing" on everybody's calendar right before lunch, so Lilly figured it was time to finally learn a little bit more about what this new auto-neurological protocol was and how it was going to mess with her job.

The scanning staff crammed into a long conference room on

the lab floor. A few people were in chairs but most were standing around the table. Lilly leaned on the wall by the radiator. Whitman talked through a slide presentation one of her assistants had put together.

"What this means," Whitman said, after discussing new mission priorities from the studio and R & D leadership, "is that implementations will proceed with a reduced QA procedure for all below-the-line characters. This is in order to ensure that we have adequate capacity for the new extraction procedures we plan to introduce next year."

Lilly knew there would be time for questions at the end, but she shouted one out anyway. "What extraction procedures?" Several other scientists nodded when she asked. Clearly everyone had been wondering.

Whitman glared at Lilly but eventually answered. "I was getting to that. As some of you know, Project Athena is one of the company's tier-one objectives. R & D have been working on it upstairs since the set went live. It is a new procedure that will allow increase in fidelity and replicability across brain models. I can't get into the details yet, but suffice to say everyone in leadership is very excited and thinks it's really going to enhance the work being done here."

Lilly, annoyed though she was by it, also admired the skill with which Whitman and the other senior scientists never directly mentioned that "the work" they were doing was making fantasy films.

Several other staffers had questions, some quite heated, about the safety implications of cutting back even further on quality control, and quite a few questions about what this meant for the neuroscanning program's already tenuous legal status, but Whitman talked them down with more corporatespeak and assurances that none of this meant anything negative for anyone's employment prospects, which was the real locus of concern anyway.

Lilly went back to her apartment for lunch. Glenn had been

at a production meeting upstairs and decided to stop by, eating a reheated burrito and slumped back on the chair opposite her. He barely said hello before he started talking and chewing simultaneously. This was the usual point—after he blew through whatever nonsense was initially on his mind—when Lilly would ask him what plans they had for storylines that week. She knew the answer, of course: The training of the Council was continuing, delayed due to the slow progress of the characters to get into fighting shape and the equally slow progress of the special effects department in constructing the animatronic monsters the Council was supposed to fight. The delay was costing the studio enormous amounts of money. They had expected a finished film in theaters by now. Spin-offs, series, and other forms of content in production were on hold until the film came out. Et cetera, et cetera.

Lilly could have asked about this, and Glenn might have talked about it, at length and in tremendously tedious detail. But for whatever reason he had been avoiding discussions of the story recently and seemed genuinely anguished when Lilly brought it up. So she didn't ask, and Glenn kept on praising her for things she didn't like or care about while she read her emails.

"You always have the best potato chips. Sour cream and onion, yum. And you got those good napkins that don't fall apart so fast."

Lilly's inbox held unread requests about spreadsheets to fill and reports to review and benefits to enroll in. After Lilly browsed through and marked them she flipped to the internal company chat page, the aptly-named-by-HR portal The Informer, because people liked to post important messages there instead of sending emails, and if you didn't check it regularly you would miss out on mandatory trainings and documentation and invitations to birthday parties. There were messages about a new CFO and other staffing changes, updated guidelines on archiving and disposal of confidential documentation, and a brand-new alert that finally forced Lilly to ask Glenn about his job.

"The Council is going out on its mission next week? Why didn't you mention that?"

"Oh, well, you know. It's been a lot."

"Is this what's been bothering you?"

Glenn's smile faded. "What? No? Yes, I mean—" He shrugged.

"You usually tell me everything," Lilly said. She tried to sound sincere, even though this was a lie. Glenn told her everything about work but very little about anything else. But she wanted to be sympathetic. How did a supportive girlfriend sound? What did her mother sound like when she comforted her father? Lilly remembered that her mother never had.

"Yeah, it's just some minor stuff. No big deal." He stood up and went rummaging through the refrigerator, even though he had said he wasn't hungry.

Lilly didn't really care to press on. She was still thinking about Whitman's presentation, about the endless drudgery she was expected to immerse herself in and then spit back out and be happy about. Everything The Company Does Is Good. That should be their motto. What was an extraction procedure, anyway?

All right, she would try. "You have to tell me what's been bothering you," she said. "I can't stand having anyone else talk around me in euphemism and metaphor today."

Glenn nodded. "Sure, okay. I mean, it might be nothing. But it's been nagging me, and he's come to me about it a few times now. Kip, the Council hero. He doesn't think he's a warrior. Like, he's convinced of it. He doesn't want to fight or be part of the Council or do any of the things he's doing. I don't know what he wants, but he keeps coming up to me and begging me to let him leave. I've tried to talk him down best I can, but he thinks I'm a wizard with some real authority. I don't know, it's just weird. It's like he's not implemented right."

"Well, he's not wrong, is he?"

"What do you mean?"

"He's not a warrior. He's an actor. A comedian, right?"

"Yeah, Gerry Alderbiest. He's played Kip for years, used to be on *SNL*. But he doesn't remember that. He doesn't know he's a comedian, he just knows he's not a warrior."

"You should have told me sooner. Could be a sequestration problem. I can look at his profile, maybe we can get him back into the lab. There could be something neurological."

"Jules isn't going to like that, with them leaving on their mission soon."

"Let me talk to Jules, to the producers. From a scientific perspective. Let me help." Let me be useful.

Glenn agreed, and on the producers' call the next day Lilly logged on from her lab office, turned her camera off, and waited. The meeting began full of prep talk about the Council's quest. The demon monster animatronics were nearly ready, and the stunt and FX teams were busy laying down the pyrotechnics. The fight was scheduled to take place in the first village that had been retrofitted to appear as the monsters' breeding ground. A great deal of discussion was about rushes and dailies. Half the film was already finished, a teaser trailer was being released the next week, and Larry wanted to make sure Jules and the other writers were ready to go with the next film more or less immediately after the conclusion of the current story.

"I'm not sure how much rest time the cast is going to need after this," Clinton Maxwell, the director, said.

"Make any rest into an opening montage of the Council killing time before their next assignment," said Larry. "We can't stop or else they won't have anything to do."

Lilly waited patiently for the agenda item Glenn had added. "Character Memory Issues" was all he had called it.

"Okay, what's this?" Larry asked, apparently not having looked at the actual agenda before that moment. "What memory issues? Who flagged this?"

"I added this one," Glenn said. "Kip approached me with concerns he's not capable of fighting."

"Ah yeah, I saw those dailies," Maxwell said. "You handled it well!"

"Well," Glenn continued, "it might be a bigger issue. I asked Lilly to speak on this."

"Who?" Larry asked.

"Lilly Kaminsky. She works in implementations."

Lilly flicked her video on and cleared her voice to speak. "I looked over Kip's chart. He's our third-oldest active A-level character, after Prion and Heloise, but the oldest biological body. Gerry Alderbeist is the oldest of all the Council actors."

"Yeah," said Jules. "Gerry's, what, sixty-five?"

"Sixty-seven," corrected Larry.

"Yes," Lilly continued. "So it seems probable that his brain synapses were more degraded to start with. And then add to that the fact that we had to neuroscan him twice—"

"Twice?" Larry shouted. "Why?"

"Didn't take the first time," Glenn said, inserting himself back into the conversation. "Happens a lot, actually."

"Yes, that's correct," Lilly said. "So I think it might be good to keep Kip back, if possible, for his own health. Stress may exacerbate his sense of dislocation. Frankly, it would probably be a good idea to restore his original—"

"No," Larry said. "The whole Council is going. Or else the movie doesn't have an ending. This is a reunion film, a team-up film. Kip's a fan favorite, he has to come."

"I understand the story needs," Lilly said, her voice steady now. "But I'm talking about the health of one of your actors."

"But he's not an actor," Jules interjected. "He grew up in a northern swamp castle and fought with Prion on his first campaign. His best friend is Jip, a fellow knight with a drinking problem. These are all *real* to him, you get it? He's a knight."

"It's real because that's what he's been told. But you know it's not. He's an actor. He's from Cleveland."

"Not anymore," said Jules, "thanks to your team."

There was a long silence. Jules's gaze pierced the screen.

"Why not just rescan him?" Larry asked.

"Because we've already done that," Lilly said. "It's not how it works, anyway. If there's some underlying issue then you can't fix it with more scanning. That's the science. There's nothing we can do via neuroscanning."

"She's right for once," Jules said. "There's nothing to be done. He's been fine in training and he'll be fine on the quest. We can talk about retirement after this arc."

Jules and Larry were united against interfering and the meeting ended. Lilly got a text from Glenn moments later: **Sorry that got heated.**

She didn't respond, and went back to filing through emails.

Glenn texted again. **They're just really concerned about this story.**

Bullshit, she texted back. **You hardly said anything. You have to stand up for me.** Then she turned off her phone.

The next day Lilly finally got a full lesson in the lab's new extraction protocols.

"This is the new input channel," Whitman said, pointing to the red cord that had been installed on each of the neuroscanners, feeding into the same port where the original green cord also emerged. "We can still load PersMats from the servers the old way, but now we can also read scans from live individuals and load them straight onto the hard drive. This data can then be fed back into our databases, giving us more realistic PersMats with more diverse thoughts and memories than ever before."

R & D had retrofitted every machine with the new technology, and wide-scale extraction would soon be rolled out. The entire workflow for implementations was about to change. Every personality could be built from someone else's actual memories, which meant memories could be more specific. It also meant they could more easily build and add technical skills to the cast.

Lilly was pulled off regular implementations management to help calibrate the machines. They started by bringing in a group of outside consultants, people who had been selected and flown to the Malicarn set because of some special skill they possessed. They had to do it in the lab. There was no chance the studio was going to let a neuroscanner off the island. The first man who came worked at a summer camp where he taught kids how to make baskets—a skill the producers noticed no one in the Malicarn actually possessed and had led to a stark shortage of suitable baskets throughout the realm.

"Sounds ridiculous," Whitman said, "but it turns out it's actually important to have baskets."

Lilly sat the man down in the observation room, asked him to think about basket weaving very intently for several minutes, working his mind step-by-step through the process of making a basket. Then Lilly attached the red cord to his forehead and flipped a new switch on the scanner's box that had been hastily labeled INPUT with a sticker and marker.

The man blinked a few times but sat mostly still, staring at the table in front of him. A couple of minutes later the buzz of the machine slowed down, and clicked off, and Lilly told him he was finished.

"Is it really safe for them to be awake?" Lilly asked Whitman when the man left.

"They have to be, otherwise who knows what the scanner will pick up? We need them to think about specific things. But the machine is only programmed to scan them for about three minutes. We don't want anyone getting brain cancer." Whitman laughed at this, but Lilly did not.

They spent the morning gleaning information from more outside consultants: a doula, a musician, a man who knew how to skin a bear. The downloads all went smoothly, only one or two people complaining of a slight headache after.

After each subject, the scanners were carted over to the Brain Coders, who uploaded the data into their servers and started building them into what they were calling PersMat Supps—Supplemental Personality Matrices, which could then be mapped on to preexisting characters.

"We'll start with the extras," Whitman explained. "See how the new information binds. Writers think it might be a good tool to build up B-levels with more backstory when and if they get more story time."

Lilly thought the whole exercise was lacking in scientific rigor. It felt messy, and Whitman seemed to be rushing through it in order to finish up and report back to the studio. The original scanning procedures had been developed by the Pentagon, rigorously peer reviewed, and had even gone through several rounds of questioning by the House Intelligence Committee on the ethics involved. When the studio picked it up and the whole program fell into legal limbo, it was at least a well-understood scientific process.

This new Supps procedure was no such thing. The entire protocol was researched, documented, and deployed only within the Citadel lab. The American studio heads were briefed on its progress, but none of the technology had been developed in the United States, which Lilly knew was necessary due to the neuroscanners' questionable legal status outside of Madeira. Lilly's colleagues were doing cutting-edge research with very little oversight, and no one beyond the walls of the Citadel knew anything about how it worked. Lilly did not even have proper documentation about the machine modifications. But her concerns went unheeded, Whitman sighing when she brought it up and waving her off with a condescending eye roll.

Even Glenn, when she texted him about what was happening, did not provide the expected concern or remorse.

Oh, yeah, Jules is really excited about that. Gonna help with being able to do rewrites on the fly. Hey, you want to get dinner later?

The first character brought in for supplemental implementation that afternoon was an extra named Jasper, a middle-aged man who had been working as a hired hand on various farms. Today he was going to learn about tanning hides. The tanning information had been downloaded from a Colonial Williamsburg employee and retired history teacher who spent many summers in historical reenactment camps demonstrating dead trades for bored children.

Lilly looked over Jasper's implementation history. Real name: Aaron Limt. Hometown: Chicago. Age: 47. Former political activist. Had an arrest when was twenty-five, unusual for an extra. Usually those got filtered out. But no convictions. Seems like it was vacated due to police brutality, so the studio probably gave him a pass when he applied. Under a long-term contract now. Lilly had implemented him originally, though she couldn't remember that.

Jasper was drugged the night before and carted away from the set by a team from the props department. They rolled him into the observation room and prepped him. When the scanner came in, recalibrated with the Supp ready and loaded, Lilly entered the room and placed the green wire onto the nodes. Whitman came in to observe and supervise.

"I'm only running this for sixty seconds," Lilly said. "That should allow plenty of time for the Supps to be implemented while not overwhelming his synapses. It's not clear what will happen to the memories he *does* have."

"Nothing will happen," Whitman said. "Do you forget something every time you learn something new?"

Lilly bit her tongue. She dialed up the Supp on the scanner's console, checked the settings one last time, and then turned the switch.

The subject jerked violently, which had never happened with new implementations. He started to groan and shift on the gurney.

"Is he really drugged enough?" Whitman asked.

"Call the anesthesiologist down here," Lilly shouted through the door at an assistant. She switched the scanner back off.

"What are you doing?" Whitman asked.

"I can't continue if he's—"

"Turn it back on!"

But Jasper was already awake, sitting up on the gurney. The

wire was still strapped to his head, but his eyes were open and he was looking around the room.

"Get security," Whitman bellowed.

Jasper did not run. He did not even try to stand. Instead, he began to cry. His head fell into his hands as he sobbed.

"She's dead, oh God she's dead!" Jasper bellowed. "Why, why, why! I didn't mean to, I just thought, oh no, oh no!"

He fell off the gurney, started slamming his head onto the ground, and continued to shriek.

"I'm sorry! Oh no, I'm sorry! No, no, no!"

By the time he could be sedated, cuts on his head had covered his shirt in blood. It took a few days until the casting department discovered that the tanning expert had been convicted of manslaughter for killing his wife. It was why he had "retired" so early from teaching. In the haste to hire experts for Supps, a proper background check was never conducted. Evidently, when asked to concentrate his mind on how to tan hides during the download procedure, the man had focused on the night he murdered his wife instead.

"What will happen to Jasper?" Lilly asked Whitman at the end of the day. Whitman sat at her desk scrolling through emails and trying to finish the day's reports. Lilly stood in the doorway, and Whitman did not look at her.

"Who knows? The writers will figure something out. Maybe a dragon will eat him."

"That's not funny. It's not fair, what we did to him."

"What does that mean?"

"These people. We're messing with their minds."

"Come on, Lilly, you're a scientist. Grow up. He'll be reimplemented and forget all about it. We'll give him a nicer job, make him a blacksmith or something. You want him to be happier? You do the implementation yourself. Give him a daughter or something, one of these orphans on set. See, everyone wins."

Lilly didn't say anything else. That night, she took an Ativan and fell asleep on her couch. She dreamed about her father, yelling at her in the laboratory observation room, screaming like Jasper, but she couldn't hear what he was shouting about.

3.

"What strength we have, we carry with us," Prion boomed. "We fight not for ourselves, but for all the Malicarn. May this be the first day that the Necromancer fears our wrath."

He stood with the Council on a platform in the Old Village square. They were all dressed for battle, horses waiting for them at the gate. The crowd let out a *huzzah* and cheers erupted. Buglers blew their trumpets. Prion turned and embraced Kreek, and then the Council began their slow trek out of the village. It was a circuitous path that looped around the outer square before turning south toward their destination, but it was more cinematic and allowed more time for the editors to add in a rousing score.

Evangeline waited by the gate, and Prion embraced her in an impassioned kiss. Tears streamed down Evangeline's face as he rode out. Glenn waited at the last turn on the road before it broke south. Prion and the Council slowed their march as they approached him.

"Remember, it is not who you are," Glenn said to them. "It is what you do that defines you."

Glenn thought the line was pure cheese, but Jules wanted a big "morality" quote and had spent several days thinking of it himself. Glenn knew he stole it from one of the *Batman* movies.

The Council marched on. As Kip walked past, he turned his head away from Glenn to look at the ground. Glenn leaned toward him, reaching out his arm to offer some solace, but he didn't actually have anything to say. Kip walked on. Glenn raised his staff and pressed the small button to set off the static sparkling—another request from Jules, thinking the Council would appreciate a small magical token from the wizard—and then watched the heroes march until they were out of sight. It took a long time, as the road was flat for nearly half a mile before turning down and behind a small hill.

Once they were gone, Glenn walked back into the town square. He saw Evangeline standing by her flower booth, and he knew that the kiss she had shared with Prion was going to make Jules very angry. There would be no way to edit around it without losing a large chunk of the scene.

"Good morning, sir," Evangeline said to Glenn as he approached. Her voice shook. "What an honor to meet the wizard Gregorian. A . . . a bouquet for your trouble?" She held out a clutch of flowers.

Glenn smiled. "No need. I do not believe we have been properly introduced."

"I am Evangeline. But oh, I know who you are, of course. I have heard so much about you."

"From who?"

She looked at him and didn't speak.

"Do not be scared," Glenn said. "You have nothing to fear. I know that you and Prion have formed . . . a, well, a friendship, yes?"

"He has been quite kind to me."

"What is your story?" Glenn asked.

"Well, my mother and father were murdered by the Necromancer. His armies burned down our whole village. I fled with my brother, but he went off to fight in the wars. I haven't seen him since. So now I live alone in the Old Village."

Glenn knew half the extras in the square had almost identical backstories, but as Evangeline described hers it sounded very sad.

"I am a friend of Prion," Glenn said. "If you need anything, come to me, all right?"

Evangeline nodded. "Thank you, sir."

"Do not call me 'sir.' Just Gregorian is fine. Good day."

Brian Doyle was still standing on the podium as Glenn left Evangeline, staring off in the direction of the Council.

"Hi Brian," Glenn said.

Doyle continued to stare. "If only I could have accompanied them," he said. "I could have helped shield them from harm."

"I mean, I don't think the animatronics are going to be that hard to defeat."

"You do not have faith in our king, Gregorian. That is why he does not truly trust you and never will."

"All right, Brian, nice to talk to you, too. I hope you can take a break. I'm going to nap."

Glenn returned to his apartment but didn't sleep, instead spending the afternoon filling out paperwork and reviewing notes. Lilly showed up after dinner, tired but talkative. Glenn couldn't predict her anymore—when she would come over, what mood she would be in. But he still liked his apartment more when she was there. She was the only person who didn't really care about the story or character arcs or how the movie was turning out. It was refreshing.

In bed that night, Lilly lay on her back staring, oddly intently, at the ceiling when Glenn suddenly rolled over.

"Oh, I forgot to tell you," he said. "The premiere is going to be in LA. The first week of June, most likely. Postproduction won't take that long but they want a summer release. I'm getting an invite, and they're letting me have a week off to go. You should come with me. Visit your parents?"

Lilly remained silent.

"I'll have to do some press," he said, "but maybe we could get away for a few days? That would be nice?"

"Sure," Lilly said. "Sure, that would be nice."

The next morning the sun was rising over the village when a shout went up from a group of children sitting in the church tower. "The Council has returned!"

There was a rush as the villagers made their way toward the southern gate to meet the arriving heroes. A minstrel band struck up a tune, and decorative candles were lit and hoisted on strings above the town square.

Lilly stayed in bed but Glenn dressed, barely making it to the square in time. He pushed his way ahead to stand near the front of the crowd at the gate as Prion approached—covered in mud and blood but beaming—and the two embraced in an actual hug. Jules had explicitly allowed an embrace on just this occasion.

"The demons are defeated!" Prion cried out.

"Victory!" went up as a shout from the crowd.

Evangeline emerged from the crowd and fell into Prion's arms. The other Council members hugged the villagers in turn, hooting and hollering and breaking out casks of ale. The party moved inward toward the town square, where the producers could get good footage for a final scene. Someone handed Glenn a pint. He smiled and took a large gulp. Bariol and Ravela danced with a child.

Only one person stayed outside the village. It was Jip, and Glenn could see him through the gate as he slowly climbed off his horse, then pulled down a large wrapped package. A body. The crowd parted as he approached. Glenn turned toward him.

"What happened?" Glenn asked.

"He could not outrun the monsters," Jip said through tears. "But, oh, Gregorian! Oh, how he tried!"

Glenn leaned over and pulled back the cloth covering. He covered his mouth to stifle a cry. Kip's faced was smashed in on the left side, dried blood all over his hair and cheeks, his eye missing. His right eye lay open, and his jaw was agape, as if he saw something terrible and didn't know what to do.

THE MALICARN LOWLANDS

THE FIRST YEAR IN THE REIGN OF KING PRION V

Another pig was dead. Marion found it in the morning on her way to collect eggs. It had collapsed in the night on top of the trough, knocking it over and pouring slop all over the ground. The other pigs slurped up the food, standing over their dead friend and eating.

Marion told you right away, but you had to finish milking the cows before you could walk over to the sty and inspect the situation. By then the flies were buzzing around the dead animal, and the heat was baking the leftover slop into the mud. It took most of the morning for you to hitch up the horse to a cart and back the cart into the sty. You tied the pig's hooves together with rope and lashed the other end to the cart. The horse dragged the body away, and you led it to the refuse pit at the far end of the pasture behind the barn. There was no sense saving any of the pig, not just because of how long it had sat out but because of how sick it had been the day before. Pus streaming out of holes in its side, walking deliriously. Not safe to eat. The final payout would be less, but you figured that would be all right. There were still three other pigs.

Your parents used to take you to a farm down the street from the high school, one of the last ones that hadn't been turned into tract housing yet, where they sold ice cream and let you look at their show pig. The pig was always sleeping and you ordered butter pecan in a waffle cone.

Marion fed the sheep and tended to the other horses. She was feeling better now in the mornings, but her belly was large and she moved slower than she used to. Most afternoons her feet swelled and she had to sit down in the house. You carried on alone, checking on the blueberries and hanging ribbon to scare off the birds. You might need to hire a hand, but with one less pig there likely wasn't money for that anyway. You already waited too long to hang the ribbon, and the blueberries were half eaten.

At dusk you returned to the one-room house and found Marion asleep in your bed. A half-eaten peach pie sat on the table, but you didn't feel like eating it. Instead you wiped as much mud off your boots as you could and walked up the hill toward the old mill. Just past the mill was the Black Crow, a cramped pub on a cliff overlooking the sea, with a fireplace that put out too much smoke, and not enough seats. The ale was cheap, however, and you usually found a handful of other veterans commiserating in the corner.

You didn't use to drink much. Even in college, that was never your scene.

These men, this special breed, recognized each other at once. Even from a distance, they walked with a certain haggard bearing. A dull-eyed glassiness, the look that said, *I have seen what normal men dare not dream.* If a man fought in the Wizarding War, had seen lightning fry a company of soldiers, fields choked by frozen bodies, men transformed into beasts by their wizarding overlords, he carries that with him. That night you brought your past into the Black Crow, where you and your fellows drank pints of ale and sang the songs of youth into the night.

"I counted out his money and it made a pretty penny. I put it in me pocket and I took it home to Jenny. She sighed and she swore that she never would deceive me, but the devil take the women for they never can be easy."

You stood on a table, slapping your knee while Tibalt, who had one arm, and Kilwin, the butcher who screamed in his sleep, harmonized.

"Mush-a ring dumb-a do dumb-a da, whack fall the daddy-o, whack fall the daddy-o. There's whiskey in the jar!"

No one asked about your pigs, or your farm, or your wife, and you never brought them up. You didn't remember walking home or falling into bed. You did remember that you dreamed of crying during Little League practice and your dad shaking his head, saying, "Terry, you have to be tougher." Then you dreamed you were wearing your soldier's robe from the Wizarding War, and there was a mirror, like in your bedroom on the Chestnut Drive house, and when you looked into it you were not your father. Or rather, the you in the robe was not you the father but you the son. Marion jolted you awake.

"Another pig is sick," she said. It was midmorning already. You had forgotten to milk the cows, and your head felt split wide open. You stumbled into the daylight. The pig was stumbling worse than you were, foaming at the mouth.

"Shit."

Marion did what she could, herding the two healthy pigs out of the sty and into a separate pen, which you had hastily erected with leftover wood from a fence built the previous winter. It wasn't very big but it would hold.

You then returned to the sick pig, looking him over for sores, and tried to clean out the sty as best you could, hoping that the infection would slow in a cleaner pen. As you shoveled week-old pig shit out of the pen, the pig waddled over and sniffed your leg.

"Get on away, now. Get away."

You heaved a shovelful over the fence and lost your footing, falling on your back and spooking the pig. It leapt away, its rear hoof smashing against your skull. You yelled out and grabbed your forehead, blood running down your hand. Dizzy. Slowly you stood and climbed out of the pen, walking with one eye open. At the house Marion wrapped your head with cloth and you drank from the bottle of spirits you kept in a cupboard. The bleeding stopped but the pain didn't, shooting down the side of your face. You had been injured plenty of times. Falls off horses, arrows clipping your arm during the war. You broke your leg crashing your bike in seventh grade. But somehow the kick of a pig's hoof was like nothing you had felt before. Sharp and bright. You sat inside the house for a long time.

This wasn't what you had hoped for, what you expected. Every day was this same nonsense. You never saw knights or wizards or monsters. Had never even been far from the farm, this little patch stuck on the edge of a hill by the sea. Why won't you leave, go out for some grand adventure? You try to tell yourself to do this, to go become a hero of the Malicarn, to fight with the great men of the realm, but you just sit inside and nurse your head.

When you finally returned to the pen, a man stood against the fence. It was Jack the pig buyer, holding a length of rope.

"Morning, Frank. Thought I could stop by if the pigs were ready. I don't have payment with me but I can come back with it tomorrow." He looked over the nearly empty pen, and saw the pig lying on its side, breathing heavily. "What's going on here?"

"Some trouble," you said. "Sickness. Killed two already. Now this one's got it."

"I was hoping for five hogs."

"Well, I can offer three."

"Two, I'd say." Jack walked to the separated pen and looked over the two healthy pigs. "Not spreading, I hope?"

"Not anymore. You come back with that money tomorrow and you can have the pigs."

"How about I come back next week, see what's left?"

"I could use that money sooner, Jack."

"I could use healthy pigs. I'll be back next week. I'll bring the money with me."

There was nothing to be done. Jack left and you went to milk the cows. Too late today. They were going dry. Marion was afraid to ask you what you planned to do, because what you planned was simple: You would go back to the Black Crow that evening and then sleep until midday.

Two days later the pig was dead and another was sick. You separated the two remaining pigs, moving the sick one back to the original enclosure and dragging the dead one out with the horse again. You worked through a headache that would not abate. But Marion's back was hurting, along with her feet, so she rested and you said you'd go into town to look for a farmhand to help, at least for a little while. You didn't tell her you planned to sell the horse.

The Old Village took half a day to ride out to, and the markets were already closing down when you arrived. Finally, a place where something interesting might happen. You found a stable near the wizard's tower. You waited outside with your horse, looking up at the tower, wondering where the wizard was, if he couldn't come down and help a poor farmer cure his pigs. Or whisk him away on an adventure.

The stable boy didn't like the look of your horse.

"We'll give you two sols for him. But he's old, ain't he?"

"He's old but he's strong!"

"Two sols."

You didn't haggle. You took the money and asked if he knew anyplace you could find farmhands looking for work. He recommended the inn on the far side of town. "Always men looking for some kind of work there."

You found the inn by following the sounds of singing. Inside you saw a group of old men, all veterans of the war. You could tell instantly. They stood, arms on each other's shoulders, singing and swaying as pints were passed from man to man.

"*While the world did gaze, in deep amaze, at those fearless men, but few, who bore the fight that freedom's light might shine through the foggy dew.*"

You ordered a pint, and found your way into the circle. You recognized Denny Porter, who served in your old company, and Olly Tenyson, a former pikeman who owned a farm not far from your own. You and Denny sang your company anthem, and you fell to talking with some of the older men, who had served in wars as far back as the old Mages' Rebellion. You saw the movie about that one with your dad at the theater with the sticky floors and the burnt popcorn.

At some point night turned to day and you stumbled out of the inn, half a sol lighter, and without a night's sleep under you. You had no horse now, but were so drunk you would have had trouble steering it regardless. You walked out the village gates and up the road slowly. You were hungry but too far from the Old Village by the time you realized it, so you continued home.

Marion was in bed, her feet particularly swollen, when you arrived in late afternoon.

"Where were you? Where is the horse?"

"I sold the horse." You didn't explain, and she didn't ask. "No help to be found."

"I nearly fell over milking the cows this morning. That other pig's dead, by the way."

That night, when you went to sleep, you looked at Marion for a long time and realized you had no idea who she was. You knew married men got jealous, or bored, but you didn't realize they could grow ignorant. Ignorant not just of what they thought a wife was but ignorant of the whole idea of her in the first place. Why was she beside you at all? What did you ever think you could understand by being with her?

And why were you still a loser? You thought you left that behind in Sacramento.

You hitched the mules to the wagon in the morning, tied up the dead pig, and began to cart it to the refuse pile. The last pig watched him from the other enclosure. You had only made it halfway when you heard Marion shout from the house. You ran to her. She stood beside the bed, piss or something all down her leg.

"The baby!" Marion yelled. "The baby is coming!"

You ran up to the old mill, where you fetched the miller's sister, an expert midwife, who followed you home with an armful of blankets, towels, and a kettle. She made you fill it with water and heat it on your fire, then she banished you from the house.

You don't know anything about babies. You don't now and you didn't before. You don't want to, it's not exciting, not interesting. What if there is a war, an adventure to be had? You'll have to stay home, because of the baby. Run away, you tell yourself. Leave now, go somewhere. But you don't. You do what you can on the farm, trying not to stray too far from the house, and it was several hours before the midwife reemerged and told you to come inside.

"It's a son," Marion said, sitting on the bed. "His name should be Buck."

You looked at the boy, barely a person at all, and wondered how it was you ended up a poor man on a poor farm with a wife and a son who looked like a potato.

You didn't need to buy any drinks that night. Your friends at the Black Crow treated you in honor of new fatherhood.

"I don't know," you said to your companions, head hung over the table. "What will I do? My pigs are sick. The crop is infested. There's not enough rain. What will I do?"

"Sell your horse," said a man named Brighton. "You can get by with the mules."

"I've done that already."

"Learn a trade, Frank, give up the farm."

"I have a compact I signed with the local magistrate. I have to work the land fourteen years or I face a royal inquiry."

"Oh no, you don't want that. Better just to steal some money."

It was an enticing idea, and it got you to thinking. Jack would be back soon, no doubt returning from a visit to other farmers and breeders off west. He would have the money with him, he said so.

Yes! Here, at last, a quest.

"Hey, Brighton? You want some extra change?"

The plan was simple. Jack would arrive with money for three pigs. So what if there was only one? He would take the one, no matter how mad he'd be about it. Then on his way out, a mile or so down the road, Brighton would ambush Jack and take the rest of his money. At least two pigs' worth. Jack didn't know Brighton, wouldn't connect him with you. You and Brighton could split the rest—doubling your profits. Brighton liked the plan.

"I can beat a man real hard and let him live," Brighton said. "I'm good at that."

On the day Jack came Marion had been up all night with the baby. Buck wouldn't stop crying and you started yelling at her to quiet him down, do something to make him shut up.

"It's good he's healthy," Jack said, when you told him how loud your new son could be. "Crying means he's strong. You want a strong child."

"Yes, of course. You want them to be strong."

"How's your head doing there?" he asked, pointing to the gash on your forehead.

You ignored Jack's question and took him to see the pig. You didn't explain why there was only one left.

"So the sickness spread, did it?" Jack clicked his lips together, shook his head sadly. "Well, that's a shame for you, Frank. But it's not my problem. I wish you a good day."

"I still got the one!"

"Last month you had five healthy pigs. Those I was interested in. Fetch a fair price for them. But now you got one pig that's liable to be sick any day. I can't truly bargain with that, no sir. Good day."

Jack tipped his cap and walked off whistling. You could hear the baby crying from the house.

You spent the afternoon pacing around the farm, surveying the dying blueberries and the overfed chickens and the sheep who weren't growing any wool. You looked at the barren wheat field you needed to seed and the rotten apple trees you needed to cut down. You thought about all the farmwork you needed to do and how little you actually understood about farming. How mad you were that you were a farmer at all, how much you hated it and never wanted to do it, but how you somehow had to do it anyway. You looked at your last pig, who was idly searching the dirt for food, and you waited on Brighton.

But Brighton never showed up. You waited a bit longer, thought about going up to the road yourself. Finally, as dusk fell and Marion fed the young child, you marched up the hill to the Black Crow, where the old vets were singing their songs and telling their tales. Brighton was among them. You walked right up and grabbed him by his shirt.

"Where's my money?"

"Whaddya mean, Frankie?"

"I mean where is it? It was my job, where's my share?"

"Oh, that. Yeah, yeah, sorry Frank. I was helping the missus, if you know what I mean. Plum forgot."

"Liar! You buy rounds tonight? You buy for everyone? You buy with my money?"

"Calm down, Frank. It's not like that. I just forgot is all. That fellow's probably spending his money buying rounds for some other fellas somewhere else. Nobody's ripping you off."

You swung your fist into the side of Brighton's face. He fell backward over the bar, and cries and huzzahs rang out across the pub. A few men pushed through, grabbed you, lifted Brighton.

"Now Brighton's allowed to take a swing at you, Frank. That's just fair."

But you refused to stand for it and so they took the sol and a half you held in your vest and they threw you outside, into the dirt. "You come back when you can take a punch, Frankie."

Marion was asleep at home, baby Buck in her arms. They were both quiet. The farm was quiet, the land quiet. You sat in a chair at the table and listened to the farm. Your trousers were caked in mud, the gash on your head still stung, and you picked at the meat pie, thinking about what to do, how you could make the best of it. Find another buyer for the pig. Get back your horse. Something.

You didn't want to sleep, didn't want to be near Marion or the baby. You walked out to the pigsty. The last pig wandered around the large pen, all alone, sniffing the ground, hoping for scraps. In three days it would be dead, too, but it didn't know that yet. It was just looking for something to eat. You remembered how, when you heard about the opportunity to join the Malicarn, you expected to be riding horses and shooting arrows on some battlefield. You thought you'd be a different person. The pig snorted as it sniffed the mud, and you found the whole scene very funny.

Frank Douglas, for reasons he could not fathom, began to laugh.

LOS ANGELES

June 2043

The sun hit differently in California. Lilly forgot how afternoons felt hotter, somehow. The sunlight made her anxious, the sense that the day was always going on, things were happening, she needed to do something. It made her remember the passage of time and how tomorrow she was supposed to visit her parents. Her parents, who had no interests and no hobbies and no friends, were bound to love Glenn, who shared their lack of passions. She also knew that at some point her father was going to say something racist and Glenn would either not notice or not react.

The lights illuminating Grauman's Chinese Theatre were blindingly bright even though the sun was still out. (It wasn't really Grauman's anymore, Lilly noted, though Glenn still called it that. It was the FedEx-DraftKings Chinese Theatre.) Two floodlights, one on each side of the entrance, shot bright beams into the sky, while a series of LED screens covered the walls, rotating through photos of actors and sets. Several large faux-marble columns made of plastic and rubber lined a red carpet that led out of the front of the theater and rolled down Hollywood Boulevard. Lilly watched the mass of crowds standing in the risers outside the theater, with even more fans lined up against a rope that cordoned off the street. She stood a few feet behind Glenn, who waved at them.

"Hey!" shouted a woman behind the rope at Glenn. "You're in the trailer!"

She asked for his autograph and Glenn fumbled for a pen. He scratched his name onto the piece of paper she held out—a receipt from Starbucks. He signed a few more autographs before the crowd's attention suddenly shifted to someone behind him. The fans screamed and Lilly turned around to see Marvin Powell, the real Marvin Powell, personality restored for the premiere, in a double-breasted tuxedo, smiling and shaking hands. He radiated the calm magnetism of someone who knew that everyone, everywhere, wanted to speak to him.

Glenn walked back toward Lilly. She held his hand but he stood limply, watching Marvin. Lilly began to walk forward, toward the theater, but Glenn dragged behind. Eventually Marvin noticed him, gave another wave to the crowd, then walked over and placed an arm over Glenn's shoulders.

"How's my wizard?" he whispered into Glenn's ear.

They continued up the red carpet, stopping for publicity photos in front of a large canvas poster of the film, Marvin smiling widely while the camera flashes forced Lilly into a spasm of blinking, teary eyes. Eventually they arrived at the theater entrance. Once they passed through and out of sight of fans and cameras, Marvin sighed loudly.

"They're still making me do the publicity racket," he said. "Contracts only go so far."

Glenn nodded. "Uh, yeah. It's really nice to meet you, like for real."

"You've done a good job. I've seen it all, you know. You hardly flub lines at all."

"Oh, thank you," Glenn said, taking the compliment. "It's been a real honor to work with you."

"Well, not with me really, right? I've found it to be pretty relaxing, personally, not having to think all the time. Still feel every blow and bruise, though. What about this new chick of mine? She's pretty hot, eh?"

Lilly doubted Marvin actually found the act of being sequestered as Prion relaxing—she knew he'd feel every strenuous or uncomfortable action Prion participated in. On the other hand, what *would* actually be relaxing was the enormous amount of money Marvin was making and could daydream about as Prion went about his business.

They stepped up to a small bar cart in the corner of the lobby. Marvin asked for two whiskeys, neat, handing one of them to Glenn. Lilly ordered a glass of wine herself.

"I think this movie is going to be really good," Glenn said, "just based on the work you and the others have done."

"No, it'll probably be shit," Marvin said, "like the last two. It's okay, I make five percent gross. And after tonight I'm spending two weeks detoxing in Palm Springs before they ship me back to set. You going anywhere?"

"Uh, Pasadena?"

"Want some advice? Don't get comfortable. The fans will always want your autograph but that doesn't mean they don't hate you. They'll love your character but you can get in the way of that for them."

"I'm more worried about the executives," Glenn said. "Maybe one day they'll fire me and replace me with another scanned actor." He laughed, but Marvin just gulped down his whiskey.

"Don't worry about the suits," Marvin said. "They don't care about you."

"Yeah, that's what concerns me."

"No, you don't understand. They. Do. Not. Care. About. You. So what? Maybe you'll get fired but you'll still exist. The fans, though, they'll turn you into a monster and never let you breathe. Even later, years later. If I go to town? I visit a restaurant? Then I'm not me anymore, I'm Marvin Powell."

"But you are Marvin Powell?"

"Just be careful."

Marvin winked at Lilly, then turned and stumbled toward the auditorium with his glass in hand.

"Charming," Lilly said.

"He's so famous," said Glenn, still watching the door Powell had walked through.

"You've spent most of the last two years with him."

"Yeah, but not *him* him, you know?"

Glenn and Lilly took their seats, a row behind Jules and a few of the producers. Jules was reading the first press review of the film on his phone, shouting out lines he especially hated.

"'. . . The story is a conventional team-up plot, so remarkably underwritten it must be intentional.'" Jules waved his phone in the air. "He doesn't understand how difficult it is to do this!"

"Oh, is this the review from the *Times*?" Glenn asked. He leaned over the seat to look at Jules's phone. "I thought it was pretty positive. Three stars. Look here: 'Instead of giving us simply another fantasy adventure, director Clinton Maxwell and the enormous crew working behind the scenes have instead birthed something new.'"

"Clint didn't do shit."

At just that moment the theater lights flickered, and Clinton Maxwell himself climbed the stage. He had clearly overheard Jules, as he spent his entire walk to the center microphone glaring at him. He droned out a list of thank-yous as Jules kept muttering under his breath, "Thank you to our dear leader for orchestrating such an incredible, real-life experience."

Glenn continued whispering to Jules, too, but Lilly gave up on the two of them and spent Clint's speech staring at the carpet. When Clint finished, he left the stage and the lights dimmed. Applause rang up at the sight of the studio logo.

Lilly found it hard to explain what felt wrong about the images projected above her. Nothing was ugly, exactly. The cinematography was dynamic enough, given so much was sourced from hidden cameras. The shots of the island were detailed, the opening a long push in from a drone in the sky to a rider on a horse below. A fight scene followed, quick but efficient. The audience applauded at the reveal that the rider was Prion. Lilly heard Marvin Powell drunkenly laughing a few rows ahead.

But there was something else. And maybe no one there noticed, because no one else worked with the scanned characters every day, watched them think and process a little too long, watched them follow orders even when they weren't quite sure why. But Lilly did. She quizzed them on lore and backstory that they already knew. She followed them around sets, testing behavior, ensuring they knew how to be people. She gave them their personalities, exactly as they needed to have them, and she knew when they deviated.

So when Prion said one of his signature lines and the audience cheered, Lilly could only think about how many times he was coached on exactly that line, how the implementations team struggled to get him to remember it, how his delivery was wrong nine times out of ten, how even on the tenth time it was said at inappropriate moments. The casual, easy way the line ended up onscreen rested on weeks of prep that did not feel light and carefree.

Glenn's own performance seemed odd, too, though it was for different, more understandable reasons. He was stiff where Prion was natural, deliberate when other characters were free. Every time he was onscreen, Lilly could feel him shifting in the seat next to her, his hands gripping the armrests, his body slowly contorting itself against the back of the chair. But his funny lines got laughs and his emotional scenes were not met with snickers, so at least it wasn't a disaster.

What was artifice for Lilly, however, was transfigured into an electric charge for the audience. They laughed and hooted and screamed and cried. The tears—actual loud sobs that Lilly could hear from multiple corners of the large auditorium—came mostly at the end, during the big battle. Kip's scene.

Watching Kip throughout the film literally repulsed Lilly. Every time he was in a scene, cracking jokes, Lilly could only see the bloody corpse a prop assistant had wheeled down to the lab. When the climactic battle commenced, she looked away from the screen.

The scene was straightforward. The Council approached the demon trolls, who sent out a legion of spiders and giant insects.

A long fight ensued. If the Council of Heroes moved somewhat more slowly than in earlier, CGI-assisted films, the filmmaking at least could be called "visceral." It cut often, keeping close to the action—the monsters had cameras built into them—focusing on grit and dirt instead of theatrics. But Kip made it out of the fight all right, and Lilly wondered if perhaps they had reedited the end of the film.

But then the demon trolls themselves attacked. Most of the preplanned pyrotechnics were used: fire spurting out of the ground, bolts of lightning shooting across the sky. This battle was tougher, longer (too long, Lilly thought), and by the end of it the heroes were exhausted, not yet victorious. There was a brief pause. Bodies of the enemy littered the ground. Kip turned toward Prion, breathing heavily but smiling. He was opening his mouth to deliver some witty banter when a long claw burst out of the ground and impaled him.

Someone in the audience shrieked. Kip fell over, his head splitting against a rock. He died instantly.

The rest of the film was perfunctory. Kip's death rallied the Council, who defeated the Final Big Monsters and returned, triumphant, to the valley they protected. There was a brief stinger setting up future installments right as the film ended—a hooded figure, who Lilly knew was supposed to be the Necromancer, walking among the corpses of the demon trolls. And then the credits rolled and the audience clapped. Glenn and Lilly sat still until the lights went up.

"I thought you were very good," Lilly said to him.

Glenn nodded and did not respond. Glenn had the vacant expression he held whenever he was thinking very hard. It was the same expression he had when thinking about nothing at all.

Everyone was buzzing as they walked out of the theater, snippets of "How interesting!" and "So engaging!" and "Enchanting!" No one mentioned that they had seen a man die onscreen.

Jules and Clint stood in the lobby mobbed by well-wishers, people trying to get to the Great Men behind the production.

"You wanna skip the after-party?" Glenn asked Lilly, looking blankly at the crowd. "Just head back to the hotel?"

"You should still go," Lilly said. "I might go see my parents."

"Aren't we going to see them tomorrow?"

"No, I think I want to go tonight."

"Are you . . . ready for them?"

"Yes. Go on. Call a cab for Jules. He looks like he needs one." Glenn nodded but didn't speak. "Are you all right?" Lilly asked. "Or would you rather come with me?"

"No, no," Glenn said. He shook his head, and the long gaze he'd held since coming out of the theater vanished. "No, go see them. I'll look after Jules and make sure he doesn't drink too much at the party."

Glenn laughed softly, and Lilly squeezed his hand. It was truly impossible to tell if he was upset or not.

Lilly didn't want to take a cab and risk talking to a stranger, so she spent the next hour hopping on and off buses until she made her way out to Pasadena. She walked the last few blocks to the house with the yellow door, a screen still missing from the first-floor window, and knocked.

Her mother said nothing at first when she opened the door. Lilly realized her mother and Glenn shared the same blank expression.

"I thought you were coming tomorrow?"

Lilly stretched open her arms. "Surprise!"

"I don't have any food for you."

"I already ate."

There was a long pause. "Well, come in I guess."

Lilly shuffled into the house. It still smelled of stale bread and burnt eggs. The kitchen had several empty boxes of takeout scattered across the counter, and the table was piled with unread mail, mostly coupons and flyers. A mess.

Her mother rubbed her hands and looked her over. "You should have called. I'm not ready."

"Ready for what, Mom? I just wanted to see you."

"Well, we're watching the news now. You can visit but your father can't hear if you talk."

"I'll sit then."

They walked past the kitchen and into the family room. Lilly's father was sitting on a recliner, the television turned to whatever right-wing pundit was their current favorite. The volume was deafeningly loud. An angry man on the TV complained about liberals burning down cities.

Lilly and her mother sat down on the couch. Her father looked very thin. "You saw the postman?" he asked instead of a hello. "Did you get the mail?"

"Um, no," Lilly said. "I just took the bus here."

"You need to get the mail before they steal it."

She wasn't sure what he meant. Lilly tapped her fingers on the edge of the couch. Her father didn't move his eyes away from the screen. Her mother rubbed her arms but kept looking forward. The pundit played a clip of a congressman speaking on the House floor, then a commercial for hearing aids began. Lilly leaned forward.

"Hiya, Dad. How've you been?"

"Where's my soup?"

"Did you want soup? I was just—"

"Lisa, I asked for my soup!"

"I'm not Mom, I'm Lilly."

"This is ridiculous!" He slammed his hand down on the side table. Lilly looked over at her mother, who turned away back to the kitchen. Lilly followed.

"I'm sorry, Lilly," her mom said, holding back tears, "but this is the way he is. It's worse at night, the doctors say—"

"The doctors? Mom, what's wrong?"

"It's a form of dementia. Crosfolt, uh, Jacob—"

"Creutzfeldt–Jakob disease?"

"Yes, that's it. It progresses very quickly, the doctor said. There's nothing you can do about it, just try to make it easy on him. Watching the news makes him less agitated."

"That was *less* agitated? Jesus, Mom, when were you going to tell me?"

"I wanted to tell you in person, so I was waiting until tomorrow."

"You should have called me."

"Why? What would you have done? There's nothing to do."

"I'm a neuroscientist!"

"The doctor says there's nothing to do."

Lilly knew that was right. Creutzfeldt–Jakob moved fast and there was no way to stop it. Her father would be dead in a year.

She walked back into the living room and sat near him. He was watching the screen, unaware that Lilly was even beside him. She reached out and laid her hand on his arm.

"Hey, Dad. It's Lilly. I wanted to stop by and say hello."

He turned to her and smiled. "How's school, honey? You did your English homework already?"

"Yes, I finished it. School's good, Dad. It's real good."

"Don't forget to tell your mother to get the mail. The Mexicans will steal it."

Lilly sighed. Her father's brain, what was left of it, was still his, and the racism and aggressive ignorance was not, she had to admit, anything new. But the idea that whatever *was* left of her father, the remaining and functioning synapses, was literally dissolving in front of her made Lilly surprisingly sad. It wasn't as if her parents ever had particularly deep or interesting thoughts about the world, but at least she could always imagine that her father had a meaningful inner life she just didn't have access to.

"He talks about Iraq a lot," her mother said when they were back in the kitchen. "His own childhood is confused. Sometimes he thinks I'm his mother. But he'll start talking about the war and that's still clear."

"The most important things go last," Lilly said.

"Is that true?"

"No," Lilly said. "But it sounds nice. I think I dreamed about this."

"About your father?"

"Yes. He was yelling about something."

"I thought you didn't believe in that kind of thing?"

"I don't."

"Will you still come tomorrow?" her mother asked.

"Well, I—"

"Because I'd rather not cook anything, you know, if you're not coming."

"Do you want me to come?"

"Doesn't matter to me either way. I'd just rather not cook."

"I won't come then."

"All right."

"I fly back the day after next. I'm not sure when I'll be back. Keep me in the loop about Dad?"

"There won't be a funeral. He never wanted one."

"Mom, please. Just keep me informed."

"I'm just saying. We're not even going to sit shiva. He doesn't want any of it. Don't worry about flying back when it happens."

"Of course I'm going to be here." Lilly said this and knew it was a lie.

She went to say goodbye to her father, but he was still focused on the television. The pundit was on a rant again and he had leaned forward in his chair to listen closer. She hugged him and he didn't move.

"I'm going to get the mail now, Dad."

"I said I wanted soup."

"I'll get that, too."

Lilly's father didn't say anything else.

As she walked to the bus stop, Lilly texted Glenn.

Well, I saw them.

It took several minutes for Glenn to text her back with a picture of him and Jules at the after-party, smiling with their arms wrapped around each other. The picture was a selfie, and off-center. They were drunk.

Come join us!

She wouldn't tell him about her dad. Or maybe she would. He would feel bad, and that would make Lilly feel a little better. She let her fingers hover over her phone for a long time before she wrote back.

I see you're finding ways to forget about Kip.

Glenn's next text came back quickly. **What the fuck, Lilly. Why would you say that? Do you even know that I'm . . .**

She stopped reading, but Glenn was still texting out angry, half-coherent messages when Lilly finally turned her phone off. She thought back to a pathology class she took in graduate school, about diseases of the brain, and thought about what it felt like to be the person whose mind was warping and shutting down. But she knew that after a certain point it didn't feel like anything, that the disease itself took away your ability to be aware, to even know that you were sick, or alive. An image of Kip falling and hitting the rock flashed before her, and she began to cry.

She sat at the bus stop and waited for nearly an hour, with nothing to look at except the stars, barely visible through the Los Angeles haze.

THE MALICARN

THE SECOND YEAR IN THE REIGN OF KING PRION V (MADEIRA—DECEMBER 2043)

1.

The killer did not look threatening under the fluorescent lights of the infirmary. Partly because he was dead, but also because the lights made his skin look pale and waxy, washed out. The body lay on a metal gurney. Glenn and Jules stood over it, Jules prodding the arm.

"He was implemented six months ago," Jules said. "Totally normal, QA controls checked out."

"Did Lilly implement him?"

"No, one of the other techs. Valerie, I think? It wasn't a scanning thing, far as we could tell. Guy just wanted to kill."

The character had spent most of the previous week wandering the countryside, murdering. He killed six people with an axe. He didn't steal anything, didn't even threaten anyone. But he proved elusive, disappearing into the woods between killings. Glenn had asked to make the killing spree into a subplot for Gregorian.

"Detective Wizard," Glenn jokingly—but also sincerely—proposed. "Could pull in some true-crime fans."

Jules overruled him, and they tracked the killer down using the camera feeds. A pair of cops from Funchal cornered him in a church and shot him dead.

"Who was he, before?" Glenn asked, trying not to look at the bullet holes in the dead body's chest.

"Oh, just some volunteer. Former teamster. Guy didn't have a criminal record, if that's what you're asking."

"Are you going to tell his family that he was a murderer?"

"Uh, no. Worksite accident, like anyone else who's died here." Jules prodded the body again. "Would be nice to have some idea what was going through his head, though. You know, for storytelling purposes."

Jules smirked, and Glenn already knew what he was thinking.

"There's no way," Glenn said.

"You can ask her?"

"She's going to say no."

"I just want to use one for a little while. Off the books."

But Glenn wasn't even going to try to ask Lilly. He could imagine her reaction perfectly.

"You want to borrow a neuroscanner?" she'd say. "For Jules to do what, download memories of murder? That sounds like a productive use of creative energies."

Lilly was only ever sarcastic and mean when talking to Glenn now. He hardly saw her unless her team was at a meeting that Glenn also happened to be at. He didn't eat at the Citadel cafeteria often, and more and more avoided sitting near her when he did.

It had been this way ever since the premiere. They hadn't broken up, at least not technically, but of course if you don't see somebody and you don't talk to them and then they make fun of you when you do see them, it's probably not the case that you are in an active relationship.

Glenn never asked her about borrowing the neuroscanner. Jules brought it up again during a video call the next week. "I'm not sure she'll want to talk to me," Glenn said.

"Well, she's a bitch," Jules said. Jules never did date anyone for very long.

The meeting was full of detail but dominated by Jules's monologues. There were currently plenty of little subplots that the characters were in the middle of: brigands that the Council fought, threats of foreign invasion that King Prion dealt with in meetings. They were still building up to showing the Necromancer onscreen, but so far neither Jules nor anyone else had worked out how best to introduce him, where he came from, what he wanted.

Jules was obsessed with crafting something more spectacular for the next film. "There should be sacrifice, there should be tears. Something that really changes the balance of power. People have to see that this isn't a controlled environment. Stuff happens, you can't do anything about it. Just like real life. You gotta push the envelope, make them see the chaos of it all. Props is working on a new device. You won't believe it. When it's ready, it will blow your mind. Story *is* chaos."

He spoke quickly, rocking in his chair, gesticulating and drawing invisible diagrams with his fingers in the air. The depleted writing staff consisted of only half a dozen people now, many of them fairly new, all lorded over by Jules, who made most of the decisions and always had final say. Even Glenn's ideas were shot down most of the time. There didn't seem to be a way to stop him. *The Return of the Council* had been such a financial success—indeed, a genuine cultural event, given the amount of discourse generated about it by everyone from heads of state down to the loneliest internet troll—that Jules essentially had free rein over the set. Larry still found him annoying, but Larry was in Los Angeles. Jules ruled the Malicarn.

Glenn decided to spend more time on set itself, where he could avoid both Jules and Lilly for a while. But Jules's influence was everywhere. After the meeting Glenn traveled to Kingstown and visited the king's court, where an advisor was reading a missive about the threat of the Necromancer. Obviously Jules was trying to push this new storyline forward. The letter was hastily and sloppily written, and it wasn't having the desired effect.

"And so at once," read the advisor, "the king must surrender his crown to the Necromancer or else face the consequences."

"Ha!" Prion bellowed. "Why would I ever treat with such a fool? Send no response. If the Necromancer wishes to parley, let him come himself."

"But, Your Majesty, should we not—"

"No! This Necromancer is all bluster. He will do nothing. Come, let us enjoy our feast."

Tables were laid out, plates of food were brought forth, and a band of minstrels began playing harp and lute. The chefs prepared a delicious array of roasted chickens and vegetables. It was Malicarn-raised chicken, not factory-farmed birds plumped up with hormones and flown in to the island. Glenn found it gamey. The court—which now included Evangeline, members of the Council of Heroes, various ladies-in-waiting, and a number of new royal characters—sat down to eat. Gregorian took a seat across from the king.

"So is there any truth in these matters, Gregorian?" Prion wore a long-sleeved cloak, despite the warm weather that day. He wore long sleeves all the time now, because Marvin Powell had decided to get a Buffalo Bills tattoo on his upper arm during his California vacation. He hadn't told the producers, and when Prion reemerged on set with a blue-and-red buffalo on his arm, Jules threw a computer across the room and threatened to kill the king himself.

"The Necromancer is a real threat," Glenn said, "but I do not believe he has any immediate plans to strike." Glenn had been given very little detailed information about Jules's story plans for this arc, so he hoped it was true.

"Good, good. I thought not. We have enough to concern ourselves with in the realm."

As Prion ate, he passed cuts of meat to Evangeline, sitting across from him and next to Glenn. She sat in her chair, hands resting on her belly. Glenn had only recently realized she was pregnant when, embarrassingly, it was brought up at a production meeting. Of course Jules was enraged at this unplanned development, just as he was when Prion and Evangeline were married soon after the Council's return. Prion had spent much time ensuring Evangeline comfort and preparing for the new child, whom he hoped would be a son. He cared very little about all these vague threats from what he assumed was far beyond the Malicarn.

The minstrels performed in the middle of the hall. "I hear you once were an actor," Evangeline whispered into Glenn's ear as they ate. It was an odd rumor to have somehow gotten out into the Malicarn, and Glenn suspected Jules planted it on purpose as a prank.

"Only a little, in my youth," said Glenn. "Before I was a wizard."

"I am so happy you could join us tonight, Gregorian," she said. "Prion will not ask you, but is there some sort of spell? To protect our child?"

Glenn got such requests often. He had a standard little act he did, which seemed to put most people at ease. He leaned toward Evangeline.

"Of course, my lady. Do you mind if I—" He gestured toward her belly, and she moved her hand. He softly placed both of his hands on her, closed his eyes, and whispered, "Yivarechecha Adonai v'yishmerecha." Glenn didn't know Hebrew, but had searched online one night for something that soundly faintly mystical, and had used it a few times on set. He thought about asking Lilly how to pronounce it, but figured that would annoy her.

Only Jacob the cobbler ever noticed it. He had once laughed under his breath when he heard Glenn giving the blessing to another woman in town. "You're pronouncing it wrong," he told Glenn afterward. "You're saying the last syllable like the *ch* in *child*, but the sound is in the back of the throat. Believe me, my bar mitzvah tutor used to yell at me for the same reason."

Glenn still couldn't pronounce it right, but figured there was no way Jules would use it in a final scene so it didn't matter. Evangeline was happy all the same. "What does it mean?" she asked.

"It means I hope your child is blessed."

"Do you know if it will be a boy? I would like to give Prion a son."

"I cannot tell that."

"Ah, I thought wizards could."

"Perhaps some wizards. But it is beyond my powers."

"I hope this Necromancer business will not be so dire. Some peace and quiet around here will be nice. No more adventures, no more fighting."

"Well, I am sure Prion will do his utmost duty."

"Oh, of course, Gregorian! I do not mean to take him from the important work of leading the Malicarn. My husband is a just man, I know. He will reign as a peaceful king."

Jules already had three different adventures planned for other Council members. Glenn did not know which of these Prion would be a part of, but he knew the king would not have much time to rest, or for peace.

"Surely, you agree that Prion will be a peaceful king?" Evangeline asked. Glenn's silence disturbed her. "Gregorian, you know him well, but I promise you that he wishes for there to be no more war. You must believe that."

"Oh, I do, my lady. I believe he will strive for a peaceful reign."

Evangeline softened quickly, smiling again. "Yes, he will. He wants peace for our children above all. This I know."

She was comforted easily. Glenn looked over at Prion, who was chatting and laughing with one of the visiting knights, and felt a horrible knot in his stomach. He didn't really know what Jules was planning. He didn't know anything. He wished he could talk to Lilly. Even when she didn't have any advice to give, just talking to her had always helped.

"What is wrong, Gregorian?" Evangeline looked up at him with concern. "Are you ill?"

"I am fine, my lady. Let us enjoy this meal."

The next night, Glenn attended another feast, this time at the office Christmas party. There was no Christmas in the Malicarn—the generic religion that operated in the kingdom had no holidays at all, as far as Glenn could tell—but the Citadel still managed to throw a pretty good holiday bash in the production offices. Glenn spent most of it dodging Lilly, who wore a Hanukkah sweater and seemed to be avoiding most of her colleagues, as well, by constantly sneaking behind the cash bar and mixing herself new martinis. Jules cornered Glenn before the karaoke started.

"Let's get out of here," Jules said.

Glenn didn't protest and followed him into the elevator. He was finishing his spiced rum when he realized they were in the infirmary. And the murderer's body was still waiting there.

"What are we doing here?" Glenn asked. The body was on a gurney in the middle of the room. No one else was there except Jules and Glenn.

"Might be time to start lining up our timeline with the original films," Jules said, ignoring him. "Institute a ban on magic throughout the Malicarn. Not yet, but soon. We're too reliant on tricks. We need a second set, a second land where everything is dark and evil. Like a Mordor, with scanned characters who can just be villains."

"Are you drunk?"

Jules was fiddling with the body, and Glenn was going to ask again what he was doing when Jules pulled out a neuroscanner from a cabinet and began placing a node connected to a neuroscanner wire onto the dead killer's head. Jules connected another one to his own head.

"Um, what are you doing?" Glenn asked.

"Whitman said the current from the machine should generate enough electrical activity in the brain," Jules said.

"Was *she* drunk?"

"Come on, Glenn. This is the fastest way to find out."

"Find out what?"

Jules adjusted some dials, but Glenn was sure he didn't know what he was doing. Jules turned the machine on. It happened quickly. A spark shot out of the node attached to Jules and into his forehead. The corpse remained still. Whatever was in there, among the decaying synapses, flew straight into Jules's own brain. Jules yelped, tore off the cord, then bounced around the room as if he had had a hit of cocaine.

"Did it work?" Glenn asked. "What did it feel like?"

"Like lightning," Jules said. "Like a movie, but the movie's in your veins, in your lungs, in your fucking heart."

"That's interesting," said Glenn. He almost meant it, too.

2.

Somebody tried to kill the president. They took a shot at his limo. A dumb idea. The car was bulletproof, impenetrable. But it was enough for a protest in Knoxville to turn to a riot.

Somebody else had made a viral video of their dog dressed up as Groucho Marx. And there were a number of clips from a match between Arsenal and Tottenham. ASMR videos of shipping containers being unloaded in Shenzen. The Rose Parade canceled due to poor air quality. And tips on grilling flank steak. Also there was a winter cyclone forming in the south Atlantic that was headed north-northeast, expected to clip the Azores although no one in Madeira was worrying about it yet.

Lilly watched it all from her computer in the corner of the implementations lab. It was the middle of the night, her other colleagues off for New Year's Day. Whitman was visiting California and sending emails about upcoming implementations from her hotel room in Burbank.

Most of the lights were off, save for a lamp over Lilly's desk and the glow of the computer screen. She was supposed to be going through prechecks for tomorrow's implementations, but instead she cycled through the news and social media feeds. She watched a press conference about the assassination attempt on MSNBC. She did a crossword puzzle and took a quiz explaining which *SpongeBob* character she most resembled. She clicked "like" on a picture of a college friend's baby on Instagram without really looking at the baby or the friend. She browsed through some porn but decided it was all produced for a primary audience of fifteen-year-old boys and watched clips from *Bridgerton* instead. She didn't really feel horny, so she watched more MSNBC.

She closed her browser and looked through the implementation notes. Lots of subjects for the new arc. Guards for the king. A group of thieves pledged to the Necromancer who would terrorize the farmers. A number of new fighters for an upcoming battle. Their personalities were thin, barely sketched in. "A traumatic past," or "raised an orphan," or "spent a year as a mercenary across the sea." The writers were rushing now, in need of bodies more than coherent characters.

There was an email from Jules, replying to an earlier one from Whitman, who had cc'd Lilly. He had borrowed a neuroscanner again and was keeping it a few more days. Lilly objected but no one responded to her directly. She didn't want to lend it out but Jules had permission from the producers to borrow it, doing God-knows-what with his writer buddies.

We're gonna use the extractor to get some ideas together, he wrote, **see what our collective intelligences assemble!** He sounded giddy, but Lilly knew that most of the writers had been fired.

You should do this down in the lab, she wrote back. **It would be safer.**

Whitman responded almost immediately. **You're too busy. Jules can handle it. @JulesWalker: The documentation's all in the share folder.**

Lilly reopened her browser. Five new series to stream this weekend. NBA statistics. Best funds to grow your IRA. A video of a kid whose home was bombed. Cheesecake recipes.

She opened a new tab and looked up her father's obituary. She read it again. She had read it almost every hour.

> *Herbert Kaminsky, 67, of Pasadena, died Tuesday after a brief illness. Mr. Kaminsky was born and raised in Riverside. He served eight years in the Marines, including a tour in Afghanistan and a tour in Iraq. He then attended California State University, Northridge, where he studied electrical engineering. He worked as a quality-assurance*

specialist for Lockheed Martin for over thirty years. He is survived by his wife Lisa, daughter Lilly, brothers Victor and Alan, and several nieces and nephews. Funeral arrangements are private.

Eighty-four words, that's all you get in the end. Lilly admired the portrait it painted: a man without passions, without ambitions, without mistakes or flaws. A man with no interior life or exterior charms. A man who never had nightmares or played golf or cut the grass or drank bourbon or badgered Lilly to clean her room or missed her dance recitals or forgot her name because his brain turned to mush. The obituary was the précis of a life without the mess of living.

Another tab in Lilly's browser had a news alert about the arrest of several members of a drug cartel.

A bouquet of flowers, still in their paper since she couldn't find a vase, sat next to her computer with a note that read, "I'm sorry for your loss. Thinking of you. Glenn." Maybe she should call him. Tell Glenn about Jules's behavior. About how quickly everything was spinning away from her. But she wouldn't know what to say. He would want to console her and she didn't want to be consoled. He was so immediate, so focused on the task in front of him. He had to be, constantly improvising through his day while still trying to follow the beats and story points Jules laid out for him. She needed him to be a bit more hands off, opaque, unemotional. Plus, if she talked to him about anything he would probably interpret it as an excuse to get back together.

Lilly was too busy, anyway. She had so much work to do, but that morning she simply stopped doing it. She didn't fill out any reports, didn't handle any quality assurance, didn't prep any implementations. She just sat at her computer and read the news. Her inbox filled up. Whitman wouldn't notice for a day or two.

She watched lip-sync videos. She read essays about the challenges of new motherhood. She played online chess. And as she did all this, the bank of servers against the back wall of the lab, full of PersMats and data and algorithms waiting to be people, suddenly began to make a noise. Or rather, now without the constant barrage of tasks needing to be cleared, Lilly heard the noise for the first time. She heard the hum of the servers. And the less work she did the louder they got.

Herbert Kaminsky, 67, of Pasadena, died Tuesday after a brief illness.

Soon they were deafening, a groan that stretched around the room, enveloping Lilly and the computers and tables and equipment and everything else. When the lab was empty the only sound was the hum of those servers against the wall, terabytes of future work sitting and waiting for deployment. Lilly stood up and walked across the room to the closet where the neuroscanners were kept. She entered the closet and closed the door, hoping to shut the sound out.

There was a light in the ceiling. The closet was a small circular room of shelves, all holding gray neuroscanner boxes, each box plugged into the wall behind it, charging itself up. Nearly a dozen of them, each with a blinking red light. Charging, charging. The lights grew brighter, redder, filling the room. They were worse than the humming, they were blinding. Lilly blinked, tried to close her eyes, couldn't get the brightness to stop.

served eight years in the Marines, including a tour in

She left the closet, walked back across the room. She didn't look back, didn't want to see the red lights. She held her hands over her ears as she passed the servers. She walked into Whitman's office. The large corner office, enclosed by glass walls. She shut the door.

The room was cold, an air vent in the ceiling too strong for the little space. With the door closed it became even colder. Lilly put her head down on Whitman's desk, a glass table empty of pictures or trinkets or any sign of personality. But she could feel it now, the cold, against her face on the glass. The cold took over the table, pushed against Lilly's cheek. She could feel it creeping into her, grabbing her from within. The whole building felt cold. A heavy cold, a dry cold, like an old corpse, one that wouldn't move or escape.

he studied electrical engineering

The lab was too loud, too bright, too cold. Lilly went to the break room, whose door opened onto the lab but at least provided some separation. Once inside she kept pacing.

I can't talk to Glenn, she thought. What will he say? He'll talk about work and about how Jules is a hard-ass and how he isn't sure the story is working. He'll be unhappy because he's always unhappy but he won't be sad, he won't be upset, he won't be distraught. He won't hear the humming or see the lights or feel the cold.

Lilly opened the break room refrigerator. A leftover pizza box inside. Lilly took it out and opened it. Double cheese and mushroom. The smell wafted out of the box, and pulled at her shirt, her hair. A sickly smell, the smell of staleness and rot and decay. She threw out the pizza, but the smell was in the lab now, all over. She couldn't get away from it. She hurried back to her office.

for over thirty years

The smell hadn't reached into there yet, and the neuroscanner closet door was closed, the light hiding behind it. She stayed away from Whitman's cold office. She could still hear the servers, buzzing against the wall, and she had to decide what she hated worse, what she could stand the least. The sound, the lights, the cold, the smell.

It was only then that she tasted something. She hadn't eaten. Still, there it was in her mouth, rolling over her tongue. Something inside of her that she couldn't ignore. It was subtle. A sharpness, a tartness, sucking the moisture from her mouth. Drying her out. And it was growing. And she couldn't make it go away.

survived by his wife Lisa, daughter Lilly,

She turned her computer back on, loaded the news, and saw

images of fires. A wildfire in Simi Valley. There was a smoke warning in Los Angeles County. Dangerous to be outside.

Funeral arrangements are private.

It was in that moment that it first occurred to Lilly that all of the world's neuroscanners, all that tech, all of their data, all their documentation, had made its way through the circuitous and terrible logic of litigation and politics into this very room. And nobody was there except for her.

A fire in Los Angeles. A fire to celebrate her father. Fire was bright. Fire was hot. Fire smelled strong. Depending on what you burned, fire could be very loud. Get close enough to fire, you could taste the embers, let them singe your tongue.

Get close enough to fire, and you wouldn't feel anything else anymore.

3.

After he poured his morning coffee Glenn tried to read his email again. Earlier he couldn't connect to the internet, but this time his inbox refreshed.

> *TRAVEL PROHIBITED. No studio staff, crew, or cast are permitted to travel to or from the Malicarn set until the tropical storm has passed. Winds are expected to be in excess of 95 kph with heavy rains through Sunday evening.*
>
> *Essential on-set activities relating to food, medical, housing, and other basic services may continue, but no storylines are to be advanced at this time.*
>
> *Further updates to come.*

The weather in Madeira continued to flummox him. It was January and they had to worry about hurricanes. Or maybe Madeira had nothing to do with it and weather itself was just weird now. Glenn wasn't sure.

So far, it was still sunny outside. Glenn wondered if this meant he could skip a trip as Gregorian to the castle. He tried to email Jules but his internet went down again, and his phone wasn't connecting, either. It'd be nice to have a Saturday that was actually a Saturday but half the staff *was* coming off a holiday and he decided it was better not to miss their morning production meeting by feigning ignorance. The last time he tried that he got an official reprimand from Larry. So he threw on jeans and a shirt and slipped down his tower into the service tunnel, unplugged a golf cart, and drove it himself to the Citadel. It was still very early, and traffic in the tunnel was light. When he got to the Citadel, he took the elevator up to the production offices. Despite the hour, Jules was already in the writers' room, his legs propped on a box covered with a blanket. He was reading a thick book, *The Collected Letters of J. D. Souard.*

"I thought maybe this would give me some story ideas," Jules said as Glenn entered, putting the book down. "You know, information and tidbits Souard cut out of the novels or something? But it's just lots and lots of blather about publishing contracts with his editor or whatever. There's like twenty pages where he bitches about de Gaulle. Why are you here anyway?"

"Happy New Year to you, too. I'm here for our meeting. I tried to call in but the internet's down."

"Oh yeah, the storm! Good news, huh? The suits were badgering me about story before Christmas. But they can't fly in to berate me now. We can run this one completely on our own, no interference! Once they see it, they'll understand why it had to be this way."

"So you still want me to go to the castle today?"

"Oh, you have to. Important stuff to set up. The props department has cooked up something special. Probably wait for deployment until after the storm, not sure what our timeline is there, I don't want to rush it."

A fire alarm, blaring and shrill, emitted a shriek throughout the floor. Lights began strobing over the exits.

"Ah, shit," Jules said. "The security system is all tied together on the network. You said it was down, right?"

"Yeah. Should we evacuate?"

"It's probably nothing. It happens sometimes."

"What about our production meeting?"

"We just had it. This was it. Go back, look over your notes, plan to be at the castle this evening."

"But the server's down, I don't have any notes."

"Ah!" Jules barked, then shook his head, blinked a few times, and reached for a sheet of paper with handwritten scribbles. "Sorry about that. Here. Take this, look it over. I'll text you if service is restored. You'll be fine."

Glenn tried to take an elevator back down, but it was inoperable, so he walked all the way to the tunnel using the emergency stairs. A few security guards were giving orders, directing people to the lobby.

"What're the alarms about?" Glenn asked one of the guards.

"Not sure, something in the lab I think. Can't get down there now."

Glenn rode a cart back down the tunnel to the Old Village. The emergency lights were on, and the tunnel was extra dim. Glenn didn't think much of it, though he thought he smelled smoke.

He still got back to his apartment before his servant had even made breakfast, and jumped in the shower. When he came out, only a towel wrapped around himself, he was surprised to find Lilly pacing in his kitchen.

"Um hello," he said.

"I'm sorry to drop in like this. I have to tell you something," Lilly said. "I'm leaving. The Malicarn, the lab. I'm quitting."

"Is this because of me?" Glenn asked.

"What?"

"What did I do? Honestly? I'm not in charge here, Lilly, I—"

"Christ, Glenn, no. This isn't about you."

"It clearly is! At least a little bit!"

"Am I mad, Glenn? Yes. Am I mad at you? Probably. And I should probably be over it by now but . . . Do you think you could put on some clothes?"

"Oh, yeah, sorry." Glenn ducked into the bathroom and reemerged clothed a minute later.

Lilly was sitting on the couch. "You don't even know, do you?"

"Know what?"

"I snuck out. If they find me . . . God, don't you see what they've done?"

"Who? Jules?"

"All of them! Jules, Larry, the executives, everyone who bought into this shit. You! What are we doing here, Glenn? Art? Science? What have you been doing if you don't even understand what's happened?"

"I don't know what you're talking about."

"We make people and then we tell them who they are and what they are supposed to do. And we fuck with their minds and then eventually we kill them."

"It's not like that."

"I got out of a boring life and into one where I could be smart and people treated me like someone who was smart. I think I was happy, Glenn. Maybe, I don't know. But this fake thing. This fake world with real people."

Lilly's voice trailed off. Her eyes were puffy and red. Glenn wanted to hug her, to pull her close to him. But he just stood, watching her. She shook her head and stood up.

"I wanted to see you. But I'm going now. I'm leaving."

"To where? You can't travel anywhere right now. It's not safe with the storm." He said the words and then realized it was actually true.

"I'm leaving. I have to. I can't let them catch me. Not after what I . . . not after this."

"After what?"

"I couldn't let them keep doing it." She hugged him. "Be good, Glenn. Don't forget to look at the stars sometimes."

Glenn had so many questions, but Lilly didn't wait for him to ask. She grabbed a small backpack, threw it over her shoulders, and walked toward the door.

Before she opened it she looked back at him. "There's one more neuroscanner left. I don't know where. Jules borrowed it. Find it, please. For me."

She vanished through the door. She didn't run, she just floated away, leaving Glenn alone in the apartment, silent but for the hum of the refrigerator and the fluorescent lights in the kitchen.

Glenn finished putting on his costume and then sat on his couch. His computer, phone, and TV all didn't work. He tried to read Jules's notes but the page was indecipherable. Just erratic scribbling. Glenn wondered if the lines on the page had ever meant anything at all, even in Jules's brain before he wrote them down. He wouldn't need to leave for the castle until after lunch. That part of the day's script needs had been made clear. Showing up early could throw off whatever plans Jules had written for the day. With nothing else to do, Glenn reached for the only book he had in his apartment, the illustrated edition of *The Malicarn*. He opened it to the first page and began to read.

Chapter One

The Necromancer never forgot the Great War, the times when

"Glenn, open up, goddamnit." Someone was banging on the door.

Glenn stood up, put down the book, and opened the door. Jules and three burly men—security from the Citadel—pushed themselves inside.

"Where is she?" Jules asked, the other men searching the small apartment.

"What?"

"Where's Lilly?"

"I don't know. She was here this morning for a few minutes, but she left. I haven't seen her. I don't know where she is."

"What did she tell you?"

"Nothing? I don't know, she was nervous about something, said she was going to leave. Went on a rant about ethics."

"Did she say where she was going?"

"I don't know where she is, Jules. What happened? Is she all right?"

Jules shook his head. "She blew it up, Glenn. The lab, implementations. Early this morning. No one was hurt, thank God. She must have timed it. All sorts of research is lost. All the neuroscanning data, templates, protocols. The machines, too, all their documentation. Firebombed, all of it. Christ, Glenn, we're finished. Years of work lost. There's no way to program any more characters now."

The security guards went through Glenn's drawers, closets, cabinets. It was a quick search. Glenn had very few things.

"I'm sorry, Jules. I didn't know. I swear."

"The execs are going to be furious. We have to finish the film. Now. If they see it, maybe we can keep our jobs."

"*Our* jobs? But . . . I didn't do anything!"

"Exactly, Glenn. You did nothing. Nothing to stop her. You're supposed to be my guy on the inside, but lately it feels like I've been running things all by myself out here."

"What do you need me to do?" Glenn asked.

"Okay," Jules said, nodding his head, thinking out loud. He rubbed his hands together, but his arms shook as he did. "We're going to push ahead with the finale. Today. A last-minute rewrite, but we can do it. We can splice in some B-story with the Council later to extend the running time, if need be. Maybe make it an exclusive short film for streaming. The props department already put the device in the field, so I can get it up and running today. I'll get the king to travel out to the canyon in sector three. He'll investigate the Necromancer, think he's hot on his tail. Then I'll activate the device."

Glenn was not, self-admittedly, very insightful. But he had seen a lot of movies. He had read a lot of plays. And as he stood in his apartment he all of a sudden realized what Jules was going to do.

"No. No, you can't do this."

"And then," Jules continued, "you show up just before his death—"

"No!"

"Yes, that's the big twist! He's going to have to sacrifice himself to save his bride."

"You can't do that."

"Why not? We killed Kip."

"That was different. That wasn't planned."

"Wasn't it?"

"What does that mean? No, Jules, you'll . . . you'll ruin the franchise. Prion's the main character, the star, he—"

"He *was* the star, of this phase. But this is a prequel. He's not in the original films, he has to die eventually. The next phase can have different heroes. We have plenty of Councilors, and before Lilly destroyed the tech, we created quite a few promising new characters. And I have . . . I have ideas. Think bigger, Glenn! This is how we make history, make something of our own! Are you with me, or not?"

The security guards finished their search and hovered behind Glenn.

"I'm with you."

"Great. Wait until noon, then ride to the canyon. Follow the smoke, it won't take you long to find us. I can make the fight last as long as I need, so that just when you arrive I will finish."

"You'll be there?"

Jules smiled. "I'm the Necromancer, baby! Ha! Remember, try to stay back, and just look horrified. I don't need any dialogue from you. Your presence is enough. We can always film your coverage later."

Glenn nodded. "Sure thing."

"Good boy."

Jules left with the guards. Glenn watched them walk out into a square from a window in the staircase. The guards turned north but Jules climbed onto a horse and rode south, toward the castle. Glenn knew he would take the main road, looping along the creek before riding across the meadow. It would take him over an hour, but if Glenn was fast enough, he could cut across the forest, straight and off the road, and beat Jules to the castle. There was no tunnel between the castle and the Old Village. This was the fastest way. He could warn Prion. He could stop this madness.

Glenn rushed to the stables, hitched a horse to a cart, and set off by himself. He drove quickly out of the village and down the main road, across an open field and into heavier woods. He guided the cart around exposed roots and bumpy stretches of rock. To the west, Glenn saw a mountaintop, moving steadily closer before slowly receding north behind him. He cut a diagonal route toward the pass. Even moving through the forest, Glenn knew he could beat Jules.

Then there was a sudden loud crack from up ahead, and Glenn pulled the cart to a stop. The horse reared back.

"Whoa, boy," Glenn said.

There was another crash and someone shouted. Emerging from the brush, stomping noisily, was a man holding a spear. Behind him was a very young boy, barely more than two years old. The boy waddled slowly.

"Let's see your hands!" the man shouted. He was covered in mud, barefoot, missing teeth. "I don't want no funny business, just whatever coin you have—" The man stopped when he recognized Glenn.

"Well, well. Look here, we have a wizard. Hey, Buck, come

here. See that? That's a real wizard, like the ones I used to fight with."

"Mawic!" the young boy said.

"Sir, I am on an urgent errand for the king, if you let us pass, I promise I will compensate you—"

"Shut up! Get on down!"

Glenn climbed down, keeping his hands raised. The man approached him slowly. "My son said he wanted to see a magic trick, think you can show him one?"

"No, I cannot. I have no magic here, now. Maybe later, if you let me go."

"Could you bring back my wife? My little girl? She was still suckling at the breast when the fever took them both."

"I'm sorry. No. Please. I am sorry, but we have—"

"What about my farm? Can you make it prosper?"

"No."

The man poked Glenn's chest with the spear point. He held it steady, and looked up. His eyes flickered, and he spoke, his voice slightly slower, higher pitched, afraid. "Can you give me back my life?"

"Daddy?" cried out the little boy, and the man blinked away, shaking his head as if forgetting a terrible memory.

"How about this? I take your cart, and you do a little magic and just disappear?" The man raised his spear and swung the shaft against Glenn's head. He fell back and rolled off the road. His head throbbed, and by the time he could turn to look back at the cart, the man and his son had climbed on board.

"What a nice wizard," the man said to his son. "We needed a horse, didn't we, Buck?"

The cart turned around and began rolling away. The father and his son sang a song as they bounced out of view.

"*Waltzing Matilda, waltzing Matilda, who'll come a-waltzing Matilda with me?*" A minute later they were gone, and Glenn was alone.

Glenn stood up, picked up his staff, and started running south. He kept the mountain on his right as best as he could, jumping over brush and roots, trying to ignore the throbbing of his head. He still had time. He could still make it.

Without the cart and horse Glenn moved slower, cutting himself on thorns and tripping once over a stone. He hit the ground hard and skinned his leg. He hobbled forward, until he emerged from the forest into an open plain at the southern spur of the mountain. The castle was a mile ahead, the high tower peering out above the grass.

He ran. Jules might have beaten him there, but perhaps he and Prion had not left yet.

At the castle gate the guard looked at him with concern. "Good sir Gregorian, are you all right? Where is your horse? Let me find you some help."

"No need. Where is the king? I must speak with him."

"Oh, the king left with a messenger. You just missed them. There was a matter of some urgency."

"Damnit. Do you have a horse? Please, I need to follow them."

"Yes, sir. Stay here, I'll find the stablemaster."

The guard shuffled off, and Glenn sat on a ledge, inspecting the rivulets of blood pouring down his leg.

"Gregorian! Gregorian!"

He looked up. One of the nursemaids from the castle ran out to him, waving her hands.

"Oh, Gregorian! I'm glad you've come! Please, quick, come this way!"

"I am waiting on a horse, I have urgent business with the king."

"No, no! The queen! It is too soon. Please, my good sir!"

Glenn's heart fluttered and he followed the woman into the castle and up a flight of stairs to the queen's chambers. Evangeline was lying on her back in a large bed, several women attending to her. She was sweating.

"Oh, Gregorian," she said. "It hurts. It hurts so much."

"When—" Glenn stammered, looking down at the young girl. "When did this start? Does the king know?"

"No," said the nurse. "The birthing pains began only after he left." The nurse moved toward him, her voice in a low whisper. "It is too early for the child, Gregorian. You must delay it."

"I don't—I don't know how." He walked up beside Evangeline and held her hand. "How were you feeling this morning?"

"I was fine. I could feel the baby kicking."

"Did you . . . eat anything? Maybe you ate some spoiled food?"

"She has eaten nothing poor, my lord," said the nurse. "She was about to dine with the king just now when a messenger arrived."

"But I did not eat," Evangeline said, breathing heavily. "Just a little bit of wine, that is all. With the king when he was here."

"Who prepared the wine?" Glenn asked. "Was it the messenger?"

"I do not know," the nurse said. "I suppose so, why?"

"That man . . . he was the Necromancer." There was a long pause, and Evangeline yelled. "I cannot help her. I do not have the magic. But I can find the king and bring him here."

"The Necromancer!" The nurse shook her head. "I might have known. These are dark times."

"You can take care of her?" Glenn asked. "I will find more help, but you must take care of her."

"Of course."

Glenn knelt beside Evangeline, his face level with her eyes. "My queen, I am off to find your husband. He will come and you will be safe. Do you understand?"

"Yes. Please hurry, Gregorian. It hurts so much."

"I will be back soon. Just rest. All will be fine."

A horse waited for him outside. Glenn told the guard to close the gate and let no one else inside. Then he rode off.

Glenn was not a strong rider and had not spent nearly enough of his time in the Malicarn practicing. As the horse bounded over the hill Glenn did his best to grip onto the reins, accidentally pulling too hard when he meant merely to adjust himself. The horse slowed but then Glenn dug his heels into its side and it sprang forward again. It was a bumpy, jerky ride, but at least the path was clear.

Sector three was a series of hills and cliffs that overlooked the sea. They were about as far south from the castle as the castle was from the village, just on the edge of the set's territory and never used in story. Characters did not travel there due to legends of monsters, but those legends were fake. Not far beyond were a hotel and the main road to Funchal.

It was well past noon when Glenn reached the foot of the cliffs. He followed echoing booms all the way down toward the river. The sounds grew louder and clearer. They were groans, animalistic. Roars. Glenn followed a dirt path next to the river, and was turning around a bend when he finally saw the source of the noise, the device Jules had bragged about. A dragon.

The dragon was built of metal, though it still looked very lifelike. It had a wingspan of thirty feet, red and black scales up its body and long neck. Its eyes were large but black, teeth long and sharp, and the screech it let out was cold and piercing. It could fly, like a large drone, and hovered in the air above the water. It bent its neck down, a plume of smoke and flame spouting from his mouth.

Prion stood waist-deep in the river, a sword held over his head. Mud caked his body and blood was trickling down his skull. As the dragon dove toward him, he lunged and tried to slice at its neck, but missed. He limped and nearly fell over but righted himself and prepared for another attack from the dragon.

"Prion!" Glenn yelled, and drove his horse forward. He heard a cackling laughter, and up atop the low cliff that flanked the river stood Jules, waving a remote control fashioned to look like a wand. He was guiding the dragon, controlling its dives and bursts of flame.

The horse stopped as it reached the edge of the water, and Glenn jumped off. He had no weapons, no tools at all except his staff.

"Prion!" he called again as he began wading into the river. Prion turned and saw him approaching, waving him off.

"Get back, Gregorian! The beast is too powerful!"

"No, Prion! It's not a beast. You have to run."

"No! It will destroy the entire Malicarn if I flee. You do not understand. This man, he is—"

"The Necromancer. I know." He trudged through the water, close enough to Prion that he didn't have to yell. The dragon rose up high, circling above them. He knew Jules was holding it back to allow for this conversation, but Glenn did not know where the microphones recording them must be hidden.

"How do you know that?" Prion asked. "Are you still in league with him?"

"Please, you must leave. The dragon is not real, and Evangeline is not well. Your child may be born tonight!"

Prion lowered his sword and looked at Glenn. He opened his mouth to speak, but nothing came out. Then his eyes searched Glenn's. He twitched nervously, like his brain did not know how to respond.

"I know I should say something, but I cannot think what it should be."

"Say you'll come back with me," Glenn said. "Marvin, please."

The dragon roared, turned, and began to fly down toward them. Prion snapped to attention, as if suddenly he remembered who he was.

"Glenn?" he asked, in Marvin Powell's voice. "Please, make it stop."

But it was too late. The dragon broke toward Prion and opened his mouth. A ball of flame shot out and surrounded him. He gave a great shout but the dragon flew directly into him.

Glenn pressed down on the trigger on his staff and pointed it at the dragon. Dozens of sparks shot out in a dazzling display. The dragon buckled and collapsed on the shore beside the river. There was no sign left of Marvin.

A cloud of steam rolled across the river and over Glenn, cloaking the shore in a haze. He stood there, silent and still, watching the spot where Marvin had stood only a moment before. He turned only when he heard the sound of someone else's boots walking on the sandy riverbank behind him.

"Good idea to use the static," Jules said. "It had no effect, of course, but it looked cool. Dragon was almost out of power anyway, so you gave me a good excuse to set it down. The rest of it, I'm not sure. Might take some clever editing. Maybe we can do a reshoot where I reveal myself to you or something earlier."

"You killed him."

"Glenn, come on. We discussed this."

"And you're killing her."

"Her?"

"The queen. She's in labor. You poisoned her."

"Wow, what a twist." He smirked. "You know, it could be a good ending, assuming she lives. A dead king and a live baby."

"She needs a doctor, a real doctor."

"This is the middle ages, Glenn. Come on. She can't have those things."

"She could die. The baby could die!"

Jules sighed and took out his phone, punching in something. The dragon mechanically lifted and began to fold into a ball, packing itself up to nearly a quarter of its size.

"Don't be so dramatic, Glenn," he said, then dialed a number. "Hello? Bill? Can you arrange to come get the dragon? Yeah, right now. I'd like to beat the weather." He hung up. "I have to go back to the Citadel. Lots of shit to clean up from your girlfriend."

"What about the baby?"

"Jesus, Glenn. Go deliver it yourself. Don't you see what we just did? We wrote our own blockbuster! We're like Lucas and Spielberg. And with no interference from the suits. It'll be like nothing else we've done before. Isn't that exciting enough for you?"

Glenn walked out of the river and approached Jules. "You killed him. He's going to be a father, and you killed him."

Jules shook his head and turned away. "Your horse wandered up to the road. I'm going to take it back, if you don't mind? Mine's dead, and I could use the ride. Regular writing meeting tomorrow, all right?"

Jules walked up the shoreline and away toward the road. He vanished behind the bend. Glenn looked over the river at the decommissioned dragon, thought of walking over and tearing it apart by hand, then remembered Evangeline, lying in her bed, waiting for Prion to return to her.

Glenn ran. He ran back to the road, following the cliffs north, and up through the hills and forests toward the castle. There was no sign of Jules. Glenn dropped his cloak and staff, sweat pouring through his shirt, and kept running. His legs burned and he didn't slow down.

The gate of the castle was still closed when he arrived. "It's Gregorian!" he shouted, banging loudly on the metal door. "Open up!"

The gate creaked open and the guard poked out his head.

"Gregorian? Where is the king?"

Glenn did not answer. He walked into the courtyard, passing the worried looks of court staff as he walked straight into the castle, hopping up the stairs and running into the queen's chambers.

He was met with the sound of a crying infant. The nurse was holding her, a small child with a wisp of black hair, wrapped in a blanket. The nurse swayed back and forth and looked up at Glenn, tears on her cheeks.

"It is a girl," she said, then glanced at the queen. "But there is too much blood."

Evangeline was lying on her side, the bedsheets glistening red. She breathed slowly, her eyes locked on the small child in the nurse's arms. Glenn walked over and leaned beside her.

"It is a princess," Evangeline whispered. "A little princess."

"That's good," Glenn said, placing his hand on her shoulder. "That's good to hear."

"Her name is Hannah," she said. "Do you like it? It was my mother's name."

"It's lovely."

"Where is Prion?"

"He is coming. I saw his horse over the hill. He will be here soon."

She closed her eyes and smiled. "He will be so proud of his daughter."

"He's proud of you, Evangeline." The baby cried again.

"You will make sure they are safe?"

"The king is safe, my queen."

"No." She shook her head. "My little Hannah. Make sure she is safe."

Glenn turned and looked at the nurse, who was bopping the child to calm her down. Glenn had never seen a newborn baby before. She was very small, with black hair and light brown skin. She had dark almond eyes, like her mother. She was alive where before she wasn't alive, and her name was Hannah, which somehow wasn't her name yesterday but today it was. Glenn reached out and touched the child's head but was overcome by an intense feeling of shame. He pulled his hand away. He didn't deserve to touch her. The child was going to be an orphan and that was his fault, at least a little. Maybe more than a little. Suddenly all Glenn wanted to do was talk to Lilly.

When he looked back at Evangeline, she was still.

"I did what I could," the nurse said. "But the child was stuck. I think her leg might be hurt. And the queen . . . I could not stop the blood."

"It's not your fault," Gregorian said.

"Where is the king?" the nurse asked.

"He is not coming."

The nurse closed her eyes and cried fresh tears.

Glenn thought about what he would do. He would go to his

apartment. His phone was there. If he could get service, he could call Lilly, call someone, let them know what was happening. Jules was killing people. Murder. And now there was a baby, and a dead woman, and they needed doctors, real doctors. They had to do something, stop production. Anything, he just had to get word out. Get word to Lilly. She would know what to do.

He tried to imagine where Lilly might be, if they had found her or if she was still hiding. If she was on the island, or if she had gotten away. Maybe she was safe, already somewhere far away. Glenn tried to picture her, what she was wearing or what she was thinking. But he couldn't. He couldn't think, couldn't imagine. Lilly was like a void, a distant object he could never comprehend.

That was the moment Glenn understood he would never do anything at all.

The baby cried. Glenn looked back down at her. Hannah, the little princess. No, the little queen. She was so very small. And with no one to protect her. Outside, it was storming. Rain pelted the windows. Winds thrashed tree branches against the castle's stone walls. The hurricane had arrived.

LONDON

May 2059

Roger was running the Kyiv desk when it all went to shit. It wasn't his fault, but it was, at least a little bit, his responsibility. Moscow rolled up Odessa, compromising every asset, every agent. Roger's networks ran those networks, so somewhere down the chain they got fucked and the Russians wasted no time. Worse was how it compromised the Americans, as well, which at the end of the day was the real problem. Roger had to write three different reports, speak to a dozen different interrogators, and even sit for a confidential inquiry with the foreign secretary. He was transferred back to Head Office, placed in the pool, and told to cool his heels. When he got operational status again, all he did was debrief agents coming in from Budapest or Karachi or wherever. Kid stuff.

His section chief never let him forget about Odessa, either. Anytime Roger was read into an operation, the old man would immediately shut him down if he ventured an opinion.

"Pendleton," he'd say, because he called only people he respected by their first names, "if we wanted to fuck this one up we'd listen to what you are saying, but until then I'd advise just letting the adults talk."

It was all nonsense, anyway. Computer hacks and reams of data analyzed by algorithms. Little men in little cubicles, in the deep recesses of SIS, writing reports about what other reports might mean. Foreign desks weren't finding fresh angles, weren't training Joes, weren't working through one asset or another until they found the piece of treasure that actually mattered. They tried to catalog everything and in the process learned nothing.

Roger still wore a suit and vest into the office, still smoked tobacco out of a pipe, and still followed supper with a brandy. He did these things not because he particularly liked them. The suits were uncomfortable, the pipe a pain to clean, and he had recently concluded that he actually did not enjoy spirits at all. No, Roger did these things because it's how things ought to be done. Carefully, deliberately, with the best of ethics and intentions. Men had served Crown and Country well for quite a long time before deciding it would be all right to wear khakis and vape and drink seltzers, and maybe there wasn't a correlation between the lax standards and the denuded mindset of the analysts and agents of the Secret Service, but it bloody well didn't hurt to try to give a shit. Roger wasn't old-fashioned, he was just practical.

That was also why he still took time every day to practice his street work, walking down alleys and into the Tube, out of the Tube and down other alleys, working his way circuitously home to his flat in Islington in order to throw off any shadows. It wasn't that anyone from Head Office was going to follow him—they knew where he lived, of course—or even that there was much chance that the Russians or Iranians were trying to find his residence. They, again, probably already knew that if they wanted to. You could find it online. But you could never be too careful. And it was good practice. A spook had to be good at these things.

An idle mind was a recipe for imprudent action, as Roger knew from too many empty afternoons and weekends at the racetrack. So when he had nothing else to do after a day of accomplishment, he put his mind to work, reading the classics. John le Carré's bickering bureaucrats were eerily recognizable, but it felt excusable when you had an actual enemy to fight, out there somewhere. Graham Greene made him nostalgic for real men, and Fleming was silly but romantic. Alan Furst and David Downing gave him an appreciation for the old-timers. Even Patrick O'Brian had plenty of espionage amid the sailing and cannon-fire. Oh, how Napoleon's eagerness so inspired the science of spycraft! He read Eric Ambler and John Buchan for historical perspective, and even as far back as Robert Louis Stevenson you could find secrets and the men who made them prowling the Scottish Highlands. Roger didn't go in much for general mystery and crime. He didn't want detectives solving murders on the moors, he wanted men fleeing on trains and preventing war. He also didn't care for what became of his intelligence-gathering heroes once the Wall fell and the Cold War became a War on Terror or War in the Assistance of a Morally Compromised International Ally or War Against Our Own Citizens For Their Own Good. Those more recent books had a lot of moralizing, first of all, but also there were too many computers. There were fewer trains. People didn't write down coded messages in newspapers anymore.

He also preferred his spies British. A bit of national chauvinism on his part, perhaps, but that was simply the truth. Unfortunately, when he got tired of reading and instead switched to a movie—usually after the brandy made him drowsy enough to nod off mid-page—he found most of the spy movies he preferred were American. He could watch a Bond or a le Carré adaptation or even something a little more contemporary, but by the time the telly was on he really preferred a steroidal idiot from Iowa or Texas or some other dumb place in the United States smashing people through windows. He was not proud of this personal preference, would never tell anybody, but the truth was that he ended almost every night falling asleep with tobacco dust from the pipe all over his vest while Jason Bourne tried to remember who trained him.

It was in one those half-awake bourbon-induced film binges that Roger recalled a task force he was briefly on, many years before. This would have been not long after Sandhurst, when he was early enough in his military intelligence career that SIS had not yet even reached out to him. It was a technology summit with the Americans, a knowledge-sharing conference in good faith. The British had some new drone system, something technical but dull. And the Americans had discovered how to map and program neurons.

They were, it seemed at the time, trying to make real-life Jason Bournes. Trying to calibrate superspies who went undercover without even realizing they were undercover. Roger was seconded to a committee, his only purpose to aid senior staff in their discussions, and briefly had eyes on a preliminary précis of what the Americans were cooking. But the entire event was canceled at the last minute and the technology never deployed. Some civil liberties issue in the United States.

But Roger also knew that the tech worked, that subsequent American administrations would, if they could, give it another try, and that the tech did in fact still exist. The vagaries of international law meant it was sold to some film directors in Portugal for some fantasy show, that even the studio had seemingly abandoned the use of it, and that the Americans would, no doubt, like to have that technology back in their hands. What better treasure, what better way for Roger to rebuild his reputation with Head Office, than if he could find a neuroscanner as a gift for our dear, beloved American friends.

Roger sat up in bed. Bourne was crashing his car into a bollard. Roger had one of those ideas people really only have once or twice in their entire lives. If you are lucky, that idea is the internal combustion engine or general relativity and you can change the world. Roger's wasn't quite so ambitious, but he knew it was still a good one. But if he was going to see his idea through to fruition, he was going to have to do everything himself. Off-the-books. Old-school.

He was methodical. First he read every publicly available bit of information he could about this fantasy series. He watched all the films and put together a timeline. In 2040 they announced a new series of movies made with "unique neurological technology." He read Portuguese news reports about fires on the island of Madeira, he watched behind-the-scenes documentaries of early films shot on the island, he read about special exemptions the Portuguese government made to the studio to help revitalize the Madeiran economy, and he read hundreds of fan blogs, wikis, and subreddits from the early 2040s about the production of the films. Learned how people were volunteering to move to Madeira to participate, found a deposition with families suing the studio after no one had heard from their children and spouses. There were online fan communities dedicated to "Finding Your Lost," combing through stills from movies and identifying extras in the background who looked like your family members.

Roger used his discretion, though, and skipped reading the original novels. Too long. Not really important.

He read interviews with film producers, directors, set designers, production assistants, sound editors, and even actors. Everyone was a little bit vague about how the movies were made, but clear enough that the characters were "real" now, that the fantasy world actually existed, that if you visited it you felt transported. He looked at *Variety* and *Hollywood Reporter* stories about the productions, watched a documentary about Cristiano Ronaldo visiting the set, saw photos of press junkets and film premieres. Here's the guy who played the king. Here's the guy who played a wizard. Here's a crowd on Hollywood Boulevard outside the Chinese Theatre screaming at them.

He began looking through the clandestine materials, too, sneaking through old files at work from the Portugal desk, reading up on what he could about their political situation, Madeira's economic woes, information on what activities the studio might be up to. There wasn't a lot. No one thought the island was very interesting, intelligencewise. But there were hints and whispers everywhere. Some major setback in production around 2044, shortly before the family of actor Marvin Powell settled with the studio for an undisclosed sum, rumored to be eight figures. He looked at visa applications, tried to cross-check them with people's online profiles. Here's a props assistant who moved from LA to Madeira in 2041, and returned in 2046. Here's an IT specialist who left Chicago in 2042 and returned in 2050. Here's a neuroscientist who left Stanford in 2040 and returned in 2044. That's a lead. Except, she was dead. Sue Whitman, deceased 2053.

There was only so much you could learn from documents, though. Roger knew that well. That was what the old-timers would have told him. He increased his anti-surveillance techniques, hiding his research inside flowerpots placed in the back stairwell of his building, and making his walk home after work longer, more difficult to track. Nobody from Head Office could know what he was doing, not yet. Not until he hit the streets and sourced some human intelligence.

You had to do that. It was the only way. But he couldn't travel to Los Angeles or even Madeira. Way too conspicuous. Leaving the country without clearance was the easiest way to see you packed up and sent away on early retirement. Even leaving London was suspicious. Roger didn't holiday much, so any trip at all would be a problem. He had to start in London. See what he could see.

Easiest place to begin was the studio's London offices. He faked a job application, faked a delivery, faked being a tourist. The London office handled a lot of publicity for the series, negotiated distribution rights in Europe, but otherwise had very little information about production itself. No one knew what was happening on that island.

He tried a new tactic. He spent many hours reading production updates and rumors from fans. Who knew more about anything, after all, than a committed fan? The best place to find human intelligence in Odessa was always with native Odessans, after all. Why not find the people most invested in this fantasy world, find out what they had to say?

There was a Facebook group advertising a monthly meetup of superfans. They watched the movies together, talked about what was coming out soon, dressed up, and had discussions about the films and their history and whatever else someone could possibly find interesting about them. Roger could hold his own. By now he had probably watched and read as much as anybody. More even. All he had to do was fake passion.

The first meeting he attended, in a community center in South Croydon, was focused on the topic of "wizard lore." This consisted of a speaker detailing the history of wizards and wands and other magical shit, followed by tea and cakes. Roger introduced himself, acting a little shy, and explained how he was looking for some new social activities since he had been caring for his sick mum the past few years.

"And how is she doing? Oh, I am so sorry to hear. Yes, it's good to get out and meet new people after all that."

Seated next to an older married couple, Roger watched the group's speaker prattle on about early editions of the books and continuity errors in the films.

"But these days it's pretty well regulated. So when you see Gregorian use any magic—and granted these days that's fairly rare—he'll always turn his staff about forty-five degrees before doing any spell. That's not a signaling or special effects requirement. That's to line up with the lore as originally described by J. D. Souard."

The audience was rapt, for some reason, which meant Roger could easily turn his head from side to side and observe the crowd without anyone noticing. There was a group of teenagers, all dressed up in some homemade costumes. There was a group of middle-aged dorks, bespectacled and wearing logo T-shirts. There was a woman, seated by herself, not looking at the speaker but at the floor.

Roger could not see her well from his vantage point, so when the question-and-answer session ended after an interminable amount of time, he sidled over to the tea and began preparing a cup when the woman approached the table and picked up a biscuit.

"Hi," Roger said, extending a hand. "I'm Roger. Roger Pendleton. This is my first time here."

"Oh, hello." She shook it, and almost walked away with her biscuit before adding, "I'm Lilly Kaminsky."

Roger smiled and watched her sit back down and eat her biscuit alone. She was familiar, and Roger knew that any sense of familiarity in his line of work could never be coincidence. He didn't believe in coincidence. He glanced at her one more time, capturing an image in his mind of exactly what she looked like: brown hair in a messy bun, brown eyes, short, no makeup, no jewelry, what one could call a "hard face."

As he traveled home, taking extra care to slip in and out of shops, two Tube stops this way, four bus stops the other, Roger worked back through his memory archive, the thousands of documents and videos and photos. That face was from somewhere. He shed invisible shadow after invisible shadow, working back north through London slowly, zigging and zagging across the Thames and across his mind. As he entered his building and began walking up the steps to his door, it came into focus, a lens from far away, telescoping in on exactly what he needed.

He retrieved a USB drive from the second hidden flowerpot (old tech was still the most secure), went into his flat, and powered on the air-gapped laptop he had purchased with cash for his own research. He put the drive in and opened a folder of photographs, scrolling through quickly. He knew what he was looking for. They were chronological, publicity stills from the studio and the press, arranged by film and year. 2037, 2038, 2039. He kept going. 2041, 2042.

Here, 2043. June. Los Angeles.

A red-carpet premiere. A large canvas backdrop. Words, in an elaborate font, emblazoned across it. *The Malicarn: The Return of the Council.* Three people standing in front. Smiling widely is the actor Marvin Powell. Beside him, smiling much less confidently, another actor named Glenn Mackey. And beside him, barely smiling at all, eyes squinting and watering under the lights, an unidentified woman. Brown eyes, brown hair. Short. A hard face.

Roger opened the file's metadata. He added a note. "Woman on right: Lilly Kaminsky."

That's some good sleuthing, Roger. The old-timers would be proud. You really are a spy.

THE MALICARN

THE SIXTEENTH SPRING IN THE REIGN OF QUEEN HANNAH I (MADEIRA—MARCH 2060)

Folks in the little villages that now dotted the Malicarn would say to one another, as Glenn walked solemnly through their communities, "What does that old wizard Gregorian think he is up to? Magic is gone, what else could be on his mind?" It wasn't longing. And it wasn't regret. It was something else. As Glenn spent the years traversing the sets' valleys and rivers and mountains, dispensing prewritten lines and acting out scenes, interacting with characters and keeping the illusion of that imaginary world a reality, he felt shame.

If the villagers had asked him, "What is it that drives you onward, Gregorian, without your magic or purpose?" he would have said, "Shame! I am driven by shame!"

But Glenn would never actually say that. Instead, he would spit out some boilerplate about "protecting the Malicarn" and keep walking. It was a subtle shame, he had to admit.

His shame from within the Malicarn was far worse than his shame from without, however. In the outer world, Glenn was beloved. The day of the plane crash, Glenn was in Funchal as part of a goodwill press promotion, hoping to foster some cooperation with the local government. A new crop of elected officials faced backlash for the Cameroon-resettlement program, and now had begun to support a platform of "Defund the Malicarn." Stress between Madeira and Lisbon had reached a fever pitch, with the Madeirans accusing the prime minister of corruption and dirty dealings with Hollywood. But Glenn charmed everyone he saw at the Children's Hospital and the restaurant grand opening and the airport-terminal-expansion groundbreaking, talking about the old movies and showing off props. He stood for photos and signed dozens of autographs. Most of the younger officials had grown up watching him onscreen, and despite their political reservations were awed by his celebrity. That was the cost of defending the realm. Glenn never felt bad about himself after such days.

The dozen or so fire engines that roared out of Funchal that evening, all heading north, were odd, but Glenn didn't think much of it until he had been driven back to the Citadel's underground parking garage, where Jules and half a dozen Madeiran officials were yelling at one another.

"I am telling you, no one can enter the set until we clear the sector of characters!" Jules said.

The man Jules was yelling at was the fire commissioner, whose English was poor but whose anger was great. "If we cannot stop the fire soon, forests will burn. This is a serious issue. You have not seen Madeira burn before, I have."

Glenn found one of the other writers, hanging back by the elevator, and heard the whole story. A fighter jet from what appeared to be the Chinese air force had crashed in one of the northern sectors. No word on casualties, but it was burning pretty good.

"Wow," Glenn said. "What were they spying on?"

The crash site was not very exciting, when Glenn and Jules joined the firefighters to survey the damage the next morning. The plane was charred, little more than a crumbled mess of metal. No bodies were found in the wreckage.

"No characters killed," said Jules, "as far as we could tell. Pilot must have ejected. Could have happened over the water. Who knows, but he's probably floating in the ocean somewhere."

"Did a camera catch the moment of the crash?" Glenn asked.

Jules was evasive on this point. "I dunno. Who cares? We couldn't use the footage anyway."

When the pilot continued to not turn up, the Malicarn had its very first foreign policy crisis. Larry was getting pressure from his contacts in the Portuguese Ministry of Foreign Affairs, who in turn were getting pressure from various high functionaries within the European Union and a slew of members of the Chinese Central Committee. Everyone wanted to know where the pilot was, if he was alive, and if so, why hadn't anyone given him back yet?

Glenn had no insight into any of these things, mostly because nobody told him anything and also because he was consciously avoiding the discussion of the plane as much as possible. He had worked in the Malicarn long enough now to know nothing but shame could come of it. Indeed, Glenn had other things to worry about, like placating Hannah. She was skeptical of the plane from the beginning, which didn't surprise him. She was a smart girl. The day after the crash, she called him using the trick he'd taught her: shouting his name loudly and demanding his presence, which would get picked up on the feeds and forwarded to his inbox, via a little program Glenn had paid one of the tech guys to write. And when he rode out to the castle she was indignant that no one was keeping her in the loop about "the dragon."

"Sanderson and Quentin did not know much about it," she said to him in the castle courtyard. "Took their time even telling me."

"Well, there's not much to tell. What is left of it is well charred."

"You have seen it?"

He probably shouldn't have mentioned this. It would just stoke her imagination.

"I think I should see the remains. Reassure the people—"

"No, it is really not necessary," Glenn said. "Trust me, the faster the people forget about the dragon the better."

He gave her points for tenacity, but even Glenn didn't expect she would try to sneak out to view the wreckage. Jules or someone else in the Citadel noticed her on the feeds and shut that expedition down quick. Glenn didn't like when they controlled

Hannah in that way. She was very angry with him after her attempted escape, scoffing each time he visited the castle. Glenn tried hard to assure the rest of the court that everything was fine, the dragon didn't mean anything, it was nothing to worry about, but she continued to doubt him. And the commoners weren't buying the story, either. Rumors continued to fester.

Today would provide some distraction. It had been over two months since the plane crash, and Glenn was off to a production meeting to figure out if there was any story business he needed to prioritize. He left his tower, did some standard mingling among the commoners, and then snuck off to the underground tunnel and headed for the Citadel, where Jules was waiting for him to talk over some upcoming story beats. Jules sat alone in the writers' room, surrounded by televisions and paper and handwritten notes. His writers, mostly freelancers at this point, only met sporadically, but Jules stayed in the conference room all the time. Glenn thought he slept in there.

When Glenn walked into the writers' room Jules was hunched over a series of photocopies. He hadn't showered in several days. His beard was long and unkempt. In the corner sat a mound, covered hastily in a blanket. Classical music played loudly from a speaker.

"What's on for today?" Glenn asked, looking up at the bank of TVs cycling through camera feeds all over set. Glenn could guess but Jules liked it when he asked. The court was hosting the Kingstown Players, and Glenn had been invited by Hannah to come watch.

"Huh? Ah!" Jules sat up as if realizing Glenn was in the room for the first time. He picked up the papers he was reading and waved them around. "You see these? Beinecke Library sent them over, from their special collections. All this correspondence from Wendell Highsman, stuff about Souard's early drafts, what they changed, what Souard was thinking. I mean, a lot of it is

Wendell bitching with his lawyers, trying to get out of his contract with Souard, but some of it is good."

Jules's quest for story ideas had long rested on nuggets from Jean-Danton Souard himself. Whenever Glenn thought he had probably exhausted every possible avenue of inquiry, Jules found some other tidbit, some other note, some other scrap of information.

After Prion's death and the fire in the implementations lab, the studio brought in a new producer to help right the ship. Jules wasn't fired, but only because he had way too much knowledge about the inner workings of the set, and if anyone replaced him the entire operation might just fall apart. Jules did find himself in quite a bit of legal trouble with the family of Marvin Powell, however, and nearly lost his visa. Fortunately, extradition was never enforced, the family was paid off, and Jules was allowed to remain on set, though he was rather forcefully warned that returning to the United States was not in his best legal interest.

The Return of the Necromancer, the film that resulted in Jules's shenanigans, was not very good but managed to make even more money than *The Return of the Council* and so, as far as the studio was concerned, nothing bad really happened. Oh, there was plenty of online discourse about the film's ethics. But it turned out, as much as people thought it was incredible to watch their favorite characters become "real," even more than that they wanted to watch these real people die.

Jules remained the series showrunner, with even more producer oversight, but the years following *Return of the Necromancer* ushered in a new and unique writing approach to the franchise. It was born out of necessity. With the neuroscanners destroyed and the lab in shambles, Jules and the writers couldn't introduce new characters with specific story purposes, so Glenn and the other Reals became more important in shepherding along character and story. Brian Doyle, in particular, began driving the Council of Heroes onward toward various quests and adventures. Glenn, on the other hand, became a living exposition dump, always available to explain to a scanned character some bit of lore or backstory. Fans jokingly referred to Gregorian as "the Wikipedia Wizard." His recent tour around the Malicarn, speaking to guilds and churches and children in town squares about the lost art of wizardry, was partly about shoring up goodwill for the queen and partly about making sure characters remembered basic backstory for future films.

"So, what are we doing?" Glenn asked again, shouting over the music. "Could you maybe turn it down?"

"Ah, ah." Jules reached over, tried to turn the speaker off, and when he couldn't he bent down and unplugged it. "Sorry. Messiaen. It's a recording of a German quartet in the seventies. They did it in West Berlin in front of the Wall. You like it?"

"Sure. What are we doing today? I'm supposed to go to the castle but I have no notes."

"Okay, yes, let's talk about that. I'm done with notes, Glenn. You're constricted by them, they are bringing you down. Let go, let go. That's what I say. No more notes. Just live, be in the moment. It's all real, it's all happening."

"But don't you have the Tristan and Heloise thing—"

"No!" Jules's face twitched, and he spasmed in his chair. "You don't have to worry about that anymore. Just be a wizard. That's what you're good at."

Glenn wasn't sure if that was true, but he also didn't feel like arguing with Jules. Talking to him felt like talking to a chatbot. He spit out human-sounding language with very little sense behind the words.

Glenn knew Jules was stressed. The act of running the realm became as important as the job of telling stories, and the weight of ensuring harvests didn't fail, housing was available, and people had enough money to live became a real headache. Jules hated dealing with it, even though he had become the point person for all the Madeiran officials who needed some political cover for their constituents, upset about Malicarn land or water or road use. The Madeirans were always asking for more from the Malicarn, and after Jules ran out of no-show jobs and money to bribe the politicians with, he just started ignoring their requests entirely. Why should he care? They weren't part of the story.

Plus, he had plenty of Malicarn-based problems. Food production was dangerously low, and every year they ended up importing more food to avoid famine. But Jules hated it, said it wasn't a "story outcome." Plenty of farms were failing or left vacant, and finally Jules found a solution that pleased the local politicians as well as his own sensibilities. A Portuguese MP set up a work exchange program with the Cameroon government and allowed a few hundred people a year to move from Cameroon to the Malicarn under the condition that they work the farms and pay a very steep tax to the Madeiran authorities. They were mostly placed on vineyards. This consoled the politicians concerned about the dip in productivity of the Madeira wine economy, provided essential farmwork in the Malicarn, and didn't interfere with the story, since Jules kept the Cameroonians offscreen as much as possible. They were only there to farm, to prevent the set from totally collapsing. It was easy enough. No one in the Malicarn spoke French, so they treated the Cameroonians as outsiders. Glenn had nothing to do with the program, except that Malicarn farmers consistently blamed him for it anyway.

The native-born characters, never scanned, were growing up, too. This was an opportunity. Unaware of their world's fabrication, they didn't see the Malicarn as anything except reality, and in a way it was. Jules called them "our best untapped resource," and looked forward to when the Malicarn was majority-native and a whole new set of stories could be built around them.

The young queen was the most prominent native-born character of all. Hannah was inescapably involved in most plots at least tangentially, though Jules had never given Hannah much in the way of her own story. She was mostly in the background. Even now, as she was entering adulthood and with the regency soon to end, Jules hadn't planned anything significant for her. She was sharp and clever and knew how things in the Malicarn worked. Glenn assumed Jules would want to use her. But maybe he agreed with certain vocal fans that the Council of Heroes provided more traditional role models, and that a disabled mixed-race girl wasn't the model the Malicarn series wanted to project. Or maybe Jules was just running out of ideas.

In truth, Glenn found Hannah's absence from storylines a relief. If she wasn't being written into an ongoing arc, there was little chance she would encounter real danger. She could stay mad at him for now, that was fine. It meant she could also, at least for a little longer, stay safe.

The queen's safety had been assured when Jules figured out a way to resolve the issue of the Necromancer quickly after Prion's death. It was his idea to make Gregorian "negotiate" with the Necromancer directly, ending the threat in exchange for the banishment of all magic in the kingdom. This would align the prequel story they were telling with the beginning of the original films, still some decades ahead in "story time." But there were practical considerations, as well. It was cheaper not to worry about so many special effects. The studio could lay off a number of technicians and engineers. Jules's only regret was that he could no longer use his mechanical dragon.

Glenn didn't protest to any story beats. He didn't even continue to express his outrage about Prion. He didn't want to draw attention to Hannah. Glenn saw Hannah as often as he could, making excuses to visit the castle on royal business. The tutors, nurses, and advisors who raised her meant well, but they were scanned characters and knew barely more about the world than she did. Glenn tried to let her in on what knowledge he could without totally disrupting the reality of the set. He slipped her little nuggets of truth, comic books, and facts about science. If Jules or a producer ever saw him doing this on one of the camera feeds, they never mentioned it. Maybe Glenn could explain more to Hannah about the reality of the Malicarn, if he ever managed to find a spot on set that wasn't being observed and recorded. He had no particular obligation to the girl, he knew, but wanted her to have as normal and safe a childhood as possible. Perhaps Glenn did this for whatever responsibility he felt toward Prion and Evangeline, but on his more lucid days, when the shame stung especially hard, he knew he actually did it for Lilly.

Glenn never found out what happened to Lilly after she burned down the lab and ran away. Perhaps she was dead. Perhaps she was hiding in Marrakech or Hong Kong or even back somewhere in the United States. Maybe the studio knew where she was and was waiting for the right moment to retaliate. Glenn didn't know and was too afraid to ask. And so he agreed with Jules's wild story ideas and all the other changes that occurred.

"Goddamn teens!" Jules yelled at one of the camera feeds. A pair of Madeiran teenagers were driving a car around a farm in one of the southern sectors. They weren't hurting anyone, though the farmer and his wife were yelling at them as they ran over a vegetable patch. "It's so easy to keep people from leaving the set, why can't we invest in keeping people out?" The teenagers had become a hobbyhorse for Jules since their vandalism had increased over the last year.

"Any future plans you can fill me in on?" Glenn asked, trying to redirect. "I have a convention in the States next week, I could use some guidance. Something to pepper in during my talks with fans?"

"No, I don't care about all that." Jules turned his focus back on the letter in his hands. That was Glenn's cue to leave. Annoyed that he had traveled all the way to the Citadel for nothing, Glenn made sure to get out the last word before leaving the room.

"You know, anybody who walks in here can see the neuroscanner," he said, and pointed to the covered mound in the corner.

Glenn returned to his apartment and spent the morning looking over emails and planning his upcoming travel. There was no one else left for these publicity events. The other Reals had long since quit. Jacob and Darryl took a job back in California, and all of the fight trainers one by one followed other opportunities. Technically, the Cameroonian farmers were Reals, but of course that was different. The only original Real who remained other than Glenn was Brian Doyle. And Doyle hated publicity. He hated leaving the Malicarn in general. And without the neuroscanner, scanned heroes couldn't be temporarily de-sequestered and carted out for the media. That left Glenn as the last character who would attend conventions, press junkets, premieres, and anything else the studio wanted. Next week was a Comic-Con. Cons were the worst—physically exhausting, with the traveling, the taking of pictures, and the signing of autographs—but at least they were mentally quite easy. Nobody ever asked anything surprising.

Not that Glenn loved to travel but it did get him off the island a few times a year. And it was obvious how the Malicarn no longer consisted of the carefree strolls and nature excursions he and Lilly had once enjoyed. When he arrived at the castle in midafternoon, Glenn had to push through a crowd of commoners who had camped out before the main gate. They were dirty, emaciated, and Glenn thought they would swamp his cart before he could make it inside. The city of Kingstown, whose growth Jules had encouraged, had nevertheless taken on a life of its own. Glenn preferred the old days, when there was just the castle and nothing else, but the people of the Malicarn were inventive and tenacious, and Kingstown had grown into a sizable urban center, with all the drawbacks that entailed. He struggled through the crowds and onward to the castle gates. Hannah was sitting inside in the main courtyard, watching the Players unload their sets from their cart.

"It might be better if you were in a somewhat more secure area of the castle," Glenn said to her.

She rolled her eyes. "Nothing's going to happen to me, Gregorian. But look at the Players. One of their backdrops got smashed by the crowds in the street."

A few of the actors were huddled around a slashed canvas,

arguing with one another what they should do. Glenn considered offering a helpful theatrical pep talk but thought better of it.

"Well, all the more reason to keep you safe."

Just then someone shouted from a window in the nearest tower. Glenn looked up to see Sanderson gesturing down at the queen.

"Get back into the tower at once!" he shouted, before hastily adding, "Your Majesty!"

Hannah groaned and stood up. "You know, you said the dragon wasn't a big deal but everyone's still on edge."

"I think everyone has been on edge since you tried to run away."

"Ah, there it is. Thank you, good sir!" Hannah had been especially sarcastic to Gregorian since her escapade, and he wasn't sure to chalk this up to the dragon situation or general teenage malaise.

He gave Sanderson a thumbs-up as Hannah headed back inside, but Sanderson just shook his head and disappeared back through the window without a word. It had been Glenn's idea to appoint several regents to assist the young queen, characters who could actually run the kingdom, and while Sanderson and Quentin didn't seem to like Gregorian very much they did a decent enough job of keeping things in order.

Glenn ate in the hall with the rest of the court, stuck next to Bariol, who droned on about his gout. Glenn was relieved when the tables were cleared and the stage erected. He sat next to Hannah, and the actors took their places as the hum of conversation in the hall dimmed. The oldest of the actors, costumed in kingly fashion, walked forward and took the hand of the actress standing center stage. "Now, fair Hippolyta," he began, "our nuptial hour draws on apace."

Glenn chuckled aloud to himself as the players leapt into a production of *A Midsummer Night's Dream*. The actors were good, hitting the right comic notes, keeping the action fleet but engaging. The actor playing Nick Bottom was bossy but buffoonish. Sanderson laughed loudly at his antics. The characterization reminded Glenn a bit of Jules.

Hannah was delighted, and her earlier annoyance seemed to abate. She leaned over and whispered into Glenn's ear. "Gregorian, what are they doing?" Hannah always liked to ask Glenn questions when the court hosted a play.

"They are actors putting on a play."

"Obviously, but what is happening?"

"I am sorry, I was not clear. The actors in the play are also playing actors, who are also putting on a play."

"That is strange."

But she enjoyed what she saw. When Bottom's head was transformed into a donkey's, and the actor playing him put a large donkey-shaped mask onto his head, Hannah burst into hysterical giggles, unable to control herself. It was an infectious laugh, the carefree laugh of a young woman still partially a child, and Glenn was soon laughing as well.

"Oh!" Hannah squealed. "He's human again!"

The actor playing Bottom stretched and woke up, groaning and holding his head. "I have had a most rare vision," he said. "I have had a dream past the wit of man to say what dream it was. Man is but an ass if he go about to expound this dream."

Glenn began to feel better about things. Theater could do that. Yes, Jules was acting strange. But when wasn't he strange? And soon people would forget about the plane. Glenn would be around to help shape whatever story came next. His contract was up soon again, but he could extend it. Or not? Maybe he could do some other kinds of movies, ones where people cry a lot and win awards? There were possibilities. Lilly was long lost, that was clear, but whose heart hasn't been broken? There were other girls. Maybe Glenn would ask Jules to introduce him to one of the production assistants who worked at the Citadel. There was a cute redhead in the props department. And even on the set, things were good. They had a strong core of characters. Glenn considered many of them genuine friends. Oh, sure, they didn't know who Glenn really was, but not all friends do. Hannah was like a niece. How lucky he was, living in an interesting place doing interesting things. And it was he who helped make it all. Even the bad parts were something he could be proud of.

At the end of the play, when Bottom and his troupe acted out their failed production, and the other characters mocked it, Hannah began laughing so hard she fell off her chair. The characters filed off the stage, leaving the fairy Puck alone at center.

"If we shadows have offended," the actor said, "think but this and all is mended: that you have but slumbered here while these visions did appear."

The cast bowed, the audience clapped, the musicians returned, and the court broke out into a dance. Glenn's shame melted away.

THE SOUTH FLORIDA OFFSHORE TOURISM REDEVELOPMENT ZONE (FORMERLY MIAMI BEACH)

April 3, 2060

1.

"Science is not about certainty. It is about deductions, tested and retested, until we are satisfied enough to deduce some more. You can never really know anything for certain."

Lilly remembered the way her dissertation director looked when he said those words, leaning back in his chair with his neck craned up, eyes staring at the ceiling. The words came out strained, like he was quickly cobbling them together as he spoke, though he had said the same thing to dozens of other graduate students before, in the same office with the same expression on his face, stretched out in his chair with his neck in the same position.

Still, it was good advice, and Lilly never forgot it.

The loud groaning and cracking sound that startled her out of bed, for example, led her to deduce that a condominium building on the mainland had collapsed. Some old, abandoned tower that had been rotting in the surf for years. Hilton-over-the-Beach looked eastward, and guests couldn't see the ruins on the other side of Biscayne Bay, so Lilly deduced such collapses happened often, the hotel deliberately constructed to obscure the rot. No alarms went off in her room, and her view toward the ocean showed nothing amiss. A few cruise liners and megayachts sailed past slowly, and a cargo container floated on the horizon. Lilly couldn't be sure that *nothing* was wrong, but she deduced that everything was still going to plan.

She made a cup of coffee from her room's machine and leaned

against the large window, which stretched from floor to ceiling, and watched the sun rise. Leaning forward, she tried to peer down to the water below her. The hotel was built as a cascading series of shrinking floors, each one smaller than the one below, like a wedding cake, so her view of the large steel stilts on which the entire edifice sat was blocked by the floor beneath. She couldn't see the stilts entering the water below, which at high tide completely covered Miami Beach and made the hotel look like a large luxury oil derrick from afar.

Lilly checked her phone for messages. There was just one from Roger: **12:00 PM confirmed. Hall B.**

It was on then.

Lilly finished her coffee and dressed quickly. The convention halls would not open for another hour but she could do a slow walk around the promenade and continue her reconnaissance. She put on her pass and lanyard, hung the DO NOT DISTURB sign on her door, then took an elevator up to the convention center.

Even at this early hour there was a buzz among the handful of attendees who milled around the lobby, talking excitedly over breakfast and looking at photos and videos from the previous day's panels. A few were already in their cosplay outfits. Roger suggested they should wear costumes, too, partially as a joke and partially because, as Lilly knew, he really wanted to. But it was never practical. Too cumbersome. Lilly kept her outfit simple: sneakers, jeans, and a T-shirt that read FOR THE MALICARN! with an outline of Prion's profile. Roger thought the shirt was corny and old, but that was why Lilly liked it. It looked authentic.

A complimentary breakfast buffet for hotel guests was laid out, featuring lots of fruit, an omelet station, and several trays of sausages, blintzes, and eggs. Lilly stuck with her coffee. She still felt ill when she ate rich foods. Anything with too much sugar or fat made her nauseous. That had been the case for years, ever since the boat.

When Lilly escaped from the Malicarn, it took two months for her to cross a little less than five hundred miles of open ocean.

Of course that was never the plan. She expected it to take two days, but even the man who sold the boat to her in Funchal had warned her not to head out, that there was no way she could beat the hurricane. But Lilly was desperate to stay ahead of whoever was almost certainly going to be chasing her, so instead of waiting she overpaid the man for the twelve-foot dinghy, packed it with cans of beans, vegetables, and bottled water she purchased at a nearby market, and took off just before the rains started.

She should have died. She knew that. There wasn't any sense in it. She had never navigated a boat larger than a kayak, and the dinghy's little GPS monitor shorted out as the rains hammered down. She nearly capsized multiple times, finally lying down on the bottom of the boat, gripping the sides, hoping not to be turned around. When the storm finally passed, she had no idea how far she had been steered away from her original course, and so simply started heading east, best as she could make it out, which went fine until the boat's engine began smoking and shut down. Lilly was adrift at sea.

The rationing of the cans and water was easy. She could space that out well enough to make it a couple of weeks. What was hard was the counting down, each can a literal marker for how many days she had to live. Most people didn't die with so much certainty, but Lilly was able to deduce with extreme precision how much longer she had to live based on the amount of food and water left in the boat.

Deduction, however, was not certainty. And two nights after her last can of corn, with a single water bottle left, Lilly lay down in the boat, flat on her back, and watched the stars above her, bright and glorious in the middle of the dark ocean. The night had never seemed so full of stars, even in her college astronomy classes where they would hike out into the woods, camp under a clear sky, and stargaze all night. She knew she was at the very end of whatever life she was going to get to live, and only now could she see the entirety of the universe so clearly.

She thought to herself that she did not want to die alone.

The next morning a Moroccan fishing boat sighted her, pulled her in, and brought her to land. She didn't have the stomach for rich foods after that.

There was not, she was fortunate to discover upon her return to civilization, any kind of global manhunt for her. If the Portuguese government knew about the arson at all, they weren't advertising it, and the studio didn't seem to have any resources to do much about it. Lilly was still wary about returning to the United States. They'd find her eventually. Maybe she wouldn't go to jail but there were other ways of ruining your life, and a bunch of lawsuits didn't sound like Lilly's preferred way to spend the future. Best to steer away from the European Union as well, in case Portugal decided to follow up about her property destruction. The UK was still easy enough to get into, however. Lilly's bank accounts hadn't been frozen or anything, and Norman fishermen still took bribes in American money so she could avoid customs. In London, Lilly sublet a flat in an outer suburb and found a job as a cashier at a grocer. She remained as invisible as possible, abandoning her old social media accounts, emails, everything. She didn't have a phone. She never even tried contacting her mother to tell her she was alive.

Lilly didn't speak of her time in the Malicarn or her dramatic escape—not to coworkers, not to customers, not to anyone. It was like it never happened. She made no friends, intentionally staying away from pubs and parks and even the lobby of her apartment. She kept expecting someone from the set to sneak their way to London, to find her and capture her and bring her back, to answer for her destruction of the neuroscanners, her immolation of the lab.

It never happened. Two years after her escape, she saw an article online: "First new *Malicarn* movie in three years premieres in the United States." In one publicity photo, Lilly recognized the soft, out-of-focus profile of Glenn, standing in costume behind a row of warriors in a still from the movie. So at least he hadn't changed at all.

Lilly didn't go to the theater to see it. Instead she pirated a copy and watched it one night on her computer, lying in bed under the covers, ashamed someone might see her and know that this lonely woman who worked a double shift stocking produce had an interest in a long-running fantasy franchise.

The film was garbage. King Prion is betrayed by the Necromancer and killed by a dragon. This spurs Glenn, as Gregorian, to seek an audience with the Necromancer. He returns to the Malicarn and announces that magic is banned forever from the Malicarn, and peace is pronounced throughout the land. The plot was uneven, the ending drawn out and anticlimactic, with the queen giving birth to a baby girl and then dying, and Glenn was forced to do a lot more acting than ever before. And though the previous films were professional-looking, *The Return of the Necromancer*—as it was called—felt sloppy and slapdash. Lots of digital effects were applied to make the fight scenes more intense. Gregorian ended the film with a long monologue about peace, which made Lilly laugh, as she could clearly tell Glenn's heart was not in it.

But it was only a movie. Lilly's unremarkable life continued. Every day she went to her job and then back to her apartment and the next day back to her job. Every few years another *Malicarn* movie was released and she watched the bootleg and cried under the blankets and then tried not to think about it again.

There were eventually men, some she saw only for a night and others that became temporary boyfriends, but Lilly never gave much of herself to them. She met them at pubs, late at night, when it was dark and they could never see her well. Most were forgettable, less charming even than Glenn. For a few months she dated a doctor, an endocrinologist named Charlie, who was funny and smart and caring, and seemed interested to learn more about Lilly even though she spoke very little. He was the nicest person she had ever dated and it creeped her out. Why was Charlie so genuine? Who was Charlie to be with someone like Lilly, poor and sad and lacking in any prospects? He didn't know she had a doctorate, had been a scientist. He thought she just worked at a grocer. Wasn't that strange? The mere fact that someone could be with Lilly was evidence that Lilly should not be with them. Charlie was too good, and so she broke up with him and went back to being alone.

Lilly spent time on message boards and in chat rooms, discussing Malicarn lore, the latest releases, rumors of what was happening on set. She picked an anonymous moniker, "WizardGirl26," and started posting, parlaying her own theories and ideas. Sometimes she drew on what she knew from her time there, sometimes it was just speculation, but she never told anyone who she was or what she used to do. The fans did a lot of heavy lifting justifying ruptures in continuity, trying to explain how the prequels could ever line up with the original films. There were multiverses, they theorized, or the original movies were de-canonized, or there was time travel. Lilly never reminded any of the commentators that it was all made up.

There was a big, heavily marketed anniversary rerelease of all the *Malicarn* films, one a week for several months. Lilly decided to go see a recent one—*The Malicarn: Demon Spawn*, a horror-like film featuring a few minor Council members and barely any Gregorian. She went on a Saturday afternoon. One of the accounts she followed shared a post about a London-area *Malicarn* fan group that would be assembling, in costume, to watch the film, and Lilly wanted to see them. To meet, in person, another group of *Malicarn* fans, people who thought the ongoing travails of a living land of make-believe actually mattered.

She took a bus to Croydon and walked to the theater. The fans were not hard to identify. They were dressed in homemade costumes of robes and capes and mail. Even from far away they looked cheap and fake, nothing at all like the clothes Lilly remembered from the Malicarn set. The fans sat together, over a dozen of them in the front rows, hooting and hollering throughout the whole film, quoting lines and clapping at every minor moment. When the credits rolled, they gave a standing ovation.

In the lobby afterward Lilly walked up to one of them, a girl dressed in a white simulacrum of Heloise's traveling gown.

"Are you guys *Malicarn* cosplayers?" Lilly asked.

"Oh yeah! Do you cosplay?"

"No," Lilly said. "But I'm interested."

"Oh, you should come to our meetings! We're the Reapers, we meet once a month."

The girl gave Lilly information on their next meeting, and two weeks later Lilly found herself back in the back of a pub, with a group of very motivated, excited *Malicarn* fans. They played trivia and Lilly won, instantly endearing her to her new loud and opinionated friends.

There weren't really her people, of course. But they were something.

Hilton-over-the-Beach had an open-air balcony that wrapped around the front of the hotel. Lilly walked out onto it while she waited for the convention to open. It hosted a wide promenade with grass and trees, much like the parks Miami Beach once had. Hardly anyone was out here except for a few landscapers and maintenance staff. From the southernmost tip, Lilly leaned over and could see a mass of dust and debris rising over the edge of the hotel. She heard the buzz of helicopters circling the fallen building on the mainland.

Hilton-over-the-Beach was one of a dozen resorts, hotels, and privately owned golf clubs that had been erected above the water after Hurricane Jason. The State of Florida gave the land away for nearly nothing, as long as the developers promised to bring in some tourist dollars. The land was barely even land anymore, except for a few hours a day when sand emerged from the low tides. But the development deals didn't work as the state had intended. Without the ability to leave their hotel, any tourist's money was just going to a single corporate owner. And it didn't take long for businesses to get a special tax exemption so that each sky palace operated as its own individual fiefdom. Some were geared toward families, some honeymooners, and some to rich guys who wanted to get away from their wives and have a prostitute pretend they were good in bed.

Hilton-over-the-Beach was the largest resort and the convention hub. People came by boat or flew into the new floating international airport. Some even took water taxis from the mainland, though the high crime and poverty of what remained of southern Florida made it an option only for the most frugal.

From the southern edge of the promenade, Lilly looked down at the layers of balconies and hotel rooms. Ten down, three to the left. She had studied the architectural plans thoroughly, knew exactly which window it was. As long as they hadn't misidentified the correct room in the first place.

Lilly walked back into the main lobby. It was nearly nine, and the room was filling up with con attendees waiting for the exhibition hall to open for the morning. Lilly was moving through the crowd slowly, counting security guards and cameras, when she noticed a man in a blue windbreaker leaning against a column, chewing gum. Without his usual suit and pipe combination he looked almost normal.

"No tea this morning?" she asked Roger.

He shrugged. "Trying to cut back. Makes me jittery."

The doors to the exhibition hall opened and the crowd began moving inside.

"We should line up at Hall B early," Lilly said.

"Not too early. Easier to leave when we are toward the back."

"Well, let's do a loop. And try to seem interested, okay?"

Roger shrugged again, and they walked together into the convention hall. There was a large plastic castle constructed at the entrance, and beyond that a fake cobblestone path that wound between the aisles of booths. There were hundreds of stalls, filled with writers or comic book artists, C-list actors from old TV shows, retailers hawking T-shirts and tote bags. Large studios had bigger booths with more interactive features. The smaller guys had a table and maybe a few posters.

They walked up to the largest booth of them all, with elaborate decorations and life-size cutouts of characters. The *Malicarn* exhibit always gave out free swag. Lilly walked up and took a pen, the end of which was shaped to look like a wizard's staff.

"I think they are setting up a resurrection storyline, definitely," said a fan standing behind Lilly. He was a young man, barely out of school, talking excitedly to a friend. "You can see it because of the Easter egg from the last movie, with the face in the lake."

"Oh, who was that face?" Roger asked, inserting himself into the conversation.

"What do you mean?" the young fan asked. "It was Prion, obviously."

Lilly turned around. "Where are you from?" she asked the fan.

"Uh, Dublin."

"See, they reedited that scene. They always include some bit that still seems like magic in the international releases, even though they're not supposed to. But that wasn't in the original cut."

"Ah," the young fan said. "Bummer. I wish they could make all these timelines match up somehow."

They wandered away and Lilly turned to Roger. "You sounded like an idiot."

"I dunno, you told me to be enthusiastic."

"It's easier to actually be enthusiastic than it is to fake it."

"Hey, I've seen every one of these movies."

"But you don't remember any of it."

"I remember things that are important, okay?"

"Don't be snarky. This is your idea." She pointed to a video screen hanging from the *Malicarn* booth. "Look. You can't even get the time right."

The screen had a picture of several characters from the *Malicarn*. Underneath the photo were the words:

***Secrets of the Malicarn.* New Time: 11:00 AM, HALL B.**

"Now we're going to be late," she said.

Lilly had attended meetings of the Reapers for years and never told anyone a thing about her past. They knew that she was from America, of course, but Lilly didn't want to divulge any more than that, and no one asked.

Then Roger showed up. Tall, superficially handsome, and amiable, his accent a very studied Received Pronunciation. Roger began coming to meetings even though he didn't know anybody and never explained how he discovered the Reapers' existence. The more he hung around the more it seemed that he had absolutely no interest in the *Malicarn* at all. He never talked about the movies, shows, or books directly, and when others brought up iconic scenes or characters, he seemed annoyed. It was as if he joined the club just to learn what the *Malicarn* Expanded Universe was, though in all his time at club meetings and events he seemed to be growing actively more ignorant. The other Reapers liked him but he made Lilly nervous. She avoided talking to him whenever possible.

But Roger was interested in her. He liked to sit next to her, always bought her a pint when they met at pubs. He offered to accompany her home on more than one occasion, or call her a cab when she refused. One of the other Reapers teased her, thinking Roger was clearly crushing on Lilly. But Lilly knew better. A fifty-something-year-old man like Roger does not crush on a fifty-something-year-old woman. Guys like him lean younger. No, he was after something else.

After two months of Roger's flirtations, he changed tactics. One Saturday night, a few hours after she'd returned from trivia night with the Reapers at a pub, there was a knock at Lilly's door. Hard, loud, with a gruff voice shouting behind it. Not the kind of knocking one could ignore. Peering through the peephole, Lilly saw Roger, wearing a suit. He had been wearing a polo shirt earlier. She opened the door.

"Hi, Roger," she said.

"Lilly, hello," he replied. "I was worried about you. I didn't have your number. I couldn't call."

"I don't have a phone."

"What if there's an emergency?"

"Who would call me in an emergency?"

Roger smiled, not in the flirty way she had seen him smile before, but with a malicious delight.

"Can we talk?" he asked.

She let him in. Lilly sat on the couch, pushing aside the old, crusted plates of food. Roger stood over her, uncomfortably close.

"How did you know where I live?" Lilly asked.

"It's not very difficult to find people," Roger said. "Also I followed you home tonight."

"Christ, Roger."

"Don't worry. You know the British Secret Service? That's MI6. You know, MI6? I'm with them."

"Well, of course," said Lilly, almost relieved to be caught. "I haven't done anything else, you know. I haven't hurt anyone. It's been years, I've stayed quiet, I—"

"I know," Roger said. He spoke with the confidence of a man who had never believed himself to be wrong. "I'm not here on behalf of the studio. I'm here because I need your help."

"With what?"

"Tell me everything you know about neuroscanner technology."

Roger and Lilly filed into the large, hot convention hall. They sat in small, wobbly folding chairs set up in the very back of the room. Roger had worked out down to the minute the timeline, but if they weren't in the hall then they couldn't be precise. All Roger had to do was confirm the start time, but he screwed that up.

"Lilly, calm down," he whispered as they sat down. "They changed it, it happens. You know how many times I've done this?"

"Are you trying to sabotage us?" she hissed at him. The crowd erupted in applause as the lights dimmed. "This is your idea anyway."

"Yeah, you keep saying that."

"Hellloooo, Miami!" The voice boomed out over the loudspeakers. Hall B was set up for speakers and guests, and it was the largest room at the convention. Hundreds of people crammed into it. At the front, on a raised stage, were two large chairs, facing one another. Behind the chairs were projected images from the *Malicarn* films.

"Now if you direct your attention to the main stage . . ." The voice introduced some studio official, a diminutive man who spoke softly. He droned on about the importance of *The Malicarn* and how excited he was about upcoming projects. Nobody listened to him.

"The schedule for the meet and greet is still the same, though," Roger whispered to Lilly. "So we actually have more time than we thought."

"You sure? Don't you think you should double-check that too?"

The official introduced a celebrity journalist with a popular video blog, then left the stage. The journalist, a man named Bob Pickering, worked the room with jokes and hype. Then he pointed at the crowd and began to shout. "Now, are you ready to learn 'the Secrets of the Malicarn'? Well, put your hands together for the most famous wizard of all time!"

The crowd roared.

"Ladies and gentlemen, the Great Gregorian himself: Glenn Mackey!"

From stage left emerged a tall, thin, balding man, with a short, messy beard, dressed in a blue suit. He waved and smiled at the crowd, then sat in a chair opposite Pickering. Lilly was shocked at how old he had become.

2.

The woman in the row behind Glenn took three selfies before she got one that didn't crop out his face. The furtive scurrying of fans toward the first-class cabin started up again now that the plane was in the air, but after the woman's photo Glenn placed his headphones on and squinted at his laptop, hoping to ignore them by playing the part of a man in deep concentration.

Glenn's inbox was all notes of fury and despair. He read the ones from Jules first.

We need to do something about the lack of progress with Maximus. Search for lost dwarf kingdom???

More info coming soon on logistics with the planned pestilence. Will make major appearance.

The sons of Ravela continue to be the center of the next arc, so we ought to introduce them to the queen soon. ASAP if possible. For their benefit, not Hannah's.

Jules's emails were always short messages, written down in haste and sent without much thought. Notes for future discussion.

The other emails, from Larry or an executive or a journalist fishing for sources, were even more direct. The entire set had been on high alert since that morning, when some intern flagged a shot of a man running through the woods, and a producer noticed that the man was the missing Chinese pilot. So he wasn't floating dead somewhere in the Atlantic. He was alive in the Malicarn. Glenn had just arrived at his layover when the news broke, and he decided to put off reading those emails as long as possible.

It didn't have anything to do with him, he reminded himself. If Jules knew, that's on Jules. They'll find the pilot soon enough. It's a good thing, isn't it? He's not dead. The Chinese will be happy. Everything's fine.

An email from Larry's boss's boss, a former White House press secretary: "I'm told the president is fielding calls from the Chinese general secretary. This could blow up real fast, why isn't anyone briefing senior execs?"

Nothing to do with me, Glenn thought.

He looked out the plane's window. The view below was cloaked by a thick blanket of cloud cover. It was the third time this year he left the set, but the first time he was going to the United States. He hadn't been back since attending the Emmys three years earlier, another compulsory publicity event. His first flight that morning, an early charter from Funchal to Atlanta, was choppier, so even with the fans bothering him he preferred this commercial flight. Flying commercial took longer, however, and once they landed he would not have much time to rest.

Two days of my life for this, Glenn thought. He refreshed his emails and looked over them again. Jules hadn't responded about the pilot. Instead, he was complaining about the Madeiran teenagers who lately had been vandalizing the set. "Need to liaise with local police ASAP." But Jules had long ago alienated the locals. Meanwhile, there were several additional panicked emails from the studio. Glenn tried not to worry about it, it really wasn't his problem, though he wasn't sure how the Malicarn population would act if they discovered that the "dragon rider" was real and alive. Ideally Jules would institute some measures to tamp down on the rising tide of anger in the commons. Some extra food would go a long way. At least Hannah was smart enough to leave for the Mountain Keep. She was clever. It would serve her well, once her character came of age.

The plane landed on a large floating tarmac and disembarked

into a busy terminal, where Glenn spent several minutes taking pictures and signing autographs for the excited crowds that formed around him. Eventually he made it to the helicopter gate, where he was the only passenger for a brief ride from the airport to the large red hotel hovering over the water in the east. The other passengers would have to travel by ferry.

A concierge met him on the hotel's roof helipad, where Glenn's bags were taken and he was led to his room, a few floors below the convention hall. His room was a large, comfortable suite. Sterile, yes, but quiet. But before Glenn could fall asleep there was a knock at the door. He opened it to find one of the convention producers.

"I'm very sorry, Mr. Mackey, but it appears there's been a change in the schedule and now your interview is moved up to eleven."

Glenn sighed. "That's fine. I'll be ready in a minute."

Fifteen minutes and a quick shower later, Glenn was back out in the hallway, some intern leading him to a service elevator and up to the convention hall. He fiddled with his tie. His suit was tight and uncomfortable. Glenn rubbed his eyes and tried to remember who he was speaking to, and about what. It didn't really matter.

In the wings of the main stage, someone applied stage makeup to Glenn as Bob Pickering walked up and shook his hand, made a ribald joke, and then bounded out to the stage to introduce the session. Another intern clipped a mic to Glenn's shirt as he watched Bob pace under the bright stage lights.

Showtime, thought Glenn.

"Now, are you ready to meet the most famous wizard in the history of the Malicarn?" Bob shouted to the crowd. "Ladies and gentlemen, the Great Gregorian himself: Glenn Mackey!"

Glenn walked out, waving at the large, cheering crowd, then shook hands again with Bob before sitting in one of the chairs in the center of the stage.

The cheering eventually died down. "Thanks for joining us,"

Bob said, as if Glenn had done him a personal favor. "So you've been playing this role on the live Malicarn set for almost twenty years now. That's incredible."

"Thank you," Glenn said. "Nineteen years next month." He wasn't sure what he was thanking Pickering for.

"What are some of the things which have changed in those years? What's different now from when you started?"

"Well," Glenn said, "the structure is different. In the early years everything we did was really in purpose to an ongoing story. That first live-set film, *The Return of the Council*, was very planned out. Now the films are much more improvisational. We find them in the editing. It means that day-to-day life on set feels more chaotic, but also more lived in. Most days people are just going about their lives."

"You say 'people,' but you mean the memory-scanned characters?"

"Well, yes. But most of these characters have been on set now for nearly two decades. So they are pretty well integrated. And there's a whole generation of children and young adults who've grown up on the live set."

Pickering, the good PR fluffer that he was, did not interrogate the longevity of the scanned characters, all of whose contracts technically expired years ago but were extended after Lilly's arson through legal chicanery that Glenn decided was better for him, intellectually and ethically, not to understand.

Pickering looked out toward the audience as he asked the next question. "Now, this is an interesting concept. Because these younger characters aren't prewritten. You have to interact with them in unexpected ways, right?"

"That's true. The most recent film, the Bariol solo picture, was built around his relationship with a group of orphans. The orphans' parents were all scanned, but the children aren't."

The whole conversation was short, less than thirty minutes, and almost immediately after it was over Glenn could no longer remember much about it. He took some audience questions, waved again at the crowd, and exited stage left. The convention producer was waiting for him.

"Because we moved up the interview, you have a few hours before the autograph booth."

"Great," Glenn said. "I could use a nap."

A different intern accompanied him to the service elevator, and by the time Glenn made it back to his suite, he was so happy to be alone to rest that he didn't notice the window was open. It wasn't until he was in the bedroom and one of them spoke that Glenn saw the two other people waiting for him.

"Hello, Glenn."

Her voice was the same: dusky and serious, though wearier than it once was. When he turned, he noticed her hair was shorter, the lines under her eyes deeper, but she looked more like his memories than he could have hoped.

"Lilly?" Glenn asked. "You're here? What's—what's going on?"

Next to her stood a tall, dark-haired man with a scowl on his face.

"You better sit down," the strange man said. "We're going to have a conversation."

Glenn leaned back on the bed, and it was only then he noticed that the man was holding a gun.

3.

Glenn's conversation with Bob Pickering was vapid and inconsequential. A few preprepared questions were asked by attendees in Hall B.

Glenn answered one about future storylines with some empty platitude. He was surprisingly soft-spoken, Lilly thought, and clearly a little uncomfortable. Perhaps he wasn't used to being out in front of so many people, away from the false anonymity of the set, or perhaps he was just a coward. Lilly suspected the latter.

Bob Pickering announced that the session was over and that

a special meet-and-greet line for Glenn would be available that afternoon, for the low fee of two thousand dollars a person.

"Let's go," Roger said, and they stood up and made for the back of the theater. They were in the lobby ahead of the crush. Roger grabbed Lilly's hand and pulled her close, a little too comfortably. But he wasn't paying attention to her. He was looking for the left maintenance corridor, the one obscured from security cameras. Lilly and Roger ducked through the mass of people, slipping past the door when the crowd was at its thickest. They walked down the hallway, a member of the catering staff rushing past them without a thought. Lilly and Roger dipped through another door and then another—third left, second right—arriving finally in a small storage room filled with foldable tables and chairs.

The room was empty. This had been no guarantee, only an assumption that the crowds in the hall and the lunch rush would mean no new tables needed to be set up. The window was right where Roger's architectural plans said it would be, in the southwest corner. It was bolted shut, and Roger opened up his watch face and removed a small foldable screwdriver.

"They sell those at the MI6 gift shop?" Lilly asked.

He ignored her and quickly unhooked the screws and smacked the edge of the window frame until it popped out. The ocean breeze blew into the room, and Lilly pulled from the lining of her backpack a pair of leather gloves with nonstick palms.

They both tucked their pant legs into their shoes, stuffed their jackets and bags behind a pile of folded tables where they couldn't be seen, then crawled through the window. A sloping ledge was immediately outside, about two meters long, and Lilly rested herself on the edge of it as Roger reached back through, pulled the glass up, and rested it back in the frame. He pulled on the window just enough to jam it back in.

"Is this really the easiest way you could find?" Lilly asked.

Roger looked down at his watch. "We have about two minutes," he said. If he could have blasted action-movie music he would have.

They climbed down the side of the building. Because of its pyramid shape, each drop from one level of the hotel to the next was only about ten feet, followed by another two or three yards of sloping rooftop. Lilly guided herself down with her gloves, trying not to think about slipping down the incline and into the water below.

When Roger first came to visit her, Lilly said nothing about Glenn. Roger didn't force her to talk but she knew she didn't really have a choice. She sat on her couch while he paced around, fielding his endless questions. She told him everything. Her career, her work in the Malicarn, tech specs and protocols, what she did to destroy the technology, and how she escaped. They talked about neuroscanners, the implementation process, even the science behind the scanning.

"So there were twelve neuroscanners on-site, correct?"

"Only eight were operational by the end. They were always glitching."

"And you destroyed eleven of them?"

"Yes, one was missing."

"Where was it?"

"I don't know. One of the writers borrowed it."

"Jules Walker?"

"Yes, I believe it was him."

"Does he have it still?"

"I don't know."

"Who would know?"

The only thing she kept private was her relationship with Glenn. When she mentioned him at all it was only in passing, another figure among the many she used to work beside. Lilly didn't owe Glenn anything. What was Glenn doing, what was he thinking, year after year, working for those people, putting on the same old farce? Lilly didn't have to protect him.

"I know who to contact on the inside," Lilly said. "Find Brian

Doyle. He's one of the actors. A Real. He plays Kreek, a swordsman and trainer. He's been there a long time. He might know."

"Yes, I am aware of Brian Doyle. You think he knows about the neuroscanner?" Roger puffed on his pipe as he spoke. Lilly had to open a window to let the smoke out.

"Yes, I believe so," Lilly said, but she was not sure if she did.

"What about Glenn Mackey?"

"Oh, yes, well, I suppose he might know something too."

Roger smirked and nodded.

Lilly did not miss Glenn, did not miss his indecisiveness and lack of strong opinions about anything. There was not a nostalgic romantic spark she hoped to rekindle, certainly not since Glenn had clearly taken no action in the years since she left to change the Malicarn in any way. What Lilly did do, however, was wonder. Wonder if Glenn ever thought about her, about what had happened, about how things had changed and how they might change again. Lilly had spent a short but momentous period of her life tied to a man who had never once thought anything important, and in the years since she had become a person of little significance herself. She was like Gregorian, bereft of magic or purpose and wandering a world where she was no longer needed. So she wondered if perhaps, somewhere on an island in the middle of the ocean, Glenn had spent the ensuing years finding something, anything, inside himself that mattered even a little bit.

But Roger, still smirking, wasn't going to let Lilly off so easily.

"Brian Doyle is a dead end. I looked into it. He doesn't leave the island anymore. Not a single press event in twelve years. But Glenn Mackey travels all the time. I'm sure he'll want to talk to you."

"Talk to me? Why?"

"Because you used to fuck each other."

Lilly couldn't deny it. Roger produced photographs of the two of them, some from a premiere or a press event, some from Glenn's old social accounts, which while not updated often did include several pictures of the two of them camping or hanging out with Jules in one of their apartments.

"Here's how I see it," said Roger, "which is that you are hiding because of what you did to undermine the neuroscanning program for the studio. There's a lot of back chatter on this, and I've pieced together a pretty clear timeline. You destroyed the laboratory—*arson* is the word I've heard used—in January 2044, then found some way to smuggle yourself off the island. You arrived in England that same year. You have never left, even when your already questionably obtained visa expired. You've kept yourself anonymous, but you don't want to go to the United States, not even to visit your mother."

Lilly said nothing.

"Well, it doesn't matter. Your mother is dead. Did you know that?"

"No."

"Yeah, who would have contacted you? Who could have? Right, nobody? Now what I can't figure out exactly is why you are hanging out with these nerds who are obsessed with the characters you used to create. Guilt? Perversion? I don't know, I don't really care. But I do need you to help me."

"I've told you everything I know."

"Not really. You didn't tell me about Glenn. But that's okay. Now you can help me talk to him. It would be a shame if your visa became an issue."

Roger wanted the neuroscanner. To what end, Lilly wasn't sure. Not to use it, she divined that much. But he seemed to think Glenn could help him get it, and Lilly would help him get Glenn.

That was how Lilly found herself poring over stolen schematics and preparing to climb down the outside of a hotel that rose a hundred feet above the sea. Roger forced Lilly to go with him. He suspected no one else would be quite as effective in interrogating Glenn. He arranged her travel and gave her a phone, reminding her that it was important to maintain constant communication and that running away would not, at this juncture, be in her best interest.

The Miami Comic-Con was their best chance, but it was also a busy, high-profile affair. The plans were clear: The VIP suite was exactly ten floors below the conference center, and exactly right beneath the window in the southeast corner of the surplus storage room. One of Roger's contacts confirmed that the VIP suite would be housing the special guest, a secret *Malicarn* star being flown in for the weekend, and Roger's agent estimated that the average time a person could travel from the stage in Hall B to the VIP suite, assuming some delay for security protocols, was just under three minutes.

Roger didn't want to leave earlier and risk walking in on a housekeeper. He also wanted to visually identify Glenn himself first. "That's what old-timers would do," he said to Lilly the night in London he came over to lay out the details of his little operation.

"Why aren't we meeting at your office?" Lilly asked.

Roger gave a rambling response about how this operation was off-book, how he had to travel quickly so as not to raise any red flags, but don't worry it's all on the level and Head Office will really appreciate everything you're doing in the end, and Lilly suddenly realized that she was once again at the mercy of an idiot.

Roger procured fake passports, transportation, a little bit of money. Lilly thought her cover persona—Penny, a computer systems analyst who grew up in Toronto—was lazy, but she certainly wasn't interested in traveling to the United States under her real name, in the event someone from the studio was still on the lookout for her.

It took sixty seconds for them to climb down ten floors, ten seconds for Roger to use a pick—also hidden in his watch—to pop the window, and ten more for both of them to slide inside. Roger forgot to shut the window and they both crossed the large living room and waited in the bedroom. Twenty seconds later the door opened. Roger took out his gun.

They heard the door close, and a man let out a long sigh before walking into the bedroom.

"Hello, Glenn," Lilly said.

He turned and saw her, his face blank, almost without expression. That was the Glenn she remembered.

"Lilly?" Glenn asked, after staring at her for an obnoxiously long time. "You're here? What's—what's going on?"

"You better sit down," Roger said. "We're going to have a conversation."

Glenn sat on the bed, his blankness turning to anxiety and eventually alarm. Roger walked to the other side of the room and Lilly sat on the far side of the bed, facing Glenn.

"We're not going to tie you up or anything," Roger said. "Technically you're free to go. *If* you can go anywhere."

Glenn rocked on the mattress. "What do you want?"

"First of all, nice to meet you," Roger said. "I'm Roger, you know Lilly." He waved. Lilly did not move.

"The convention security will find you. If you think you can ransom me or—"

"Oh, don't think so highly of yourself," Roger said. "We'll be gone in about twenty minutes, if you cooperate. More than enough time to take a nap before you sign autographs."

"Okay, that's enough, Roger," Lilly said. "We don't have time for this. Glenn, where is the neuroscanner?"

"What?"

"The neuroscanner? When I left the Malicarn, I told you one neuroscanner remained. Do you know what happened to it?"

Glenn looked back and forth between the two of them. "I don't understand."

"Jesus, Glenn," Lilly shouted. "Roger is with British Intelligence. MI6."

"Like James Bond," said Roger.

"He thinks the neuroscanner still exists and he wants to find it."

"I'm just, I'm confused," Glenn said. "But you . . . you're okay? They didn't hurt you? Where have you—"

"Glenn, goddamnit, what do you know?" Lilly shouted, surprising herself. His passivity still angered her. Whatever pity she felt for Glenn onscreen or onstage was gone.

"But you're all right?" Glenn asked.

"She's fine," Roger said. "She's living her best life, or something."

"You made her do this?"

Roger groaned. "I thought you would be really vain, but not dim."

"Glenn," Lilly said. "If you tell us what we need to know, I'll tell you everything."

Glenn nodded but didn't speak for several seconds. "I know where the neuroscanner is. It's still in the Malicarn. It even works. Jules uses it, all the time, but he's kept it secret."

"What does he do with it?" Roger asked.

"He writes scripts. He's been using it to help him write for years."

"He has a machine that can remake minds," Roger asked, "and he uses it write scripts?"

"Yeah, he's a writer. That's what he does."

"Where's Jules usually at?" Roger asked. "Does he travel with the scanner around the island?"

"No, not at all. He hardly goes anywhere. He's mostly in the writers' room at the Citadel. That's the administration building. He doesn't leave for meetings, anything."

"Do you ever use the scanner?" Roger asked.

"Of course not. I try to stay away from the Citadel as much as I can. It's always a bit dramatic there. The pilot is only making things worse."

"The what?"

"The Chinese pilot? You're British Intelligence, I thought maybe you knew."

Roger did not, and after Glenn filled them in, Roger left the bedroom to make a phone call. He was giddy. Lilly and Glenn were left alone.

"Lilly, I just need you to know," Glenn said, "that the queen is safe. Don't worry, I kept her safe."

"The fuck do I care if she's safe?"

"I just . . . I tried."

Lilly couldn't think of any possible response that wasn't filled with curses before Roger came back. "All right, well now who's laughing at Roger Pendleton, right? This is big, this really turns the entire operation up a notch. There's not even time for them to ream me out before we deploy."

"Roger, what are you talking about?"

"The Portuguese are already sitting offshore of Madeira with two battleships. They have two tanks in Funchal, a couple of companies of marines, and an air force helicopter. A Black Hawk! A big one! They've been ready to invade their own territory for over a month to extract the pilot, which they seem to have known was there all this time. Evidently the Americans know all about the pilot, too, so the Portuguese are ready to go in. My colleague in Lisbon tells me he can get me onto the helicopter in exchange for whatever intelligence I have about the pilot's location. You can get that for me, right Glenn? They want to get in and out, avoid a mess. And while they're nabbing him, I go in on the chopper, get the neuroscanner. How about that, eh? Head Office can't stop me now."

Glenn nodded, trying to seem enthusiastic. "Yes, yes. I could probably find the pilot, if I could see the feeds. The camera feeds. Jules doesn't like me watching them anymore, because it makes the story fresher, or something."

"So I really need to talk to Jules, not this chump."

"Oh, please don't kill me!"

"He's not going to kill you," Lilly said. "You don't really know anything."

Glenn looked at her, but there was no way for her to read his face, to understand what he wanted. Did he want to leave the Malicarn? Maybe not. Maybe he was happy being a wizard and running that little kingdom. Maybe he wanted nothing at all.

"I can help you get onto set," he said.

"I don't need you," Roger said. "The Portuguese will let me do whatever I want."

"But Jules will see you coming. If he knows you're coming for the neuroscanner, he'll destroy it, or blow himself up, or something, and you won't have it. He's not right in the head."

"Why should we trust you?" asked Lilly.

"Because, Lilly . . . because I'm not a bad person."

"Now, listen," Roger said, moving back to the foot of the bed, totally uninterested in this, "we're going to leave you here in your hotel room and then you will go back to the Comic-Con. But if we let you do that, are you going to snitch on us?"

"No, of course not! I really can help. I can get the neuroscanner, it'll be easy for me to take it. And I can find out where the pilot is. Then I can meet you. I know a spot. It's a meadow on the northeast end of the set. The river runs half a mile or so east of it. There used to be a gas station there. They demolished it but the land is all poisoned or something, and there's no grass. You can still see the concrete slabs where the station used to be. They don't ever do scenes there because it looks too modern, so there's no cameras. It's a day's walk from the Old Village, and it's usually deserted. It's about as far northeast as you can go before you leave the set. In and out, right?"

"You can get there?" Lilly asked. "With the neuroscanner?"

"Yes."

Lilly looked at Roger. "And you could meet him there? Would that be hard?"

Roger shrugged. "Not particularly. Quick is good. I don't care what Jules or anyone else does after we leave. Frankly, for my purposes I don't even care if the Portuguese rescue the pilot or not, long as they think I helped them. You fly back tomorrow, right? Can you be at the spot in two days?"

"Two days? That's not much time, I—"

"Two days," Roger said. "Dawn. I can hold the op off until then but no longer. If you're not there I'm going to assume you've snitched."

Glenn nodded, trying not to shake too much. "You'll be there, right Lilly?"

"What? I don't think—"

"Do you not trust me?" Roger asked. "Is it going to be a problem?"

"I don't know," Glenn said. "Are you holding her? Is she your prisoner?"

Roger sighed. "She'll be there, if it means you cooperate."

"Wait, what?" Lilly asked. "Roger, I—"

"You'll be there, goddamnit. Now let's go, and let's all hope this pilot isn't killed before we arrive."

Lilly stood up, but Glenn reached out and grabbed her hand.

"Lilly, please, I need more time."

She pulled her hand away. "I asked you to destroy it and you never did. You've done this to yourself. Get the neuroscanner, meet us in two days, and then we'll talk."

"At dawn," Roger said. "We'll fly in under cover of darkness. It'll be fun!"

Glenn opened his mouth to plead something more, but Lilly turned and walked away before he could speak.

Ten minutes later, Roger and Lilly had climbed back up to the storage room, had packed away their gear, and were mingling once again in the main convention lobby. They split up and went back to their own rooms. Lilly didn't see Roger again until that afternoon, when they climbed aboard the ferryboat taking them to the airport. Lilly stood at the bow of the ship, watching the hotel shrink into the distance. Behind it, a faraway shore was smoking with rubble and debris.

"Sorry to volunteer you." It was Roger, who appeared suddenly beside her, leaning over the ship's railing. "But there's not much time to set up this op. We'll have to fly straight to Lisbon, and the Portuguese navy will get us onto their ships. Plus, you know the terrain. Useful, on-the-ground intel. We'll pay you, if that's what you want."

"I don't care about that. I didn't want to go back there, to that place."

"It'll be fast. You can tell people you're a secret agent now."

"I don't want that. I don't want anything else."

Roger shrugged. "Well, we'll pay you anyway. Makes me feel better when I don't owe you anything." He pulled out a pipe, loaded it with tobacco, and lit it. Then he chuckled. "You didn't tell me he was so gullible, though. I wish I could get more people to do what I want by making them think I'm going to screw them."

"You're a fucking asshole, Roger." Lilly turned and walked into the ferry's cabin, where she ordered a gin and tonic from the bar and decided not to watch the horizons shrink away behind her anymore.

CURRAL DAS FREIRAS, MADEIRA

April 4, 2060

Many years later a journalist would ask Major Wu Zihao how it felt to be a hero, but Zihao thought the question was based on a false premise. "I am not a hero," he would say, "I just did my duty." It wasn't humility or false modesty on his part. A hero has to take action. Zihao had only followed orders. Zihao only ever did exactly what he was ordered to do, nothing more and certainly nothing less. He was ordered to fly a sortie over the eastern Atlantic, he was ordered to photograph the French fleet, he was ordered to ditch his plane in case of mechanical failure, and in the event of capture he was ordered to wait for his superiors to handle the negotiations of his release.

He didn't have any orders for or against learning new skills while in captivity, however, and so Zihao was pleased that his English was improving even though he still had trouble understanding the new guard's accent. This guard talked slower, but with a sort of lisp that forced Zihao to concentrate longer on each syllable. He explained he was "An outsider, not Malicarn," and that English wasn't his first language, either. His name was Afonso, but the other guard kept calling him "Alfonso." Even Zihao knew this was wrong.

The other guard's name was Wallace. He had watched Zihao many times. "More and more of them like Alfonso's going to help us," Wallace said to Zihao when Afonso showed up, the day after Zihao's failed escape attempt. "Kreek finds them. He knows all sorts of folk."

Wallace was a talkative man, though Zihao couldn't understand half of what he said. It wasn't because of the language barrier, but rather was because Wallace talked mostly nonsense. He and his friend Buck had both talked lots of nonsense when Zihao was in the granary tower, but since his recapture Zihao hadn't seen Buck at all and only Wallace was left to talk and talk and talk.

"Kreek's pretty sure soon it will be time soon to get you out of here, don't worry on it. He's quite sure of it, oh yes, what with the anger and all. Lots of anger, they're all saying. The Queen ran away, people are mad. Now there'll be magic coming back, yes, because of the dragon. You must have lots of dragons, where you're from. These other fellas from outside the Malicarn don't have dragons."

"No dragons," Afonso said. "We have planes, I explained to you." He and Wallace had stood guard over Zihao in the granary all night. They had rifles with them now, not just swords, and Wallace liked to hold his with both hands. Afonso kept his slung across his back. Outside it was raining hard.

"Yes," Wallace said, "you have many great things." He looked at Zihao. "Alfonso showed me his, what you call it, phone, yes? Phone. He's no wizard, neither. See, outside the Malicarn, magic's just all over the place. You know this, right?"

Afonso sighed. "It is not magic, Wallace."

"You speak another language. In the Malicarn it's magic."

Whatever was going on, Zihao could tell there were multiple factions and agendas and it all seemed rather political. Zihao wasn't political, or at least tried not to be. He had heard enough stories about politics to know it wasn't for him. Before he died, his grandfather used to whisper sad stories to Zihao about Tiananmen. Stories where people suffered and his grandfather carried guilt about what he should have done instead. Zihao didn't want that, so he joined the air force. He could take orders. *That* was easy. Orders meant you didn't have to be political, you just had to do what you were told. Simple enough. Stand straight, shine your shoes, salute your commanding officer. Attend briefings, fly your route, land where you were told.

Zihao knew that Afonso wasn't one of these brainwashed movie characters, and once Afonso began to use his phone to translate, they spoke easier to one another.

"We're not with the Portuguese government," Afonso said. "Fuck them. They took our homes away from us."

"But there's got to be someone coming for me?"

"Probably, I don't know. I'm part of the Madeira Resistance. We're going to help these Malicarn rebels throw down the studio shitheads in charge, and then we can have our island back."

"Who were the other people? They helped me when I tried to escape hid me in their home."

"There's lots of people in the Malicarn trying to do what we're doing. Doyle's probably coordinating with all of them."

"Doyle?"

"The guy Wallace calls Kreek. He's leading the rebels."

"What are they going to do to me?"

"I don't know. Sorry, bud, I don't much care."

Afonso was young. A boy, a child really. Zihao tried to explain that he was a father, he had a wife, but no one listened.

It was a stupid thing, stalling out like he did. He knew better. He shouldn't have been climbing his aircraft so steeply. But then he shouldn't have been doing a low pass over those French cruisers in the first place. They weren't going to shoot him down, they were probably just messing with him, warning him. Or maybe they thought he was a drone—that was what Zihao would have thought. Anyway, he got out of there quick, stalled on the ascent, and didn't bail out in time. Fortunately, or so he thought, there was land ahead. An island. Pretty rocky, but he found a patch, hard-landed the plane, and made it out before the flames consumed him.

It took Zihao another couple of days before he realized his rescuers were, in fact, his captors and that they seemed to have no idea who he was. It was a few more days after that when he remembered a series of films he once watched on bootlegged DVDs, the films themselves never released in China. Bad American fantasy films, the kind he'd been watching in various formats for a long time. And then he remembered the reason they were banned, because the Americans had created the fantasy world in real life. The Party said they were "dangerous propaganda, about Americans twisting people's minds." Zihao had a good laugh at this, but when he realized he *was* in the fantasy world, he began to get nervous. Why was no one coming to save him? After so many months, maybe nobody could.

"Where is your friend?" Zihao asked Wallace.

"Wow, you're learnin' to speak real good."

"Yes. And your friend?"

"Oh, you mean Buck? I dunno. Kreek's pretty mad at him. He's the one let you get away, you know. The Guild's kicking him out. Too bad. He's a nice guy. Want an apple?"

When the rain stopped, the other men outside who had been watching the granary, friends of Wallace and outsiders like Afonso, were practicing shooting. Zihao could hear them, training on their new guns in the predawn hours. The outsiders were teaching the Malicarn men, who had never seen guns before.

Zihao was already thinking about his next escape. Afonso's phone was the obvious solution. He could make contact with someone. Send an email, a text, something. Afonso wasn't very careful with where he kept his phone, always leaving it about. Surely, Zihao could distract him, steal the phone. He didn't need it for long. Just to get word out, to get—

"Time to go." Kreek, or Doyle, or whoever he was, stood at the top of the stairs. Zihao hadn't seen him since the escape attempt. "The hour is upon us."

Wallace bound Zihao's hands behind him in a rope. "Just for now, just for now," he whispered. Afonso made a phone call, speaking excitedly to someone in Portuguese.

"What now?" Zihao asked Kreek. He wanted to ask what he was planning on doing with him, but Zihao didn't have the words.

"Now you help us become free."

They carried him outside, where a carriage was waiting for them. Kreek and Zihao climbed aboard, and they began to roll away. It was still dark out, but the dawn was creeping over the treetops. Zihao smelled smoke in the distance.

They rode all morning. Men and women emerged from huts and cottages, cheering them on, joining in a march beside and behind. They wept when they saw Zihao, reaching hands toward him, shouting, "Magic! The rider! Magic!" They handed Zihao bread they had baked, fruits and vegetables, pints of beer. They threw flowers onto the cart and in front of the horses' tread. They sang and danced as the carriage rolled forward.

By early afternoon they arrived at a walled city. Stretching around in front of the wall on all sides were hundreds of people living in tents on the ground. Within the city Zihao could see many tall buildings and, in the center, a castle. The gates of the city were opened wide, and the carriage rode inside, flanked by adoring, desperate crowds on all sides. Every street was thronged with people weeping for joy.

In front of the castle gates, still shut, the carriage stopped. Kreek stood up and stretched his arms out toward the square in front of him.

"People of the Malicarn! You have asked, and I have answered! Behold, the harbinger of your deliverance! A man of great magic: the dragon rider!" He gestured to Zihao, who clumsily stood up and looked out at the sea of faces before him. He did not know what to do, so he bowed slightly. The crowd quaked with jubilant fury.

"Now," continued Kreek, "we will enter the castle and take back what is ours! Bring forth the Goblin Queen!"

"Kreek, stop this madness!" A man stood on top of the castle walls, flanked by several knights. "You have sworn fealty to the Crown!"

"Oh, Bariol," Kreek said, turning to the man, "how far you have fallen. You were once a mighty hero."

"And you were a great man, but no longer."

"Where is the queen?"

"Far from you. Kreek, do you remember what you told the Council of Heroes, once? To never turn your fear to hatred?"

"Yes, and I do wish you had remembered that lesson." Kreek nodded at Wallace, who raised his rifle and shot Bariol in the chest. The old knight collapsed. The mob's anger boiled over and they rushed the castle gates. Kreek smiled.

Zihao was not a political man, but he thought again of his grandfather and another whispered story, about the Cultural Revolution. His grandfather was a small child then, but he remembered standing in the crowds, yelling at the traitors paraded in front of them. Cheering when they were executed.

"Why were they killed?" Zihao asked him once. "What did they do?"

"I do not remember," his grandfather said. "But we all imagined it was for something bad."

THE MALICARN

THE FINAL DAY OF THE REIGN OF QUEEN HANNAH I (MADEIRA—APRIL 4, 2060)

The Revolution of the Malicarn, as they would eventually call it on film and in canon and even in actual history books, was a mass, voluntary uprising of the people. It was a coordinated strategy of the filmmakers to shake things up. It was a subversive campaign by the Portuguese government tired of sharing the sovereignty of their land. It was a mob of dissolute Madeiran youths who hated their parents and their teachers and any authority whatsoever. It was a false flag orchestrated by the Americans. It was a fake war shot on soundstages in Burbank.

When it started, Glenn Mackey was across the ocean, in a Miami hotel signing autographs. Glenn worked his way through his second meet-and-greet session in as many days in a haze, eager smiles pushing at him a host of paraphernalia. Posters and comic books and action figure boxes and copies of the original *Malicarn* novels. He signed people's arms and chests. He signed photos and T-shirts. He took pictures with fans young and old, a few squeezing their arms around him very, very tight. He remained gracious and pleasant, answering stock questions ("What's your favorite *Malicarn* film?") with stock answers ("Probably *The Return of the Council*, since that was our first one on the live set"). After nearly two hours he finished and was escorted back to his hotel room.

In Kingstown, the remainder of the Council of Heroes assembled and pledged to fight off the rioters who had occupied the castle courtyard. They marched out of the tower and at once were overrun by the angry mob. Their throats were slashed and their bodies hung above the castle walls. Glenn packed his suitcase and took a private helicopter to his chartered plane.

Coincidence, in Glenn's opinion, was very lazy. He didn't like it in a play when two characters who needed to meet just happened to do so under strange circumstances. How many times did Shakespeare pull off that trick? The comedies did it all the time. The whole finale of *Romeo and Juliet* was built on just such a horrifying coincidence. He didn't care for it even in *The Tempest*, where at least the Duke ending up on Prospero's island could be explained away by magic. No, coincidence meant that the writer needed to work on another draft.

So the fact that the day they had discovered the Chinese pilot was the same day Lilly showed back up in his life made Glenn nervous. Was this Roger person really with MI6? Was this just some elaborate part of Jules's story plan? Did Lilly know? Was she compromised?

Lilly, angry and jet-lagged, did not consider this coincidence at all as she sat in the back of the briefing room on a Portuguese naval frigate. Roger stood next to a Portuguese colonel who filled in his marines about the unfolding political situation on Madeira—how the studio was losing control of the set, how the locals were assisting the rebelling characters in overthrowing the existing leadership. Lilly assumed that Jules was more than likely aware of and perhaps orchestrating the whole revolution. It would be a good story, and that was what Jules cared most about.

To Derek, one of the studio security guards waiting with a car at the Funchal airport, the chaos in the city streets reminded him of his years in the NYPD. He had seen this kind of lawlessness before, had cracked a few skulls in his time to keep it from escalating, and had taken his pension and left for a job on an island with the intention of never having to see this again. But everything is always the same shit, he thought, no matter where you go.

After Glenn's plane landed he met up with Derek, and as they drove out of the city Glenn tried to work out his plan of attack. He could go to the Citadel, make as if he was just checking in on Jules, and confirm the location of the neuroscanner. Who would doubt him? No one would question—

His train of thought was broken by a handful of fruit, which hit the side window of the car and burst open, pulp and juice sliding down the glass.

"Ide! Ide!" Derek shouted at the crowd harassing the car. "Sorry, sir, these protestors are getting worse."

"Ah, yeah, it's okay." Glenn had not noticed them.

As the car wound its way out of the city and up a mountain road toward set, Glenn finally concluded a big coincidence was the simplest explanation, however unsatisfying and emotionally manipulative that felt. Sometimes more than one important thing happened at once. It was only the promise of Lilly—of seeing her again, knowing she might be safe—that convinced him, or rather allowed him to convince himself, of Roger's true intent. If he was wrong about that, well, he would find out sooner or later.

Lilly thought about Glenn, too, but desperately tried not to. She was putting on a camouflage outfit, military issue but a size too big. She had a radio clipped to her belt and an earpiece in her ear. Roger was babbling on about protocols and rules of engagement and other stuff, and Lilly was thinking about what Glenn was going to look like, what he was going to say, what he was going to do. All she had to do was meet him, get the neuroscanner, and then she could leave. Right off the helicopter then right back on. She could leave the Malicarn forever and never see Glenn again, if that was what she wanted.

In Kingstown, the mob completely surrounded the north castle tower, still bolted shut. In the castle courtyard, they looted whatever they found. Weapons, food, horses. They smashed the royal menagerie and burned the stables. Inside the tower Sanderson and Quentin yelled at one another and tried to devise a means of escape. The cook and kitchen staff hid behind barrels of ale. Fennick the tutor collected as many books as he could in his arms. On the castle walls, commoners walked the perimeter, mooning and flashing those below for laughs. They made lewd gestures at the bodies of the Council heroes. Kreek deputized Wallace to lead the people inside the final tower, and then Kreek rode his carriage out of the city, the dragon rider still in back, waving at the adoring crowds as they made their way to another town, another village, to spread the revolution further.

Glenn asked Derek to drive toward the set's northwest entrance, which allowed them to travel the road with direct access to the Citadel. He could follow his plan, visit Jules, then get everything ready for that morning, when Roger would arrive. He could spend the rest of the evening at his apartment in the Old Village, come back that night to distract Jules, maybe get him drunk, then take the neuroscanner and meet Lilly at the rendezvous point.

The wind carried a cool breeze. Glenn should have packed a jacket. All he had on was a Philadelphia Eagles T-shirt. After the car pulled into the underground garage, Glenn left his luggage in a locker by the garage entrance. He left his phone with his luggage, too. Reception was always poor in the Citadel. But Glenn never was very good at thinking ahead.

Derek walked to the security office on the first floor. His coworker Paul sat in the chair, head in his hands.

"I don't know what the fuck to do. I can't get LA on the phone. No one upstairs is talking. Look at this shit."

He pointed to a screen showing the security feeds. Portuguese teens driving all over the set, running people down, setting fire to buildings. Rioting in Kingstown. The security teams were spread thin, all over the island.

"I can't get local police on the phone, I can't get anybody. Derek, what do we do?"

Roger's Black Hawk helicopter had an automatic machine gun. Not that he needed it, but it was nice to have. He was so eager to be in the air, the operation underway. His contact in

Funchal was reporting a sighting of the pilot. There were riots all over the studio-managed sectors, but their rendezvous spot was still clear. This would be easy, and it would be fun.

The Citadel was quiet now, because it was so understaffed. Glenn rode up the elevator past the old dorms, cafeterias, and conference rooms, all closed now. Most of the admin was offsite, housed in LA, and hardly anybody lived in the apartments. The old implementations lab was used for storage. The walls there were still charred from fire. By the time he arrived on the thirteenth floor, a single knight, large gash across his belly, stumbled to the topmost room of the highest tower in Kingstown and lit a beacon. An hour later, Sir Kellington noticed the mountain beacons burning from the Mountain Keep. Buck Douglas, covered in mud, woke from his hiding spot behind a rock and saw the beacons, too, but he did not know what they meant and continued his vigil of the keep.

Hannah did not yet know Kingstown had fallen, had not yet realized that the very end of her reign as queen had already begun, and though these portents of doom were increasingly concerning, she sent the royal stablemaster to ride back to Kingstown for news and then spent the afternoon reading the book of astronomy she had borrowed from the keep's librarian.

"Stars are pinpricks in the veil of Heaven," she read from the book, which was very old but heavily illustrated. "The whole Globe is surrounded by the protective blanket of darkness, within which circle the planets, the Sun, and the Moon. And in the center of all is the Earth itself. It is a system of perfect balance and symmetry."

Hannah already knew this was nonsense, but she liked the idea of a perfectly calibrated system with everything in its place because that's where it was supposed to be. The book was later burned with the rest of the keep.

On the thirteenth floor, Glenn entered a long white hallway with every other lightbulb burned out. The old writers' offices were empty. Even the reception desk acted as a repository for leftover packages and papers. Glenn saw one intern making copies. At the end of the hall was a large oak door. Behind it was the old writers' room, where in the early days a few dozen people would congregate and bat around story ideas, fleshing out arcs and discussing how to make them work in the live, improvisatory set they were building in the valley below. Now only one person sat there, and he hardly ever left.

Glenn knocked, though he did not expect an answer. When he didn't hear anything, he pushed the door open and walked through. The room was very dim, all the light coming off a dozen or so LED screens arranged in rows on the wall. Empty boxes, backpacks, and computer bags were stacked in the corner. At the table in the center sat several more monitors, keyboards to multiple machines, and a host of half-eaten snacks: chip bags, soda cans, used napkins.

Sitting in a large desk chair, his back to Glenn but facing the myriad screens, was Jules, bent over a keyboard. His long beard was a tangled mess, his eyes beady, face pale. He did not respond at first, but when Glenn walked toward him he suddenly jerked and removed something from his head. Glenn thought it might have been headphones.

"What, what?" Jules shouted, annoyed, his expression softening only slightly when he turned to see it was Glenn. "Oh, Gregorian. Hello. Do you have an appointment? Please check with Darla."

"Didn't Darla quit, like, five years ago?" Glenn asked.

Glenn sat down in another chair a few feet away and looked Jules over carefully. He was red-eyed and manic, his fingers tapping incessantly on the table in front of him. Jules's clothes were stained with food and sweat. His beard grew out in every direction. He looked like shit.

Jules smiled. "Yes, yes, of course. I forgot. I don't have a secretary anymore. Should probably get one, don't you think? They gave me an intern. Some kid from Dartmouth. Wants to be a *writer*. What nonsense! I told him to become an engineer instead. But he said he hates math. Well, too bad I guess! Hahahaha!" Jules laughed as if he were faking it.

"I just got back from the con," Glenn said, looking around the room. "It was a pretty good trip. Nice change of scenery at least."

"What, what?" Jules jumped, as if hearing Glenn for the first time.

"The Miami trip," Glenn said. "Remember?"

"No. How's Miami?"

"Different from when my grandmother used to live there."

"Nice to visit with her, eh?"

"What?" Glenn could never tell when Jules was actually listening to him. "No, Jules, she's been dead for years. Her condo's probably underwater by now, anyway."

"Why cry about it, then? Ha!" Jules didn't laugh, just shouted loudly.

"Are you all right?" Glenn looked up at the camera feeds. No sign of the pilot. There was a lot of activity going on, though, more than Glenn expected. He couldn't quite tell what was happening.

"Fine, fine. Look, I want to show you something." Jules pulled out a box from underneath the table. The neuroscanner. So at least Glenn knew where Jules was keeping it. "I've almost finished it, Gregorian. You know how long I've been working on it? It's loading now. Gonna take a few hours to render properly, but then I'll have it, finally. The complete digital re-creation of Jean-Danton Souard. Right here, in this scanner. And then I can understand him."

"Did you build a character on your own?"

"Not a character! Not a character, Glenngorian. No, it's a real approximation. It's everything ever written by, about, and in relation to Souard. Every word of his, every scrap of information anyone said about him. His son, his colleagues, random fans who met him. Plus everything he saw: Paris, the war, what Boston smelled like in the 1960s. It's all here!"

Several miles away, Buck Douglas watched a large spider climb a tree. As he waited for night to fall, he could smell fire.

"There's no way you captured everything," Glenn said.

"I captured everything we know, which is the same as everything! Once I scan myself with it—"

"I don't think that's a good idea."

"Once I scan myself with it, I'll be able to write a real story. I'll finally bring something to the Malicarn, something new. What Souard would have written."

Glenn wasn't going to have to get Jules drunk to distract him. He was so revved up Glenn wasn't sure Jules would realize a nuclear bomb going off on one of his screens.

"I really don't know, Jules. I think you are doing a fine job writing as it is."

"Rubbish! This whole revolutionary storyline is bonkers. Kreek's been running it all himself, basically. Didn't even ask permission. I let him do it, because I recognize opportunity. But I would have pushed it forward sooner. He has no sense of timing. No need to kill those guards, just release the rider and get on with it."

"He did what?"

"Moving now, though. The riots are on in Kingstown, probably in Old Village by this afternoon. You shouldn't go home for now, I need you for this next stage. See!" He pointed to a monitor. A large mob was marching up a road away from Kingstown. For the first time, Glenn looked at what was happening inside the Malicarn. "Those ones are probably heading for the Mountain Keep to grab the queen. When she's dead I'm going to need you to negotiate a peace, we can start over fresh."

"What are you talking about, Jules? What the hell is going on?"

Kreek and the dragon rider arrived at the Old Village. "Where is the wizard?" Kreek shouted. "Come forth and be counted!" The villagers surrounded Gregorian's tower and began banging on the door.

Wu Zihao was afraid, but he tried not to move. He did not know if he could run.

Roger and Lilly's Black Hawk took off from the battleship. It was loud and shook violently, and Lilly had to use all her willpower not to be sick. But that was all right. The motion sickness distracted her from thinking more about Glenn.

Derek and Paul used their radios to communicate with staff across the set. Production assistants, tech specialists, Cameroonian farmworkers. "If you can make it back to the Citadel, that seems to be the safest place right now. Hello? Hello?"

In Langley, Virginia, the director of the Central Intelligence Agency received an urgent cable from the Lisbon desk but he was leaving to play golf with the Senate Intelligence chair and so he didn't read it.

"We need a strong man as the hero," said Jules, "not a crippled girl. It's boring. And well, you know diversity casting doesn't really work."

"We didn't cast her, she was born."

"I know, I should have been more proactive about her mother's romance with Prion. Too bad. But she needs to go. She is such a *boring* character anyway, like her mother was. You know this, Glenn."

Glenn sat quietly for a long moment, watching Jules jitter in his chair. He saw a screen of the Old Village, of the library in his tower, overrun by characters. His servant had let them in. They were tossing furniture out the window. "Why did you let this happen, Jules?"

Jules sniffed the air and coughed. "Ah, gads," he shouted, and shuffled in his chair.

"This storyline can't keep going. Jules, listen to me, there's a—"

"Wait! Let me tell you about the guns! Listen to this! I just got a message last week, you know I really should write them back, but listen! New props! The studio thinks it is time to move the

Malicarn into a more modern mode. Progress is very compelling, they say! So, guess what we're going to get to use!"

Glenn shook his head and didn't say anything.

"Guess, guess!"

"Are they bringing back magic?"

"What? No, magic is banned. Come on, Glenn! We're getting gunpowder! Rifles! Cannons!"

Glenn looked into Jules's eyes, which were fluttering around as if unable to focus. "Why on earth are we—"

"Progress, Glenn, progress! Think of the story possibilities! They even gave me a rifle to use, to try out and think about ways I could incorporate it into stories. This is how the revolution ends, do you see it? Kreek's men are already using them. A new world! New tech!"

Jules was vibrating in excitement.

"But all these people. Hannah—"

"The queen is nothing!" Jules shouted. "She's a dead end! Let me do the writing, Glenn. You'll say the lines. They gave me a gun, and you'll get to use it too. How about I write it so that you invented it, eh? Some glory to an old wizard, yes? Ha! Of course!"

On the screens: People rioting, burning buildings. Pissing on the bodies of dead Council heroes. Lining up in formation for a march, like an army. He saw Hannah sitting in her room reading a book. A man chasing a monk with a sword.

"Jules, you can't. They're coming."

Jules's vision was fixed on his keyboard as he tapped away. "Who, what?"

"They're coming for the pilot. British Intelligence, the Portuguese navy. Real soldiers. People with real weapons. They'll be here tonight. You can't keep doing this."

Jules straightened up. His eyes were clear, and for the first time since Glenn entered the room, Jules was completely cogent.

"What did you do in Miami?"

"Nothing. They found me. They're going to come in here and rescue that pilot and stop this."

"The rider is part of the story now. They cannot have him."

"You've known where he was this whole time, haven't you? Jules, he's not a character, he's a person. Hannah's a person, too, they're all people."

"You never were committed to the project. Okay, fine. I can't protect you." Jules pressed a button on the intercom on the desk. "Please escort Mr. Mackey from the premises."

"Jules, don't do anything stupid. Just hand the pilot over when they get here."

"They want to come into my story and tell me how to write it? Well, this isn't a revolution anymore. This is a war."

Glenn looked at the neuroscanner, thought about jumping for it, but he wasn't sure of his next move. He wasn't going to fight Jules, that was ridiculous. Everything was ridiculous.

Derek and Paul entered the room. "What's the problem here. Glenn? Jules?"

"Escort him to his apartment," Jules said.

"It's real hairy up there. We've actually been telling all staff not go out on set."

"Do as I say!" Jules barked.

The guards grabbed Glenn and pulled him up. "Jules," Glenn said, "this is a mistake."

"No, it's just part of the story."

The guards pulled Glenn out to the elevator and down to the lobby. "Guys," Glenn pleaded. "You don't have to do this. Why are you scared?"

The guards stopped, looking cautiously at the security cameras in the empty lobby. "The other day they thought they found that Chinese pilot. Gene and Ken went to pick him up and never came back."

"Then let me go. Don't take me to the Old Village. Try to keep any of the characters from entering the Citadel. It'll be a few hours, but I'll be back with help."

"What about Jules?"

"The safest place for him is in that room. Keep him there. Don't let him talk to anyone else."

He had until dawn, when he was supposed to meet Lilly. The Mountain Keep was half a day south, if he was quick. He didn't have his phone, but he didn't have time. Rocky terrain, he'd have to walk. But he could be quick. He could get to her first.

Derek and Paul watched Glenn leave up a northern road. They waited for more staff to return to the Citadel, but nobody did.

"I'm taking the car back to the airport," Derek said. "Fuck this." And the two of them left.

As men and women pulled out bottles of Diet Coke and yogurt from Glenn's refrigerator, marveling at his appliances and electric lightning—anger rising more than ever, they had been cheated and deceived—Kreek continued on his journey with the dragon rider, taking the carriage through little hamlets and farms along the river. He made his way west, where he had told his new army to meet him.

Glenn still did not know what had happened within the realm, not entirely. But Lilly knew enough. As the sun set, she sat in the back of the helicopter, approaching the mountains of central Madeira, and she reflected on the colonel's intelligence briefing. Brian Doyle at some point forgot his name and place of birth and social security number and decided that Sir Kreek the Swordmaster's destiny was to free the Malicarn people of their oppression under the yoke of Wizard and Crown. Roger found the Revolution a convenient distraction for their operation, but Lilly thought he was underestimating Doyle's commitment.

A Madeiran teenager named Afonso turned his car around and began driving home when he saw the helicopter. A big one, like in the movies. He didn't realize there would be an army coming in.

Roger sat next to Lilly and relayed the intelligence he was getting from his contacts over the radio. It was confusing. No one knew what was happening. A dragon had been brought out and was being paraded around Malicarn villages. No, not a dragon. A man. "Do you mean the pilot?" Roger yelled into his radio. "Can you acknowledge you have confirmation about the pilot?"

The common man's anger over Gregorian and the queen's lies spilled over. They ransacked armories and burned churches and slit the throats of highborn knights. They organized into large mobs—not mobs, but militias, armies—and stormed castles and keeps from one end of the Malicarn to the other. They took their country back.

People weren't really mad about the dragon rider, though. They were mad about being poor and being sad and not understanding who they were or why. Lilly knew that a lot of them were mad, deep down somewhere, for still being stuck playacting as shepherds and innkeepers and millers, when they were really college dropouts or frustrated accountants from Montclair or aging romantics who taught high school and directed the spring musical. They were mad because the Malicarn was going to be an escape from their lives but there was no escaping your life.

Glenn snuck into the Mountain Keep through a false door the production department had installed when the place was first built. He raided a hidden prop closet, found a bottle of chloroform, and drugged the guard standing outside Hannah's room. He surprised the girl—she was wielding a knife, he should be more careful—but he convinced her to follow him. She was scared, more scared than he'd ever seen her before. As they snuck back out the production exit, Buck Douglas, sitting on his rock, saw them turn northward into the woods. He followed. He was going to be a hero.

Lilly's helicopter landed in the dark hours before dawn. The marines from Funchal, two tanks and a couple of jeeps, began their offensive into the interior of the island to extract the pilot. Lilly climbed out of the helicopter, Roger told her she had thirty minutes, and the chopper lifted off again and circled around behind a hill.

When she arrived at the old gas station, Lilly waited in the brush. She did not want to be here, again, in the Malicarn. It smelled the same, and she had a buzzing in her head that would not go away. The sooner Glenn got here, the sooner she could take the neuroscanner from him, call back the chopper, and leave.

On the other side of the mountain, an army of common men armed with spears and knives and torches broke down the gate to the Mountain Keep. Among them were members of the Wizarding Reenactors Guild. They ran inside, slashing and hacking at stable boys and chambermaids and Abbott the old librarian. The Queen's Guard ran to find the queen, but she had vanished. Sir Kellington jumped over the wall and ran into the woods, but the mob tortured the others, asking them to hand over the queen. When they didn't find her, they burned the keep down.

The tanks made their way out of the city, but immediately stopped when they realized that the road they were on led in the wrong direction. Roger could not get a clear link to their comms. Kreek and the dragon rider had ridden through the night, emerging in a large field. Hundreds of people followed behind him. Jasper and the underground waited for him, amassed in a uniform line.

Zihao woke up, sore from bouncing all night in the carriage, and recognized the field they had arrived at. It was the same field where he had crashed his plane.

The final tower of the castle in Kingstown was overrun. The mob threw Fennick from a high window. Sanderson and Quentin were dragged out, robes ripped and bloodied, then flung onto a hastily erected stage in the courtyard.

"Your charges," Wallace bellowed to them, "are treason, murder, and bestiality." He made those up on the spot. "How do you plead?"

When Glenn arrived at the meeting spot, and did not have with him the neuroscanner or even information about the pilot, Lilly was not upset. It was almost a relief to find he let her down.

How correct she could be about him, even all this time later. And as Glenn led them back to the Citadel and was attacked by Buck Douglas, Lilly still wasn't upset. She let him go. Why should she stick her neck out for him?

A woman in Funchal listened to a morning news report, which was trying to make sense of the helicopters and tanks all over the island. "There is some crisis on the film set," the broadcaster said. The woman cooked her children breakfast.

Buck Douglas had never been so happy. He had captured a wizard! He dragged Gregorian to the Dollories Monastery, not so far from the Morlon Kastaun, and tied him up beneath the altar. He must find the Guild. They would be happy. Buck did not notice at first that the monastery was empty, and it took him a long time to consider the reason why.

Roger's commands over the radio were cloaked in static. "Are you sure it's him? I want visual confirmation that it is Major Wu. I do not care how many people are surrounding him. If it's actually Wu just march right in there and take him. They don't have any weapons! Rifles? We have fucking tanks. What the fuck are they going to do?" He did not have command authority over the ground units and he was growing frustrated.

Lilly and Hannah arrived at the Citadel to find it nearly empty. They went upstairs. Roger cursed at everyone over the comms. The entire operation seemed to be going sideways. Of course it was. Roger had planned it, and he had relied on Glenn to help them. Lilly could have predicted as much, if anyone had asked her. When they entered the writers' room and found Jules hunched over the neuroscanner, muttering under his breath and twitching violently, Lilly wasn't surprised about that, either. Jules had always been this way.

"I'm going to take that now," Lilly said to him, as he adjusted some dials on the neuroscanner—banged and dented and dirty, but still the same machine she remembered.

"Yes, yes, it's ready," Jules said. "I have him all loaded now. Watch, watch, I'm going to see it now. I'm going to see!"

Lilly didn't have time to find out what Jules was talking about. She picked up a chair and swung it at Jules's head. He fell back, yelling, tumbling over a mound of trash and debris scattered all over the floor. He grabbed his face and moaned, but Lilly didn't hesitate. She grabbed the neuroscanner, turned to Hannah, and said, "Let's go."

Lilly never could trust any of these men.

Wallace held a sword above his head. A royal sword he had stolen from the castle. Sanderson and Quentin were on their knees in front of him. "In the judgment of the people of the Malicarn," he said, "I find you both guilty, and sentence you to death!"

Lilly wrapped the cords around the neuroscanner and held it under her arm. It was warm, its internal drive humming with its malicious intent.

"We have to go save Gregorian," Hannah said. "I saw him. Back in the citadel. Those mirrors on the wall. I saw Gregorian in them. He's in the Dollories Monastery, I'd recognize it anywhere."

"No," Lilly said. "We're getting out of here."

"No, please, we have to help him."

"You don't have any idea what's happening here. It's not safe."

They walked back through the lobby, but beyond the front door she heard yelling, saw the torches, the spears held aloft.

A stone flew through the door, glass shattering over the lobby floor. Lilly held the neuroscanner tight and began running for the stairs. She didn't even realize Hannah was still behind her until they reached the bottom and the entrance to the underground tunnel.

"What do you mean, an army?" Roger yelled into his radio. He had half a dozen people embedded all over the island and each of them was saying something different. "It's a mob. They're not organized."

"Well, I'm looking at it right now. Sector fourteen. Gotta be a thousand of them. Swords, horses. Even rifles. It's a real army. The pilot is with them."

The tanks stopped again. Something blocked the road in front of them. "Jesus Christ," Roger shouted, watching them from the Black Hawk, endlessly circling. "What now? And where the hell is sector fourteen?"

Lilly heard voices, angry voices and dim lights, some ways down the tunnel. The mob had found an entrance beneath the wizard's tower. Lilly stopped at a service exit half a mile down, and she and Hannah climbed up a ladder to emerge in an abandoned hut. Nobody but staff had probably used this building in years.

"Gregorian can help us," Hannah said, as Lilly looked out the windows and tried to see if anyone was nearby. "You can trust him, believe me."

"I know him a lot better than you," Lilly said. "He can't help with anything." She tried her radio but there was nothing but static. "Roger, can you copy? Roger? Shit."

They had to go back to the extraction point, but now they were down the mountain and way off course. They could go west, avoid passing back by the Citadel, and hope not to run into any more rebels. The Dollories Monastery was not so far out of the way, Lilly remembered. Maybe new homes or towns had been built between here and there in the last sixteen years, but if not the road would be relatively barren. Glenn was probably going to die, Lilly thought. She didn't owe him anything.

Who was Glenn to her, anyway?

"How fast can you walk on that leg?" Lilly asked. "Can you make it to the Dollories?"

On the field of the Morlon Kastaun, Kreek addressed his troops. "They are coming for us, my friends. Men of great evil. They ride beasts of metal, they ride monsters of steel. They have come for the dragon rider. They have come to tell us that we do not control our destiny. That we do not deserve magic. That the Malicarn does not belong to us. That we must bow to their will. Well, I say to you today: We will not be cowed! We will not be made to suffer! We will not be ground under the heels of our oppressors anymore. Today, we stand tall. Today, we say that we are Men of the Malicarn! Today, we fight!"

Jules wiped blood from his forehead as he listened to Kreek's speech over the feeds in his office. It was a good speech. Doyle delivered it well. Jules couldn't have written it any better.

Hannah and Lilly emerged from the hut, cutting as straight a path as they could toward the monastery. Buck tightened Glenn's bindings. A Portuguese soldier climbed out of his tank, yelling at a man to move his cows off the road. A family from Cameroon, living on their Malicarn farm for only six months, watched their house burn down as they hid from the mob in the woods. Derek and Paul waited in line at airport security, hoping to catch an outbound flight. Roger banged his fist against the helicopter door. Kellington ran through the woods, hoping someone at the north mountain garrison was still alive. Men took their family swords down off the mantel and marched out to join their brothers. Kreek raised his sword above his head, an army of patriots cheering before him. Glenn tried to remember where he had seen Buck before. Children wept as their fathers promised to return. The royal stablemaster fled over the hills with a carriage filled with the children of castle staff. Quentin watched as Wallace beheaded Sanderson in front of the burning castle. Zihao hoped the sound of the helicopter meant he was being rescued. Each road and hill Lilly passed was drenched in memories she didn't know she still had. Hannah looked at the rising sun and convinced herself that Gregorian could save them. A red flag of freedom was hoisted in the Old Village, atop the tower of the Great Wizard.

All of this happened at the same time, with you alone to comprehend its enormity.

QUARTET FOR THE END OF TIME

Buck

There was fire to the north, in the woods, and a great noise beyond it. Creaking and cracking, like stone breaking apart. He spied a dozen men, two dozen, three, all running toward the fire and the noises, carrying spears and swords and shouting angrily to one another, looking for a fight. Buck couldn't be sure, but he thought whatever was going on was his fault.

The monastery was empty from the moment he arrived. The monks had left in a hurry and left no sign of where they went. Buck tied Gregorian to a pillar in the chapel, just under the altar, then walked the grounds to see if anyone was left. Only the gardener's son, no more than five, was sitting underneath a poplar tree.

"Where's everybody gone?" asked Buck.

"Went fighting in the war." The boy was poking at a scorpion on the ground with a stick.

"When will they be back?"

"Don't know, didn't say. Magic's coming back, that's all I know."

"They're all fighting? Even the monks?"

"Monks wanted to fight most of all."

"Can you deliver a message for me?" Buck asked the child to go to Otto's farm and tell Kreek, or whomever from the Guild he could, that Buck had captured Gregorian. "They'll want to come back here straightaway," Buck said.

"Doubt that very much," the child said. "Sir Kreek? He's the one came by here with the Guild and some dragon man. That's why everyone left."

"How long ago? Can you follow them?"

"Father said not to."

"You have to. I can hear the armies, they're not far. Find Kreek and tell him I have the wizard."

The boy hesitated, but Buck searched his pockets for a silver coin and handed it over. The boy ran off north.

Buck returned to the monastery and slumped into a chair in the chapel beside the wizard.

"I remember you," Gregorian said. "You're one of the reenactors, right? One of Kreek's men?"

"Not anymore," Buck said. "I screwed it all up."

"Where is Kreek? Let me talk to him."

"He's gone to the war."

"War?"

"He's taken the dragon rider and gone to free the Malicarn."

Gregorian tried to sit up, but the ropes around his wrists held his arms awkwardly above his head. "What's your name?"

"Buck."

"Buck, listen. I'm not a wizard. There's no Necromancer, there's no dragon rider. Kreek isn't really a knight. His name is Brian Doyle, and he's lying to you. He can't bring magic back because there is no magic."

Buck noticed for the first time that Gregorian appeared very scared. "Is that why you haven't tried to fight me off with magic?"

"Exactly. I can't, because there isn't any. The Malicarn isn't even a real place. It's all made up."

"Maybe you can't use magic because the dragon rider has broken your hold over the realm?"

"No, Buck, please. This is for your own good. You don't have to listen to any of this—"

"I used to think you were nice," Buck said. "But now I see you're not. When I was a child you leant my father your horse and cart. You probably don't remember. You walked alone through the woods so that we could ride. I always thought that meant you were very wise, and kind. Maybe I was wrong. You're just an old man."

"I don't remember that. Perhaps you're right. Maybe I'm old now and nothing matters, but Buck, please. Listen to me. Let me go. By this time tomorrow the Malicarn as you know it will be over. There's no sense being rash here."

"The Malicarn's greatest days are ahead. Kreek will show us. That's what he's doing with the dragon rider."

"But you're not with them. Why?"

"Because I was foolish. Not anymore."

Buck stood and looked out the window. A haze was wafting across the field, smoke from the trees. Then he saw the gardener's boy emerge, skipping back toward the monastery. A dozen men followed on horseback.

"See?" Buck said to Gregorian. "They have come!"

Kreek entered the chapel, brushed right past Buck, and grabbed Gregorian by the chin, forcing him to look into his eyes.

"This day has gone better than expected," he said, and patted Gregorian on the cheek. "I owe you an apology, Buck. You have proven your worth to the Guild. We will have to look into your reinstatement."

"Thank you, Sir Kreek. That honor means much."

"The Guild's armies have defeated a small company of queen's men who were hiding in the woods. We smoked them out. Kingstown is ours, the Old Village, too, and a dozen more towns all along the river."

"Brian, I—"

Kreek slapped Gregorian hard across the face. "Quiet. We have already assembled our forces and will face off against the remainder of the queen's fighters massing against us. The dragon rider is held with our men on the field of the Morlon Kastaun. He must remain in the open, to inspire the people. But Gregorian, you are too sneaky. I suspect a plot. Buck, I want you to keep him here. Watch him. When the battle is won I will return."

"I would like to come to fight," Buck said.

"No. You have regained my trust but you must do as I say. Afterward we will deal justice upon the wizard."

Several of the other Guild soldiers milled about the inside of the chapel, each holding a long knife or a spear and trying to look threatening.

"Please, Brian," Gregorian pleaded, "you have to let me go. There's a deployment of Portuguese and British troops on the island. They're coming here now, and they are going to take the pilot back by force, if they have to. You can't fight them."

"None of this concerns me," Kreek said. "Sixteen years ago you decreed an end to magic as part of your deal with the Necromancer. This has led to poverty, grief, and the loss of our farms and homes to goblins. We want magic back. It is our birthright, our holy inheritance. The dragon rider is the key. He will inspire the realm and show us how to fight back these invaders."

"Brian, stop it!" Gregorian yelled. "This isn't part of the script, this isn't part of the show. It's not the Necromancer, it's not Jules. It's a goddamn army, a real army. Jesus, Brian, why the theatrics? Why is this necessary?"

Kreek stood up and circled the room, gesturing at eroded statues and gaps between stones.

"Are you speaking to me?" asked Kreek. "I do not know a Jules, or a Brian. I am Kreek, the royal swordmaster, and though I have traveled to faraway lands in service of the Malicarn, I have never met these people before. I do know you, though, Gregorian. I know you are wicked and false. Most of all, I know you are a coward."

"You're insane," Gregorian said. He turned to the other men in the room. "There is no magic, there never was. Look, up there!" Gregorian pointed to one of the distressed gargoyle statues hovering on the wall behind Kreek. "In that statue's mouth! Buck, look! There is a device called a camera. The Necromancer is watching us. He knows where we are. There are at least six more in this very room. Kreek knows this, too. His real name is Brian Doyle. He knows the truth of the Malicarn, even though he treats you all like fools."

Buck looked with concern toward Kreek, who remained unfazed. "Gregorian," Kreek said, "this is why you were never a true hero. It is why you are a failed wizard. And it is why you live a lonely, forsaken life. You never believe in what is before your eyes. You try to control it, but you must let go and accept what you see. This land is not false. I can smell it, touch it, hear it, taste it. I *see* it, and my perceptions do not lie. What I see is a world bereft of magic, men who yearn for what their fathers had, and the wizard who took it from them."

"Hear, hear!" Buck shouted.

"Spare the queen, at least," Gregorian said. "She is not involved."

"Of course she is," said Kreek.

Another man walked into the chapel and rushed up to Kreek. "The Queen's Guard is on the move. We saw a company of knights riding toward our position on the Morlon Kastaun. We have more men waiting outside to join the others."

"They will be searching for the rider," Kreek said. "Buck, stay here and guard the prisoner. He is not to be moved, understand?" Kreek looked back down at Gregorian. "You were a fine wizard once. Shame you have forgotten your heritage."

"What do you think is going to happen here, Brian?" asked Gregorian. "Magic isn't real! It's all an illusion!"

"No, Gregorian. You are the one who lives inside an illusion. I see things as they really are."

Kreek left the chapel with the other guildsmen. The clanging of sword and spear followed them as they marched away outside. Buck hovered anxiously by the doorway.

"I wish I could go with them," Buck said. "Soldiering's part of my heritage. My father fought with wizards."

"No, Buck, he didn't."

The soldiers had all marched off, the sound of their steps fading in the distance, when the gardener's son walked into the chapel.

"They said they was asking about you, sir?"

"Who?" Buck asked.

"They said to come and see."

Buck turned to follow the boy, then looked back at Gregorian. "You come, too. Don't want you out of my sight again. Can't afford any more failures." He untied the rope from around the pillar and pulled Gregorian outside, as if on a leash.

"Told ya he was in there," the gardener's boy said to the woman waiting for them out front. Buck recognized her as the wizard's companion in the woods.

"Run along now," she said to the boy, who darted off away from the monastery. "We've come for the wizard," she said to Buck. "We don't want to hurt you."

Buck took out his knife and held it at Gregorian's throat. "I don't want no trouble, either," Buck said. "But I'm keeping this here wizard. For the Guild."

"Lilly?" Gregorian asked. "You came back for me."

"Would have been here earlier but we had to wait for Doyle and his friends to leave."

Another person stood behind Lilly, and when she walked forward Buck nearly let the knife slip. "My queen!" he gasped. "I didn't mean you no harm, Your Majesty. But the wizard here is deceiving us all, you understand."

The queen held a large gray box. "You can let the wizard go," she said. "It's not safe for you here, I promise."

"I'm sorry, Buck," Gregorian said, pulling a little on his rope leash, "but you have no idea just how sheltered you are. Even the queen doesn't know, but I do."

Lilly laughed. "Do you?"

"Don't be cruel," Gregorian said.

"Be quiet!" Buck said. "I don't want to kill him, either, lady, but I will if you try to take him."

Hannah walked forward. "Please let him go. I'm just starting to understand, too, but there are a lot of lies in the Malicarn."

"What's that? What are you holding?" Buck asked.

"It's a, well . . ." Hannah paused and looked at the box. "I don't know really. Some kind of magic."

"See, Gregorian, there is magic!" Buck laughed. "You said there ain't but I knows the truth. Wizards lie. My father fought in the wars. He told me all about wizards. He didn't trust wizards neither, not really. They used people as shields, as tools, children even. He told me this story once about searching for rogue mages in a village. They found a kid in a house, in a hideaway, watching over magical artifacts, but the kid tried to kill my pop and his buddies. Killed one of them with an arrow, then my father struck him down. The wizard set the kid up, believe that? Damn shame they had to kill the kid. Got the mages in the end, though. Found them and killed them."

"Where did you hear that story?" Lilly asked.

"Like I said, my father told me."

"What was your father's name?"

"Well, his right name was Francis. But folk called him Frank. Frank Douglas."

"It's not real, Buck," Gregorian said. "It's like I've been trying to tell you, none of it is real." Gregorian moved a step back, but Buck held the blade closer to his neck, the tip poking the skin.

"No, it's real," Lilly said.

"What?" Buck asked.

"There really was a child. He was hiding, he probably didn't want to trick the soldiers. But the soldiers killed him anyway. The child was real. He lived. My father told me that story, too."

"Lilly," Gregorian asked, "what are you talking about?"

"I don't understand none of this," Buck said. His eyes teared up, and his voice cracked. He pointed at Lilly. "How do you know these things?"

"This box," Lilly said, taking it from Hannah's hands and

setting it on the ground. "It's a, um, a dreamtalker. It creates memories. I gave your father that memory with it."

"Never heard of a dreamtalker," Buck said. "I know loads about wizards but ain't never knew of that."

"That's what this is," Lilly said, kicking the box softly with her foot.

"I don't think you should touch it," Buck said.

"It's real magic," Gregorian said. "Let us go and I will show you."

"How will you show me if I let you go?"

"I will come back," Gregorian said. "I promise. I just want to get the queen to safety. As soon as the queen is safe, I'll come back and I'll still be your prisoner. I'll even show you how magic works."

Buck smiled. "No, no. Kreek says you are a schemer. No, no, no. How do I know you'll come back? Never trust a wizard, that's what my father always said. You're lying still."

"Show it to him now," Lilly said. Her eyes were fixed on the box. "Go on, *Gregorian*."

"Lilly?" asked the queen. "What are you doing?"

"The wizard is going to do some magic," she said.

Gregorian nodded. "Yes. Buck, please, come. The dreamtalker can tell a wizard what's in another man's head. Would you like to see what I know? I can give you some real wizarding knowledge, directly from my mind to yours."

"Sounds like dark magic, maybe."

"No, no. It's quite safe," Lilly said. "Please, let me show you."

"I'm gonna have to watch you close, though. You try to run and I'll have to cut him." He waved the knife at Gregorian.

Lilly knelt on the ground beside the box. She touched it, and the box began to hum. Buck laughed. Lilly uncoiled two cords, one green and one red, as lights shone out from the box.

"Incredible," Buck said. "Magic light."

Lilly took the red cord and placed one end of it on her forehead. Then she pressed one of the lights on the box and there was a loud buzzing sound. The dreamtalker shook. After a moment it ended and Lilly removed the cord from her head.

"See? The box just read my mind. I am fine. It isn't dangerous at all."

"Doesn't seem much like magic," Buck said. "Does it really work?"

"It's an invisible magic," Gregorian said.

"Let me see, then. Let me see what a wizard knows!" He cut the ropes around Gregorian's wrists, then kept the knife against his throat. Gregorian knelt down next to the box. He looked up toward Lilly, who backed away. Hannah stood behind her, watching, her eyes flicking back and forth between the box and Lilly.

"The first step," Gregorian began, "is, uh—"

"You have to disengage sequestration," Lilly said.

"What?" Buck squinted his eyes and looked at her. "You are a wizard, too, aren't you?"

"She's a real dream sorceress," Gregorian said. "Knows more than anyone about it."

"Take the sequestration protocol offline with the master switch on the left."

"It's turned off already."

"Good. Now you set it for input or output. Both systems can work simultaneously, so you have to set either input or output to zero. If both are set high, then it will extract and implant at the same time."

"What wizard talk!" Buck laughed.

"Do you understand me, Gregorian? If both are set at one hundred percent, it will do both at the same time, and at the same rate. *Both at the same time.* And with no sequestration."

Gregorian nodded. "I understand." He made a few adjustments to the dial.

"The red cord reads. The green cord implements. You want to put only the green cord onto Buck's forehead. Not both. If you do both, it will both read and implement." She looked straight at

Gregorian as she said this. "Do you understand? It will *both read and implement*."

Gregorian nodded and said nothing. He reached the green cord toward Buck. "Here, Buck. At the end here is a flat sensor, called a node. Like a magic orb. Hold it onto your forehead."

Buck smiled. With one hand still holding the knife, he used the other to place the end of the green cord above his eyes. He smiled broadly.

"Real magic!" he cried.

"Now," Lilly continued. "You have to enter an algorithm based on the subject's height and weight. You can estimate but—"

Gregorian shook his head. "I don't know, I don't know."

Lilly slowly approached. "I'm going to show him, Buck, okay?"

Buck nodded, his eyes crossed as he stared at the cord in front of him. Lilly leaned over the dreamtalker.

"I'll tell you what to enter, okay?" She read out some numbers to Gregorian, who messed with the lights on the box. The box began to sing a high-pitched note. Gregorian held the end of the red cord against his temple.

"Are you ready, Buck?" Lilly asked.

"I want to feel what it's like to be a real wizard!" Buck shouted. "I'll be like you, Gregorian!"

"When I say to"—Lilly looked between Gregorian and Hannah as she spoke—"press the yellow button to commence program. Ready? On three. One, two, three—now!"

Gregorian hit the yellow light, but as he did so Lilly leapt forward, grabbed the red cord away from the wizard, and thrust the end onto Buck's head. The box's internal metallic hiss screamed, and sparks ignited across Buck's face. Gregorian grabbed Buck's shoulders to keep him still and Lilly held both cords in place on his forehead. Buck swung the knife wildly in front of him, digging it into Lilly's side. She screamed as he pulled it out. Gregorian grabbed Buck's arm, kicking away the knife as a white bolt of energy sparked out between the two cords, snapping back Buck's neck.

Lilly rolled over and grabbed her side. Blood flowed out between her fingers. She shut her eyes, groaned, breathed deeply.

It would be hard to describe what Buck saw in the instant that followed, as by the time it was over he had no memory of any of it ever happening in the first place. There were sights and smells: fires in the village during market festivals, fresh fruit from the farm, his home before the flood. He was in an inn, reeking of alcohol and sweat and full of song and dance. There was the master mason, showing him how to use a whetstone to sharpen his tools. A dirt path that ran down from the old farm, toward a creek. The Reenactors, talking in a circle at the back of a church. His mother, alive, washing clothes in a tub outside their house on a summer morning. His father, dead, lying in a cold bed waiting for the grave. His baby sister in a crib. Buck jumping into a puddle.

All parts of his life at once, rushing past him. "No, no, please, no," Buck said. But he didn't know why. When he spoke again, it was only screams.

All the memories were gone, and all Buck knew was that his face was on the ground. A cold, muddy ground, where someone's blood pooled among dry tufts of dead grass. But he didn't know whose blood it was, why it was soaking the dirt, or where the grass came from. He didn't know anything, anymore.

Jules

He was a poor man begging for scraps on the side of the road. He was a child unable to sleep because she feared the night demons. A woman who missed her sister, now married and living far away. An old man who thought about his youth in the King's Army, fighting beside wizards. A Council hero, who had been through many campaigns and missed his old friend Prion.

He was a blacksmith and a carpenter and a knight and a weaver and an innkeeper and a farmer and a housewife and a priest and a physician and a king.

When he was just Jules, or tried to be, he wrote alone and kept to himself, to his own mind. The writers' room didn't help anymore. They had no good ideas. He hated the conferences, the pitches from young, ambitious writers, the meetings spent hashing out executive displeasures. Staff to manage and assistants to placate. Jules preferred to compose his symphony on his own terms.

He was always dreaming and never asleep. He watched, and reviewed, and relived. He relived every life they had built and sent out into the world, every constructed memory, every implanted personality. Into the conference rooms he brought in screens, dozens of them, linked to every camera and location across the land. On the table in front of him he kept the neuroscanner, his dream maker, always charged, always linked to his own mind.

On the screens he followed his characters, saw their movements, tracked their conversations. And from the neuroscanner he saw their pasts. Saw their oldest thoughts and desires.

Into a recorder he spoke his notes.

Cleo is spending a lot of time with the baker, but only when his wife is running errands. The baker reminds her of her dead husband. This should be discouraged. Will lead to unsuitable complications.

Maximus has been bored lately. Drinking too much. Must devise mission for him soon. Will coordinate with ongoing Council plots.

Too many children in Kingstown. Will result in unacceptable numbers of casualties following attack by Eastern Riders next spring. Consult Percival the blacksmith; he has fondness for children from memories, can be induced to travel with children on some sort of to-be-determined adventure.

Footage recorded by cameras came through at all hours. Jules flagged them, annotating notes about what was useful, what was needed, what was disposable for Clint or Larry or someone in Burbank who would package it for mass consumption. But Jules had bigger plans now. Not just an edited digest. Everything needed to work. Too much of the story was simply extras, people wandering around their little lives and worried about the most undramatic and least interesting things. Food and work and family squabbles. Jules only had, perhaps, a dozen interesting characters. The few remaining Council heroes, a couple of knights, and one or two new young fighters. But those kids were born and raised within the Malicarn, and Jules did not have any memory banks on which to draw from, or understand them.

The first time he implemented himself, the way forward became clear. The body was dead, but it didn't matter. Jules saw the killer's life clearly: childhood as an orphan, brother eaten by a troll, loneliness in a monastery. He saw the old memories, too. Ball games at Camden Yards. Jump-starting a car battery. Sitting at home, scrolling through streaming channels, looking for something to watch. But what struck Jules were the recent memories. Stabbing a woman through the heart. The fluttering in his stomach when she went limp. The mad desire to kill again. Those were useful. Jules could do something with that.

The task of creating new memories started as an experiment, a way for Jules to get inside the head of the young, unscanned characters and understand them. Such characters were popular, notes from the studio always giving them glowing reviews. "Wholesome, pure," they said. Which meant "Feature them more."

Jules reverse-engineered a method to program simple memories pulled from his own mind, using the surviving R & D computers. Strong smells, like flowers. Or the feel of the hot sun. Simple enough nodes that Jules could upload them into the neuroscanner and build it onto a preexisting profile. But writing a whole new profile, a new personality, was much harder.

So he uploaded himself. At first he only did a little, memories of his own time in the Malicarn. But soon he added the rest:

early days in LA, his stint teaching college writing, undergrad nights bouncing around New York, childhood summer camp and trumpet lessons and his uncle's sailboat.

Once Jules put himself into the neuroscanner he could build up other memories. Ones he created based on the new characters' actions, or what he imagined they might be thinking. And then he would turn off sequestration, plug himself into the neuroscanner, and watch them again, receiving his own memories back with additions and embellishments and new thoughts.

The new memories made Jules a better writer. More empathetic. And also more precise. He would test out storylines with these memories, see how they worked, if they made sense. When they didn't, he'd try again, layering on slightly different versions of the same events into his head. Now when he thought back to his childhood, after soccer practice or a day at school, he remembered jumping over caverns, running from dragons, fighting trolls.

Not all memories were for story. Sometimes Jules just enjoyed things: wielding magic, flying, seducing beautiful women. He spackled over his actual memories with these new ones, replacing drunken nights at bars with hours tutoring young magicians in training at a special school. Instead of hopping on buses across a city he remembered a torrid romance with a devilish witch. When he developed a crush on a farmer's daughter he watched on the feeds, he replaced his college girlfriend with memories of the farm girl instead. So he knew the crevices of her body, what it felt like to lie naked with her under the covers. When the farmer's daughter drowned in a pond, Jules retooled her fate in his memory so that she killed herself, so grief-stricken that Jules could not be with her she would rather die. Jules never really met her, never saw her except on cameras, but he didn't remember that anymore.

The process of loading his head with memories became second nature. He could run the neuroscanner without fear of collapsing, sitting upright in his chair while keeping an eye on the camera feeds at the same time. Eventually he could even record script notes as he uploaded scans, existing in the past, present, and future all at once.

"Jules, I am trying to talk to you."

His name was strange now. Like an old dream, one you are jolted awake from and barely remember.

"Jules, please. I need more guidance here."

The voice was Glenn's. He knew that voice. Gregorian. Not Glenn, Gregorian. Jules was plastering those memories, too, replacing late-night rehearsals with adventures across the Mallicarn. Gregorian was an old friend. He knew that.

"Hello," he said to Glenn. To Gregorian. "How are you doing?"

"Christ, Jules, I've been here for an hour. Can you just let me know what you want me to tell the queen's advisors when I go over there?"

Jules didn't look at the voice. It was somewhere, over there, in the dark. He wanted it to go away.

"I am the Necromancer."

"Yes, I know. What do I tell the advisors?"

Gregorian was going to have to learn to be more self-reliant. That was important. No more story sessions. He needed to be able to live free inside the story.

"You should handle the situation in the most effective way you know how," Jules said.

"Yes, but what is that?"

"Do you remember Frederickson?"

"Professor Frederickson? Our drama teacher?"

"Do you remember affective memory? You have to relive a memory, to make it real. Tie it to some trigger and pull it out when you need it."

"I'm impressed you actually remember that. But I'm not rehearsing for a scene, Jules. I need to know what the scene is."

New memories: The Necromancer was born a regular child. Poor but smart. His family was killed by marauders. No, they were killed by a monster. No, he had no family. An orphan?

Sense of injustice at a young age. Traveled to the Morlon Kastaun to learn the ways of the wizards, but shunted aside because of their snobbery. Obvious? A bit. Comment on inequality by posing inequality as the origin of an evil man. Maybe he is not evil. He is misunderstood. Yes: Create a past where the heroes are actually villains. Can you make this story believable?

"We have some notes on the recent scripts."

Gregorian was gone. Another voice. Another day? Hard to maintain the balance of time when your memories are always new.

"Clint in particular has concerns."

Yes, a new voice. Larry Pine. On the video screen. Good. He wasn't here. He couldn't see the neuroscanner. Jules could't let them know of it.

"Basically, we want to know if there's any sort of long-term plan here. The shows are putting up decent streaming numbers but we need another movie. That's the main thing. Is this getting tied together? What's the plan?"

Jules pretended to listen. The notes were always the same: Feature popular characters. Less moral grayness, more heroes. Jules didn't care. He wanted spectacle, real spectacle, and he could provide it.

"Oh, and there's another thing. We've discussed the issue of the queen."

"The queen?"

"Yes, you remember. We were split on whether we wanted the young queen in a more central role or not."

"She's nearly an adult now. I can start featuring her more—"

"No, no. We don't want her. Look, it's just that, nobody wants a cripple as the hero. Especially not a weak character like her. Prion was great, but it's been sixteen years. We think you should introduce a new king and write out the queen. Make her evil or something."

"Ah, a twist."

Jules hadn't planned much for the queen, but Larry was right.

She was boring and sad. A bad character, one he had never put much time into developing. Of course, she was natural born so Jules didn't have her memories, and he never bothered to imagine them. Her life was dull, holed up in the castle. Easy enough to just write her out. Start over.

"I'll figure out a way. What if she becomes corrupted by her advisors?"

No response. The video call was over. Had been over. What day was it? No matter, back to work.

People in streets. People running. In fear? No, in play. An arrow through the heart of a comrade. Horses stampeding. Two people using one another for warmth on a cold night. A father telling his son about magic, what it was like. The son pretending to be a wizard.

But it wasn't good enough. Jules could see everything and imagine nothing. He needed help. Not another writer's assistant, not a producer. They were hacks, what did they know? He needed someone who really understood the Malicarn, inside and out. Someone who could create it from whole cloth, if need be.

Only one person was like that. Jean-Danton Souard. He was dead, but that didn't matter. Jules could re-create him. There was enough material in the world. Put it all into the machine. Biographies, letters, documentaries, old videos of talks he gave or appearances on *Dick Cavett*. Add them in. A half-finished memoir, still in his handwriting, never finished, never typed, found in the archives. Personal correspondence, memories of his family, friends, editors, lawyers, fans. Add them too. What did he know? Here's an interview where he talked about his childhood love of English mystery novels. So those go in. The first *Malicarn* film producer, reminiscing about the one time they met. Movies Souard watched, photos of Paris before the war. A newsreel about a German POW camp. The New York publishing scene in the 1960s. A photo of his home office, all his books and records visible on a shelf. Inventory those, put them all in, too. Tolkien and Dunsany and Verne and Shelley and Milton. Edith Piaf and

Cole Porter and Duke Ellington and Olivier Messiaen. Lots of Messiaen. The same piece, different recordings, bought and rebought, on his shelf half a dozen times at least. Why? Put it all in. What was his home in Boston like? What was his wife like? His son. It all goes in.

You add enough detail, you might have something approaching a real person. If Jules could put Souard into his own head, he could be Souard. He could write a real masterpiece.

"I got a visit from the NSA, Jules. The fucking NSA. If they come back and take our hard drives, they're going to see the same thing I saw." It was Larry again. How tedious. Larry from Los Angeles. Jules was compiling the Souard profile, finalizing it for implementation. He didn't have time for this. "I have hours of footage that *you* sent of the plane crashing, the pilot getting kidnapped. The Chinese are already pretty mad, imagine if they find out we've been purposely misleading them?"

"I do not know," Jules said, trying to sound genuine and empathetic. "I have not seen him on my screens." It wasn't a lie. He hadn't seen the pilot in weeks. He had seen Kreek talking to his reenactor friends, multiple trips to a farm, visiting a small granary tower that didn't have any cameras. He knew all about the Malicarn underground and Kreek's patronage of their cause. He knew about the young Portuguese anarchists who were slipping into the realm and causing mischief. He knew Kreek was connecting all of these elements, and Jules was letting him. It seemed like a good idea. Something interesting might come of it, storywise.

"I need you to be sharp," Larry said. "You're our eyes and ears over there."

No, thought Jules. I am your conductor.

Render the profile. Let it compile. A little more time, that is all. Kreek makes his move. Protests across the realm. Chaos and bloodshed. Perhaps Kreek timed it wrong, thought Jules. But no time to manage that now. Soon Souard will know what to do, how to shape this arc. How to mold these characters. Let the protestors run wild. No one can stop them. Compile. Wait.

"It was a pretty good trip. Nice change of scenery at least." The nervous voice was back. Glenn. No, Gregorian.

"What, what?" Jules asked. He could see Gregorian now, standing at the edge of the table, looking at the wall of screens.

"The Miami trip," Gregorian said. "Remember?"

"No." Jules remembered nothing. "How's Miami?"

"Different from when my grandmother used to live there."

"Nice to visit with her, eh?"

"What? No, Jules, she's been dead for years. Her condo's probably underwater by now, anyway."

"Why cry about it, then? Ha!" Jules tried to laugh. Couldn't do it.

"Are you all right?"

"Fine, fine." He reached for the neuroscanner. The memories were in there. Souard. He had to get to Souard.

"Well, anyway, you don't look well, Jules. When was the last time you were outside? In the fields, stretching your legs. Under the warm autumn sun."

Wait, no. That is a memory. Old conversation with someone else. Move it, edit it out. Back to Gregorian.

Jules tapped his fingers on the neuroscanner. He smiled and looked at Gregorian. Gregorian was talking. About what? Was he walking toward Jules?

"This storyline can't keep going. Jules, listen to me, there's a—"

"Wait! Let me tell you about the guns! Listen to this!" Jules looked at Glenn, who stared back down at him with concern. Somewhere he remembered running lines for a show in a dorm late at night and decided that this strange man was in fact his friend. "I just got a message last week, you know I really should write them back, but listen! New props!"

He kept rambling. What did he say? Gregorian was speaking. No, *Jules* was speaking. And then, then—they rope in the queen! Make her betray someone. Maybe you? Haha. Yes, then! Then you can expose her. Maybe, not sure. Lots of details. But then we find a new king. Someone tall, blond. Not crippled, obviously. And we kill the old queen. Really sad. Lots of political intrigue.

Was this how the conversation actually went? Jules didn't remember. He didn't write it.

"They're coming for the pilot," Gregorian said. Yes, he actually said that. "Real soldiers. People with real weapons. They'll be here tonight. You can't keep doing this."

A real army. Modern guns. Wasn't planned that way, Jules didn't expect it. But continuity is the hobgoblin of little minds. I am beyond such trivialities. When the story is real and good and strong, there are no flaws.

Gregorian stared at Jules and rubbed his face. Then he stood up and started pacing. Maybe this man was not his friend.

"What did you do in Miami?" Jules asked.

"We didn't cast her, she was born."

Gregorian stopped pacing and turned toward Jules. He was close to him now, close enough that Jules could smell him. He smelled like cow shit. Was that what the Malicarn smelled like? He needed more smell memories. Powerful thing, smell.

Rambling again, about spies and plots and story arcs. Gregorian was mad. "—and they're going to come in here and rescue—" Why?

Gregorian gone. Got rid of him. A nuisance. Doesn't matter. Files are rendered, compiled, downloaded. Ready to go. Someone else now, more annoying.

Lilly Kaminsky. He remembered her. Always wanted to fuck her. She was old now. Ugly. Didn't want to fuck her anymore. Forget it, delete it.

"It's nice to see you again," he said. "After all this time." The queen was with her. He's losing the plot now. Things are getting out of control. Got to implement Souard. Get Souard into my mind.

"Where is it?" Lilly asked.

"Where is what?"

"Don't be foolish, Jules. I am not here to play."

"Of course you are here to play. Whatever else is there to do?"

"I'm going to take that now." She pointed at the neuroscanner. She wanted Souard for herself, of course. But Souard belonged to Jules. Jules *was* Souard, was going to be. Any moment now.

"Yes, yes, it's ready," Jules said. "I have him all loaded now. Watch, watch, I'm going to see it now. I'm going to see!"

What did it feel like to be hit in the head? Jules had many memories of it, but not his own. Always a loud pop, a violent throw. Lilly must have punched him, or no, she hit him with something. Would be good to have a real memory like that, could recalibrate the others then. Jules missed a moment, something jumped, and Lilly and the queen were gone. Lilly should have punched him with his fist, not hit him with a chair. Jules would add it somewhere. Just layer it in over a boring conversation. Make it better. First he must program in the disorientation, then the pain. It's a good note, have to include it. Have to upload it to the neuroscanner.

Jules reached for the table. Brian Doyle is giving a speech, a good one. Reached for the neuroscanner. Stood up and searched. The neuroscanner was gone.

But no. Souard was in there. Jules needed him. He needed to see him, to be him. To live him again. Make him smarter, make him better. Make the stories work. Where was the neuroscanner? Where was Lilly?

He scanned the camera feeds, but it was all chaos. Revolution. War.

He remembered the Necromancer's backstory. His greatest betrayal, by a fellow pupil at the Morlon Kastaun. Who was it? Gregorian, of course. He had known Gregorian a long time. Gregorian who had loved Lilly. This was his doing. Gregorian had betrayed him again.

Gregorian would have the neuroscanner. He had Souard. Jules needed them back. Find Gregorian, and he'd find the neuroscanner.

Jules burst out of the room, into an empty hallway. Followed it down to the closet, next to his sleeping quarters. Old props here, old things. Things not needed anymore. If he was going to be betrayed, he would do it in character. He pulled out a cloak, threw it on. And the rifle. The one they gave him. Sitting there, ready to use. Yes, yes, not magic. He could use a gun, that was allowed. A rifle, a hunting rifle. The rebels had them. The anarchists had trained them how to shoot. It was canon now. He felt around in his cloak. His remote was there, his old one, the one for the device they said he could not use. But what did they know? Awaken it. Why not? The rifle and the device, together. Old magic and new. How did the Necromancer find these things? Did he create them himself? He would have to write a memory for it, soon. Souard would be proud. When he got the neuroscanner back. When he found Gregorian. When he killed him for his betrayal.

In the lobby the rebels milled about, unsure what to make of the Citadel. They had smashed windows, doors. They stood with weapons and fury. Follow me! Follow me! I am the Necromancer! I will free you of your bondage. And so they followed. The Necromancer led them to war.

What a scene it would be!

Lilly

Buck quivered, whimpering and hollering gibberish. Lilly slumped and held a hand over her gut. Blood was everywhere.

"We need to help her," Hannah said to Glenn.

"Garah! Mamama lollihar!" Buck spit through his teeth as he spoke, shaking his head and trying to stand up.

"The . . . scanner," Lilly said, gritting her teeth and gesturing with her head toward Buck.

Buck was holding the scanner above his head, jumping and hollering. Glenn stood up and jumped toward him, but his legs were still tied together and he stumbled. Buck swung the scanner at him like a weapon, then turned and ran. He bounded past the monastery and went north, following the sounds of battle.

"We need to get the scanner," Lilly shouted, or tried to shout, but her hands were covered in blood.

"Oh, God, Lilly, you need help," Glenn said. He knelt beside her. "Oh shit."

"No, the scanner. We need to follow him."

They saw Buck's head bouncing on the other side of a hill, and the sounds of his gibberish echoing back. "Ladela, trelolo gafidy gaf."

"What's wrong with him?" Hannah said.

"He's erased," Lilly said. "We wiped his mind."

"What?"

"The box," Glenn said. "That's what it does. It controls memories."

"What about you?" Hannah asked Lilly. "You ran the machine on yourself first."

Lilly shook her head. "No, just extraction. I didn't implement anything in myself." She grunted and sat up. "We have to follow him."

"We should call Roger," Glenn said. "Get him to pick you up, get you to a hospital."

Lilly's radio was hissing and crackling, with sounds of men barking orders and gunfire and screaming. "Roger will never come unless we have what he wants."

Glenn untied the ropes from his legs. Lilly took off her jacket and ripped an arm sleeve, wrapping and tying it around her waist. Then she started walking north.

"What are you doing?" Glenn asked.

"Getting that scanner," she said. "I'm not going to die in this fucking place."

Glenn and Hannah followed Lilly, who hobbled up a nearby hill. The morning was cloudless and bright. Buck's faint scream of "Garga hanalot!" rose from the meadow beyond. Ahead, she could see Buck jumping around and flailing. Her head ached but she didn't think she had hit it on anything. Maybe that was what extraction felt like, a dull pain like an oncoming migraine.

What had she thought about when the machine was reading her? She didn't remember. All she was thinking about was how to make this all end.

Lilly started walking faster, her hand still clutching her stomach, when another loud boom echoed across the field. She looked toward the tree line ahead and saw a plume of smoke, and the orange glow of fire. Glenn and Hannah were beside her.

"Kreek's men," Hannah said. "They're close."

"And so is the Queen's Guard," Glenn said. "Look!"

He pointed at a gap in the trees, where dozens of men in red cloaks brandishing swords ran out. Sir Kellington led in front. They were covered in dirt, retreating quickly from another contingent dressed in handmade wizard robes. The Guild warriors were carrying rifles, firing at the queen's men, chasing them back.

Buck hollered again. "Jalool! Jalool!"

A hundred guildmembers and reenactors ran out through the trees. Glenn saw the flash of steel and heard the clash of their swords.

"For the queen!" the guards shouted as they were cut down and slaughtered.

"No!" Hannah yelled. She turned toward the melee, but Glenn reached out and held her back.

"Stop! There's nothing you can do."

"They are being killed!"

Only another cry and the sound of horses trembling over the earth made Hannah pause, as over a far ridge they noticed dozens, hundreds more flocking toward the battle. They were townsfolk with pitchforks, torches, and knives forming a line, assembled at the crest of the hill.

"For the Malicarn!" they cried.

The queen's men turned toward the arrivals and formed a new line. "For the queen!" they shouted. The two rebel armies converged and rushed toward their enemy.

"Jesus Christ," Lilly said, watching the battle commence. "What the fuck have you been doing here, Glenn?"

"Baaa!" Buck screamed loudly. He was fifty yards ahead. He had stopped, still holding the scanner, and watched the battle like a film, enraptured and entertained. Lilly's knees buckled and she fell to the earth. Glenn leaned over her.

"I'll get the scanner," Glenn said. "Stay back here, okay? I'll get it, Lilly. We'll get out of here."

"Please, Glenn. Please . . ."

Glenn ran toward Buck, but when Buck saw Glenn coming he hopped forward and down the hill. Lilly groaned and was about to stand back up when the earth shook. Tanks and jeeps burst from the tree line, flanked by soldiers with automatic rifles.

A flash of light, a crack. Through the trees opposite them another figure emerged holding a rifle, a dark black cape flowing behind him. A shout of terror went up from the queen's men. "The Necromancer!"

Lilly saw Jules's face, dark and determined, searching the field before him. A man charged at him, but Jules raised a rifle and fired. The man crumpled.

Lilly's radio crackled again. "We're in pursuit of the pilot," someone called out over it. "We have visual confirmation." In front of the tanks and jeeps emerged a horse, upon which rode two men. The rider was bearded and fierce, and Lilly knew it was Brian Doyle. The man seated behind him was the pilot. The Portuguese soldiers chased them.

"Roger, the neuroscanner is at the site of the pilot," Lilly shouted into her radio. "Tell everyone to use caution until we have retrieved it."

"Lilly? Are you in the middle of all that shit? What the fuck happened?"

She had no idea. She had no idea how she had ended up back in this stupid place with these stupid people, worried once again about a neuroscanner. She looked out on the field of battle before her, men with swords facing men with rifles facing men with tanks. It was a tapestry of stupidity, a nightmare scene of everything and everyone Lilly had hated and resented for almost twenty years, all in one place.

Hannah wept beside her. "I have to help them," the girl said, more to herself than anyone else. "I should help them, I'm the queen."

"No, you're not," Lilly said.

"I have to help them." Hannah ran forward, toward the queen's men on the nearest ridge.

"Shit," said Lilly, but she couldn't stand fast enough to stop her. "Why is everybody such a goddamn hero?"

As the horse and the tanks raced toward the middle of the field, Jules shot down another man with his rifle. Lilly lost sight of Buck and Glenn, but she could tell, as Jules rapidly surveyed the bodies around him and in front of him, that he was looking for them, too.

"Where is it?" Jules bellowed. "What have you done with it?" He walked in between a line of queen's men and Guild warriors, pacing furiously. But both sides stopped cold when they saw Glenn standing on the field between them, too.

"Gregorian!" a cry went up. "Gregorian has come to save us!"

Glenn

Buck led Glenn away from the battle and into a forest. He was fast, and Glenn nearly lost him among the trees when Buck turned and began to run back. Two Portuguese soldiers were pointing their guns, yelling at him to stop. But Buck just hooted, jumped, and ran off again. The soldiers did not follow.

"Stop him!" Glenn shouted, waving at the soldiers.

"Pare!" they shouted back, raising their guns. A jeep and a tank drove out from the foliage. Everyone was rushing toward the battlefield. "Pare!" the soldier shouted again.

Glenn put his hands up above his head. The tank drove forward. Soldiers climbed out of the jeep and ran toward him. Everyone raised their rifles. Glenn closed his eyes.

"Gregorian?"

He opened his eyes again, and the soldiers had all lowered their weapons. They pointed at him, smiling, giving him a thumbs-up. One young man ran beside him and snapped a selfie. Another gave him a high five.

"Gregorian, o mago!" they shouted and cheered again as they passed him. "*Huzzah*, Gregorian!"

The soldiers, a few even pulling pens and scraps of paper from their jackets for autographs, happily escorted Glenn out of the woods, back after Buck. Everyone was headed to the same spot, on a ridgeline near the trees. As Glenn ran he jumped over stone ruins, the facades of fallen temples. They were right in the middle of the old location of the Morlon Kastaun set. The fake ruins of a fake battle.

Gunshots rolled from the center of the fighting, but it wasn't the Portuguese. As Glenn approached the center of the line, his eye was drawn toward the figure marching around, shooting whoever came near. He wore a cloak, and he carried a rifle. He was shrieking. Angry.

Glenn, without even meaning to, walked into the field of fighting, and right up to his old friend.

"Where is it?" Jules shouted at him. "You have taken it from me!"

"You're not well, Jules," Glenn called back. "Tell them to stop this and go home."

The queen's men were cheering. "Gregorian has come to save us!" Glenn looked at the damn fools and saw Hannah running among them. Glenn did not have a weapon. He had nothing, in fact.

"You tried to take it from me!" Jules hissed. "You tried to take it for yourself!"

The queen's soldiers, as if suddenly receiving orders, rose over the ridge, running toward Glenn and Jules. From the opposite side the Guild's army ran forward as well.

"No more!" Jules shouted. "I bring with me the doom of all!" He slung the rifle over his shoulder, raised a small receiver in his hand, and pressed down on it.

A loud, guttural roar echoed over the entire valley, and then there was a strong blast of wind. A red-and-black metal dragon flew out from above the trees, fire blowing out of its mouth.

"Jesus," Glenn said. "It still works."

The dragon circled above. Some of the guildsmen stopped their fighting to watch the dragon. "Magic!" they yelled, pointing at it. "Magic has returned to the Malicarn!"

Kreek stood nearby, arms held wide, cackling. "This is what it is! This is what it is!" The pilot stood beside him, looking in terror at the men running around him, the dragon in the sky, the tanks fast approaching.

The fighting near Glenn and Jules was scattered, erratic. Nobody knew what to do. The guildsmen and revolutionaries fought the queen's men, and the Portuguese troops fought everybody. Glenn saw Hannah standing on his left, at the ridge, pointing her knights toward Jules. She stood just above him, and when Jules noticed Glenn looking up the hill he followed his gaze, and smiled when he saw her.

"How is this for a dramatic twist?" Jules turned toward Hannah. "With the daughter, the Necromancer finishes the job he began with the father. It is poetic."

Above them was an explosion, and the side of the dragon blew into flames. A helicopter flew low over the trees, spitting fire from its guns at the dragon. The dragon buckled and fell from the sky. Kreek stood right underneath, and was still cackling wildly when the metal beast collapsed on top of him and exploded. The pilot dove out of the way and then ran toward the tanks, keeping his arms raised high, weeping and shouting, "It's me! It's me!"

Jules sneered at Gregorian. "Was it you who called in the goddamn air force? Enough of this!" He raised his rifle at Hannah and fired.

Gregorian jumped in front of the gun. The shot hit him in the stomach and he crumpled to the ground. Jules looked down at him.

"You fool," he said. "I would have written such a better end for you."

He lifted the gun again, but there was the quick flash of metal swinging through the air, and for the second time that day Jules was hit over the head. He fell backward. Buck dropped the neuroscanner and leaned over the fallen Necromancer.

"Papapa?" Buck grabbed the Necromancer's shoulders and began shaking him violently. "Papapapapaa?"

"Get off me, ah!" Jules howled in pain as Buck climbed on top of him and started shouting gibberish and slapping him across the face.

The guildsmen ran back into the forest. The death of the dragon and the loss of Kreek spooked them. The queen's men chased the retreating forces while the helicopter hovered overhead, slowly lowering toward the ground. The tanks surrounded the position and the fighting ebbed.

Gregorian lay on his back. The bullet had torn into his gut and lodged in his spine. He reached a hand out and found that Hannah was holding it.

"Gregorian?" Hannah asked. "Are you all right?"

"Glenn," he said. "My name is Glenn."

Beside him sat the neuroscanner where Buck had dropped it. One side was dented, blood smeared over the surface.

"Bring it here," Glenn said. Hannah dragged the box close to him.

What were they going to do to her? He hadn't taught her anything, not really. She was just a child. He had lied to her. He had done nothing to show her the world. He had killed her father and he had done nothing.

"There's no time," Glenn said. "They're going to take it away and then you'll never know, not really. You have to see."

Glenn pressed a few buttons on the box, and it started to buzz, the central display lighting up. The sound was more erratic than earlier. Glenn took the red cord, pressing the node against his temple. He passed the end of the green cord to Hannah.

"No," Hannah said. "You need help." The blood beneath them formed a shallow pool.

"Just do it, Hannah. Please."

In the final estimation, Glenn Mackey was a very selfish man. But he could show her. He was always good at putting on a show.

Hannah held the green cord's node up to her head, then Glenn held the red one tight on his as he pulled on the central switch. The machine buzzed loudly, extracting, feeding into the hard drive, and immediately implementing on the other end. As the bytes of data streamed through the neuroscanner, they took with them Glenn and everyone else they found inside its hard drive. Buck. Lilly. Souard. They clashed together and melded and diverged and converted themselves into an electrical signal that shot up the green cord and into the cerebral cortex of a sixteen-year-old girl.

Hannah took a breath. It was like the ground fell away. She leapt forward into a deep pit.

IMAGINARY LIVES

As the universe expands, any point in space appears to itself as the center, from which all else moves away. That is an illusion.

There are fifty states and sixteen ounces in a pound and eleven positions on a football team—true whether you mean soccer or the other kind—and the head bone is connected to the neck bone and you have to move the chicken coop every day and don't microwave metal and Odysseus built the Trojan horse and all men are created equal with the inalienable right to pass traffic on the left except in some countries where it's the other way around. *Non, rien de rien.* The tailor on the west end of Kingstown is a cheat. Everyone says the *Mona Lisa* is very small but it's pretty much the size you expect.

The first time you act is in fourth grade. The community theater runs classes for kids on Saturdays, and at your brother's karate class you see a poster. LEARN TO ACT! FUN GAMES! You don't really like games. Games are unpredictable. They have rules you don't understand. You try karate but cry when the instructor punches a dummy. Your mother signs you up for acting instead. It is at the same time as your brother's karate class so you have something to do and she can go grocery shopping.

Your mother hires the tutor and she's from Surrey and before the end of the year you only talk to her in English. She gives you books by Robert Louis Stevenson and you imagine an adventure in the Scottish Highlands with the deposed king, though when you eventually visit Scotland forty years later you're driven around in a car and it's beautiful but the romance isn't the same.

You read in your bed late into the night as your father and his communist friends yell about the world downstairs.

One time your father lets you go with him to the pub, one not far from your old farm. You're not sure why, maybe he is being sentimental. You are excited and when you approach the doors and hear singing inside you expect a night of friendship and camaraderie, but it is nothing like that at all. Men piss and vomit in the corner. They yell at one another and then immediately soften before yelling again. Everyone smells of sweat. When your father's friends talk to you, they shout, tapping your shoulder so hard it leaves a bruise. You are too young to drink but they let you try an ale anyway and you have a headache the next day.

You are always good at math and science so your mother expects you to be a doctor but you don't much like working with people and you tell her you want to be an astronaut. Your father scoffs and says you have to be realistic and you never hated him so much as you did then.

You smoke cigarettes with your friends on bridges over the Seine and then throw the butts in the water to see which ones float away fastest, cheering them on. You waste your summer at bars and cafés and walking along the river and sneaking into art galleries. You don't talk politics—that's for your father. At the cinema you like to watch American movies, which your friends hate. They are all dead now.

The acting games are simple. You don't overthink them. Try to act like an animal (got it, you're a monkey), now try to tell the teacher you're hungry (you're a monkey, you just eat whatever you see). You learn tongue twisters and short scenes and pick out props and costumes from a big bag the teacher brings with her each week. The props mean nothing at first but then you decide what they are and suddenly you have a whole world, one you are in the center of, that you control. At the final class, you and the other students perform a short play called *The Great Meatball Mystery* for your parents. Your brother is mad because he misses his karate class. You play a waiter.

Sine equals opposite over hypotenuse. Turkeys are native to North America. In their rematch Ali knocked out Liston in the first round. There's a goat herder named Harry on the south mountain who has three beautiful daughters and he still thinks they're all virgins. The Yangtze is the longest river in Asia. An old-fashioned is four parts bourbon, one part water, two dashes of bitters, and one sugar cube, muddled, served on the rocks. Your favorite café is on the Boulevard Saint-Germain, which was built by Napoleon III—the boulevard, not the café. Don't let quicklime get into your eyes when mixing mortar. When she says, "Let's be friends," it means she never wants to see you again.

You don't learn to drive until you move to America and you never really get comfortable with it. Wendy does most of the driving and eventually Daniel, too. You like Boston because the North End reminds you a bit of old Europe except in the winter when it's so cold you can feel it even when sitting inside by the fire. Wendy grew up in the cold and doesn't mind it, but it reminds you of the camp.

On New Year's Eve your parents throw a big party and invite all their friends. A dozen different kids hang out in the basement as their parents drink upstairs. You write a play, a one-act about a family that is attacked by a bear while camping, and try to direct all the kids in a performance. Rehearsals are at nine o'clock and showtime is right before midnight. You shout and yell and try to instill order on the production but no one will listen to you. "This is going to be great if we all focus!" you say, because you know your parents will like it, will tell you they liked it. But the little kids get bored and the older ones want to play video games. There is no show and you spend the rest of the night crying alone in your room.

There's a redhead named Viola at one of the pubs on the west end of town, and even though you pay her it's really nice to lie down next to her and smell her skin and twirl her hand with your fingers and wonder how the color turned out that way. She's nice but the other apprentices tease you. She has to be nice to you, they say, that's her job. But you can still like something even if you are paid for it. You like the walls you build. She might like you, too.

Local stations are marked with a white circle and express stations have a black dot, though that doesn't matter since the metro tunnels are flooded now. What does matter is that blackjack is when you are dealt an ace and a ten-card and it is not illegal to count cards although you don't know how to do that. Your tutor buys you a copy of *Tom Sawyer* and when you read it you decide you like America. You never learn to read, though you think your father knew how to. You can't change a tire. Actually, you can, because your father taught you how, saying you can't live your life and rely on a man to do this for you, a surprisingly sensible sentiment for him. You only like sushi rolls with the fake crab inside.

When the war starts, you enlist in the army and say goodbye to your parents and your tutor and go north, where you never fire a single shot before being captured at Sedan and sent to a camp on the Polish border. You never see your parents again. They're shot by an ambitious corporal on a road outside Paris for being on a list of known communists. They shoot your tutor, too, just for being with them. But you don't find out about that for a long time.

Junior year your father's taunts about being practical finally get to you and you change your major to biology. There's a bunch of classes you need to catch up on and so you overload and don't have time to study for the MCAT. When you bomb it, your mother is angry and your father unsurprised. You think they should just go fuck themselves but you apply for graduate school anyway. You don't even really like neuroscience that much, but you have a hunch that when you study it you'll be able to prove that people aren't actually that complicated or interesting and then your parents' judgments won't intrude on your private thoughts.

The community theater does a children's production of *Winnie the Pooh*, and you are cast as Piglet. Most of the kids are older than you, but they actually care about the show and after some light teasing you become "their Piglet." They tell you about all the good movies you need to see, the ones your mother never lets you watch but that the kids show you on their phones anyway. You like Mafia movies and horror movies, especially ones you are too young for. When the play is performed, you do two shows in one day and only forget a couple of lines. Your parents take you and your brother out for ice cream afterward and tell you they are getting divorced.

The hardest you ever work, and the sorest you ever feel, is after digging the hole for your father's grave. Carrying stone is nothing compared to holes.

The second book is much harder to write than the first book, because now your publisher is waiting on it and the fan mail is coming in. Everybody is trying to get in touch with you, all the time. Daniel talks now, too, and he's always babbling about something but to your horror you realize you don't know how to communicate with children. Wendy is patient but you don't think you ever really loved her and maybe you don't know what love is. You can't write unless you are alone and it's harder to be alone, to sit by your fire on cold nights and put words onto the blank paper sitting on your lap.

One time a traveling music troupe rides into town. This must have been the first year you and your father lived in the city. Your father passed out as usual after drinking, so you wander down to the square alone and try to get a seat near the front. They play lots of music and tell jokes and even have some puppets. When you tell your father later he grunts like he wants to tell you something but can't remember. He does that a lot.

All the best writers are Russian for some reason, but you still prefer H. Rider Haggard and Edgar Rice Burroughs and Jules Verne. Niagara Falls is only ten thousand years old. You hate coordinating plans with friends through text. You think Prince is amazing but a friend who listens to a lot of podcasts thinks he's overrated. Mix the water and lime and then add sand. The infield fly rule treats fly balls in the infield as caught when there are forced runners, even if they are not caught, so there are balls that might not be caught but by definition were already caught even before they were not caught. Wernicke's area and Broca's area were thought to be the centers of language but actually it's clear that now language is distributed throughout various neuro-networks.

The first time you nail it is junior year. Your school puts on *Singin' in the Rain*, and you play Cosmo Brown. When you perform "Make 'Em Laugh," jumping and flying all over the stage, running into walls and falling down, there is actual laughter from the crowd. Not the satisfied high-school-musical laughter of adults watching their children, but real laughter that comes from something you did. Your brother wants to build bridges and you can never understand why.

In graduate school you always stay late at the lab, and one night you walk home and see a busker strumming a James Taylor song on his guitar. "Maybe you can believe it if it helps you to sleep," he sings. You haven't listened to music in weeks and suddenly begin to weep.

You don't watch movies after the war. But you remember the old ones well. Your favorites were the westerns. They were earnest and innocent and a little bit dumb. In the last one you ever saw—you watched it in a sweltering cinema, the day Hitler invaded Poland—a bunch of strangers come together to ride a stagecoach across treacherous terrain. They bicker and argue and eventually become a kind of family. An outlaw named Ringo kept them safe. When Ringo first appeared onscreen, you gasped: The camera pushed in quickly on an actor you had never seen before. He twirled his rifle, and the camera fell out of focus and then in on him again, his face taking over the whole screen. That was a hero. There were shoot-outs and exciting escapes and in the end Ringo rode off with his new lady love, running from the law but happy together. "Well, they're saved from the blessings of civilization," the drunk doctor said, and you thought that might be the most beautiful thing you had ever heard. Your friends just laughed. Too many horses, they said.

Your brother goes to Annapolis—a good way to study engineering, he claims—and drowns at sea during one of the wars. That's something: There is always a war, somewhere. Your father fought at the Somme, in Iraq, in the Great Wizarding War.

You apply to NYU and get in, even though your mother says she can't pay for it. Your father lives in Denver now. In college you are not what they call a "natural talent." You really have to work at your craft. Some of the other students have a way of just disappearing into their roles, but your teachers constantly criticize you for trying too hard. Which is counterintuitive. Aren't you supposed to try hard?

Shakespeare is better than Chekhov is better than Ibsen is better than Williams is better than O'Neill. Oh, Pinter. Pinter is better than O'Neill. No, O'Neill is better than Williams. Arthur Miller is shit, actually, except when he is great. Ben Jonson is annoying. Your favorite writer is still Mark Twain. Still Beckett. You don't read literature. You don't read.

Sophomore year you meet Jules, who starts out on an acting track but switches to playwriting because, he says, "No one remembers actors, not really. You hear about Sarah Bernhardt but was she even good? You don't really know." Jules is very concerned about how people will think of him. Your friends in the lab—not friends, really, but people with whom you socialize on occasion—are also obsessed with status. Getting published. Getting grants. The master mason wants everyone to know his work but there's a rival mason from over the river and people keep getting them confused. Once you have true publishing success you wish you hadn't.

After college you stay in New York and wait tables between auditions. Wendy gets into wine and you travel to Santa Barbara but when you taste the wines they are all the same and you realize the cigarettes have finally ruined you. Private research pays better and you hate yourself a little but when you tell your father what your salary is he is genuinely impressed. Computers communicate in binary but you don't know what that means. You like to tell people you can talk to cows and when you're drunk enough you believe it.

Your mother is sick but you land a small role in a small play at a small theater in Ossining, and you can't come home right away. You have two lines—you run onstage and tell another character he has a phone call, and then a little bit later you tell that same character that the mayor has arrived—but the show pays real money and it feels too important for you to leave and visit your mother in New Jersey. After all, if you aren't there, who will tell everyone about the mayor? The next year you spend a lot of time with lawyers on the phone closing up the estate, a ridiculous word for the belongings of a woman who died broke. The house sells to a developer who wants to flip it. Your father calls you on your birthday, asks how you are doing, and doesn't mention your mother. He dies a year later, and you let his new wife handle all that.

You do a book signing in Dallas and decide it's the worst city in the world. The owner of the coffee place in Greenpoint is mobbed up but the Danishes are good there. You're still young so why does your back hurt so much? Elvis was a sergeant in the army and he also stole music from Black people. Sex in pornography is always so confident and aggressive. Peppermint mochas are disgusting.

Stalag VIII-A. That was the name of it, over the river from Görlitz. It had once been a camp for Hitler Youth. Ten thousand Poles were already there when the French and Belgians arrived, and you are placed in a tent while more barracks were built. There wasn't cholera or diphtheria in the camp yet, but there would be, along with British and Canadians and Russians and Americans. You spend over four years there before the Germans marched you back into the interior of the fatherland, and the whole time you try to imagine how it's going to end.

The flooding in Manhattan means a lot of closed theaters and a lot of out-of-work actors. Jules has a couple of shows produced. His breakout is a financial flop but a critical success that finally gets him a phone call from Los Angeles and a flight west. He says he'll be back but you know he won't. You move to Philadelphia and take a job pretending to be Thomas Jefferson for tourists. You have no close friends. When the lights are on, you can't even see the audience.

You're an apprentice working long hours and the musical troupe returns. Or it's a different one, you can't tell. They do their act, you make sure to catch it after working in the sun all day. You laugh a lot, louder at jokes that are familiar. You don't know if you like it or if you just like the memory.

You watch hundreds of people change their entire personalities right in front of you but decide such a thing would be impossible for you to do, even very slowly. Sometimes Glenn shows you an actually good movie and the daily slog seems less impossible. You don't tell him this because he takes too much satisfaction when you like something.

The last book is almost impossible to finish. You are breathing with an oxygen tank now. The winters are felt deep in your bones. All you can think about is the camp.

The Tempest does it for you. You have one good night and you never really act again. The Malicarn calls and you help develop the set. It is a living thing. The Malicarn isn't real but it's not fake, either. It takes you a long time to understand that. Jules never understands, not one bit. But Lilly understands, right away. You think this is because she is a scientist, but it's because Lilly doesn't like to live in her own head. In fact she hates it. That is the difference between the two of you.

You tie a slipknot by folding the rope, taking the end and looping that around the double line a few times, then pulling. Lift is achieved when thrust forces enough air under the aircraft's wing that pressure is higher than above it. Bluebirds have orange chests.

The first winter in the camp was the most difficult, because you had no idea what to expect. You are a child of intellectuals, a child of Paris. Your father would rail about the people and revolution but you never suffered for it. Now the snow blows into the barracks and you trade for extra rations and try not to look at any of the guards the wrong way. You don't have the right coat. The dying dreams start, where your body falls apart, dissolves into dust, and you try to capture the feeling the moment it happens but you always wake up. You get sick, very sick, and cannot keep down food. For three days you retch, you become dehydrated. You lie on your bunk and realize you don't have the strength to stand. You are going to die and nothing ever happened. The world ended and nobody remembers.

There are twenty-four hours in a day, three hundred sixty-five days in a year. Except in leap years. The earth is round, circles the sun, and spins on a crooked axis. The earth is at the center of the universe, surrounded by the circling planets and stars. Strawberries taste best freshly picked. People complain about the weather but that's because they are afraid to talk about anything else.

Sometimes when you look at a wall you help build you realize that the world can be really beautiful, but you don't know what to do with this knowledge.

You spent the first half of your life trying to understand things and the second half trying to forget. You're like your father, in that way. In the end he managed to forget everything. But even if you forget it, it's still true.

It is January, the first winter. You are feeling better, drinking and eating again. But you have lost a lot of weight. The cold is worse now. The guards tell everyone to come to the main yard. There is a stage, and chairs. You sit with the other prisoners. The guards are going to give a speech. No, not guards. There is a piano on the stage. Four other prisoners ascend. One carries a cello, another a violin, a third a clarinet. The fourth man, his blond hair dirtied, his round glasses hiding his serious expression, sits at the piano. He places his sheet music, handwritten, on the music desk. The musicians tune their instruments. The sun is out today, but the air is sharp and cold. There is a deep silence in the yard, as if at the opening of the seventh seal. Then they start playing.

You know now why you could play Prospero, how you made it work for just one night. You were an understudy, called up at the last minute on the last day of performances. There wasn't time to prepare, wasn't time to overthink. So you stood onstage and you didn't try to control it. Like the old sorcerer tired of maintaining his little island, you finally let it all go. You didn't work too hard. You didn't act. You just existed.

But this rough magic I here abjure,

The music is soft at first, the instruments rising together, almost as if they are still tuning. Discordant but not apart. The piano hits louder notes, erratically. Then the clarinet comes in, fliting over it. The four instruments clash and find harmony and break apart again. The sound is angry, it is sad. It searches for some way to be whole. Sometimes one instrument will fall silent for a long time, sometimes all four will sound at once. The violin takes its time to cry out a melody while the piano taps behind it. The man playing the piano closes his eyes, he does not see his own music, he does not need it. You understand this man completely. The world is over and you have already died. Someday when you are beside the fire in your Boston home, your wife and son in the next room, you will play a record and remember what it was like to live through the end of time. And so you will take out your sharpened pencils and your blank pages and you will scratch out some imaginary lives.

I'll break my staff, Bury it certain fathoms in the earth,

And that's it. What do you remember? You spend your whole

life telling made-up stories about made-up people and looking at their brains and thinking about when your father fought with wizards and wondering what it feels like the moment you die.

and deeper than did ever plummet sound I'll drown my book.

You let go.

HANNAH (AND AFTER)

1.

Jules was shouting, that was the first thing. Someone held him up, grabbing both his arms. He wanted them to let him go. Buck was hollering, as well, and two other men lifted him, holding his limbs while he thrashed about.

Hannah blinked, held her hand over her eyes, though it wasn't very bright. Soldiers—Roger's men, and she knew who Roger was—surrounded her, dragging Jules and Buck toward their jeeps and tanks. Lilly knelt next to Hannah, next to the neuroscanner. But she was checking on someone, checking for a pulse. Glenn lay on his back. He was still, and Lilly's shirt was soaked with blood.

The neuroscanner still buzzed, but it was slowing down now. Low on power. Hannah knew that somehow, too.

A few other Portuguese soldiers were barking at Kellington and the other knights, who had taken cover at the ridge. The guildsmen had run off, but there were still some rebels hiding in the tree line. Hannah could see them, so she stood up.

"My queen!" Kellington yelled at her, but the soldier kicked him. "Hannah, stay down! It's not safe!"

When she had run toward the line, as Glenn and Jules were facing off, she wanted to save Kellington, save her guard. She didn't want them to get surrounded and trapped, so she had ordered them to attack. But now she didn't want the rebels harmed, either. Nobody needed to fight.

She walked toward the trees. "Come here! Please! I must show you something!"

The man who walked out was old. Hannah remembered when he was implemented, years ago. He was a schoolteacher, or used to be. Aaron. What was his name now? Hannah remembered. When Lilly tried to fix him and failed. And she remembered when he came to the castle, pleading for her help.

"Jasper," she said. "I want to show you something. Please, come here. I won't harm you."

Jasper slowly walked out of the trees. "Truce?"

"Truce," she said. She led him back toward the neuroscanner. "Let those men go," she shouted at the soldiers. "Let them come here."

One of the officers turned toward her. "Desça!"

"No, they have to see. Kellington, come here. I have to show you." She leaned over the neuroscanner but the officer grabbed her and pulled her up. He threw her toward a younger soldier, who carried her toward a jeep. Someone else was lifting Lilly, and the neuroscanner was packed into a bag.

Hannah looked at Jasper, about to run back to the woods for cover. She looked at Kellington. "The Citadel," she shouted. "You have to go there. Take everybody. You will see." And to Jasper she yelled, "Aaron! Remember! Aaron!"

The helicopter was idling behind the jeeps, and they threw her inside. Her head pulsed, the lights were still bright. Something fell beside her. The helicopter roared to life. At first Hannah thought she was falling, but she was rising up.

Below her she could see the whole stretch of the battlefield from the Morlon Kastaun through the forest and back toward the monastery. The jeeps and tanks corralled the remaining fighters away. Everything looked very small.

Hannah felt the helicopter's angle shift, and she sat up from the cold floor. Buck, still spouting gibberish, was tied up on the other end next to Jules, whose mouth had been muffled. The Chinese pilot sat in a chair, weeping.

There was another clank, and Hannah saw a man holding the neuroscanner. "Assets secured," he said into a radio. "Tell everyone to pull back." It was Roger, who was taller than in her memory. He set the scanner on the floor and wrapped a securing strap around it, then smiled with the confidence of a man who had never failed.

"Roger, you better see this," said another soldier.

Roger walked past Hannah to two other bodies.

"Ah, shit," Roger said. "What the hell happened?"

Hannah stretched out her poor leg, just far enough that she could touch the edge of the scanner. Roger can't have it. Nobody can have it. She looped her foot around the strap holding it down, and pulled. The strap came free.

"Is he dead?" The voice was soft, but Hannah recognized Lilly. "Please, Roger, tell me."

"Looks like it. You've lost a lot of blood yourself."

The floor heaved forward, and Hannah knew they were flying fast now. She gave the box a strong kick and it slid away.

The floor tilted in the other direction and the scanner fell toward the open door. It smashed into the doorframe, the glass display screen shattering.

"No, no, no, no!" Roger jumped and reached for it, but the box fell out of the helicopter, a long way down. Roger cursed and slammed his fist. Glass shards vibrated and slid across the metal floor.

Through the helicopter door Hannah could see the Malicarn stretch out before her, its green hills dotted by huts and homes and villages. Then they passed through a cloud, and the land dissolved like a dream upon waking.

2.

The queen was gone. They had taken her, and the wizards. The metal beasts and the men with wands of fire retreated back the way they had come. The Guild's leader was dead, too, and so the reenactors ran off somewhere into the hills. Those who were left did not know why they were fighting.

"She knew my name," Jasper said. "Aaron. I remember that somehow."

"We do as she said," Kellington said. "We go to the Citadel."

They joined together, men and women of the Malicarn, and walked all day to the great black fortress. The wizards were gone. There was no one to stop them. In the lobby mobs had smashed glass and turned over tables, but no one had explored further. One by one they entered the recesses of the Citadel, tentatively at first but then with a zealous determination to discover its secrets. They wandered the halls and the offices, the conference rooms and the lab. They saw the camera feeds and the props and the piles of paper scrawled with story notes. The outsiders, the Madeiran youth who had joined their fight, showed them the computers. Together they found files with information about their lives, their homes, their whole country.

Here was a database with a day-by-day accounting of Kellington's activities. Here was a video of Jasper working in his forge this week, last week, a year ago, ten years. They found personnel files, movie clips, promotional posters. Emails with producers. Inventories of food, livestock. Interviews conducted with versions of themselves when they had different names. They saw who they were now and who they had been. Once they saw, they remembered.

It did not happen all at once. Guildsmen were still fighting in the hills. Outsiders were pouring into the countryside, young and old alike. But word spread throughout the realm and more came to the Citadel. The truth, horrible but clarifying, became known. As the violence faded, plans were made and strategies devised. They pulled the cameras out of the walls and ceilings and trees and rocks, and they smashed the computers and the servers and made it impossible to track anyone anymore. The outsiders helped, showed them how to spot a hidden camera, explained where it led, what it captured.

The older ones, those who had lived in the Malicarn since the beginning, read about their past lives. It was all in the files, electronic and paper, and in audio and video. Some eventually remembered who they used to be. Once they knew their old names and heard their old memories, they could pull into the deep recesses of their minds and recall what their lives had been like. Jasper remembered Thanksgiving dinners and the way the cold whipped off Lake Michigan in the winter. Others didn't know, didn't want to know. The Malicarn was all they wanted to remember. And some were sad to discover that there were no other lives for them, that they had lived in the Malicarn since they were born and had nothing else to return to. Kellington was just Kellington. The Malicarn was all.

Powerful outsiders arrived in planes and drove out to the Citadel, ministers from the government. They negotiated with the Malicarn. How can we provide for you? they asked. Many Madeirans demanded their old homes back, land they had been forced to sell and leave. Some in the Malicarn wanted cars and phones and electricity. Others did not. They liked their old ways. They wanted to live on their farms and in their stone homes and have nothing to do with the outsiders. No one asked the Cameroon farmers what they wanted.

A Truth and Reconciliation Committee in Lisbon spent years mediating the rights of everyone on the island. Would there be justice for those killed by the mobs? Who would pay to give a Malicarn man his old life back? Who would be responsible for the transfer and retransfer of property? What would be done with the migrant workers? Could the government provide subsidies, stimulus, some way to remodernize the economy? Nobody came away satisfied from these judgments, so there were more hearings in Brussels that took even longer to adjudicate.

Massive poverty across the island began to abate only when the tourists arrived. Many locals thought these new visitors could use their dollars to help revive Madeira. They took driving tours of old Malicarn villages and castles and battlefields. The Citadel became a visitor center. Some of the Malicarn traditionalists, who still lived as in the old days, didn't mind when outsiders came and gawked at them, but sometimes there was violence, shoving and shouting when a college kid from Ohio or South Carolina tried to take a picture while making a lewd gesture in front of a market stall.

Kellington stayed on the island, but he would go on television and plead for compassion from the world on behalf of the Malicarn. He wrote a book about the plight of his countrymen. He invited politicians and celebrities to see the poverty, to ask for help. Wu Zihao, now a colonel, came back to visit on a goodwill tour, documentary crews following him everywhere as he and Kellington hiked over the Morlon Kastaun and reminisced about the great battle they fought there.

Others left entirely, the Malicarn now an open wound, a memory of oppression and death. They formed communities, a global Malicarn diaspora. Jasper returned to Chicago, though his family did not recognize him as Aaron anymore. Wallace moved to Dublin, where many guildmembers lived as well. Today you can find someone from the Malicarn in almost every city on Earth. The Cameroon farmers stayed, and they aren't called goblins anymore.

On the island most people speak Portuguese again, intermarrying or going to the mainland as they need. Traditional Malicarn living is rare now. But there are still some who remember the old days, when men fought beside wizards. Every child knows the stories. In this country magic once was real.

3.

Hannah drank a cup of espresso on the open patio in front of a café, watching the frogs. They hopped, dozens of them, up the street. One woman pulled on her dog's leash to prevent him from chasing them. A man on his phone stepped on a frog without seeing it.

Paris was louder than she expected. In the memories, there were fewer cars. But maybe that was all wrong anyway. The Seine at least was cleaner, so they said. A busker sat with his guitar on the corner, crooning out some Bob Dylan tunes. He kicked away a few frogs that jumped into his case. The café owner's son came out to the sidewalk with a pail and a long stick. He was about ten and said hello to the busker as if he recognized him. Hannah watched him walk over to one of the frogs, then quickly stab it with the stick and drop it into the bucket.

The boy saw Hannah's expression, which must have been half amused and half disgusted, and apologized. "They have to do this in Australia," he said in French. "My dad saw a video about it. It's one of my chores now."

"Of course," she said. The boy turned to stab at another frog. It squeaked and twitched on the end of his spear, then went limp as it fell into the bucket.

Last year the frogs were accidentally imported from the Philippines and exploded in population. They didn't cause much damage, apart from being extremely plentiful. The official guidance was to kill and dispose of any frog you saw. The Paris sanitation department had installed "frog cans" around the city for that purpose. Street preachers called it a plague. Late-night comedians made a lot of strained jokes about the French love of frogs. Most people just found them to be annoying. The frogs didn't bother Hannah. They reminded her of the royal menagerie.

Hannah drank her espresso. This was what people did, right? Sit in cafés and watch other people. She remembered doing it but had never done it. It felt okay.

"Good morning, Hannah." She looked up and saw Lilly wearing a sweater and jeans, and leaning on a cane. "Thank you for meeting me."

Hannah smiled. "It's nice to see you."

Lilly shuffled across to the table and sat. The busker switched from Dylan songs to Australian folk music, joking with the young boy.

"This is how they really do it down under!" he said. The boy smiled as he stabbed more frogs.

"How are you doing?" Lilly asked.

"I am well," Hannah said. "These cities are so enormous. I mean, I thought so, from what you and Glenn remembered. But I did not really know. You had no trouble leaving England?"

"Roger helped. He has a lot of connections with the right people. Where are you staying?"

"A hotel in Montmartre. It's nice. How are you?"

"Three surgeries but feeling better. I wish I didn't need the cane, but it helps."

"I should get one," Hannah said. "I enjoy wandering the city but my leg is pretty sore most nights. But I might try physical therapy. Is that what it's called? Six months in the real world and I'm already learning new things."

Lilly smiled and looked at the ground. Hannah suspected the reason she had wanted to meet, and was waiting for Lilly to get the courage to ask, even though they both knew what Hannah was going to say.

After her extraction, Hannah was interrogated by MI6 for several days before an official apology came from Parliament and she was released. The film studio settled with her quickly, hoping she wouldn't talk to the press. There wasn't much she was able to tell the British, anyway. The whole mess turned out to be a diplomatic win for the government, with them taking credit for rescuing Major Wu and returning him to the Chinese. They made a big show of helping the Portuguese, and even without the neuroscanner were able to cow the CIA, who after all had allowed an American business to shelter a political prisoner on foreign soil without their knowledge. Roger, somehow, managed to spin the entire debacle into a significant career achievement, an example of "clandestine diplomacy by force"—a term he made up. He was given a promotion at MI6, his own discretionary fund, and even a new desk. Hannah knew all of this because Roger couldn't stop bragging about it, on the multiple occasions he interviewed her directly. He also told her that Jules was released from British custody with an apology and had returned to Los Angeles. Rumor was he already had a book deal. Buck Douglas was institutionalized somewhere in Scotland.

"I'm not even sure why that guy came with us," Roger had said, offering her tea from a kettle in his new office. Hannah already had the settlement money and was planning on leaving Britain as soon as possible, but she visited Roger at his request as a courtesy. She did not really wish to ever see him again.

"But I guess his brain patterns might still hold some clues as to how the neuroscanner worked," Roger said. "Might give our guys some good data. There's a team from St. Andrews working with Mr. Douglas now. I might recommend Lilly to them for a job."

"I doubt she'll accept that."

"Oh, you never know! She's very ambitious!"

"Where is Glenn's body?"

"That's classified," Roger said. "Same thing, they—we—need the autopsy."

"What do you want from me, Roger?"

"Oh, nothing much, nothing much. Public relations, you know? Do some talk shows, some interviews. Maybe appear before Parliament. Just talk about how heinous and terrible the Malicarn is, how wretchedly you were treated. Give us some human rights leverage against the US, you know?"

"Aren't the Americans your friends?"

"What is a friend, Hannah? It's just a person who owes you favors, right?"

"I don't think so."

Hannah refused to help, claiming that the terms of her settlement with the studio meant she couldn't do press. Roger didn't believe that, or didn't care, but he let her go anyway. Not that Paris was free of similar hassles. Hannah was in tabloids constantly, fans snapping photos of her wherever she walked. She had come to Paris out of some misplaced memory, some half-true romantic recollection of Jean-Danton's from before the war, but now she was considering only leaving her hotel at night. Maybe she would leave Paris, too. But to go where? Not back to the Malicarn.

They were figuring out their future without her. She wasn't really their queen anyway. She had too many people's memories floating around inside of her, and the last place she wanted to go to was the one location where all the memories converged.

But Hannah was lonely, and when Lilly wrote her a letter asking to meet, she agreed, even though she knew that it was almost certainly another foray from Roger.

"Do you want anything to eat or drink?" Hannah asked.

"No, I am all right," Lilly said. "You know, this is my first time in Paris?"

"I guess me, too, technically."

The busker started to play "Waltzing Matilda," whistling the melody at first and then singing the lyrics loudly in a decent Australian accent: "*Waltzing Matilda, waltzing Matilda, you'll come a-waltzing Matilda with me. And he sang as he stowed that jumbuck in his tucker bag, 'You'll come a-Waltzing Matilda with me.'*" The café owner's son bobbed his head to the music as he stabbed more frogs.

"I suppose you know why I'm here," Lilly said.

"Yes. Tell Roger I'm not going to help him."

"I have a whole speech I'm supposed to give you."

"I don't care. Did he find you a job?"

"Yes. I took it. I don't know why. I haven't done any science in years."

"Well, I certainly don't know what I am supposed to do now," Hannah said, "or what I can do. People always recognize me on the street, from the films. It feels odd."

"Yes, I imagine."

"I actually went to see the latest *Malicarn* movie," Hannah said. "I guess it's the final one."

"For now. I'm sure they'll find a way to make more. They are still very popular."

"I died in it. Well, a version of myself. Glenn and I blew up. I am not sure how they made it look like that. I mean, I do, somewhat. I remember what Glenn remembered, about digital effects. But I have never seen it myself before. In the movie, I was a coward, but that is not what happened. Not really. They show us being vicious and cruel."

"They make things the way they want them to be," Lilly said.

Hannah almost hadn't gone to see it. It was too painful. But the advertisements appeared everywhere, on billboards and taxis, and there was Glenn: older, sadder, on the side of a bus. His Eagles shirt digitally erased and replaced with a wizard's cloak. She remembered that shirt because the last time she saw it, it was covered in blood. She lay in the helicopter, looking over at the person next to her. Eyes looking back, Glenn's eyes. Still and unmoving. Lilly was curled up next to him, crying.

"I didn't want anyone to get hurt," Hannah said.

"I know."

A police officer walked up to the busker and asked him to move along. "Aw, he's not bothering anyone," the boy said. But the officer ignored him and the busker packed up his guitar, tipped his hat, and walked away. The boy continued cleaning up frogs.

"I do not know what Gregorian, er, Glenn wanted," Hannah said. "I have his memories and I do not know what to do with them, or with yours or anyone else's. They're not my memories. They feel more like stories somebody told me."

"I always wondered what it felt like to be implemented."

"Glenn wanted you to be safe, but what then? I don't even know what you want."

"I wish I knew what I want, too," Lilly said. "I definitely could never figure out Glenn. He spent a long time pretending to be someone he wasn't. Or maybe he wasn't pretending, I don't know."

"It feels impossible, being a person."

"It's not impossible," said Lilly. "You just have to remember to lie to yourself every day."

Lilly paid Hannah's bill, and they shook hands as Lilly stood up. "I'll tell Roger you turned me down. I can't guarantee he won't try again."

"I know. Thank you, Lilly. Take care of yourself."

Hannah remained at the table a long time after Lilly left. The young boy was softly singing the busker's tune, circling the sidewalk in front of the café. *You'll come a-waltzing Matilda with me* . . . Every few seconds his melody was interrupted by the sound of his spear impaling a frog and tossing it into his pail.

Hannah couldn't see the Seine from her seat, but she tried to picture it. Sparkling in the sunlight, lovers kissing over it. Maybe the river was dirty, maybe the lovers were fighting, but Hannah wanted it to be clean. There was so much in the world, she could barely manage to remember it all. The Malicarn was changing, the old ways were over. And what would come next, Hannah could only imagine.

Maybe she would stay in Paris, find all of Jean-Danton's old haunts. Or she would travel, discover a nice quiet place where nobody knew who she was and then she could become herself, become whatever she wanted.

Maybe Roger was lying. He never released Glenn's body because Glenn was still alive, held under questioning, the government learning all they could. One day Glenn would go back to the Malicarn, become Gregorian again, and show everyone the best path forward. Fix all of their problems this time, help them thrive. He wouldn't be acting anymore, he would just be.

And Lilly wouldn't take that job from Roger. She would tell the world what really happened in the Malicarn, change laws and regulations so it never happens again, and be the kind of person she always should have been, someone who cared for others and wanted to help make the world better. And Jules would go to prison, he would be vilified. He wouldn't profit from the Malicarn anymore.

And they would let Buck go, too. Release him from the hospital. Because even without his memories he was still himself, he was still a person. He could relearn, but now he would learn on his own terms. His life could be genuine. Buck would be the first truly free man who ever lived, uninhibited by the past or anyone's expectations. When he traveled, each place would be new. Each person a delightful discovery. Nowhere would he be unwelcome, because everybody in his world is kind and generous and loving. He'll climb the Alps, swim in the Maldives, ride a motorcycle across the Mongolian Plateau. He'll eat in Buenos Aires and Lagos and San Francisco. He'll dance in Mumbai, sing in Barcelona, and write poetry in Boston. When he drives, because he'll learn to drive, he'll take the lonely roads, the less traveled ones. If he's on a mesa in New Mexico, and his tire goes flat, a man will kindly tow him to his family's home. And they'll let him stay the night, cook for him in the morning, and he'll leave with new tires and new friends, riding with the windows down and feeling the dry desert air on his face, that morning breeze that makes all things new. And as he drives away the family will wave until he is out of sight, and they'll say, There he goes. Another one saved from the blessings of civilization.

Hannah leaned back, closed her eyes, and listened. Sirens, car horns, bicycle bells. A waiter clearing a plate. A man lighting a cigarette. Two women chatting on the corner. A phone ringing. *Thwomp.* The boy speared another frog and dropped it into his bucket. Then he kept singing.

ACKNOWLEDGMENTS

Every book is a record of collaboration, and this one is no exception. My deepest thanks goes to my editor, Lee Harris, who helped me shape this project into its best form and championed it all along the way. I also want to thank Matthew Rusin and all of the good people at Tor who worked to bring this book to life.

I owe an incalculable debt to my agent, Ethan Ellenberg, whose patience, advice, and steady hand throughout this book's long development is deeply appreciated. Thank you also to Lindsay Watson and the rest of the Ethan Ellenberg Literary Agency for their professionalism and assistance throughout this process.

A special acknowledgment to the literary institutions that bolstered the writing of this book: the Upper Dublin Public Library, the Free Library of Philadelphia, the Doylestown Bookshop, and the W.P.M. Typewriter Shop. Backyard Beans and Wake Coffee Roasters also deserve thanks for their caffeine and the use of their chairs. Thank you to all of my early readers, especially Jason, who deserves some credit for this book's conception since we have spent so many hours discussing what's wrong with Hollywood. (Sorry I named a hurricane after you.) Shannon, thanks for letting me borrow your Barbies when we were kids so I could act out my weird stories.

Thank you to Mom and Dad for never telling me to stop reading. Thank you to Morgan for being a pure spark of creativity and laughter. It is inspiring. And to Erica: Thank you for showing me how to be the best version of myself. Without you I not only couldn't have written this book, I wouldn't have known how.

ABOUT THE AUTHOR

Lucas Sinkinson, Sinkinson Photography

THOMAS ELROD lives in Pennsylvania with his wife and daughter. His writing has appeared in the *Los Angeles Review of Books*, *Independent Weekly*, and elsewhere. *The Franchise* is his first novel.